Chapter 1
Joe
1979

Mick staggered into the room. Joe could smell him and lay motionless as the guy blundered towards the corner and pissed into an old paint tin. With an incomprehensible mutter, he crashed out onto the blackened mattress. It was hard to tell if he even knew that there was someone else in the room. Volatile at the best of times, a heavy drinking session just made him worse. Although he had never shown a hint of violence towards his friends, you couldn't relax with Mick, and it was a relief when the usual loud snoring started.

Joe shivered and pulled the thin sleeping bag up around his chin. The clammy, dank air of the room was overlaid with the stench of urine and the yellowing curtains were permanently closed so at least the squalor was less evident in the dim light. He closed his eyes and tried to sleep, but his mind refused to shut down the myriad of thoughts that circled his tired brain. *What would he do tomorrow?* It was impossible to envisage a way out of this half-life he had sunk into. Solutions came and went. Sober nights and drug-free nights were torture. He endured hour after hour of light bulb moments, so plausible in the dark quiet that vanished with the daylight to some inaccessible place.

He had no idea of the time. *What did it matter if it was day or night?* The familiar blanket of grey lethargy lurked amid the physical gloom. It didn't pay to think ahead. So often, it all slid away, and frustration set in. It was best to take life as it came and avoid all that. Other people seemed able to shake off disappointment but not him. When things went wrong, his reaction was almost physical, as though he'd been chopped off at the knees, only to crash back down to his pit of despair. Dumbed down, he would crave the buzz of a high, desperate to get back to his typical enthusiastic self where all things were possible. But without the chemical highs that had become part of his world, the necessary energy to get from one day to the next was elusive.

Stiff from lying on bare floorboards, he sat up and hugged his knees. The sour bile that rose in his throat and the pounding head were old friends as he contemplated another day of grinding boredom. He could hear Mick's heavy breathing; he would sleep for hours yet.

Joe pulled on his donkey jacket that doubled as a pillow on the dusty floor and let himself out into the street. Victoria Road, on a dark October morning, failed to lighten his mood. Stinging rain whipped the tired faces of young mothers who pushed up the road in dispirited fashion, oblivious of the silent occupant in the buggy. One mother gave a vicious jerk on the arm of her whining toddler. An old woman, head bowed against the rain, bumped into Joe. She tutted and raised her head.

Joe attempted a smile, but her faded eyes remained expressionless. The church clock struck eleven. He decided to go to The Auckland and find someone to scrounge a pint off. He pushed open the heavy door to the tiny public bar. The smell of last night's beer and ancient carpet was comforting. It was early yet, but Frank, who was sitting at his usual bar stool, raised his head.

'You up for a game?' Joe asked.

Without waiting for Frank's reply, the barmaid reached under the counter and pulled out a battered crib board. Frank had talked about his time in the navy; he'd been a big guy at one time, and Joe watched as his large and nicotine-stained fingers manipulated the matchsticks.

'Fifteen two, fifteen four ….'

Joe loved the timeless quality of the game. Fascinated by the language and the ritual, he had spent many an hour in the cosy pub playing crib when he was supposed to be at college.

The game continued in silent concentration. For a change, Joe won and began to relax in the warmth of the pub as he drank his half of mild courtesy of Frank.

2

Frank drew on his Capstan full strength. 'You're looking pale, lad.'

'Too much scrumpy in The Apsley last night, I guess,' Joe grimaced. He decided it was best not to mention that he'd mixed the scrumpy with a wrap of amphetamine powder.

They had another game then Joe downed his drink. 'Cheers, Frank. I'm off, places to be,' he added, wishing it were the case.

It was 12.30 pm, and he could just make it to St Simon's Church Hall in time for the free lunch. He found a seat at one of the Formica tables and sat stirring the bowl of oxtail soup. He liked to dip the thickly sliced white bread and watch the cheap margarine drip oily puddles onto the brown liquid. Today, it made him think about his mother in Bath with his younger sister, Jess. Part of him wanted to go home and be looked after, but that wouldn't work. After a few days of feeling safe and surrounded by love, he would start to feel smothered and trapped. It had been like that after his 'A' levels and brought on an unbearable restlessness that was best avoided. But something had to change; he couldn't go on as he was for much longer.

He finished the mug of hot sweet tea and made his way to the shopping precinct where he positioned himself on a bench opposite Woolworth's. His legs jigged inside his jeans. He hated that restlessness. It was bloody cold; he couldn't remember the last time he'd felt warm. He slid his hand inside his pocket and drew out the handful of coins, £1.32. Not enough for some speed. In any case, the hit would only last an hour or so and just made his restlessness worse. Speed was ok when he was out with his mates for a good time, but these days, he was more often alone and preferred alcohol-induced oblivion to get through life. He rolled up the leg of his jeans to inspect his fading tan. It was hard to believe that just two months ago, he had been in Spain with Stu.

By some quirk of fate, just as this thought popped into his head, he saw Stu on the other side of the precinct with his arms wrapped around a skinny girl. Unlike Joe, Stu had gone back to college that autumn. *Maybe he would have a chunk of his grant left?* Joe wandered across.

'Hey, Stu. What are you up to?'

Stu looked at his watch. 'Apsley will be open in ten minutes. Fancy a pint?'

'Yeah, if you're paying.' Joe shuffled his feet; he was reluctant to let Stu see him in this state and found it difficult to look him in the eye. They found a seat in the window, and Stu went off to get the drinks.

'How d'you know, Stu?' the girl enquired.

'We were on the same course, and we hitched to Spain together last summer.'

Stu plonked three beer glasses on the table. 'Good times, mate; good times. Remember that last lift?' He turned to the girl. 'You won't fucking believe this. We were in Barcelona, right. And as the old money was running out, we decided to head for home, so we walked to the outskirts. I'd just stuck my thumb out when this silver BMW stops. There's this Japanese bloke driving, and he asks us where we're going. "Portsmouth," I tell him. Then he shakes his head, but he's smiling, right. "Sorry", he says. "I'm only going as far as Brighton". Barcelona to Brighton, how fucking jammy is that?' Stu laughed. 'Tell Angie about that bar in Andorra,' he demanded.

'This so-called friend sold me for a hundred pesetas to some guy at the bar while I was in the loo, then he bloody scarpered. I had to leg it when I realised what was happening. Bastard!' Stu laughed, but Joe remembered the fear. He had been frightened of the Spanish bloke just as he was often frightened of Mick. Not that he'd ever let on to anyone.

'Why didn't you go back for the second year?' Angie asked.

'It was too fucking boring.'

4

'Would be for someone with the attention span of a gnat,' Stu put in.

'There was no way I could afford to pay to re-sit the first-year exams, so it's all academic now.' Joe shrugged, and the three of them fell silent.

Joe decided to try John's place. *Why was his life so shit?* Not that long ago, some days had been about hope, excitement, even. He remembered getting the results of his 'A' level art exam, a grade good enough to secure a place on a graphic design course. It would be a new start with new experiences. He had been excited about moving to Portsmouth and being independent. The school careers master persuaded him to take the commercial design route saying there was more chance of a job at the end of it. *Bad advice, in hindsight.* After the first few weeks, he'd found the course soulless. It was all technical stuff with sod all chance to be creative. He didn't want to end up setting type on some magazine. *Why had he built up his expectations?* College had been a huge let-down, and it had been hard to pick himself up from that.

He couldn't understand why he had this extreme reaction to disappointment. His mother always said that he'd been a happy child with an infectious exuberance for life. That all changed when he was about fourteen. That was when it started to get to him, often ending in violent outbursts if things went wrong. Spiralling out of control, he blamed everyone else, believing they were deliberately out to get him. Then he would fall into an unbreakable gloom, sometimes for weeks on end.

He started drinking when he was out with his mates. They would buy cheap cider or nick booze from their parents' drinks cabinets and sit in the park or the supermarket carpark and drink whatever they could get their hands on. One of the boys had an older brother who could get hold of speed, and they experimented. Discovering which method gave the quickest and best high became their nightly quest. They rubbed the grey powder on their gums; the taste was disgusting, so they tried snorting it, but that hurt like hell, so they tended to mix it with whatever booze they had. Joe remembered that all-consuming urge for a euphoric high. He drank faster than the others, yet at the end of a night on the booze, he always craved more. It shamed him now to remember how his dad never noticed the missing whisky. Then vodka became his drink of choice which often meant a visit to Tesco on the way home from school to nick a bottle. He would stuff the vodka up his school jumper and buy a big bottle of cheap fizzy orange. It was easy to take a ready mixed bottle of vodka and orange to school in his rucksack. *Who would ever know?*

His mother had done her best to persuade him to stick with the graphic design course, but he knew it wasn't for him and why compromise? That was over a year ago. He wasn't even twenty yet, and it was dreary, this business of surviving from one day to the next. Cannabis helped when he could get hold of it; it relaxed him and made him mellow. But it was his craving for alcohol that drove his days. Apart from the shoplifting, he'd never done anything more serious. Occasionally, he got the chance to earn a few quid which would tide him over. But he'd never begged or taken hard drugs. He knew he had an addictive personality and what the craving for alcohol did to him; that panic at being forced to go without a drink, knowing the physical side effects to come – those horrendous shakes if he failed to top up his intake; the cold and the nausea. It would be suicide even to try the harder stuff.

He set off at a brisk pace towards John's flat to shake off the restlessness in his legs. John taught in the language department at college. He flogged the odd pill or dope and was often around in the afternoons. Joe could hear him shuffling around inside the flat and banged on the door for a second time.

'Come on; you lazy bastard. Open the door, will you? It's fucking cold out here.'

John wore tartan slippers and a grubby cardigan buttoned up over his bulk. He peered at Joe over his thick glasses. 'Oh, it's you. Want to come in?'

He poured dry cider into cloudy pint glasses and handed one to Joe, who slumped down on the battered settee.

'What's been happening then?' John asked, 'I haven't seen you for a while. You found a place yet?'

'Naa. I crash at Mick the Merch's when he's around.'

John reached across to his turntable and put on his much loved and crackly Bob Dylan LP. 'You ought to watch out for that one; he's a bloody psychopath if you ask me.'

'Tell me about it. He's a fucking liability; if someone looks at him the wrong way, he's in there, head-butting them and kicking the shit out of them.'

John nodded. 'So I've heard and no doubt with a big grin on his face.'

'Too right. The other day he asked some random bloke the time and head-butted him for no reason I could see. He's got to be a nutter. He buys a pair of lovebirds every Saturday from the market and has them sent by train to his mother in London. Every Saturday, for Christ's sake.'

'Here.' John handed him a joint, and they sat back to contemplate the fate of these tiny birds. 'Got somewhere for tonight?'

Joe shook his head. John was hospitable enough but drew the line at letting anyone stay the night.

'Building site maybe if I can't get into Mick's. But I can't face it for much longer it's too bloody cold.'

John heaved his bulk off the settee. 'Listen, I'm off to The Apsley so, unless you want to tag along, I'll see you around.'

Joe shrugged. 'Right then, I'll be off. Cheers for the cider and the weed.'

Dejected, he walked back to the precinct and managed to scrounge a couple of fags before returning to his bench opposite Woolworth's. He didn't feel good; it was hard to hold his head up and his breath came in shuddering gasps.

There was a drumming noise in his head, a mindless drone that he couldn't silence. He jiggled his feet; it would be dark soon.

His mind drifted once more to thoughts of home. Mum would be making Christmas puddings as usual. She always did this in half-term week and since his dad died routine and tradition seemed more important to her than ever. Joe could picture her trying to persuade Jess to stir the pudding mixture and have a wish. His sister, at fifteen, would no doubt pull a disdainful face while secretly enjoying the annual tradition. Sometimes, he'd been roped in to help tie up the greaseproof paper over the basin. The pudding was then boiled for an incredible six hours which made all the windows steam up. It seemed a world away now. Mum would love him to go home for Christmas, but he couldn't face the reality of a cosy family Christmas without his father. Last year, the first Christmas since he'd died, had been overwhelming. Joe tried and failed to break through the suffocating sadness inside him only to end up morose and unforgiving.

He leaned his head back on the cold bench, ashamed of his behaviour. He had spoilt Christmas for mum and Jess, and he couldn't let that happen this year. He walked to the phone box outside the Post Office and asked the operator to get his Mum to agree to a reverse charge call. He knew what she was like. She'd get her hopes up, and he needed to tell her that he wouldn't be there. Jess would be disappointed as well, but it was better this way.

'Oh, Joe, that's a shame. It's not because of that row we had last year, is it?'

'No, Mum, it's nothing like that. I've just got other plans, that's all.'

She would know that he was lying but how could he explain that he was ashamed of the state he'd got into; that he couldn't cope without alcohol or drugs even for a few days.

'Are you sure I can't persuade you, Joe? Jess and I miss you so much; you know that don't you?'

8

'Of course, I do. I miss you too. Please don't keep on, Mum.'

'Sorry. I know it's your life and you're old enough to make your own decisions, but I can't help worrying about you, Joe. I never know where you are or if you're in trouble. I can't bear to think of you vulnerable and lonely.'

Joe heard the break in her voice, but he couldn't reach inside himself to ease her pain.

Chapter 2
Maisie

Maisie glanced up at the clear, night sky. *Why hadn't she worn a warmer coat?* She hugged her parcel of fish-and-chips, grateful for their warmth through her thin T-shirt, and walked quickly, wishing she'd parked the car closer.

Few people were about; there were several pubs along the road, but with an hour until closing time, customers were tucked up with their pints. A couple of cars drove by and an old man on a bicycle. She could see the determination on his face as he pedalled against the wind. He reminded Maisie of her beloved grandpa, who used to cycle everywhere. Further down, a woman walking her dog had stopped to look in a shop window. The long road was full of small shops, some brightly lit, but tonight the busy street had a deserted feel. Ill at ease, she glanced over her shoulder. *Thank goodness she had trainers on rather than heels or worse her new clogs.* Out of breath, it was a relief to reach the safety of her car. She patted the roof of her blue Escort and unlocked the driver's door.

Without warning, a hand clamped over her mouth; a knee rammed into the small of her back, winding her, as she was dragged backwards. The powerful smell of dirty, unwashed hands and nicotine made her gag. Desperate for air, it was hard to swallow, and she struggled to twist sideways. Her eyes watered as the blood rushed to her head. Giddy with shock, she stumbled and fell backwards into the darkness grazing her hands on some brick rubble. She lay still and tried to make sense of what was happening. Her stomach knotted into a tight ball, and she was shaking from a mixture of cold and fear. Her elbow throbbed, but she was too scared to move.

Light from a streetlamp shone through strips of planking in front of her, but she had no idea where her attacker was or even if he was still there. Her eyes scanned the darkness as she strained to listen for the slightest sound that would confirm his presence. Her hand reached out and gripped a cold metal prop. Her brain was numb with shock. She wanted to yell at him and demand to know what the fuck he was doing, but she was unable to utter a sound. She huddled in the darkness feeling small and helpless. A paper rustled, and she smelt chips. A ridiculous urge to giggle hit her. *Had she been mugged for fish and chips?* For a moment, everything seemed normal, and she struggled to her feet, not afraid anymore, just angry.

'Sit down and keep still.'

His voice was a harsh whisper; then she felt the weight of him as he pinned her to the ground. His knee pressed hard against her throat, crushing her chest, and he clamped her wrists above her head.

Unable to move, she struggled to control her mounting panic; she forced herself to slow down her breathing, but despite her efforts, noisy, humiliating sobs shook her body. As a sense of helplessness engulfed her, she tried again to scream, but he was too close, and fear had paralysed her. Her breath came in shuddering gasps. *Think, think what to do.* Overwhelmed and choking from the unabated sobbing, she hunched up and waited. Her mass of curly hair clung damply to her face, and she could smell cement and brick dust. *Where was this place?*

She remembered parking her car outside the old Essoldo cinema; the building had been demolished last year, and now they were putting up new shops with flats above. *That's what the smell was – a building site.* More accustomed to the dark now, she could just make out long, dark hair. He took a cigarette from his pocket, and as he struck the match, she caught a glimpse of his impassive face. He wore faded jeans and a black donkey jacket and didn't look very old. Irrationally, now that she had seen his face, she wasn't so scared. She groped for one of the metal supports and hauled herself into a sitting position. She sensed that he was watching her in the dim light. She strained to listen for the sound of passers-by. *Please let someone go by soon*. The pub on the corner was usually packed out with students.

'What do you want from me?' she blurted out, surprised at how normal she sounded.

He stood up and walked towards her. 'Don't worry; I'm not going to hurt you. You got any money?' He hesitated, 'or something I can flog.' He ran his fingers through his hair and Maisie sensed his uncertainty.

'I've only got some small change; you can have that.' She groped in her anorak pocket for her purse. 'Look, just take it. I've been to badminton, and I never take much money in case it's stolen.'

He snorted. 'You being funny?'

She held out the purse. 'Please take it and let me go. It's bloody freezing in here. I haven't anything else; I promise you.'

There was no reply, and she could hear him rummaging about.

'Just shut up,' he muttered and tossed her an old damp blanket.

She shuddered with distaste; it smelt of mushrooms and reminded her of the bedsit she lived in at university.

Thank God, she bit her lip to prevent herself from making a sound for, at last, she could hear people coming down the road. She sat motionless hardly daring to breathe as each thump of her heart reverberated in her ears. She fought to control the shaking and opened her mouth to scream. But she had left it too late. She choked and spluttered as he shoved his bundled-up coat into her face. She thrashed from side to side, gripped now by a wild panic. With one hand, she managed to grasp a lump of brick and threw it at the wooden planks which shielded them from the road. The voices were now a few feet away, and she was desperate to attract their attention. But the brick hit the plank with a dull thud. She kicked her feet, scrunching them back and forth on the rough ground. But no one heard, and the voices grew fainter.

After what seemed an age, he removed the coat and retreated to his corner. I should have just slammed the bloody brick into the back of his skull, she thought. She drew her legs up and hugged her knees as she rocked back and forth; tiredness and the biting cold were making her light-headed. All she could think about was being back in the safety of her warm flat. Drawing the smelly blanket around her shoulders, she wiped her nose on her sleeve and rested her head on her knees. There was nothing for it but wait and try to remain alert. She guessed he had been sleeping rough on the building site. She could make out some old paper cement bags spread on the ground, and he had organised a bed of sorts. She could see his shadowy figure as he leant against a wooden crossbeam and smoked another cigarette without urgency.

She recognised the familiar cannabis aroma.

Trembling and stiff with the cold she stayed hunched up. Her eyes were heavy, and she shook her head as a wave of nausea and dizziness swept over her. She must have been there for several hours and, as more time elapsed, the situation took on a surreal quality.

The drone of a milk float woke her with a start. In the dawn light, she could see a curled, motionless shape covered by an ex-army sleeping bag. Terrified that she would make a noise and wake him, she tiptoed towards the gap in the planks and once out on the road, she ran noiselessly after the milk float.

'Police.' She was struggling to breathe. 'Please, call the police. I've been attacked. Call the bloody police, will you?' She screamed at the amazed milkman and grabbed his arm.

At the police station, a young policewoman put a blanket around her shoulders and passed her a mug of hot tea. Maisie sniffed; she was tearful and leaden with the misery of exhaustion. The girl passed her a box of tissues and Maisie scrubbed haphazardly beneath her eyes and blew her nose.

13

'I must have dropped my car keys somewhere,' she began. 'Is my car ok?'

The policewoman promised to send someone over to check.

'Right, when you're ready, I shall need to take a statement from you.'

Maisie did her best to get her head around what had happened, but it was now half-past eight in the morning, and the details floated off like some vague dream.

'Just start from the beginning and describe in your own words what happened.' The policewoman smiled at her encouragingly.

'I'll try. I'd been to badminton and bought some fish and chips from The Seafarer for my supper. I'd just reached my car and was trying to get the keys out of my pocket when he grabbed me from behind; his arm was around my chest, and he dragged me backwards.'

'Was he someone known to you?'

Maisie shook her head.

'Ok. What happened next?'

'I'm not sure. I remember smelling cement dust and thinking that I was on the site of the old Essoldo, but it was dark.'

'Did he say anything?'

'He asked for money, but I didn't have much.'

'And did you try to scream or to get away from him?'

'I think I just froze; I couldn't do anything. It was horrible.'

'Did he hurt you in any way?'

Maisie nodded. 'Yes.' She choked with tears as she described how he had held her arms so she couldn't move and thrust his knee into her throat.

'Can you describe the man? How tall would you say he was?'

'Average height with long curly dark hair. It was difficult to tell in the dark.'

14

'What about his voice? What sort of accent did he have?'

'Local, I suppose. He didn't sound foreign, but he could be from the West Country.'

'Do you think you would recognise him again?'

Maisie shrugged. It was hot and stuffy in the sparsely furnished room, and she longed to go home, have a long hot bath and sleep.

They asked her to look through some police photographs and to her surprise, she recognised two or three men from around town, but her attacker wasn't among them.

The pillar-box red front door opened straight into the living room. Although it was daylight, Maisie switched on all the lights; she hated gloomy rooms. As a child, the dark had terrified her, and she had to have a light on in her bedroom until she was eleven. Dark corners still frightened her so whenever she saw a lamp that she liked in the shops she bought it to go somewhere in the flat. Her latest and most extravagant purchase from John Lewis depicted a reclining bronze cherub. Then she put her favourite James Taylor tape on the stereo and ran downstairs to the kitchen.

She shared the ground floor and basement of the Victorian terraced house with Sally, who was a teacher and away for half term. Maisie couldn't decide if this was a good thing or not. The kitchen was her favourite room and was often her first port of call when she got home. The pine shelves were a jumble of books, plants and scented candles and had become a general dumping ground. The corkboard above the cast iron fireplace was crammed with a hotchpotch of bills, photos, invitations, and general reminders not to forget her mum's birthday, book the car for service and so forth.

She rummaged in the cupboard for some food. A strange exhilaration had replaced the tiredness, and she was starving hungry. She decided on sardines on toast and sat at the big pine table. The warm, fishy butter dripped between her fingers as she tried to read yesterday's evening paper. Without warning, the cat flap banged. Her hand shot to her mouth, and her stomach lurched. Sick with nerves, she started to shake again. Perhaps she should have let the police contact someone instead of trying to ignore it all. But it was just Sally's cat attracted by the sardines.

Feeling sorry for herself, she filled a hot-water bottle. She clutched it in much the same way as she'd done with the fish and chips earlier and curled up in bed. She tried to sleep, but her mind refused to let go and incessantly replayed the events of the previous night. It seemed incredible that he had just leapt out and dragged her off the street. Sometimes she had imagined what she would do if she were ever attacked and had envisaged herself, possessed with enormous strength and determination, putting up a violent show of resistance. The reality was different. It all happened so fast. She had been taken by surprise and, once the initial attack was over, the shock had paralysed her. She tossed about in bed. *Who he was and why he had attacked her?* At twenty-six she looked like many of the female students who lived in the town, hardly rich pickings. She vaguely contemplated the idea that he'd been stalking her, and maybe it wasn't random at all. It was a scary thought.

Next morning, she dragged herself out of bed. She would have to leave earlier than usual to pick her car up, so she skipped breakfast and grabbed the tray of folders she needed for her first lecture. She groaned, remembering that she had intended to prepare for the lecture last night. Now she'd have to wing it again. Nor had she marked any of their essays. She wasn't ready to talk about what happened and would have to invent some excuse. *Why did she always leave everything to the last minute?*

For much of the day, she was too busy to concentrate on anything other than work. But as soon as she was in her car and alone, she couldn't help mulling over the smallest details of Tuesday night. The image of the guy's face loomed over her as she relived the smell of damp brick dust and his

16

grimy hands so close to her face. Her vulnerability was still shocking. *Why did she freeze?* It had been a horrible ordeal, not helped by her claustrophobia, but she hadn't ever been in real danger.

On impulse, she drove to the police station anxious to find out whether they'd caught him. She was sure he was local and had been sleeping rough around the area. But there was little the desk sergeant could tell her and his attitude, bordering on sarcastic, irritated her.

'Silly old fart,' she grumbled as the heavy glass doors of the Victorian police station banged behind her.

Tired and dispirited, she decided to skip badminton and drive straight home. She made her weary way up the six steps to the front door. A hot bath and a large glass of red wine were called for. Refreshed after her bath, she opened the fridge, but she didn't feel hungry. Instead, she reached for the wine bottle on the dresser. She glanced around; she ought to tidy up before Sally arrived back on Saturday. She collected up dirty coffee mugs, stored away old newspapers and threw away the screwed-up tissues, which were evidence of the bouts of weeping she had indulged in over the last two days. All this activity made her hungry, so she fixed herself a deliciously indulgent, fried egg sandwich and settled down to read the evening paper. On page four, a small column described the mugging of a twenty-six-year-old local woman. At least she hadn't been named. She still hadn't told anyone apart from the police about her attack. She wasn't sure why as she tended to tell all the world and his wife everything that was going on in her life. An uneasy part of her brain was telling her that it hadn't been some big ordeal but, instead, a piece of thrilling theatre; not that she could admit that to anyone else.

Chapter 3
Joe

Joe wiped the spittle running down his chin with the back of his hand. He had just thrown up in the gutter, and his stomach heaved once more as he struggled to control the violent shaking throughout his body. He shook his head, desperate to clear the cloying fuzziness. Wild-eyed and staring around him, his chest heaved with shuddering gasps. *What the fuck had he done?* Amidst the blur, he had a sense of violence and fear – his violence, her fear? *Yes, he'd had a joint and drunk a couple of pints but not enough to explain his actions.*

He had watched the girl through the planks as she unlocked her car. Even in the dim light, he could tell she was pretty. He remembered feeling sick with hunger and the smell of her fish and chips in the cold night air. *Why the hell hadn't he just grabbed the girl's purse and legged it?*

He walked fast, barely able to feel his legs in the biting wind. It was light now, and more people were around on their way to work. He kept his head down, conscious of the stares of strangers watching him. He had to get away from here fast; the police would be looking for him. Although it had been dark, she must have got a good enough look at him to give them a reasonable description. He needed to disappear for a few days, but without money, his options were limited. Mick might be at his flat, but he'd never wake him up this early, and he couldn't risk going to John's place. Instead, he wandered around the shopping precinct. He ran his fingers through his tangled hair. He felt light-headed as though a tight band was gripping his head.

Then he spotted a dealer he knew leaning on the wall of Boots and persuaded him to let him have two wraps of speed on account. Behind the bins, at the back of the precinct, he snorted a wrap knowing the effect would come quicker than swallowing it. He felt his heart rate quicken, and he started breathing rapidly. A burst of energy swept through him as he paced up and down, rubbing his hands together. The crazy unrealistic ideas came thick and fast. *He could sort this.*

He didn't know how long he had sat on the wooden bench in the precinct. *Had he slept?* He couldn't remember if he had eaten, but the wide-awake buzz was wearing off. He got up to stretch his stiff legs and shuffled around like some old man. As usual, the hurrying shoppers ignored him, and he remained anonymous.

That night, he huddled in Boots doorway and tried to sleep until he became aware of the breaking dawn. Heavy with tiredness, he longed to continue sleeping, but the aching cold ruled that out. Besides, he had an urgent need for a pee and a drink. His hands shook as his body craved alcohol. He dragged himself to his feet; but dizziness made him sway, and he leaned against the tiled wall for a moment, struggling to remain upright. Rain clouds mired the dawn sky, and the icy wind swirled yesterday's rubbish around the deserted precinct. After a few minutes, the giddiness cleared. But he couldn't shake off a sense of utter panic about what he had done. It was a moment of madness. He hadn't even been desperate for money. It was almost as if he did it because he could because, at that moment, he was invincible. Now he was just in a panic about what would happen if he got caught. There had been no time to pick up his few belongings from the building site, but surely there was nothing to link him to the old blankets and stuff.

He waited until opening time. Mick was already at the bar, and he broke into a big grin when he saw Joe come in and punched him on the shoulder.

'Where've you been then? You old bastard.'

Joe shrugged. 'Nowhere much. Anything happening tonight?'

Mick pulled a tight wad of pound notes from the pocket of his black jeans. 'I fancy...' he said, screwing up his eyes, 'I fancy tipping a load of beer in my head followed by a big fat curry. You up for it?'

Joe nodded. Mick knew he didn't have any money, but it wouldn't matter. Mick liked to have mates around him; he was generous like that.

They all met up at The Apsley as arranged. Andy produced a gram of speed for the four of them and just before leaving, they mixed it with the last mouthful of beer. Stu held his empty glass aloft.

'Here's to a good night. Right gentlemen, let's go.'

The Rendezvous Club quickly drew them into its heady atmosphere. Joe relished the wide-awake buzz from the speed and jumped manically around the beer-sticky dance floor. When the club kicked out at 2 a.m., Mick suggested a curry at The Bombay. It stayed open late at weekends, so they wandered off in that direction. They were walking past the church when, without warning, Mick grabbed hold of a girl coming in the opposite direction. His mouth slobbered over the girl's astonished face and chaos broke out. The girl's boyfriend landed a skilful punch on Mick's jaw; another grabbed Stu by the throat and threw him up against the rough flint wall.

The girl's screams were shrill and insistent. 'For Christ's sake, don't hit him. He's got a weak heart,' she sobbed, screaming at Mick to stop.

Joe observed the brutal little scene, struck by the irony of the girl's words. Stu lay in the gutter with blood oozing from a split lip, and everyone was running around and shouting. Joe bent down to see if Stu was ok just as the police cars, three of them, screeched to a halt. Cold fear shot through his hunched body.

Chapter 4
Maisie

Maisie heard a knock at her front door. She stretched and yawned; it was Saturday morning, and she had been enjoying the luxury of a lie-in. A policeman stood there while his colleague waited in the car opposite. Her heart lurched at the prospect of some news.

'Miss George, hi, how are you doing?'

Wide-eyed now, she raised her eyebrows in expectation and smiled at him.

'We have picked up a possible suspect for your attack, and it would help us if you could come down to the station and identify him.'

Maisie couldn't help smiling; he was younger than her, but his tone was formal and earnest.

'Yes, sure. Can you give me two minutes to get dressed?'

'No problem, we'll be outside in the car.'

Her fingers fumbled to do up her jeans. All her comfortable indolence gone; she was riddled with apprehension. She pulled on a thick sweater, brushed her hair, and ran down the steps, slamming the front door behind her.

At the police station, she peered through the two-way glass window as instructed. He was slumped in the chair and staring straight ahead. *Surely, he was the same bloke?* She nodded at the policeman.

'Yes, that's definitely him. Where did you pick him up?'

The policeman explained about the fight in Kingston Road. 'You were lucky he didn't hurt you, miss. His mate put someone in hospital last night; he's a nasty piece of work.'

'What happens now?'

'If you come down to the interview room, I'll take some more details. He'll be up in front of the Magistrates at a preliminary hearing probably on Monday morning and he'll either get bail or be remanded. Then, it will be a question of waiting until the full court hearing.'

'How long will that be?'

He shrugged. 'A month at least could be after Christmas. It depends how long the CPS take to put a case together.'

Maisie drove along the seafront on the way home. She didn't know what to do with the rest of her Saturday. Reluctant to go back to an empty flat, she parked the car and gazed across the dull November water to the island. She watched a couple of dog walkers and a dad teaching his little boy to skim the flat stones as a melancholy mood full of creeping loneliness descended.

There were plenty of things that she could be doing. She could go to Alice's Café and treat herself to a coffee and a cake. Instead, she decided to do a bit of shopping then head over to the pub for a lunchtime drink. There was bound to be someone she knew in The Apsley. *But not today.* She paid for half a lager and looked around undecided whether to perch on a stool at the bar or sit conspicuously alone at an empty table by the window. She chose the bar stool and was playing idly with a beer mat when the door banged. She hoped it was someone she knew, but it was only a couple of students.

'Stuart, my boy. How's tricks?' the barman enquired. 'Usual, is it?'

'Please, and a half of mild for Angie.'

He downed most of his pint before he spoke. 'Have you heard that my mate, Joe has been arrested?'

The barman shook his head.

'We were out with that psychopath Mick and got into a fight. Turns out Joe was wanted for another offence. He tried to mug some girl in Albert Road. He dragged her on to the building site where he was sleeping rough and kept her there all night. Christ knows what he was thinking?'

'Where did you get all this from?'

'We just bumped into Mick, who was there when they arrested Joe. The cops let Mick go because of lack of evidence, or so he claimed.'

Maisie's heart pounded, and she gripped her glass to stop her hands from shaking.

Chapter 5
Joe

Joe dialled his mother's number. He felt like shit and was alarmed at how much his hands were shaking.

'Hello, love, that was good timing. I've just walked in the door.'

'Thank god it's Friday'.

Joe heard her let out a sigh. He clutched the receiver to his chest for a moment. *How was he going to tell her that he was in police custody?* His mind was racing, and as he struggled to get it straight in his head, he kept rushing from one bit of the story to another, then tailing off mid-sentence.

'Slow down, love. I can't understand you if you talk ten to the dozen like that. What are you talking about? False imprisonment, what's that supposed to mean and who is this girl? Do you know her?'

'No, she was just walking by. I can't remember what happened, Mum. Why would I do that to her?'

There was an agonising pause while his mind flashed from one scenario to another as he waited to hear her voice.

'Listen; don't worry, love. Just hang in there and try to stay calm. I'll drive down to Portsmouth in the morning. Jess can stay at her friend's house for the weekend, so I'll see you tomorrow, old thing. I suppose they'll let me see you?' Her voice rose in agitation.

'I think so, don't know really,' he muttered. 'Must go now, mum; love you.'

He leant against the wall by the phone. *It was a long time since he'd told her that he loved her.* Always cheerful, always practical, she gave him her unconditional love, and he'd let her down once again. At least they'd let him speak to her. He chewed his bottom lip to stop the tears welling

Joe sat opposite the duty solicitor, a cheap metal table between them. He tried his best to concentrate and struggled with an overwhelming urge to stand up and pace about the room. It was twelve hours now since he'd had a drink and he had a stinking headache. *Why couldn't he remember?* He remembered that he was hungry and that he hadn't eaten. The need to get money for enough booze to get him through the night had been there, and more acutely than before. He remembered seeing her walk along the road and deciding to approach her for money. After that, it was a blank.

The solicitor told him that he had held the girl against her will for several hours.

'There is no evidence of any sexual assault, which is good for us,' he continued. 'But she sustained some minor injuries, bruising and a few deep scratches. The charge will be one of assault and false imprisonment, but I understand that, subsequent to the victim's statement, they have dropped the robbery charge.'

'How come?'

'Well, it appears that you didn't actually steal any of her money or personal possessions.'

Joe clenched his hands in his lap and looked down at his battered desert boots. He was scared, none of it made sense. *Why would he hurt her?* It was hard to breathe as he rocked back and forth.

'You'll be held here in the cells over the weekend and be taken to the Magistrates' Court on Monday morning.'

'What happens then?'

The solicitor paused as if weighing up the situation. 'Monday will be a short hearing, and as it's your first offence and you intend to plead guilty, I'm hopeful that you'll be bailed until the sentencing hearing. That's what I will be pressing for.'

Next morning, after a restless night, Joe woke drenched in sweat. He felt sick and couldn't shake off an overwhelming feeling of anxiety. When a female officer brought him his breakfast, his hands shook so much that he couldn't hold the plate. She took the plate back off him.

'Whoa, steady on.' She guided him back to the bed. 'Do you need to see a doctor?' Her tone was gentle.

The police doctor took his blood pressure and asked him about his drinking. Joe calculated that it was nearly thirty hours since he'd had a drink. *No surprise that he felt so rough.*

'I'll prescribe 30 mg of diazepam a day. They should help you to feel less anxious and should stop the trembling. That dosage may make you feel sleepy, but the effect should last for a few days.'

Joe survived the endless weekend in the police cell, and by the following morning, the clenching anxiety had lessened. His mum would put up his bail, and no doubt take him back to Bath until his sentencing.

But it was not to be, and the Magistrate informed him that he was to be remanded-into-custody to Winchester prison. The solicitor explained that it was a category B prison which meant nothing to Joe and that it would probably be for three or four weeks at the most, but this was of little consolation. The Magistrates also asked for medical and psychiatric reports.

As a remand prisoner, Joe could wear his own clothes and was allowed a few toiletries. He sat opposite his mother in an airless interview room next to the Magistrates' Court.

'Where's your stuff, Joe?'

He could tell that she was close to tears. 'I don't have any stuff, Mum. Not anymore.'

He couldn't look her in the eye and shook his head as a shuddering sigh travelled down his body.

Chapter 6
Lily

Driving back to Bath Lily worried about how she would she tell Jess? She adored her brother and missed him almost as much as she did.

'Don't be ridiculous, mum. Joe would never do that; you know he wouldn't.' Jess laughed a little too loudly. 'Unless he's gone completely bloody mad.'

Later that evening, Lily pulled on a cosy jumper; she couldn't seem to get warm. Jess had gone out to a firework party and wouldn't be back until after eleven. She was still upset and hadn't wanted to go, but Lily had persuaded her that it would be a welcome distraction. She was anxious to hide from her daughter how frightened she was for Joe. *If only Jack was here, and they could talk it through together.* There wasn't much he could have done except support him as she had tried to do, but Jack would have helped her to cope with all this. On her own, she felt lost.

There was nothing she wanted to watch on television, so she poured a strong gin and tonic and settled down to listen to a radio play. Occasionally, she pulled back the curtains to watch the firework displays. When Joe and Jess were small, they had always let off a box of fireworks in the back garden and eaten steaming hot jacket potatoes followed by mugs of hot chocolate. Jack hadn't favoured organised displays and the children always seemed just as excited by their amateur efforts. Tears ran down her cheeks as she remembered Joe in those days. He would spend hours inspecting the different fireworks, reading the leaflet about them, and making lists of the order they were to be let off. Now he was in prison. She was gripped with sadness that her bright, exuberant son should have found adult life so hard.

As a child he'd been so full of life, bounding around like an exuberant puppy but by the time he was in his mid-teens he became less predictable and prone to big mood swings. Lily knew what teenagers could be like but living with Joe was never easy, and he was often volatile and unreliable. He upset people, often unintentionally. Even when he was away at college, when they talked on the phone, she never knew what to expect. His take on life was always so extreme; it was either the best party he'd been to; the best group of friends and life was fantastic, or he would gloomily report that he hated college; couldn't bear so and so, and life was complete shit. She could never understand how his mood could switch like that when nothing in his life seemed to have changed. At times he was incredibly talkative, describing his student life in minute detail or he would be morose and monosyllabic. Either way, she learned to handle him; learned never to criticise, knowing that if she did so, he was apt to fly off the handle and even mild comments became taboo.

When Joe had sat opposite her in that ghastly room in the magistrates' court, it had been a struggle to hide her emotions. *How had it come to this?* He had seemed so bewildered; trapped in some empty, meaningless life. Lily bit hard on her lip to stop the tears. *He may not have much, but he's got me and Jess who love him so much. But would that be enough?* She was at a loss to understand him and was shrunken with fear for his future.

Chapter 7
Joe

Joe woke in the narrow prison bed. The speed of events made it hard to focus, and it took him a while to realise where he was. With his head pounding, he stretched out his arms and stared at his shaking hands. He was desperate for a drink or anything to help him relax. *The diazepam must be wearing off.*

He wondered where Mick was. *Perhaps he was here too?* Mick had been inside several times, so was unlikely to escape with a fine or probation. Joe tried to imagine some poor bastard from the probation office, having to deal with Mick. He remembered Mick's weekly trip to the pet shop to purchase the lovebirds for some sad, old woman in London who worried and wondered about her son. *Perhaps, she was mad too, sad, and mad.* Joe decided he didn't care. He had heard scare stories of rape and humiliating initiation rituals in prison. *Did they put remand prisoners in with those already sentenced?* He didn't know what to expect or how to act.

By the time he'd arrived in the prison transport yesterday and been processed, he'd missed supper and was given a cheese sandwich and a packet of crisps which he ate sitting on his bed in the cell. The other occupant was nowhere to be seen. Unsure what to do next, Joe crawled under the scratchy, grey blanket and fell asleep.

When he woke, he had no idea what the time was. There was no window, but from the corridor lights, he could see well enough to make out his surroundings. The bloke in the opposite bed was snoring. The greyish, thin face and short, dark hair told Joe that he was not a remand prisoner. He fingered his own springy locks. At least, for the moment, he wouldn't be subjected to a prison haircut. He lay back on the narrow bed with its thin greasy pillow and lumpy mattress. At some point, he realised that he was being observed.

'Alright?' The guy was propped on one elbow grinning at him. 'I'm Tony and you?'

'Joe. How long are you in for?'

'Three years this time but I've done five months, so I should be out by the summer.' He paused to roll a joint. 'This nick's ok as it goes. My mates reckon I put on weight and look healthier when I get out. If you keep clear of the psychos, it's not too stressful. None of that fear of getting caught, I guess.'

'Caught doing what? What are you in for?' Joe wondered if his questioning would trigger a reaction.

'Male rape. I can't seem to help myself.' With that, Tony gave a soft chuckle and drew deeply on his joint.

The noise on the wing grew louder as the warders unlocked doors, a signal for other prisoners further down the corridor to begin their relentless and pointless banging on the cell door and the catcalling of loud, challenging voices. Plunged into this hostile and chaotic environment, Joe was out of his depth and vulnerable. He took a deep breath. He mustn't show that he was scared.

'What happens now?' he asked, already pulling on his jeans.

Tony grinned. 'Breakfast will shortly be served.' He cocked his head on one side, listening. 'Ah, here we go.'

The airless cell was unlocked, and an orderly thrust a tray at Joe. Breakfast it appeared, consisted of a single portion of cereal with UHT milk and a hard, crusty roll accompanied by a pat of margarine and a portion of jam.

'Tea urn will be along in a minute.' Tony informed him.

'Do we eat all our meals in here?' Joe was finding the stench from the slop bucket hard to stomach.

'No. In some nicks, you have to, but in here we go to the dining hall for lunch and supper.'

Ten minutes or so later, a warder arrived for Tony.

'Bye, sweet pea, work calls.' He turned to give Joe a cheery wave.

Joe sat on his bed, wondering what to do next. He was used to his own company but not this feeling of isolation, and he missed being able to people watch. He spotted a rolled-up magazine on the cupboard next to Tony's bunk. He didn't think Tony would mind if he borrowed it but having resolved to trust no one decided against it. *Maybe he could get a book or something from the prison library, anything to pass the time?* Then, a warder arrived to escort him to the prison doctor; this was welcome news as he needed more diazepam. A bristly chinned nurse took his blood pressure and took a blood sample before ushering him into the doctor's room. Joe took an immediate dislike to him. He had the same grey haggard look of many of the prisoners and made no eye contact from start to finish. He asked endless questions about how much alcohol Joe drank, what drugs he took, and how often. Then interview over, he waved his hand dismissively in the direction of the door.

'The nurse will give you what you need for now, and you will be brought here every other day to receive your meds. I'll review in four weeks, that's if you're still here.'

The rest of the morning dragged; he lay on his back listening. It was quieter now as most of the inmates were either at work or in the education unit. According to Tony, both were optional if you were on remand, but anything was better than this void. He couldn't help glancing at the clock on Tony's bedside cabinet. Shortly before midday, he was escorted to the r for lunch. In the queue, he could feel the breath of the guy behind on his neck.

'Got any fags?'

Joe stared straight ahead and said nothing. Next moment he was struggling to breathe as the guy's muscular arm came around his throat in a stranglehold and a knee jagged his kidneys.

'Ignoring me, are you, pretty boy?'

Just as suddenly it was all over. If the two warders had noticed, they chose to ignore it. Joe collected his lunch of cheese sandwich and crisps, same as last night's supper, and made his way to a table. He managed to get a surreptitious look at the guy who intended to make his presence known and resolved to ask Tony about him tonight. No one at the table spoke to him at all and very little to each other.

During supper, Joe learned that Tony was serving time for burglary and that he had to share a cell with him because there was no space on the remand wing. His informant was a quietly spoken convicted fraudster with a bland expression.

'They come, and they go,' the man sighed, looking around the dining hall. 'You get all sorts in here. They could be on trial for murder, violence, rape, or other sexual crimes. It's anyone's guess.' He licked his puffy lips.

Tony knew straight away who had tried to intimidate Joe.

'You did the right thing ignoring him. There'll be plenty more of that and worse. They've all got their different ways. Some will ask you to lend them money, and others will offer to lend you money or give you a fag. Just don't give them anything or accept anything for that matter, right?'

'Why's that? Isn't it better to keep them happy and go along with whatever it is they want?'

'Fucking hell, mate. If you do that, they will know that you're weak and they've got you then. You don't know who you can trust. If someone talks to you, think to yourself, why are they talking to me? What do they want from me?'

After lights out, Joe pondered on what Tony might want from him.

The next few days easier and Joe, who had always been observant of his surroundings, soon learned who to avoid. Although work and education courses were optional, he volunteered for both. He was sent to the laundry room where he was hit by the incessant noise and stifling steamy atmosphere. Nobody spoke; it would have been pointless with the constant whirr of the large industrial washers. That night, Joe rubbed his aching back; he was exhausted after three hours of lugging heavy wicker baskets.

His second visit to the laundry room confirmed his suspicions that it was a dangerous place to be. There was one warder and plenty of places to remain out of sight. That morning he'd witnessed a sickening attack and heard the crack of fists on a man's jaw and his cries for help. At the end of the shift, the guy was discovered lying semi-conscious in a pool of vomit, blood, and teeth. In bed that night, he relived the awful sights and sounds he'd witnessed. The fear of violence was almost worse than violence itself, and it made him vulnerable.

Joe smoked the occasional joint, less as the days went by. Instead, he became obsessed with his predicament and was locked into a cycle of endlessly going over events and re-inventing the outcome. His intrusive thoughts kept him awake at night. He'd never had so much time to think before and it was driving him mad. When he had been on the streets, there was always the distraction of how he was going to get hold of enough alcohol or where he could crash for the night. In prison, the incessant noise and lack of sleep just made him exhausted and irritable.

He and Tony, along with the rest of their wing, were trudging around the exercise yard.

'What's the date today?' Joe asked.

'Must be the twelfth, I reckon.'

Joe groaned. 'Great, that means it's my birthday. Twenty today. I hope you've remembered my card.' He attempted a grin, but inside he felt shame and despair. This was as low as he could have sunk and the prospect of falling into a full-blown depression terrified him.

When they arrived back at their cell, there was a parcel waiting for Joe. Security had opened it, but he recognised his mum's writing. *Bless her; she'd not forgotten him.* There was a card with an eagle soaring over snow-capped mountains as well as a warm grey jumper and a packet of chocolate digestives. It was a timely boost for Joe as his solicitor, the nondescript and exaggeratedly disinterested Mr Parr, had

33

told him to expect a custodial sentence of a year to eighteen months. This was not what he wanted to hear. He also warned him about the forthcoming psychiatric report. *What would that involve?*

Three weeks later, he was to find out.

'Had you planned to attack the girl,' the psychiatrist asked. 'What was going through your head at the time?'

Joe clasped his hands in front of him. It was important to make a good impression, make the right noises.

'I didn't plan it; it was just a spur of the moment thing.'

'And what prompted this spur of the moment action.?'

Joe hesitated. The truth was that he had no idea why he'd done it. Maybe it was better just to make something up.

'I'd been drinking all day, and I knew I needed something to get me through the night. I was desperate to get hold of enough cash for that. I'm not violent; I hate violence, but I was desperate.' He raised his head and looked the psychiatrist in the eye. 'I guess I need help; don't I?'

The questions continued. How had his violent behaviour made him feel? Did he feel remorse now? He realised that he had been blocking out the level of violence he was capable of. The feeling of self-loathing which crept across him was almost physical in its effect.

When he returned to their shared cell, Tony's head was wrapped in grey, smoke gossamer. Languidly, eyes half-closed, Tony turned to face him.

'What are you looking so fucking pleased about?'

'I've just had my session with the psych, and they told me that my hearing's next Tuesday.'

Tony looked disconcerted. 'So? They're hardly going to let you out; are they? You'll probably be shunted off to another nick. The longer you are on remand, the better. Christ, don't you know anything?'

He lay back down on his bed. Like most of the inmates, he spent significant amounts of time either asleep or wanking. Joe shrugged. He didn't know why he was so wound up about the trial date. *At least, it would make a change, a break from the mind throttling routine.* He couldn't explain it to Tony, though. He was fond of Tony, especially now that he was better acquainted with some of the real nutters on their landing. The creepy fraud guy unnerved him, and Joe guessed that there was more to it than fraud. Then there was the usual collection of psychopaths; the worst offender occupied a cell on his corridor. He was covered in tattoos with a shaved head. Just the sight of him was intimidating. There was a cocky swagger about him, and Tony described how he'd witnessed him forcing another prisoner to eat his shit after flushing his head down the bog just because he looked at him funny. Lockdowns were quite common on Joe's wing, and this guy was often at the heart of any trouble.

Lockdowns terrified Joe initially because he didn't know what the hell was happening. The first time, he was on his way back from lunch when the violence erupted behind him. Turning, he saw the weaselly serial burglar guy slumped on the floor and two warders trying to restrain the psycho. The noise was deafening as whistles were blown and prisoners banged on their cell doors, shouting and jeering. One of the warders managed to press the emergency button, and prison staff from all over the building ran in wielding their batons. Some piled in to help restrain the guy while the rest locked the remaining prisoners in their cells. It was a tense situation with men, already wound up with adrenaline, resentful that their limited freedoms had been temporarily curtailed.

Joe knew how lucky he was to have Tony as a cellmate. He took off his trainers and threw them at him one at a time.

'Going to miss me then?

'Piss off,' Tony replied and carefully spat into each shoe.

Joe ignored this and lay face down on his bunk; he needed to think.

Next Tuesday was five days away. The likelihood was they would send him back here. It was three weeks now, and he reckoned he could cope if he had to even with the boredom.

Joe had always needed to be busy. One of the worse aspects of the past year was having no money and nothing much to occupy his time. Some days it got to him. His brain would buzz with a jumble of random thoughts and his legs throb with restlessness. On those days, he walked as fast as he could, going nowhere in particular, until his throat and chest hurt. Other times, when he could get booze, he'd drink himself into a state of oblivion.

When he was younger, and at school in Bath he was always on the go, playing football, skateboarding, whatever came up. It made him smile now to think he had enjoyed going to the youth club for a while. That was before he started drinking and taking drugs. Too often, opportunities slid away from him, and he'd made bad choices. *It was a funny old life.*

'What do you reckon will happen when I'm in court?' he asked Tony.

'How the fuck should I know?'

'What about the girl, will she have to give evidence?'

Tony exhaled deeply and scratched his scalp through the short hair. 'Don't suppose so, you pleaded guilty, didn't you?'

Joe wondered if she would be there. *Would he even recognise her?* When he tried to picture her face, he was left with an image of a mass of blond curls.

Chapter 8
Maisie

Maisie glanced at her watch; five minutes more and they could break for coffee. With a start, she realised that one of the students had been talking, but her mind had drifted to how Joe was coping with prison life. It was claustrophobic in her cramped room. Only four of the seven students had turned up for the seminar; even so, the central heating made the room stuffy. Afterwards, one of the girls asked for an individual tutorial to discuss the next assignment.

'Are you ok, Jodie?' Maisie could see she was close to tears and was very pale.

The girl shook her head and burst into tears. Haltingly she explained that she wasn't coping with the academic side of university life. Maisie passed her tissues and made her a cup of coffee.

'Not to worry; we can sort it,' she smiled. 'I can give you a couple of one-to-one sessions and give you some pointers. Honestly, it's not uncommon for students to feel like that.'

'Thank you so much, that's really kind of you,' Josie blew her nose loudly and gave Maisie a weak smile. 'I've been so worried.'

After she'd gone Maisie clutched her coffee cup. She had a stack of essays to mark but pushed the pile away unable to summon any enthusiasm. She usually enjoyed the intellectual challenge of the job but with so much going on in her head it was difficult to concentrate, and her brain felt like cotton wool.

She stared out of the window. November was dull, damp, and unremarkable. She was glad that she had eventually plucked up the courage to tell her closest friends what she'd been going through. She'd told Sally straight away. She had arrived home on the Sunday night at the end of her half-term to find her either weeping or slamming stuff about in a foul mood. Sally, although shocked, was a good listener and it was good to get things off her chest. At work, she'd said nothing for a few days but had eventually spilt it out to Fran, a colleague in the psychology department, and asked her to keep it quiet. No one else at work knew, at least she hoped not. They probably realised that something was up because she'd been snappy and absent-minded.

Will had been a help though. He was Fran's partner and was a probation officer. He had patiently answered her questions about the police and the court. The same questions that went around and around her head at night.

'Coffee?' Shaun, who was the Admissions Tutor, poked his whiskery face around the door, making her jump.

Maisie nodded.

'How's the paper going?' He gave her a meaningful look.

'I'll get there. Don't panic. I've just come to a bit of a standstill; that's all.' She tried to sound reassuring.

'Hmm.' Shaun stirred his coffee. 'Well, let me know if you want to talk it through.'

She was due to present a paper on aggression at a child development conference at Sussex University in a couple of weeks. Shaun was her line manager; how could she tell him that she could barely even recall what she'd submitted as her title?

In the car park, that evening, she bumped into Fran.

'You coming to Pebbles tonight?' Fran rested her forearms on the handlebars of her man's racing bike. She was tall and angular with a pale, serious face beneath short and currently, mousy hair. She could be a real laugh and Maisie had liked her straight away. She was also an exceptional teacher, and the students loved her.

Maisie thought about her pile of marking and the elusive paper. 'Oh, sod it, why not? I'm not going to get much work done anyway.'

'Good decision. See you there about nine unless you want us to pick you up?'

'No, that's alright thanks. It's not far to walk.'

38

'OK. If, you're sure? See you later.'

She watched as Fran donned her helmet and pedaled vigorously away.

A group of about six of them from the department met up once a week in Pebbles wine bar. The place had an easy-going, relaxed atmosphere and they would down several bottles of red wine and pick idly at the dishes of fat olives. As the evening wore on their conversation would become increasingly animated. Sometimes they discussed work or the latest film, but usually, it was just easy gossipy banter.

Maisie leaned across the pine table. 'Hey, Will, have you managed to find out about my mystery attacker yet?'

His eyes narrowed, and he raised his eyebrows at her. 'Now, now, you know I couldn't possibly comment.' He spoke in a high, camp voice, mimicking Kenny Everett. 'Bedsides, now you know his name he's mystery man no more. You're such a drama queen.'

Maisie had drunk too much; she rested her chin in her hands and wrinkled her nose at him. 'Ah yes. Joseph Oliver, what do we know about him?'

Will shook his head. 'It's no good turning those big blue eyes on me; it won't make any difference.'

'Spoilsport.' She picked up her glass and tilted her head to one side. 'You have very long hair for a probation officer. Do they allow such things?' There was a hint of mockery in her voice. She put out her hand and touched his floppy, fair hair. 'I like your hair.'

At that moment, Shaun appeared. 'We're going back to my place for coffee. You going to join us?' He nodded in the direction of Will and Fran who readily agreed.

Maisie groaned and made a face at Shaun. 'Not for me, thanks; I must finish some work.'

Wanting to continue their conversation she turned back to Will. 'When do you think his court case will be? Surely that's not classified information?'

Will shrugged. 'He's already been on remand for a fortnight, so it should be in the next two to three weeks. It depends how much of a backlog there is in the Magistrates' Court. I can have a look at the list if you like and let you know.' He held her gaze. 'Promise,' he smiled.

She touched his shoulder. 'Thanks, Will.' She stood up unsteadily and, hoping no one had noticed, said her goodbyes.

Outside, the cold air hit her, exacerbating her tiredness. Thankfully, it wasn't long until the end of term, but she had a ton of work to do. Then it would be Christmas. She always went home to her parents for Christmas; at least it was something to look forward to.

Next morning, she received a letter from the CPS to tell her that the guy was pleading guilty. She felt cheated, knowing that she wouldn't be required to give evidence. The letter unsettled her. There was nobody she could share all this with, and she dreaded going to court on her own. Perhaps Will would go with her?

She dialed his number. It was Friday, so with luck, he'd be in the office.

'Will Stevens.'

'Oh, Will, I'm so glad you're there. The court date is sooner than we thought. I've had a letter from the CPS, and it's next Tuesday at ten o'clock.'

'You don't have to be there if you don't want to you know. You won't be called now he's pleading guilty.'

Not going wasn't an option. 'Of course, I want to be there. I want to hear what he has to say. Presumably, there'll be psychiatric reports won't there? It might be interesting.' She gripped the phone to stop her hand from shaking. 'Would you come with me, Will?'

She could hear a rustling sound.

'Sorry, just checking my diary. I could juggle things around if it helps.'

'Oh, yes please, if you can? You can hold my hand, as it were, and explain what's going on.'

'OK but be prepared for quite a lot of waiting about. They get everyone there for ten, but we won't know until the day what order they're going to hear the cases.'

Maisie found his use of we re-assuring.

It was stuffy in the small courtroom. Maisie had been inside a court once before when she was doing 'A' level Law and the lecturer had taken them to sit in the public gallery for a morning. She had been a carefree seventeen-year-old and blithely unaware of the consequences that faced the sad individuals in court.

Today, she was a spectator again and this time felt unnervingly conspicuous. Joseph Oliver was sat next to his solicitor, behind a polished, light wooden rail and opposite the magistrates. *What was going through his head?* As if aware of her scrutiny he raised his bent head and looked over to where she sat beside Will. A smile flickered around his mouth. She wasn't sure if this was some acknowledgement, a recognition. *Surely it wasn't a smirk?* She wanted him to know that he had frightened her; that she couldn't concentrate at work and often had sleepless nights. She was angry too, angry that he had picked on her and frustrated that she'd been powerless against him.

As expected, he pleaded guilty, and Maisie listened intently as details of his background and history of alcohol and drug use emerged. A report from the Headteacher of his school was read out to the court. It described changes in his behaviour at school from the age of fourteen, notably: poor attendance, poor concentration when he was there and a decline in his grades. No surprise there. A report from his family GP was of more interest to Maisie in her role as an academic psychologist for it came to light that there had been concerns about his mental from the age of sixteen when he was seen acting irrationally, jumping off walls and shouting to the world that he was Superman; he was invincible. Then, when his mood slipped into an unreachable lethargy, the GP had prescribed anti-depressants. A year later he received a

41

police caution for being drunk and disorderly in Bath city centre.

It was a sad story and felt intrusive when read out in open court. There was a dark-haired woman a few rows behind, and Maisie wondered if she was his mother. Maisie clasped her hands together and sat motionless as she often did when concentrating. She was aware of Will beside her and could feel his warmth as one long leg brushed hers.

The Chairman of the Magistrates declared that having listened to mitigation from his solicitor, they had decided to give him a community sentence of 12 months on the charge of assault and battery to be supervised by the Probation Service. The sentence included a condition that he reside at Alpha House, a local drug and alcohol rehabilitation centre. He was also given 120 hours of community service.

'You will remain at Alpha House until such time as the substance misuse workers and your probation officer deem it appropriate for you to return to an independent life in the community,' the Magistrate informed him.

Maisie watched him clench his fist with relief. Unexpectedly, she felt sorry for him. By rights, she should be feeling anger towards him, but he was so clearly not your average druggie.

The dark-haired woman was hugging him. She must have been his mother, and Maisie felt relieved on her behalf. She shook her head. *Where had all that mixed emotion come from?* Will was looking at her. Misreading her feelings, he squeezed her hand in sympathy.

'Fancy a drink and some lunch over the road?' Will checked his watch. 'I don't have any clients until after 2 pm, and I could do with a pint.'

Maisie shook her head. 'Sorry, Will. I've got so much marking to do, and I should get back to the department.' She touched his arm. 'Let's do that, soon. But to be honest, this is a good chance for me to catch up. I cancelled my lectures today because I didn't know how long I would be here.' Trying to ignore the disappointment on his

42

face, she kissed him on the cheek. 'See you at Pebbles tomorrow,' she told him breezily.

As she walked up the road towards the Psychology Department, she could feel him watching her. Will was a good friend; she enjoyed his company and his, at times, quirky sense of humour but for her, there was no more to it than that.

'Damn, damn, damn,' she muttered as she ran up the stairs to her room. She didn't want any complications to spoil their friendship. If she was right about Will's feelings for her, it was her fault for flirting with him. She was aware that she used flirting to her advantage. She was capable of doing it in a cold and calculating way, and it was not something that she was proud of. She had always got a thrill out of flirting. Ever since she turned thirteen, men had been responsive to her and with this came a feeling of power. Pity, she mused, that she wasn't more successful at real relationships. She bit her lip and smiled despite herself. *Poor Will, if he weren't careful, he'd be trapped in her thrall.*

Once sat at her desk her thoughts turned to her attacker. He was taller than the image she had of him from that dark night. She walked across to the window to distract herself. He was nothing to do with her anymore, and she was supposed to be working this afternoon, not speculating about him.

Next morning, feeling more positive, she gave a big, satisfying stretch. It was about time she got organised, so she decided that a plan was needed. She brewed fresh coffee and sat at the table in the basement kitchen, pen and paper in hand. She heard Sally coming down the stairs.

'Mmm, thought I smelled coffee.' Sally poured a steaming black mugful from the red enamel pot on the gas cooker. 'What are you up to today?' Without waiting for an answer, she sank on to the battered two-seater settee. 'God, I'm exhausted.'

'What time did you come in? I didn't hear you,'
Maisie asked.

Sally pulled a rueful face. 'That's because I didn't go
out. I had a shower and fell asleep watching Minder, and
after that, I couldn't be arsed. Friday night too, I'm definitely
getting old.'

Maisie laughed. 'Well, I'm going to have a productive
day. Planning my dear, it's all in the planning.' She waved
her notepad at Sally.

'If you say so. I'm off back to bed.' Sally yawned and
shuffled off in her fluffy slippers.

Maisie knew she wouldn't see her again until 1 o'clock
at the earliest and began her list.

1. 10 am to 12 read background stuff for paper -
note refs and further reading
2. Go to Alice's for baguette at lunchtime
3. 2 to 6 pm write first draft of paper
4. 6 to 8 pm mark essays and coursework
5. 8 pm shower and go to Will and Fran's for
supper.

She collected the necessary books and settled at the
table. It was mostly turgid stuff, and she was struggling to
find an interesting new angle for the Brighton conference.

'Shit.' She picked up the phone.

'Hi, Maisie; it's Amanda Draycott, Buckley as was,'
the voice giggled.

'Oh, hi. This is a surprise. What can I do for you?'

'Well, I'm ringing round as many of the old crowd as
I can. A few of us are organising a school reunion to
celebrate being a quarter of a century.'

Maisie made a face in the mirror. *God, what a
prospect.* She could hardly remember ever speaking to
Mandy Buckley, and Bruton High seemed a long time ago.
Her best mate, Chris, lived in Scotland and probably
wouldn't be able to come down. *Still, it might be fun.*

'Why not? Any excuse for a booze up. When did you
have in mind?'

'First week in Feb at the Bear Hotel. We decided it would be nice to have something to look forward to once Christmas and New Year are over.'

'Sounds good to me. I'll put it in the diary.'

'Excellent,' Amanda replied. 'We're putting together a newsletter with the details and a list of names of old girls that we've contacted so far.'

'Sounds most organised who else is helping?' Maisie wasn't sure she cared to be referred to as an 'old girl'.

Amanda reeled off a list of four or five names Maisie remembered as being Amanda's cronies from school.

'If you know how to contact anyone missing from the list, do drop us a line; there's a darling.'

After the phone call, Maisie made fresh coffee and contemplated what her peers might be up to nowadays. *How much would they have changed in nine years? Who was earning a pile? Who looked like a dog these days? It would be interesting to see.* She hoped Chris would make it and they could enjoy a superbly bitchy evening.

The next call was from the library to tell her the new William Golding book she'd reserved was now available. Ten minutes later the phone rang again.

'Bloody hell,' Maisie muttered. It was Richard, her older brother, wanting to know when she was going down to Somerset for Christmas. Other than a brief enquiry about how she was coping, Richard didn't press her further, and she was grateful for that.

What with the distraction of her reminiscences and the phone calls, she had no time to go to Alice's for lunch. Fortunately, the afternoon was more productive. Feeling happier about the paper, she was able to mark several essays before getting ready to go to Fran and Will's flat.

'Hey, I like this.' She ran her hand over an ancient leather armchair.

'Isn't it gorgeous? I bought it at an auction on Wednesday afternoon, only £12.' Fran told her.

Their flat managed to be both homely and stylish. Fran had bought colourful rugs to hide the manky carpet, and throws transformed the cheap second-hand furniture. Maisie looked around admiring the cleverly placed lamps that set off the whole effect. She was always relaxed here. Hunger-inducing smells drifted from the small kitchen. Fran and Will had entertaining well organised. Fran, whose mother was French, loved to cook and had spent a happy morning munging around the market for fresh ingredients and the afternoon preparing them. Tonight, it was coq au vin with huge chunks of wholemeal bread from the deli in South Street. Will was a sweet tooth man and made disgustingly fattening puddings to which he added granulated sugar to his own bowl claiming he enjoyed the crunchy effect.

Maisie found him whipping cream while he listened to Blondie on the radio.

'You always did fancy Debbie Harry,' she teased.

He looked across at her and smiled. 'I see you've recovered from Tuesday. I was surprised the case came to court so quickly.' He ran a finger over the whisk, licked off the thick cream and offered her the whisk.

Laughing, she shook her head. 'You're like a big kid. Did you know that?' she perched on a stool opposite him.

'How did you feel when they gave him a suspended sentence?

She shrugged, uncomfortable in the intensity of Will's gaze.

'I don't know.' She shook her head, causing the blond curls to bounce around her face. 'You're a probation officer; what did you think?'

He didn't respond so she continued. 'I don't suppose locking him up would have done much good, and he couldn't pay a fine, so that doesn't leave many alternatives.'

'He got 120 hours of community service as well,' Will reminded her. 'Actually, there's something I wanted to discuss with you.'

'Sounds very formal'. Maisie was curious.

'Look, it's no big deal, but it's hectic here tonight. Can you call in at the office sometime next week?'

She was dying to discover more but the doorbell rang announcing the arrival of Shaun and his wife Kay, and they all retired to the main room.

The bed was covered with cushions and a throw. There was no table, so they ate their meal balancing plates on their knees. The talk turned to politics then Will and Fran began raving about the film *Apocalypse Now*.

The evening fell into a familiar pattern of good food, good craic and much wine.

'Fran, that was delicious.' Maisie used the last of her bread to mop the rich red wine sauce.

'Pudding anyone?' Will asked as he collected up the plates.

'Yes please,' they chorused, all well used to his extravaganzas.

Maisie turned to Fran. 'Have you two made plans for Christmas?'

'Certainly, have. The routine has become boringly established – Christmas Day at one set of parents and Boxing Day at the other. This year we are going to my Mum's in London. Are you going to your parents again this year?'

Maisie nodded. 'I'm looking forward to the break, but it's going to be stressful as I haven't plucked up the courage to tell them what's been happening.'

'You told your brother though, didn't you?' Fran enquired.

'Yes, but I just can't face a lot of explanations and sympathy, particularly from Dad.'

Later, in bed, Maisie reflected on the evening. It never usually bothered her, but tonight she was overly aware of being the only single amongst established couples.

Will's office was housed on the floor above the magistrates' court. He looked different, older, and more mature, in his working clothes of black trousers and a grey herringbone sports jacket. She was used to seeing him in faded Levi's and a baggy jumper.

Indicating a seat, he kissed her on the cheek and handed her a leaflet. 'It's a new pilot programme we've been operating for a few months. A sort of meet the victim scheme.'

Idly, she fingered the glossy paper.

'Meetings are strictly supervised by the probation service, and you are free to pull out at any stage if you are uncomfortable. Anyway, take it away and have a read and, if you are interested, Mike Green's his Probation Officer. He can talk it through with you.' He paused and put his hand on her arm. 'It might help you know.'

Maisie didn't reply. She had told all of them, her friends, her brother and anyone else who inquired, that she had been scared half to death; that she still freaked out after dark, waiting for the next screwball to leap out at her. It might be the expected response, but it wasn't true. *Why had she done that?* She'd been in a state of shock at the time, but her encounter with Joe hadn't made her fearful after dark. More alarming was the number of occasions his face, with that beguiling smile, would appear as she tossed and turned at night. It was ridiculous; he was just some mixed-up boy.

Next morning, she sought out Fran. 'What do you think Fran? Do you think it's a good idea to get involved with Will's victim scheme?'

Fran considered for a moment. 'Well, you don't want him to think you're still scared of him, do you? It will be a good chance to turn the tables and let you call the shots. It will do him good to appreciate what he put you through and how it's affected you since.' She touched Maisie's arm. 'Go on, what have you got to lose?'

Chris, however, immediately dismissed the idea. 'What's the point? It seems like a waste of time to me. It's not like he's a serial mugger or anything so I doubt it will have much of an impact on him. Much better to forget about

48

the whole thing and move on. Why would you want to see him?'

'That's more or less what Sally said,' Maisie told her. 'Fran thought it was a good idea though.'

'Well, that's no surprise, given she's Will's girlfriend,' Chris retorted.

Maisie was reluctant to reveal to any of her friends the real reason for her quandary. She was becoming obsessed with him and given her track record of persuading men to do as she wanted, she ought to be cautious. She gazed into the darkness of her bedroom. *That way lies danger.*

Next day, feeling less emotionally charged she considered the proposed meeting in Mike Green's office. *What would she say to him? Would he look her in the eye and apologise?*

Chapter 9
Joe

A taciturn warder on reception handed Joe his donkey jacket and a jiffy bag containing the possessions he had brought in with him - 31p, a packet of green Rizla papers and his treasured Zippo lighter which he had found in a bar in Spain last summer. It was a glum thought that this small pile was all he had. He'd left his sleeping bag at Mick's; there was no point trying to retrieve that. Mick was no doubt banged up somewhere, and the room in Victoria Road would have been taken over by other squatters by now or even reclaimed by the landlord if he were on the ball.

Regret weighed heavily on Joe; regret for the things he hadn't done and the wrong choices he had made. His lecturers said he was wasting his intelligence because he got bored and didn't stick at things. *Why he was so volatile?* When a dark mood struck, he'd over-react; often walking out of lessons at school or feel compelled to leave a family gathering knowing it would hurt and disappoint others When he was like this, he often refused to interact with those around him for days at a time. Yet when he was on a high, he was easily led and liable to do stupid, dangerous stuff. It would be easy to blame his mates for providing the where-with-all to get high, but he knew he had an addictive personality. He should never have gone anywhere near drugs or allowed himself to end up with acute physical cravings full of booze. It was no one's fault but his. It was all very well, deciding to be a better son or a better brother. He needed to become the better person he knew was within him and get to know his real self again. *Perhaps this Alpha House place was his chance to start again if he had the balls?* The alternative was to end up dead like his friend Ned who had lived in the flat above. Finding him like that had a profound effect on Joe at the time, but it hadn't changed his behaviour.

The court had appointed someone called Mike Green to be his probation officer. The warder handed him a letter to that effect stating that Mr Green would drive him to Alpha House.

'Hey, nice car.' Joe raised his eyebrows appreciatively at Mike Green's mustard coloured MG.

'Do you know much about Alpha House?'

Joe shook his head.

'It's an old country house about twelve miles away so I thought we'd go the scenic route over the hill.'

Joe nodded and sat back on the leather seat.

'It's a good place; it's a bit run down, but there's some nice countryside, good for walks and such.'

'What's the setup? How does it work?' Joe asked.

'Well, put simply, it's a self-help programme. The idea is that those best able to support people dealing with drug treatment are those in recovery themselves, and they often have visiting speakers who are ex-addicts.'

'Makes sense, I suppose.' Joe gazed out of the window; it felt strange to be looking forward to something.

A tall, rangy guy met them; he had floppy black hair and introduced himself as Ray Linnington, the manager of the unit. He shook hands then grabbed Joe's bag. 'Call me Ray,' he smiled.

'Follow me,' he instructed. 'Tea, coffee?'

In the office, Mike Green passed across some paperwork and helped Joe to complete the medical form.

'This is just a preliminary form,' Ray explained. 'You will have a full medical with our doctor as well as a meeting with the counsellor.'

At this point, Mike Green stood up to leave. 'Right, I'll leave Ray to settle you in and be on my way.' He handed Joe his card. 'I'll be in touch, but please ring if you need advice.'

When he had left the manager suggested he give Joe a tour of the place. 'I'll fill in some of the details of life here as we go.'

They walked across the hallway to the dining room, which had a serving hatch through to the kitchen.

'Breakfast is at 7 am. You'll find we operate a tight daily routine which can take a while to get used to. You'll be assigned a helper for the first week to show you the ropes.'

Joe poked his head around the door where two guys were preparing vegetables. Ray introduced them as Anton; he was a pale skinny guy who looked to Joe like a typical druggie, and Carl, who was older with a puffy red face.

'We have up to twenty residents split into five work teams – cooking, food shopping and laundry, cleaning, gardening and maintenance on a weekly rota.'

They walked back through the dining room into a lounge area.

'No one is here at the moment. They will all be involved with basic chores or meetings with the counsellor. This will be your recreation area for an hour after lunch and from 8.30 pm to 11 pm every evening.'

'What sort of stuff goes on in here?' It was the first time Joe had spoken since they began the tour. It was a lot to get his head around, and he was glad that Ray hadn't pressed him.

'Obviously, there's a TV and radio, and on that shelf is a CD player. Clearly, there must be co-operation amongst the residents about the choice of programme, music etc. Down in the rec room in the basement, you will find a snooker table, table tennis and some free weights. We also have an education unit next door, which houses a small library.'

Joe's heart sank at this news. 'Is it compulsory to go to the education unit?'

Ray laughed. 'Not your thing?' he enquired. 'No, it's optional in your free time. But group sessions, one-to-one meetings and helping your work team are compulsory.'

There was one resident in the education room, reading a book. Joe had surprised himself in prison that he had become engrossed in a couple of books. *Maybe he would keep the reading up.*

'Right, we'll collect your bag from my office, and I'll take you up to your room.'

On the stairs, they met a lanky guy with greasy black hair.

'Ah, Alfie, just the man. This is Joe, your new roommate. Alfie will be your helper, and for the first week you will shadow him in his work team.' He handed Joe a booklet with the daily schedule and rules of the unit. 'I'll be in my office until 6 pm, but Alfie can sort you out if you have any questions. Alright?'

Alfie led the way down a long corridor to their room on the first floor. Joe dumped his bag of not very much on the floor. The room was sparse with two single beds plus a narrow wardrobe and a small chest-of-drawers each and looked out across the green lawn.

'OK. I'll leave you to settle in. I'm needed in the kitchen just now.'

Joe unzipped the navy-blue hold-all his mum had given him. Inside were toiletries; some clothes she'd got from the charity shop; a new pair of desert boots and a photo of herself and Jess in a silver frame. He was taken aback by how much his sister had grown. Her school skirt was short, displaying long legs. She was posing, one hand on hip. Joe smiled at her apparent confidence. He placed the photo on his chest of drawers, then inspected his mum's choice of clothes. For the first time in a long while he found himself laughing at the black cords, cords for God's sake, and a grey old man's jumper.

He sat on the hard, narrow bed to suss out his new home and picked up the information pack the manager had given him. Across the top of each page was the motto *get clean and stay clean*. He learned that as well as Ray, the staff consisted of a housekeeper, nurse and part-time gardener plus Annie, the counsellor. He studied the timetable, which was headed *keep active, keep occupied*. After breakfast, the nurse would give out any medication, carry out weekly blood tests etc. Group Therapy followed this for an hour, then

53

chores in the work teams until lunch at midday. After an hour of free time, they were expected to exercise or have outdoor time where there was football and organised cross-country runs were on offer. Then it was more chores until supper at 6 pm after which there was group discussion about how the day had gone with the opportunity to air any grievances, make suggestions and so on. Each day ended with social time when phone calls to family and friends could take place until lights out at 11 pm. Joe shut the book. It all sounded well exhausting. He decided to try and find this Alfie guy as it was now five o'clock and an hour until supper. He eventually found him in the dining room, laying up for supper.

'Anything I can do?'

Alfie shook his greasy locks. 'You're alright, lad. We've got tonight covered, and you're allowed a day to settle in. Tomorrow will be a different story. New arrivals always get the shite jobs,' he laughed.

Joe slept well; nevertheless the 6 am awakening to start the breakfasts was disturbing. It took Joe a while to tune into Alfie's Glaswegian accent and work out what the hell he was saying. It appeared that porridge and boiled eggs and toast were on offer and Joe was on toast duty. He had a surreptitious look at the others. There was a skinny girl, the sores around her mouth, livid against her white face and typical of a heroin addict. Either she'd recently arrived, or she was one of the programme's failures. She was called Cathy and judging by the number of times her name was shouted around the kitchen she had the knack of winding up the others. Team leader and head cook for the week was Carl who Joe had seen earlier. He was older than most of the other residents and was well-spoken, which belied his ravaged face. Joe took in the reddened, lumpy complexion with what he called a Rumpole of the Bailey nose, which indicated long-term alcohol abuse. The other guy was a loud and cocky Liverpudlian who indulged in cheerful if incomprehensible banter with Alfie.

Joe ate some toast, but he wasn't hungry, and the egg made him feel queasy. He struggled to stop his hands shaking when he picked up his coffee mug. *Just as well he would get his meds after breakfast.* The prison doctor had lowered his dose to 10 mg, and he was noticing the difference.

A chubby nurse handed him his diazepam then took his blood pressure and a blood sample. When he described his symptoms on the lower dosage, she made a note to order a new prescription.

Then he made his way to the lounge for his first group therapy session. It was a relief when Alfie informed him that today he would be left alone to listen to the others and get a feel for it.

'Right, for the benefit of those new to the group, my name is Harry. I have been clean for the last two years and now work here full-time. I'd like to run through the main elements of this programme. Firstly, and perhaps most importantly, the group's common welfare comes first. You will find that your personal recovery depends on the unity of the group. The only requirement to be part of the group is your desire to stop drinking or stop using drugs. Any behaviour that is abusive to others is strictly off-limits. If another resident does something you don't like, you must save it for the discussion sessions after supper. That is your opportunity to air grievances or make suggestions.'

He looked directly at Joe and the other newcomer.

'We need your agreement; otherwise, this place just doesn't work. You both OK with that?'

Not used to the spotlight, Joe grunted in reply.

By the time lunch was over he was looking forward to some downtime and was vocal in his mumblings when the activities coordinator cajoled him into a cross-country run. Dragging his lethargic body through the wintery mud was not his idea of fun, but at least he could have a hot shower before it was time to head back to prep for supper.

By eight o'clock he was too knackered to socialise and slumped in an armchair. It was an excellent spot to people watch, and he began to speculate about the other residents. *What were their stories?* Faces came back to him of people he'd spent time with in the past and thought were his friends. Memories of transient faces mingled with the smell of the squalid rooms they inhabited. There was a closeness and a camaraderie that existed in those twilight communities. It may have been a false closeness based on mutual need, but he missed it and wondered if he would ever feel such closeness again. It was important to him to have friends and people around him. *Maybe he could talk about that tomorrow in his one-to-one session with the counsellor?*

Initially, he was mistrustful of her. She sat next to him; her armchair turned towards him with her green leather boots and her wiry hair. Late twenties he guessed. *What did she know?* She was attempting to get him to explore the reasons why he used alcohol and drugs. Were there any triggers that set him off on a drinking spree? *No, you stupid bitch; I just drink as much as I can when I can find the money or nick the stuff.*

Of course, he hadn't told her this. Patiently, she had tried to help him to develop strategies or decision-making skills, as she put it, to help him overcome his addiction. I'm not an addict Joe had insisted. I'm just bored, and it helps to pass the time. He refused to admit that he was an addict. His mood swings scared him. He loved the buzzy highs and wanted to cling to that feeling regardless. Then came the inevitable plunge into deep, all-consuming despair where coping strategies were just not an option.

Joe's second group therapy session proved more of a challenge.

'OK, Joe. Perhaps you'd like to start by telling us about yourself and why you ended up in here.'

Joe shook his head. *It was personal stuff and no one else's business.*

56

'I understand your reluctance,' Harry responded. 'We all do. But group therapy is the time to think about all the shit you've done in the past and talk openly about it.' He glanced around the group. 'It's hard, but from experience, I can tell you that it does help.'

Despite the nods and general agreement from the others, Joe remained silent. Harry folded his arms and patiently waited.

'The court sent me here because I've got problems with drugs and alcohol,' Joe muttered eventually.

The group, consisting of mostly men and a couple of women, listened, and asked gently probing questions. When did he first begin to think he had a drink problem? Someone asked.

Joe stared at the floor. 'When I found it impossible to function normally, I guess. When the physical effects got so, I would do almost anything to hold of alcohol.'

'How come you ended up here?'

Joe shrugged. 'I don't know. I didn't particularly need money for booze, and I wasn't high if that's what you're all thinking.'

'I'm not thinking anything, mate, until you tell us what happened.'

Joe cupped his chin in his hand before continuing. 'I'd planned to sleep in this building site, and I saw a girl coming down the street clutching something. I meant to grab her purse, but I ended up dragging her into the site. It was just a mad impulse. She must have been shit scared, but I couldn't let her go. It was like some crazy adventure where I was in control, and I was the one with the power.'

There was silence, then Harry spoke. 'How do you feel about it now?'

Joe raised his eyes to the ceiling and bit on his lower lip. 'I guess I'm ashamed of what I did and of being so weak.'

'What is it that makes you feel weak?' Harry probed.

The room fell silent again as Joe struggled to control his emotions. He glared at Harry desperate to indicate that he'd had enough interrogation. The continuing silence was unbearable, and eventually, he spoke.

'Because I let booze take over my life; because I couldn't control it, I let it control me. I feel weak every time I give in to the physical craving for alcohol or if I let people down or am a shit friend.' He clasped his hand over his mouth as an involuntary sob escaped and tears ran down his face.

The group broke into spontaneous applause.

'You've done well today, lad. I'd say you have passed the first step. Right, see you all on Thursday, same time.' Harry stood up, and the others all trooped out, leaving Joe alone.

He looked out of the window at the Hampshire countryside in winter. Trees stripped bare – that was how the group therapy with its contrived confrontation had left him feeling. The grass dull and lifeless. This was his rock bottom moment. Not the fear and privations of prison, not the precarious existence of living on the streets but acknowledging that he was an addict; Addicted to alcohol at any rate. *Did that make him an alcoholic?* Yet it felt strangely cathartic. As in nature, the promise of change and new life was always the expectation. He remembered a booklet in his information pack about some twelve-step programme for alcoholics. A lot of it made sense, and the first step as Harry had said was admitting that you are powerless over alcohol and that your life has become unmanageable. Where he struggled was the god-bothering stuff. He was instinctively anti-religion of any description and couldn't see himself deciding to turn his life over to the care of God. If there were to be a belief in a higher power, it would have to be through spirituality and the power of nature. That made far more sense. He wouldn't pray, but he could maybe meditate.

Alfie poked his head around the door. 'Get a move on, matey; you're needed in the kitchen.'

Shaken out of his reverie, Joe immediately got stuck into the task of laying up in the dining room. The week's menu, pinned to the corkboard, told him that today's offering was vegetable soup and a roll followed by fresh fruit or gingerbread. There were two long scrubbed pine tables which seated the twenty residents although today two were out on community service.

Once the soup had been dished out, Joe brought in the gingerbread. It was in two metal trays and cut into slabs. Somehow, he'd expected shop bought stuff and couldn't imagine when Carl had found the time to produce homemade cake. Sitting next to Anton, he discovered that Carl was once a chef in the navy.

'So how come he ended up here?' Joe asked.

'You'll have to ask him. It's his story and not for me to say.'

Joe looked across to where Carl sat at the next table. He had his back to him, and Joe could see bloodied scabs through his thinning lank hair. *When he got to know Carl a bit better, he would ask him.*

Back in the kitchen, Joe volunteered to do the bulk of the washing up to make amends for his late arrival. He also reckoned that if he took long enough, he wouldn't get dragged out to do another run or worse kick a football around. Unlike Alfie who couldn't wait to get out on the pitch, Joe loathed football and most team games. He wasn't sure why because he considered himself to be a sociable person.

Group therapy sessions were held every day except Sundays and Joe was starting to enjoy them. He liked the communal aspect of celebrating success and supporting lapses. He was gradually learning about his fellow residents and where they were on their journey as Harry insisted on reminding them. There was a mix of chronic bad luck, stupid decisions, and a lack of mental strength that he recognised in himself.

59

'Today, I've asked Carl to speak to you all,' Harry told them.

There was a stillness about the big man as he rose to his feet.

'As most of you know I've been here for many months fighting my demons. But on Monday, I'm moving on to new opportunities. Before I leave, there are several new people here just at the start of their journeys, and if you'll indulge me, I'd like to share mine. As a chef in the navy, I had a good life. I saw a lot of the world and had good mates. I got married and had two kids – a boy and a girl. In the navy, or any of the services come to that, there is a culture of heavy drinking, and I was no exception. It was when I left the navy at forty-five that things went downhill in a massive way. Without the routine, without my mates, I was floundering to get through each boring day. I couldn't decide about what to do with my gratuity and just put everything on hold. Jackie, that's my wife, was out at work and I started going to the pub to fill the time. I'd be there when they opened at eleven each morning. After five, maybe six pints I'd go home and slump in a chair. I didn't want to eat dinner or indulge in conversation; I just wanted to be morose. I'd start on the scotch, drinking a bottle most nights. When I woke in the mornings, my hands would shake, and I felt overwhelmed with anxiety, so I started to pour a damn big slug of scotch at seven in the morning, sometimes earlier.' He paused; drank a glass of water and looked around the circle.

'No doubt some of you will recognise this feeling?'

There was a murmuring of agreement, and he continued.

'Eventually, Jackie kicked me out, and I can't say I blame her. I was a useless twat of a husband who was steadily drinking my way through the money. I stayed on a mate's settee for a couple of months until he got fed up with me and I ended up in hostels or sleeping rough.'

'What turned things around for you?' Harry wanted to know.

'A charity for ex-servicemen got in touch and sponsored a place here for me. I can't deny that each day is still a struggle, but the medication, the support and companionship have enabled me to take stock of myself.'

'What happens now?' Alfie asked.

'The charity has fixed me up with a bedsit, and I've got a job in the staff canteen on that big new Sainsburys in Southampton. So, hopefully, I shall find the strength to stay off the booze and make the most of this fresh start.'

There was clapping and calls of good luck, Carl.

It was another wakeup call for Joe. Carl was at least sixty, but he'd once had a good life even if he'd lost it all. Joe felt that he'd never really achieved anything. He was in trouble, and his life had barely started. He didn't know if he had Carl's strength.

By the end of week two, Joe had settled into the routine. The other new guy had quit already. Was it weak, or was it gutsy to walk away from the form of regimented support that Alpha House offered and be your own person? Joe couldn't decide. It was a surprise that some residents were there voluntarily. He'd assumed that they'd all been sent there by the courts as he had. There was no walking away for him unless he wanted to end up back inside.

Having completed their stint in the kitchen, his work team was on gardening duty the following week. Carl had been replaced a monosyllabic lad by the name of Wayne who kept bursting into bouts of weeping every time Alfie, the newly appointed team leader asked him to do something.

Joe preferred being outside despite the December cold. Not a lot of gardening went on though. They were mostly engaged in tidying up the vegetable plot, and Anton unexpectedly took on the task of repointing the brick wall surrounding the pond.

Harry had asked them to think about the saddest thing that had ever happened to them to share at the next therapy session.

'Joe is going to talk about his father's death and how this has affected him. I am pleased that he feels enough trust has developed within the group to enable him to do this. OK, over to you, Joe.'

'Dad had been playing squash in his lunch hour and was on his way back to the office in the centre of Bath. They said he was found collapsed in the gutter. People just assumed he was a drunk and wouldn't even look at him as they hurried past. By the time the ambulance was called, it was too late, and he was pronounced dead on arrival at the hospital.' Joe paused, his voice faltering with emotion.

'How did that make you feel?' Harry asked.

'How do you fucking think I felt? He was only forty-two for Christ's sake. I think it's disgusting that dad was dying, in pain and nobody tried to help him.'

Joe felt inexplicable anger, and it was hard to breathe. *Where had all that come from?*

'What was your reaction to his death? How did you cope?'

Joe didn't want to go there. 'Don't push me, man.' He gave Harry a warning stare.

'Understandably you're still angry and upset by what happened. Did you get comfort from your mother and the rest of your family?'

Joe shrugged.

'You went back home, right?'

'Just drop it. I don't want to go there, OK?'

'Get it off your chest, lad. It'll help you make sense of how you're feeling if you do.'

Joe got to his feet; he shoved his chair back and strode towards the door.

'Sit down and face it.' Harry's angry bellow stopped Joe in his tracks.

'No. I didn't go home. I did what I always do. I bottled it and ran away.' He brushed away the tears running down his cheek. 'I let them down. I let my mum and my sister down,' he sobbed.

62

His reaction to Harry's probing played on Joe's mind to such an extent that he decided to raise it that evening at discussion time. Bullying seemed to be the theme of the evening because Wayne, the tearful, complained that Alfie was picking on him in his work team. Tempers rose when Alfie referred to him as 'a soft southern git.' Then two girls on the cleaning team had a moan about people not clearing up after themselves in the communal areas.

'Sorry to end on another negative theme', Joe began. 'But to get back to the bullying stuff, I wanted to share some concerns about this morning's group therapy session. Harry made me feel uncomfortable. I think he overstepped the mark to the point of bullying.'

The responses were mostly similar – that it was par for the course, and he needed to toughen up.

'You'll have to deal with a lot harder shit than that,' Alfie told him. Leaving Joe to regret that he'd ever brought it up.

He was restless that night and woke feeling nauseous and anxious. The nurse gave him a couple of paracetamol for a splitting headache along with his diazepam. He felt negative and grumpy, and now he had to face Harry, who had asked them to come prepared to share their thoughts on particular drugs. Joe had decided to talk about his friend Ned.

'What happened to Ned?' Harry asked.

'We shared a bedsit,' Joe began. 'One day, I came up the stairs, and he was sprawled half in and half out of the door.' He closed his eyes in a frown before continuing. 'I'll never forget the look of him. His mouth was open, and his lips were all blue with white vomit trailing onto the manky carpet. There was a spilt bag of greasy chips in front of him. It was such a fucking sad sight. When I found him, he was already dead from a heroin overdose, and that night I resolved that no matter how bad it got I'd never go down that road.'

Anton and Cathy, both ex-heroin addicts themselves were in sombre agreement with his description.

'I guess it was a good lesson,' Joe continued. 'I know that I have an addictive personality, and it would be suicide for me to start using that shit.'

The weekend passed without incident, and Joe welcomed the break from the intensity of group therapy. Sunday was a crisp, bright day, so he took himself off for a walk. The team were on cleaning duty next week, and he wasn't not looking forward to cleaning the loos.

Joe tried to go to the education unit whenever Mac was there. Mac was a retired teacher who went to Alpha House a couple of times a week as a volunteer. He discovered Mac didn't drive and had a twelve-mile bus journey each time. At first, Joe was sarcastic and always ready with a quick put down, but Mac demonstrated a dry sense of humour and was patient and easy-going.

'Christ, man; does that guy know a lot?' Joe told Alfie.

They were in the lounge. Joe had just finished reading *Brighton Rock* and held it out to Alfie.

'You should try this. You never know you might enjoy it and it helps to pass the time.'

Alfie raised his eyebrows. 'Do you seriously think I'm going to sit still long enough? I don't read, never have,' he told him.

Mac had started borrowing books from his local library that he thought Joe might enjoy and so far, *Brighton Rock* was his favourite. He leaned his head back with a deep sigh. He was restless tonight, but he didn't know why. Anton and one of the girls were having a noisy game of table tennis then Alfie put on his Beach Boys tape.

Joe groaned. 'For fuck's sake, not again. I can't stand the Beach Boys.'

These were the hardest times because it reminded him of nights round at Stu and Andy's flat or at The Rendezvous. He missed all that and with the memories came the craving for a drink or some dope.

Chapter 10
Maisie

Two days before Christmas, Maisie turned into the yard of Ivy House Farm. It was a relief to stop driving. She had intended to stop for coffee at Warminster, but there had been heavy traffic in Southampton, so she decided to press on. She checked her watch; just less than three hours was good going in her faithful Escort. She climbed out of the car into the familiar surroundings half surprised that her arrival had gone unnoticed.

The weather was still; it was a dull end to the day and already growing dark. Avoiding the muddy puddles in her tan leather knee-length boots, she crossed the yard to inspect the pigs. Ivy House was no longer a farm. The farmer had sold some land when they built the M5 to Exeter and had bought a larger farm a mile away.

Her father had bought the farmhouse when Maisie was fourteen, and she had transferred to Bruton High School. Richard, four years older, went straight to university in Manchester. After living in Rosyth and later Portsmouth, Maisie had been glad to stay put for a few years. Looking back, it must have been a strange time of adjustment for her parents. Her father's final posting had been to Singapore. It came at a crucial time education-wise, especially for Richard, so her mum had opted to stay in England. It was either that or boarding school; Devon for Richard and Haslemere for Maisie had been suggested, but Ruth George had quietly resisted both options.

Her husband, Derek was fifty when he retired from the navy although he had the cushion of working part-time for a couple of years as a communications instructor in Bath. He was an energetic man and not one to relish the prospect of idling away his time. He tried teaching, as a lot of ex-navy men do, but after a short spell at the local tech, he abandoned the idea. Instead, he indulged his passion for drawing by taking up glass engraving, working through word-of-mouth commissions. As far as Maisie could tell, her parents were content with life now and eleven years on, they seemed happy in each other's company. They shared the same sense of humour and tended to gravitate towards the same kind of people. Maisie envied them their closeness. *Here she was twenty-eight years old, and, despite her friends, she often felt lonely.*

She turned the black, iron handle of the back door. The kitchen door to her right was open, and the welcoming light flooded the hallway and lifted her tiredness. Smiling and light-footed, she stepped into the solid Rayburn heat. Her mother who was chopping onions as she listened to a radio play jumped when Maisie spoke.

'Hi, mum.' Maisie crossed the square kitchen to where her mother sat at the large, scrubbed table and put her arms around her shoulders. She could smell the familiar powdery smell of her childhood.

'Darling, I didn't hear the car.' She stood up to face her daughter then hugged her carefully to avoid getting her onion scented hands on Maisie's black, wool jacket. 'Good journey?'

Then releasing her, she rinsed her hands and scraped the onions into a large mixing bowl.

'Mmm. What are you cooking?' Maisie idly stirred the metal spoon in the pungent mixture.

'Oh, just the stuffing for Christmas Day. I thought I'd get it out of the way today. Hungry?'

Maisie nodded. 'Starving.'

Ruth indicated the cake tin on the side while she filled a battered, red, enamel kettle and set it down on the hotplate of the Rayburn. Maisie bit into one of her mother's rock cakes and watched as tiny balls of water shrieked across the hot metal.

'Where's Dad?'

Her mother glanced at the clock on the wall. 'He should be back soon; he went off after lunch to pick up a

Christmas tree. I think he's hoping you'll decorate it later before Richard and Lynne and the children arrive tomorrow.'

Maisie smiled. It was all too easy to slip back into the protective world of her parents' home. She wasn't sure why she hadn't told them about the attack, but for the moment it seemed the best thing to do. In different ways, she was close to both parents and confided most of the details about her adult life with them. But she kept Joe a secret.

Joe, his name came into her head with worrying ease these days. She presumed he would stay at the drug rehabilitation place over Christmas. She doubted the twenty, or so residents had anywhere else to go. Those still in contact with their families might be welcomed back for the festive season. But she doubted that Joe would be allowed to go back to his mum's house in Bath.

That evening, Maisie helped herself to a large glass of her mother's Bristol cream sherry and got on with the business of tree decorating. Each decoration reminded her of Christmases from her childhood; especially the squashed little tree crackers and bells she'd made out of egg cartons when she was at infant school. Touchingly, her parents carefully stored away these items and got them down from the loft each Christmas. For a few years, when she was a teenager, Maisie had scorned the tatty collection and implored her parents to fork out for some new stuff. Looking at them now and all the memories they held, she was glad they had resisted. She wondered what sort of the Christmas Joe would have at Alpha House. She could feel her cheeks glow pink with the heat of the coal fire and the effect of the sherry. *He wouldn't be having any alcohol that's for sure.*

Next afternoon, while Lynne settled the children for an afternoon rest, Richard suggested that he and Maisie have a walk to collect the milk. Maisie guessed that it was an excuse to talk to her on her own. The two of them donned wellingtons and anoraks that were kept in the back porch and walked up the lane. They passed a run-down, isolated caravan and Maisie tried not to appear too obvious as she peered through the yellowed net curtain windows.

'I wonder if that woman still lives in there on her own?'

Richard shrugged and walked on. Maisie lingered, remembering her teenage fascination with the woman. She was about forty and had lived in the caravan for at least ten years. There was no electricity or water, and it was just randomly parked at the side of the lane. Maisie had never lived alone; she needed company and had never been able to work out why she had this fear of being alone. She was a rational adult, a psychologist even, yet the thought of such isolation made her heart pound.

It was eight years now since she'd left home to go to university. During her first year, she shared a flat on campus with a frenetic and giggling group of girls. For the next two years, she moved into big bad Brighton where she lived in grotty houses with five sometimes six friends. Often friends of friends would arrive and stay until it was time to move on, so there was no likelihood of Maisie being on her own.

Even after she started working full-time, she always shared flats with other girls. She had never lived with a boyfriend, though. She had never had that sort of a relationship despite having had lots of boyfriends. A couple of them had been special, but there was no question of anything more permanent, and something held her back from a stronger commitment. Deep down, she knew this had to do with her fear of isolation. She didn't want to be left alone and trapped somewhere if it didn't work out.

She caught Richard up. Like yesterday, the weather was heavy and depressing.

'I wish it would brighten up; Christmas should be clear and bright and cold,' she told him.

He linked his arm through hers and turned to look at her face. 'How are you? Getting back to normal?'

'I'm OK,' she assured him. 'Thanks for not saying anything to mum and dad.'

She hadn't told him about the meet-the-victim scheme, sensing his disapproval. Nor could she explain to him why she was reluctant to tell her parents.

'You're not fine though; are you?' Richard persisted. 'You look worn out, and you're distracted half the time. Where's our bubbly Maisie gone? Mum and Dad are bound to notice that something's up. I wish you'd tell them what's been happening. You know how hurt they are going to be by your silence.'

Maisie quickened her pace, annoyed with her brother for making her feel guilty. It didn't change anything. She knew she wouldn't tell them and wasn't ready to face endless questions.

Chapter 11
Joe

Alfie was discharged a few days before Christmas and set off to hitch back to Glasgow for Hogmanay. By Boxing Day, their shared room seemed cold and empty. Since lunch, of boiled potatoes, reheated sprouts and slices of turkey covered in glutinous gravy, Joe had sprawled in front of the TV in the recreation room, and half-watched *The Poseidon Adventure*. He didn't like this growing restlessness. Despite his initial reservations, the one-to-one sessions were helping him to recognise the triggers to his extreme mood swings.

Most of the centre's staff were at home with their families, and he missed having someone to talk to. His mother had sent a card and a box containing a new *Dire Straits* tape, an expensive tin of chocolate biscuits and inexplicably a multi-coloured, woollen skullcap. Last Christmas he'd acted like a child; he saw that now. *Maybe, when he was shot of this place, he'd go up for a visit and try to make amends?*

Time was dragging with none of the usual routines.

'Someone to see you, Joe,' called Bruce. He was an Aussie who was working in England for a couple of years. He had no family here and had volunteered for Christmas duties.

Joe's dark curls swished as he turned his head. He jumped up from the settee.

'Hi, Mac. I didn't expect to see you this week.'

Mac handed him a small parcel wrapped in brown paper and took out his pipe.

'I don't suppose there's anyone around to object.' He nodded towards the list of rules on the board, one of which was a strict no-smoking rule.

Joe watched him take out a tin of Three Nuns Empire from the pocket of his tweed jacket. His large fingers pulled at the darkly pungent tobacco as he filled the bowl of an ancient, brown pipe. Then, taking a box of Swan Vestas, he laid the lit match across the bowl and sucked rhythmically. It struck Joe that there was as much ritual in this simple act as in the preparation of a fix. The smell of the tobacco smoke was comforting and familiar.

Mac peered out of the French windows. 'Feel like a walk?'

Joe shrugged. 'I'll look at this later.' He laid the brown parcel on the chair and followed Mac into the muggy afternoon.

They didn't speak; there didn't seem any need, and after a while, Mac tapped the remnants of his pipe bowl on a fence post and replaced it in his pocket. 'Time for a cup of tea, I think.'

The dull day was nearly done, and in the remaining light, they tramped over clods of heavy soil back to Alpha House. As it was Boxing Day, it was open house for family and friends, and Mac agreed to hang on for the turkey curry. It turned out to be an uplifting, if surreal, evening. Mac's present was a book called *Jonathan Livingston Seagull*, and after supper, while Mac got stuck into his crossword, Joe began reading and was soon lost in its squawking, wind-tossed world. Later, they played cards and Mac taught him a complicated game for two players called Piquet.

After Mac had left to catch his last bus back to town, Joe was calmer than he'd been for a long time. Since he had been at Alpha House, he'd been kept well away from alcohol and drugs, and there was no denying that he missed the euphoric highs. When he wasn't busy, he often felt in a state of dulled lethargy. But this was different; he felt stronger emotionally, more vibrant, and more alive. He sat up in the narrow bed to finish reading Mac's book; *perhaps, after all, he could do something positive with his life?* He just hadn't figured out what.

Chapter 12
Lily

In Bath, Lily was also reflecting on Christmas last year. It had been a ghastly time. The first one without Jack and then Joe had stormed off. But somehow this year was worse.

On Christmas day itself, she was overly conscious that it was just the two of them, her, and Jess. It felt like an admission of social failure. They both tucked into a Christmas dinner, and the walk after lunch beside the river was ok as far as a country stroll ever can be with a fourteen-year-old.

Afterwards, they had slumped in front of the television, but Lily couldn't concentrate and kept thinking about how Joe was and what Christmas was like in the rehab place.

The relief when Joe was given a suspended sentence was quickly followed by dismay that he wasn't allowed to come home but instead was to go to a drug and alcohol rehabilitation centre. She knew that Joe took drugs, but it was sobering to discover from the court reports the extent of his problems and accepting that she was powerless to help him. She felt weighed down with sadness. As his mother, she surely should be able to help her lovely boy. She pulled her cardigan closer around her. It was growing dark, and the afternoon matched her melancholy mood.

People had expected that because she was a teacher, she would be able to handle Joe's volatile teenage years. *How wrong they were*. She remembered the frustration of trying to get him up for school or to do his homework. She had never been a pushy parent believing that having taught her children what was wrong and what was right, they would be able to make their own choices. That was easier said than done with Joe, who regularly pushed her beyond any rational limits. With a shuddering sigh, she remembered being phoned by his school to tell her that Joe had climbed onto the roof. Paralysed and almost in a trance she had watched him wave

72

his arms as though he was a plane about to take off. He didn't even look like her son in that moment.

By the time Joe was sixteen, she and Jack were in despair as they watched the impact of Joe's mood swings on their family life. He was volatile and unpredictable; charismatic and beguiling on good days then something would trigger a change, and he would become frighteningly out of control or worse, sink into the depths of a depression that broke her heart.

She glanced across at Jess. She was aware that Jess would rather be out with her friends and was grateful when she could reasonably take herself off to bed with her book. But even that gave her no pleasure and her head was thick from too much telly and alcohol.

Next day was Boxing Day. Jess had been invited to her friend's family for lunch, so Lily faced the prospect of being alone.

'Becky says they always play silly games and charades. How uncool is that?'

But Lily could see her excitement and envied her daughter. It wasn't that she without friends herself; she had a good social life, but Christmas wasn't that sort of occasion.

After a mope around the winter-blackened garden, she put on her precious Astrid Guilberto record and sat at the table to write down a list of New Year resolutions. She screwed up the paper in frustration. *What was the point?* It was always the same: lose some weight, get more exercise and be more tolerant of others. *What do I actually want out of life?* Bizarrely, Jack's death had given her new opportunities. No point being negative. She was forty, only forty. The mortgage was paid off courtesy of the life assurance policy, so she had no money worries, and despite this Christmas hiccup, she had a good bunch of friends.

When she was a teenager, she had wanted to be a journalist or a high-powered PA working for some glamorous international company where she was required to travel the world and wear smart suits. She smiled; this was

73

about as far removed from her job as an infant teacher as you could get. Still, the travelling appealed; perhaps she would take an evening class next term to improve her French.

Chapter 13
Joe

Next morning, Joe's calm interlude seemed depressingly distant. Residents returned, and the staff were reluctantly back from family breaks. On the Monday morning, Ray Linnington informed him that as someone was ill, so he would be taking their place on the community service group. He explained that it would be for the whole week, three hours in the morning and three in the afternoon with a break for lunch. Joe rapidly calculated that would mean thirty hours with ninety left to complete his community service.

A minibus collected him and, after rounding up three others, they arrived at a nearby old people's home where they were put to work decorating the communal lounge. Joe had never been in a place like that before. The heat was overpowering as they trooped in after the supervisor guy, bringing blasts of the cold January day with them. It was not the low-key restful atmosphere he'd been expecting. Pans clanged from the kitchen area; several televisions broadcasting different channels blared from the residents' rooms punctuated by the buzzers for those needing assistance. Their first task was to stack the upright armchairs in a corner and cover them with dustsheets. When Joe went out to the van to collect the painting gear, he met a woman with wild white hair standing in the doorway to the lounge. She was wringing her hands in an agitated fashion and muttering 'No, no, no, no, no,' repeatedly. Joe didn't know what to do and was about to ask her if she was ok when one of the carers appeared.

'Don't mind Brenda,' she told him. 'She's just upset that she can't go in the lounge today.'

Joe was tasked with rubbing down the window frames. He gazed out onto the sodden winter garden and wondered what it must be like to be old. By now an unappealing smell of vegetables was wafting from the kitchen. Someone, obviously frightened, was shouting along the corridor. And still the buzzers went. Joe was upset by that. *Were they ever answered?*

The supervisor suggested that they eat their lunch with the residents in the dining room. Joe decided not to sit with the others but took his packed lunch and sat at a space on a nearby table. One old woman in a wheelchair, her head hanging low on her chest, was being fed by a carer. Once her cottage pie had been consumed, Joe was surprised when she started chatting. Another woman thanked Joe for coming and apologised that she hadn't got more food in for him. She said she'd be having to get home soon as she didn't like being out in the dark these days. Then to add to his bewilderment, an old boy asked him if he'd brought the car to take him home.

'I can't stay here all day chatting', he complained. 'I've got a busload of people waiting for me in Fareham.'

'He used to be a bus driver,' the carer explained. 'A lot of them live in the past. It's all part of their condition.'

That afternoon, Joe thought about their families. He hoped they still visited their loved ones. It must be so hard.

By the Wednesday, they were down to a work party of three as one guy failed to show up. Joe was feeling more comfortable in the place now and looked forward to having lunch with his oldies. Taking his cue from the staff, he quickly learned not to contradict them if they talked a load of nonsense but to humour them gently. Their requests, usually to go home or questions such as when is my son coming? were repeated several times over the course of the lunchtime, but Joe was beginning to get a glimpse of the people they had once been.

On the Thursday, Joe was excused as he was going to his first Meet-the Victim session. It was to be held in Mike Green's office, and he relished the chance to go in the MG again. They met in reception and went up to Mike's office. It was a small room, and Joe felt awkward in such an intimate atmosphere. He couldn't keep still, and when Mike introduced her as Maisie George, he couldn't make eye contact at first. But she'd persisted with her questions. She was a nice girl; pretty, with kind eyes and amazing hair. He hoped she believed him when he said that he was genuinely sorry and that it had been a stupid mad moment.

Two weeks later, the next community service stint was scheduled. The minibus arrived at ten to collect Joe and some of the others. The weather, although still dull, had lost its mild mugginess; a cold wind swirled around the house and Ted, the instructor, allowed them to wear coats over the top of their white painting overalls. Jumping down from the minibus, Joe shoved his hands in his donkey jacket pockets and stamped his feet, sockless inside desert boots.

This week they were painting a fence outside the village hall. It was mind-numbing as plank after plank was laboriously rubbed down and turned from flaked white to turgid green. Joe was daydreaming, which was his way of coping with the monotony of the task. The lad working next to him was chatting non-stop about football. It wasn't Joe's thing, and he hadn't been listening, but he turned to look at his skinny companion and grinned; his Geordie accent was almost as hard to understand as Alfie's Glaswegian.

At supper that evening, Joe was sat next to Harry.

'How's it all going?' Harry asked. 'I heard you are involved in impact meetings with the girl.'

Joe was puzzled.

'The meet-the-victim stuff,' Harry prompted.

'Oh, ok. It was alright as it goes. She did make me think about what it had been like for her. I've been so wrapped up in what was happening to me. She didn't get angry or anything and even asked about my family and how I was getting on here.'

'So, you reckon it helped, then? That's interesting.'

With that, Harry pushed his chair back and strode out, leaving Joe to his thoughts. He'd not known until that first meeting that her name was Maisie. He'd been taken aback by how stunning she was and how kind. There was something about her.

He was tired. It had been a long and boring day painting, so he decided to go up to his room. For a few weeks after Alfie had left, he'd had the place to himself. He missed Alfie's relentless banter, but it had been good to have a bit of peace.

This all changed when a new roommate, Dave, arrived. Joe couldn't take to the guy. He boasted that he was a persistent offender – shoplifting, receiving stolen goods, whatever. He cheerfully admitted that he was an alkie and viewed the Alpha House set up as a soft number. Joe didn't trust him. He was two-faced and slagged off the others behind their backs.

One evening, Joe wanted some time on his own, but to his annoyance, Dave was already in the room. He quickly hid something under his blanket and smirked knowingly at Joe. Retrieving a bottle of scotch, he wiped the neck and held it out.

'Look what Daddy's got.'

Joe snorted in disgust. 'Don't be fucking stupid. If either of us gets caught with booze, we'll be sent straight to the nick.'

'Who's going to know?' He took a big glug.

Joe could smell the whisky fumes. *Shit*. His heart was racing, and he wiped the sweat from his palms. This was his first real test. It would be so easy to give in to temptation.

'Go on, lad. You know you want to. Where's the harm?'

It had been easy to be strong when he had no access to booze, but this was different. Voices in his head were increasingly persuasive, drowning out his attempts at self-control.

They finished the bottle between them, and half an hour later, Joe was violently sick. He was angry with Dave but more so with himself for being so weak. Cold and ashamed, he shivered beneath the bedclothes.

Chapter 14
Lily

Lily touched her hair self-consciously. The tables were arranged around three sides of a square, and she down sat at an empty seat. She hadn't been inside the college since Joe was doing his 'A' levels. The class was a mixture of young and old but with few people of her age. The teacher introduced herself as Sophie. She was French and spoke perfect English with an appealing accent.

About ten minutes into the class, a man arrived late. Lily was struck by his warm, slow smile as he apologised and sat down opposite. Once or twice during the session, when something amusing struck her, she noticed him smiling at her with that lazy smile. His eyes held hers for longer than was comfortable, which made her blush and turn away like some coy schoolgirl. At the break they found themselves going out of the door at the same moment.

'Coffee?'

She nodded, delighted that he had singled her out, and followed him to the coffee lounge.

'What made you decide to learn French?' she asked. 'Sorry, you missed the group introduction bit at the beginning, and I don't know your name.' She held out her hand. 'I'm Lily.' *What am I doing?* She was amazed at her forwardness.

'Being late has its advantages,' he smiled. 'I'm Paul by the way and in answer to your question I did French at school, but I guess I'm a bit rusty now. My parents have bought a place in the south of France, near the Canal du Midi. They hope to spend six months of the year out there, so I thought I'd better improve my French.'

'It sounds wonderful,' Lily told him, mesmerised by his amused, deep brown eyes. 'And don't you just love French food.'

'I certainly do.' He stood up. 'I guess it's time we were heading back.'

He took hold of her elbow and steered her towards the door.

The next week, predictably, people sat in the same seats. This allowed Lily a good view of Paul. She smiled to herself; it was fun to behave like a lovesick teenager again, and there was no harm in it.

Subsequent weeks followed the same pattern. They would catch each other's eye at the same amusing incident and always had coffee together. She learned that Paul was thirty, ten years her junior. He looked older, making it difficult to hide her surprise.

Reading her mind, he told her it was no doubt the beard that did it. She didn't usually go for men with beards yet found herself suppressing an urge to reach across the table and stroke his. She also discovered that he owned a small, terraced house near the town centre and drove a battered, Morris Minor estate. She asked him about his job, but his answer was non-committal, and she decided not to pursue it. There was plenty of time to get to know him better.

It was a ten-week, taster course, and two weeks were remaining. Time was running out, but at the penultimate class, Sophie suggested that the following week they all go for a drink in a local pub after the last class.

Lily wore her new, black trousers and a bright red top. It fitted her well, and she knew it showed off her figure. She washed her hair and took extra care with her make-up.

'You smell nice,' Jess declared. She looked away from *East Enders* for a moment and swivelled round to face her mother. 'Wow! Where are you going? Isn't it your French class tonight?'

Don't be embarrassed, Lily told herself. You have nothing to feel embarrassed about.

'It is,' she replied casually. 'But we're all going for a drink afterwards, and it's important to make an effort sometimes.'

'If you say so.' Jess lost interest and turned back to her programme.

Sophie suggested they work through the break and leave twenty minutes early so they could have more time in the pub. Lily was on tenterhooks and the hour and a half seemed interminable. Eventually, about ten of the class trooped off to The King's Head. She resolved not to drink too much. Social situations often made her nervous, and she had a habit of knocking back several glasses of wine in rapid succession to calm her nerves. The effect would then catch up with her, and she'd struggle to hold it together and not make a fool of herself. She noticed Paul down pint after pint of bitter. By now some of the older class members had left so she slid into the empty seat beside him.

'I hope you're not driving,' she told him and immediately regretted it; she sounded like his mother.

'Well, I did bring the car, but I'll leave it in the car park and pick it up in the morning.' He leaned across and touched her arm. 'Unless you fancy giving me a lift?'

She made a mess of parking outside his house. 'It's pretty steep this road'. She panted with the effort of heaving the steering wheel back and forth until at least she was parked in a reasonable fashion.

'You get used to it, I guess,' he replied. 'Coffee?'

Lily smiled into the darkness. She nodded and followed him into the small, terraced house. The lounge was cluttered with a hotchpotch of furniture, so she sank onto a worn, two-seater settee while Paul disappeared into the kitchen. The room was typical Paul, comfortable and on the shabby side, but she felt at home here. When he returned, he was clutching a bottle of red wine and two glasses.

'This seems more appropriate than coffee.' He filled their glasses, and as she leaned forward to reach hers, she was aware of his gaze on her breasts.

Lily had always had what they call ample bosoms; she supposed it was her Mediterranean blood.

'Stop staring.' She laughed, trying to break the sexual tension between them. 'You make me feel like Moll Flanders or something.'

81

He ran his thumb across her cleavage. 'Who?' He was smiling. 'Seriously, you do have magnificent breasts. Lift your jumper up so I can see them properly.'

She burst out laughing. 'Certainly not, you are outrageous. You're worse than some adolescent schoolboy.'

Her heart thumped, and she was out of breath which didn't help the heaving bosom situation. She was surprised that she wasn't offended by his remarks. They finished the wine, and she stood up to go.

'Could you phone for a taxi? I've drunk far too much to drive home – sorry I should have thought.'

He put his arm around her shoulder. 'Look, why not stay? Just to cuddle up if you prefer but I'm not sleeping on the settee.'

She hesitated for a moment. 'It's a tempting prospect, and I have enjoyed this evening, but it's best if I go home.' She was encouraged when he didn't look in the least put out. 'Maybe I could cook you a meal sometime?'

He took her face in his hands. 'I'd like that,' he said softly. 'Sure you won't stay, Lily?'

She shook her head and kissed him on the lips. 'Go and phone me a taxi.'

Later, in her own bed, she reflected on the evening. Paul had made her feel sexy and desirable and was so easy to talk to. She hugged herself, gleeful at the prospect of seeing him again. *Who cares if he is ten years younger? What would Jack have made of it all?*

Although it was two years since his heart attack, she could see his dear face in the darkness. *'You'd find it a huge joke, wouldn't you?'*

Next morning, she fretted that, now the French classes had finished, she wouldn't see Paul again. The doubts circled. *Why would he want to?* He was a lot younger than her. She began to wonder what sort of women he usually went for. *Were they slim young things?* He hadn't struck her as overly bothered by physical appearance, but she hardly knew him. He'd given her his home phone number, but she knew she'd never and be brave enough to ring him. She'd just have to wait and see.

For the rest of the day, she had no time to wonder further as she was immersed in the busyness that is a primary school. Offering the usual thank God, it's Friday prayer; she dumped her briefcase containing the weekends marking and preparation in the hallway. She poured a decent-sized gin and tonic and had just kicked her shoes off when the front doorbell rang. Paul was leaning against the door frame stroking his beard with a wicked lopsided grin on his face.

'Where's this meal you promised to cook me, then?'

Lily burst out laughing and ushered him into the warmth of her kitchen. He helped himself to a glass of Merlot and flicked on her little transistor radio while Lily set about preparing her signature lasagne.

Jess had been at hockey practice, but by the time she got home, her mother and a strange man were acting like an old married couple. The three of them ate in the warm kitchen, and to Lily's delight, it was a relaxed and comfortable evening. Jess disappeared up to her room, but Lily and Paul carried on nattering and drinking wine, preferring the more intimate atmosphere of the kitchen.

Paul pulled her to her feet. 'Sadly, I must be making a move.' He drew her close into a hug.

'Shall I call you a taxi?'

Paul shook his head. 'The walk will do me good.' He lifted the blind and peered into the dark garden. 'At least it's not raining. I'll cook for you next week. Better be here though as my kitchen is somewhat lacking.'

The Friday night event became a regular thing, and she noted with amusement that Jess had started to invite her friend Becky to join them for supper. The amount of giggling suggested that they had a crush on Paul as they observed his every culinary move. Typically, he was unphased by this attention and used gentle humour to encourage them to help chop vegetables and, more miraculously, to wash up afterwards.

Chapter 15
Maisie

Maisie was still dwelling on the meeting with Joe. Mike Green had opened the meeting by asking them both to be as open and honest as they could.

'Maisie, I'm sure you have some questions for Joe about this incident.'

Maisie clenched her teeth in annoyance; incident was an inadequate word. She nodded and looked directly at Joe. He was jiggling one leg up and down and kept his gaze on his battered trainers. The psychologist in her had kicked in.

'Joe?' She waited until he made eye contact. A powerful wave of attraction suddenly shot through her, causing her to falter for a moment.

'One thing that I would like to know is why me? Did I just happen to be the nearest person around, or did you pick me deliberately?'

'I was watching you. I saw you pat the roof of your car and you looked nice, but I didn't select you or anything. It was just spur of the moment.'

'But why? Did you think I would have money or an expensive watch you could nick?'

Joe shrugged. 'I didn't know what I was doing, to be honest. I do stupid, impulsive things sometimes just because I can.'

How about putting yourself in my shoes for a minute. Have you any idea how frightening it was for me?'

Joe frowned and looked away. 'I have as it goes and I'm sorry that I hurt you. I promise you I'm not normally violent, but, in my head, you somehow became a threat.'

Maisie recognised his description as a form of paranoia. It was all beginning to make sense. She wanted to continue, but Mike Green indicated that the half-hour was up and that it was time to deliver Joe back to Alpha House. A second meeting was arranged for two weeks later.

True to her word, Amanda Buckley had sent the old girls' newsletter. Maisie unpinned it from the notice board and sat down with a coffee to refresh her memory about the details. The reunion was the next and, as it was a Friday, she had arranged to stay overnight with her parents. She scanned the list of names and wondered what it would have been like to go to a mixed school instead of the stuffy all girls' establishment that she had attended. She hadn't joined the school until the Upper V when she was sixteen and hadn't got to know many of the girls in her year, so it was hard to summon up much enthusiasm ten years on. Most of the interesting names seemed to be missing from the list. Some faces instantly came back others Maisie struggled to identify and gave up.

She was both surprised and pleased when Chris decided to come down from Scotland; it would be great to catch up with her. The two of them had been close as teenagers, sharing their separate highs and lows as well as some wild moments. Chris had got pregnant in her first year of 'A' levels and didn't go to university. Instead, she looked after her daughter and worked part-time in a pub while her parents babysat. Chris, effortlessly clever, was confident and outgoing. Maisie couldn't imagine her life how hard her life must have become but Chris showed no hint of resentment or regret. A few years later, she met and married a young naval officer, and they had a little boy together. Thus, at twenty-six, Chris was living in married quarters in Rosyth with an eight-year-old and a four-year-old. Maisie wondered who was looking after them this weekend and how Chris was travelling down to Somerset. She regretted not making the effort to write or phone more often, but their lives were so different now, and Chris seemed to have lost a lot of her madcap zest for living life at full tilt.

'What time are you off?' Fran asked over coffee and sandwiches in the staff restaurant.

'As soon as I can after my lecture to the P2s this afternoon. There are a few bits and pieces I need to prepare for Monday, but I want to be away before four to miss the worst of traffic.'

'Well, have a great time and don't get too pissed or they might get to see the real you.' Fran grinned at her.

'Cheers. See you later and say hello to Will.'

Maisie checked the time. The weather was mild, so she didn't have to worry about ice or wet roads. Even so, she wouldn't be at her parents before 6.30 pm. There would just be time for a quick shower. Fortunately, the letter said there would be refreshments, so she didn't need to worry about food.

'Nearly ready, Dad,' she called down.

Her father had offered to give her a lift to The Bear so she could have a drink or three as he put it. She applied her make-up with more care than usual and selected a pair of well-cut, black trousers and a sparkly top. She supposed that all the girls would want to look their best and show the world that they still looked good. She told herself that she found all the glamorising somewhat shallow. Nevertheless, it was a strong urge.

Walking into the room alone was daunting, and she wished she'd arranged with Chris, or one of the others, to arrive together. The odd shriek of laughter drifted across the room as groups of girls chatted earnestly.

'Boo!' Chris appeared behind her.

Maisie swung around and burst out laughing. Most of the girls were dressed up either in trousers suits or smart jackets with massive shoulder pads. Chris sported bright yellow, baggy, linen trousers and a multi-coloured, hippie style jacket.

Grinning in delight, Maisie hugged her friend. 'Well, look at you. You look wonderful. How's life?'

They chatted over a large glass of white wine and Maisie was relieved to find that, despite her domesticated situation, Chris was still as energetic and as much fun as ever. She leapt up and down as she spotted new arrivals and greeted them in her wholehearted, 'I'm genuinely interested in you,' way.

Several drinks later, five other close friends from school days joined them. Soon each reminiscence was greeted with increasingly raucous laughter causing a few of the staider members of the class to glance disapprovingly in their direction.

'Come on, girls.' Chris had a wicked grin on her face. 'It's truth time. We've each got to tell each other, absolutely honestly, what we secretly want in life. You first, Maisie.'

Maisie drained her glass and smiled. 'Well,' she began, 'for a start, I want to have plenty of good friends.' She looked at the bright eyes and rosy cheeks of her old school mates. 'You lot don't count. And it goes without saying that I want to have a wildly exciting sex life. I'd like the people that matter to think that I was good at my job. Actually, I just want people to like me.' She glared at the others. 'Stop mocking will you and let me go on. It's your fault for making me go first. I wish I could remember jokes. I'd like to travel and be more independent, oh, and I can't imagine not ever having children. OK, that's me done. Now you, Chris, and remember you're supposed to be honest; nothing outlandish or too over-the-top please we know what you're like.' She punched her friend lightly on the arm.

They continued to get through several more bottles of wine and grew alternately giggly and maudlin as they considered each other's hopes and dreams. Maisie found herself telling them about the Joe incident as she now described it.

She was aware of Chris looking quizzically at her.

'I don't believe you're telling us the whole story, you naughty girl.' Chris grinned at her. 'You fancy him, don't you?'

Maisie took a large slurp of her wine. She blushed and started to giggle. 'Of course, I don't, you wally; how could I fancy someone who frightened and humiliated me like that?'

Chris pursed her lips and gave Maisie a knowing look. 'Hmmm. If you say so.'

Chris had seen through her. It had taken her a lot of internal struggle to acknowledge that the frightened and humiliated line was far from true; at least not now. The court case had changed all that. At first, intrigued by Joe, she had reached the point of being obsessed with him. There was no way that she was going to reveal that to her old school friends, but Chris was different.

'You know me too well, old friend, and as usual, you are quite right. Stupid as it sounds, I can't stop thinking about him.'

'You're a daft cow,' was all Chris said.

At the end of the night, despite her reflective mood, Maisie's stomach still ached from the earlier boozy hilarity. She sought out Amanda and hugged her hostess.

'It's been great, Amanda. We must do this again. Well done,' she gushed. 'It's been a most enjoyable evening.' Then she left a bemused Amanda and set off to find her father who patiently waited in the car park.

'Have a good time?' he enquired.

'It was a brilliant night. I saw all the old gang, and we had such a laugh.'

'I can imagine.' Derek George patted his daughter's knee fondly. 'It's just like old times this Mae, ferrying you about, waiting in draughty car-parks at all hours - quite takes me back.'

'Me too, Dad; it was fun getting ready in my old room.' She squeezed his arm through the tweed jacket. 'I do miss you and mum, you know.'

'We miss you too. Still, it's good you have your own life now. Anyway, enough of all that. How long are you staying? Got the whole weekend to suffer you, have we?'

'You certainly have, and I intend to sit back and be spoilt rotten.'

'No change there then.'

Her father turned into the yard, which was floodlit by the security light. She loved the old house. An alcohol-induced blanket of peace enveloped her.

Next morning, she awoke full of energy and sprang out of bed. Drawing back the faded, floral curtains, she ran her hand over the thick, solid walls of the farmhouse. It was a crisp, sunny day and the garden sparkled with the promise of new life. Her mother had placed a large, earthenware flowerpot on the steps leading to the lawn. It was stuffed full of solemn, nodding, little snowdrops. She looked across to the big horse chestnut tree that dominated the upper level of the lawn. In the height of summer, its branches bent to touch the grass and created a glinting magical space. Maisie had sat there on many a summer afternoon when she revised for her 'A' levels. It was her peaceful, secret world.

It was an unhurried existence at the farm, and she wished she had lived there as a child. Once a week, on a Wednesday morning, the bus arrived to take the locals to the market in Weston. She looked across to the now empty pen where the pigs were once kept. She had loved the pigs and often looked in on them when she came home from school. They didn't belong to her family, but a local chap kept about five or six sows in the pen next to the garage. One evening, Maisie helped him to deliver eleven, wriggling, pink piglets; it was a special moment for a town girl.

But the pigs were long gone as were the donkeys. She laughed out loud - *that bloody jackass Franco.* He had a habit of escaping from the field across the road where he over-wintered with the beach donkeys from Weston. stubborn as the proverbial mule, Franco took to planting himself in the middle of the road, thus holding up passing traffic. Sometimes irate motorists, and once the bus driver, knocked at the farm and she had no choice but to drag and cajole Franco back to his field. *Happy days.*

Maisie thought back to last night. Now that she had told Chris and the others about Joe's attack, she would have to tell her parents.

'I can't understand why you confided in Richard but not us. We've always been able to talk you and me.' Her mother was hurt, and it made her seem stiff and unapproachable.

'We can; we do,' Maisie continued. 'I suppose I didn't want to worry you. Anyway, it's all water under the bridge now. He's been sentenced, and I'm fine, so there's nothing much else to know.' She blushed at the thought of her mother's reaction if she knew how besotted she had allowed herself to become.

She crossed the kitchen floor to where her mother was vigorously ironing and gave her a hug. 'Sorry if I upset you, Mum; it's not what I intended.'

'Oh well, not to worry, if you sure you're alright, that's all I'm concerned about.'

Shaun peered round the door of his room. 'Good weekend?'

'Fabulous,' Maisie replied.

'And how was the reunion?'

'Oh, it was a real hoot.' She leant against the corridor wall to take the weight of the stack of files she was carrying. 'It's funny, though. Some of the girls looked just the same as they did at sixteen. But some of them had changed so much I couldn't believe they were the same person.'

Shaun nodded in agreement despite never having had the opportunity or the inclination to go to such an event.

'I must get on. Are you coming to Pebbles on Wednesday?' She noticed that Shaun was looking troubled.

'What's up?'

'Things are a bit tricky on the home front just now. Kay's mother is in intensive care, so we are having to juggle looking after the kids.'

'Oh, poor Kay. Look I can do a couple of evenings if that helps. I'm sure Kay would like you with her at the hospital.'

90

Shaun gave a sad smile. 'That would be great. Thanks, Maisie; you're a good friend.'

'How about tomorrow and Thursday? If I come straight from work, I can give the kids their tea.'

Maisie drove into the school car park where she was due to meet with two of her students. *Damn,*

she'd have to block everybody in for the moment; there was nowhere else to park. Half-a-dozen youngsters were painting the fence, and with a jolt, she realised that one of them was Joe. She gripped the steering wheel in frozen fascination. He was talking to the girl painting beside him. She had a hard, pinched face, and even at a distance, Maisie could see the tell-tale sores around her nose and mouth. The girl pushed up her sleeve to scratch a scab on her arm. She watched Joe take off his coat and put it around the girl. It was a caring, almost tender gesture. She took a deep breath, slid out of the car, and walked over to him, her legs shaking.

'Hello, Joe; so, this is the latest good deed, is it?' *Why was she smiling? And what a crass thing to say.*

He grinned back at her as if she were an old friend and she couldn't help noticing the thick, sweeping lashes and the way his smile creased around his mouth.

'We're not supposed to talk to anyone outside the working party.' He laughed and nodded his head in the direction of the supervisor. 'You come to check up on me?'

Maisie stared at the dimples in his cheeks; she hadn't noticed them before. 'Actually, I've come to meet two of my students'.

'Get you.' The girl next to Joe glared at Maisie.

Without any reasonable explanation, Maisie felt foolish as her face reddened. 'Well, it's freezing out here, rather you than me.'

The supervisor was coming over, so she turned away, irritated for making another stupid comment. There was a lot she wanted to ask Joe, but it was none of her business.

91

It was a struggle to concentrate as the students discussed their projects. They were both second years and in school to carry out a small research project as part of their Child Development course. It was all routine stuff, and her thoughts turned instead to Joe, out there in the cold. She tried to imagine his life at the rehab place. He seemed cheerful enough, so perhaps it was helping; she hoped so. From their brief conversations, she knew a little about his previous life - the squats, the aimless wandering in search of companions or for some excitement to soften the edges of the numbing boredom.

She finished with her students just before one o'clock. Joe and the small painting gang were sat in the minibus. The back doors were open, and they were eating a packed lunch. Her heart pounded with disappointment when he didn't look up as she drove away.

Chapter 16
Will

'What did Maisie say about tonight?' Will called from the bedroom. 'Is she still coming to Pebbles?'

Fran poked her head around the door. 'I guess so; she didn't say she wasn't. Why?'

He shook his head. 'No reason, I just wondered that's all.'

Fran sat on the edge of the bed with her head in her hands.

'What's up?' Will's tone was gentle.

She raised her head, and he saw a mixture of challenge and sadness in her eyes.

'You can't have a single conversation without mentioning Maisie, can you?'

Will shrugged. It was a conversation he'd prefer not to have. They'd been together for five years now. Fran had been doing a PhD on juvenile re-offenders. Then Will, who had graduated the previous summer, landed his first job as a probation officer and their paths had crossed. They discovered a shared work interest and the same tastes in music, films and just about everything. They had lived in the flat for almost two years now but had rarely discussed the future.

When Maisie joined them at Pebbles, her cheeks were already flushed, and she was giggly and flirty. This was dangerous territory for Will.

'Are you ready to go?' Fran asked when last orders were called.

Maisie linked one arm through Will's and angled her head so that it rested on his shoulder.

'Oh, not yet; it's early. Why don't you both come back and have a coffee or something?'

'What do you think?' Will drained his glass and looked enquiringly at Fran. She hesitated, and he willed her to make an excuse which would allow him to be alone with Maisie.

'Oh. Why not?' Fran shrugged her thin shoulders and peered at her man-sized watch. 'As you say, it's early yet.'

'Great. Shall we make a move then, guys?' Maisie replied, linking her arms through theirs.

Will's mood plummeted. Maisie seemed happy just to cast aside the growing sexual tension between them. *Or maybe it was only on his part, and he was allowing his imagination to run away with him?* As he felt the warmth of her body beside him and breathed in her perfume, his heart quickened with desire.

Later he lay in bed, grappling with his conscience. It had been a stilted visit to Maisie's flat. Beside him, Fran was still, but he sensed that she too was wide awake. It was hard to hide his feelings for Maisie, and that wasn't fair to Fran. He owed her some honesty, but it was complicated. There was definitely a spark between him and Maisie, but she was a notorious flirt, and he had no real idea if she had feelings for him, and that was hard to bear. Besides, Maisie and Fran were work colleagues, *and what about the friendship group at Pebbles?* There would be so many difficulties if he told Fran. Feeling like a complete shit, he decided to talk to Maisie and end this agony once and for all.

As silently as he could, he slipped out of bed and grabbing his pile of clothes from the chair he quietly closed the bedroom door. Fran still didn't stir. In the kitchen, he rapidly downed a large scotch before striding, with a recklessness that was new to him, towards Maisie's flat. When he knocked at the door, he heard the uncertainty in her voice.

'Who is it?'

'It's me, Will. I need to see you. Can I come in?'

Maisie opened the door; she was barefoot and clutching a glass of wine. 'God, you're soaked.'

As if in slow motion, he reached up and ran his hand over her cheek.

'Come downstairs, and I'll make us a coffee.' Maisie turned to go, but he caught her arm and pulled her roughly towards him. He held her face in his hands and kissed her with an urgency that surprised him. She laid her face on his wet jacket as he held her close. Then she pulled away and smiled at him.

'This is not a good idea, Will. For a start, we'd never be able to look one another in the eye again.' Her tone was light-hearted, and he guessed that she was anxious to avoid hurting him.

His heart sank, and he pulled a rueful face. 'You're a hard-hearted woman, Maisie,' he declared in mock Irish.

Then, more seriously, 'Sorry, Maisie.' He held open his arms. 'Come here; I need a hug.'

They stayed locked in companionable silence until, eventually, she spoke. 'Look, why don't you stay? It's still pouring with rain. We can just talk and be together as friends. I'd like that.'

They woke early as sunlight flickered through the curtains. Will was sprawled next to Maisie, his corn-coloured hair partly covering his face. Reaching out, she stroked his broad back. Will closed his eyes, enjoying the moment. But she quickly withdrew her hand and jumped out of bed.

'Coffee and toast?' she asked. It was Thursday, and they both needed to be at work by nine. 'I can drop you off at the courts if that helps.' She picked up her box of essays.

'Thanks, but I feel like a walk.' He looked out of the lounge window. 'It looks as if it's going to be a sunny day, for a change.' He stooped to kiss her on the cheek. 'Thanks, Maisie, for everything,' he added. 'See you soon.'

The walk gave him time to reflect on what had happened. It was a relief that they were still able to be comfortable as friends, but her rejection was hard to bear.

Will was between clients when she phoned.

'You OK?' she asked. 'In other circumstances, if it wasn't for Fran, things might have been quite different. You know that; don't you?'

'Look, don't worry about it; it's not such a big deal'. He couldn't help thinking of *Catcher in the Rye*, knowing that for him it was a very big deal. He closed his eyes as he heard her say it was probably best if they didn't tell Fran.

After their conversation, he sat back heavily in his chair. He wasn't even sure he believed her about things being different. It was torture to think she might be saying that to make him feel better. *Christ, you're a fool.* Now it would be impossible to continue as if nothing had happened between them. It had been sweet delight for him to take Maisie in his arms. He closed his eyes in anguish at the memory of her warm, smooth skin and his hands in her luxurious hair. The heaviness of guilt settled over him for the rest of the day. He had to tell Fran; it wasn't fair. He longed to see Maisie again yet dreaded the reality.

Was he expected to act as if nothing had happened? He was never any good at hiding his emotions. It had been a stressful day, and he was about to clear his desk and head for home when Mike Green telephoned.

'Will, hi. I'm glad I caught you. Listen; could you do me a favour?'

'Sure, if I can; what's up?'

He heard the strain in Mike's voice when he told him that his youngest son had fallen from the top of the climbing frame at school and was now in St Mary's hospital with concussion. Will wondered how it would feel to be a father with all the responsibilities, as well as the joys, that went with the territory. He realised, to his surprise, that he looked forward to becoming a dad.

'The thing is,' Mike continued. 'I've arranged to be at the office this evening for Joe Oliver's interim review. I can't get a message to him to cancel, and it's important someone is available. Any chance you could do the interview for me? He should be there in about half an hour.'

96

Will sighed; the last thing he wanted was to give up his evening for Joe Oliver. He was also aware of the ethical issues of becoming involved. Maisie seemed intent on making a fool of herself with this Joe if she wasn't careful, and he found it painful to watch her growing obsession. It was important to remain objective, but this was easier said than done. A senior colleague had once accused him of being too gullible with the clients and too easily sucked into other people's problems.

'Thanks, Will, I owe you one. You'll find his notes in the filing cabinet. I think it should be pretty straightforward; he's done well, thanks to Alpha House.'

'OK,' Will replied. 'Love to Jan, and I'm sure he'll be fine; kids are pretty tough, you know.' He rose wearily to extract Joe's file.

Despite his reservations, he had warmed to Joe. When he had attended court to support Maisie, Joe had come across as arrogant and sullen. Will read Mike's report as well as one from Ray Linnington who ran Alpha House. Mike was right; Joe was doing well.

Joe told him about an incident at last week's community service that made Will laugh out loud. He looked at Joe's broad grin and the warmth in his eyes and had some sympathy for Maisie.

'And what about your meet-the-victim sessions?'

Joe looked surprised. 'What do you want to know?'

'Well,' he chose his words with care. 'It is a pilot scheme, so I wondered if it was helping?'

Joe shrugged. 'I haven't thought about it. It's supposed to be for her benefit, isn't it?'

It was unprofessional, but he couldn't resist probing further to discover Joe's opinion of Maisie.

Joe replied that she had been kind and had shown an interest in his life and his family. He liked her, he said.

Will and Fran were enjoying a lie-in.

'Let's organise a dinner party,' he suggested.

Fran put her book down. 'OK, what did you have in mind?'

'Oh, just the usual crowd, it's mostly for Maisie's benefit; she could do with cheering up.'

Fran didn't inquire how he came to that conclusion; she switched off the light and turned her back on him.

He lay in the darkness. He hadn't, after all, told Fran that he had gone to Maisie's flat and for the moment there didn't seem to be any point in upsetting the status quo. Normally, he went out of his way to avoid hurting other people. When it came to Maisie, the thought of her bright smile and teasing eyes, which so tormented him, overrode his guilt.

Chapter 17
Maisie

On her way home from work, Maisie saw Joe standing at the bus stop. She wound down the window.

'Want a lift?'

He came over and leant on the open window. It was a warm day for April, and the ubiquitous donkey jacket was discarded in favour of an unexpectedly white T-shirt. She stared at the muscles in his tanned arms.

'I didn't think people like you used buses.' She tried to ignore the quizzical stares from the people in the bus queue.

Joe jumped into the seat beside her. 'People like me. What's that supposed to mean, the criminal classes?' he mocked.

She was flustered. 'Don't tease. You know what I mean.'

She drove down the road towards her flat. She hadn't asked him where he was going, but it didn't seem to matter. She was tempted to turn and look at him but resisted and kept her eyes on the rush-hour traffic. Today, she had that impetuous and 'ready for anything' feeling. It was the first day of the Easter holidays tomorrow, which heralded two glorious weeks of freedom. She pulled up outside her flat.

'Fancy a beer?' she asked on impulse. *Shit*, she'd forgotten he was not long out of rehab. 'Or coffee,' she added hastily. 'Unless you're rushing off somewhere, that is.'

Joe shrugged. 'Actually, I'm living just around the corner. Social services fixed me up with a bedsit. £4 a week subsistence and I get my rent paid on top of that.'

He followed her downstairs to the kitchen. To see him there was surreal and made her heart thump.

'Why don't you sit down?' She indicated the battered settee and turned away to put the kettle on. Maybe it was her imagination, but she could sense the sexual tension between and could feel herself blushing. She handed him a mug of coffee.

'Do you fancy something to eat? I'm starving.'

They sat at the kitchen table where Joe wolfed down a pile of scrambled eggs on toast; It was gratifying to see him looking so relaxed.

'When did you leave Alpha House?'

'A couple of weeks ago. I've still got community service though, until after Easter, but my probation officer appears to think I can be trusted to turn up on time.'

'Did you have to jump through a lot of hoops before you were allowed to leave?'

'God, yes. First off, I had an interview with the doctor who updated my blood tests to make sure I wasn't still using or drinking. Then, Harry, that's the guy who runs the group therapy sessions and Annie, my counsellor, had an interview with the manager who wrote his recommendations in a report to the probation service. Mike took the trouble to drive over to Huntsford to tell me his decision in person, which was good of him.'

Maisie wanted to tell him how well he had done, but that would seem patronising. Instead, she just grinned.

'So, when is the next community service? I take it you're not still painting the school fence.'

He smiled. 'I wish; no, we've graduated to the park railings now. Scraping rust is not exactly mind-blowing I can tell you.'

While they finished their coffee, Maisie put the radio on, and they chatted in a companionable way. He told her about his bedsit, and she laughed at his tales about the Irish labourers who were working on the new sewer tunnel. He described how they would go down to the communal kitchen when they got back in the evening and heave a load of cabbage and potatoes into a saucepan to boil. Then they would fall asleep in their room until the putrid smell of burned cabbage would drive them back to the kitchen to top up the pan with more water.

Joe leaned over and took her hand. 'I'm sorry I scared you that night.'

It was unexpected but his voice was gentle, and she struggled to control her churning emotions. At that moment she heard Sally's key in the front door and stood up abruptly.

'Anyway, as you're just around the corner, no doubt I'll bump into you.'

Sally raised her eyebrows disapprovingly when she told her, in response to a 'who was that?' about Joe coming in for a drink.

'Are you mad?' She paused, 'be careful won't you Maisie, please don't get involved.' She opened another bottle of wine and flopped down on the settee. 'I can see it will all end in tears.'

Maisie remembered Sally's words in bed that night. She was to recall them many times over the coming months. In the darkness, her head was full of Joe, his face, and the touch of his warm hands as he held hers. It was the same at work. A distant look would creep into her eyes, or she'd smile a sudden secret smile. Maisie remembered a line from a favourite poem...*and snatches of thee everywhere make little heavens throughout a day.'* It was ridiculous. She knew it was, but she couldn't help it. Thinking about Joe was indeed a little heaven, both private and thrilling.

Chris would understand. Chris had always followed her heart and taken risks; she wouldn't be judgmental. Maisie resolved to phone her.

'Hi, it's great to hear from you?' Maisie could hear the television and Chris's daughter saying   'Shh, mum; I can't hear,' in the affronted way of many eight-year-old girls.

'Sorry. Is this a bad time? Shall I ring back later?'

Chris laughed. 'Don't worry about madam here just ignore her as I do. What are you up to? You haven't still got the hots for your twelve-year-old, have you?'

Typical Chris to have remembered her drunken revelations at the reunion.

'If that's what you want, go for it, I would.' Chris told her.

'That's what I love about you.' Maisie smiled down the phone, thinking about some of Chris's more colourful relationships before she married Greg.

'Seriously, be careful won't you,' Chris sounded concerned.

'Yes, I'll be careful. I'm a supposedly, intelligent woman of twenty-seven, you know.'

'I didn't just mean you,' said Chris. 'I was thinking of him as well; he's probably pretty vulnerable.'

For a long while afterwards, she was unsettled by Chris' words.

Stupidly she hadn't asked Joe his address, and it was agony not to be able to see him. By way of distraction, she forced herself to do some marking. Most of her students were doing well.

One or two had blossomed academically, but she was concerned about a couple of the girls. They were both friends; they worked hard; never missed an essay deadline and were always in lectures. She had tried to put them at their ease in smaller tutorial groups and encouraged them to contribute, but they tended to sit back and say as little as possible. When she did ask them a direct question, their answers were often garbled and missed the main thrust of the discussion. Their lab reports were way off beam too, and they were in danger of failing their second year. She decided to set up a meeting and sort the situation out.

She was sitting at the kitchen table with a pile of essays spread out before her when the doorbell rang. It was a wet, blustery night, and she wasn't expecting anyone; *maybe it was someone for Sally?* Joe stood there. Raindrops clung to his dark hair, and he was soaked. He shook his head like a dog and smiled his head on one side in that appealing way of his.

'I hope you don't mind,' he began. 'I didn't get to finish what I wanted to say to you last night.'

102

There was no hesitation; no worrying about what she was getting herself into as she held the door open. She was ridiculously pleased to see him and couldn't help smiling.

'Of course, I don't mind; come in,' her voice was soft and low with emotion.

He followed her down to the kitchen. She couldn't believe how natural it seemed for him to be here again.

'Are you allowed a beer?' She looked uncertainly at him.

'Just a coffee for me. I'm trying to be good.'

Sitting opposite one another at the table, Joe explained that since leaving Alpha House, so far, he'd been alcohol and drug-free.

'It's hard, though,' he told her. 'I just take it one day at a time and try to avoid situations where I might be tempted.' He paused. 'I'm not like that you know,' he told her, the intensity showing on his face.

She blushed and forced herself to look away. 'Like what exactly?' She laughed, trying to sound light-hearted.

'I'm not that person who goes around hurting women or anyone else come to that.'

He looked heartbreakingly young with his sad eyes. *Perhaps Chris was right about his vulnerability?* He stood up as if he had decided it was time to leave. She couldn't bear him to go like that, and his sadness just brought with it a wave of desire. She moved towards him and took his face in her hands.

'I know you wouldn't,' she whispered and kissed him on the cheek.

He stepped away from her with a look of amazement.

'Sorry, must be my mothering instincts,' she muttered. *God, how stupid am I?*

She felt empty after he left. *How could she have imagined that he might want her in the same desperate way that she wanted him?* She wanted to be near him, to talk to him, to touch him and hold him.

Then nothing. It was two weeks since she'd seen him. Distraught, thinking that she'd scared him off, she could think of nothing but Joe. She knew it was a bad idea, but she couldn't resist phoning Mike Green.

'Sorry, Maisie, confidentiality and all that; I can't give out addresses. It's for your protection as much as his.'

She bit her lip and wondered if there was some underlying meaning to this statement, a warning perhaps.

'You know how it is,' he went on. 'I can pass a message to Joe Oliver. Perhaps...' he hesitated, 'it might be more appropriate if you drop me a line and I can forward it. How does that sound?'

Maisie screwed up her face. The metaphorical patting of the head was irritating. She had no choice but to agree, and after engaging in the usual small talk, she put the phone down, and the familiar tightness of disappointment returned. A soulless, formal note to Joe was a gruesome idea, and she just couldn't do it. Nor could she walk up and down his road in the hope of seeing him. She had some pride left; that's what she and Chris might have done when they were fifteen.

They'd had many grand passions although obsessions were maybe closer to the mark. She couldn't help but smile at the memories of boys she'd once been so besotted with and wondered what they were like nowadays. Chris had been as bad, which was why they got on so well and had once been so inseparable. With hindsight, Maisie often cringed at what she had been prepared to do. She had sat on a park bench for hours on end in the forlorn hope of catching one glimpse of the latest hero. Another time she had got up at five in the morning to hang out of her bedroom window to see the current much-adored return to university on his motorbike.

Sadly, little had changed as she grew older; only last year, she had become obsessed with a visiting, research professor. She spent hours and hours in the university library reading his papers. Just to see his name had been a thrill. It was hard now, to recapture even a fragment of what had so firmly gripped her.

And now there was Joe.

Chris's theory revolved around the unavailability of Maisie's objects of desire. It was true that after each attachment had run its course, there was no regret and no sadness, just a sense of moving on.

Maisie wondered if she had ever been in love. She had adored and lusted after two men in particular; both were warm-hearted and funny. They had loved her in an uncomplicated way and in both cases the sex had been fantastic. From the start, she had recognised that there was no likelihood of commitment on either side. They could live in the moment and relish their time together. *Could it be the same with Joe?* He inhabited her night dreams, yet his face flooded her waking moments with increasing frequency. She welcomed each intrusion – longed for it. Yet deep within her, lay the hard knob of bitter realisation that this obsession with Joe was dangerous for them both. She pondered over Chris's warning about his vulnerability.

She stood up and shook herself like a wet spaniel. She wanted to shake off such disquieting notions. She wished Sally would come in, anything to distract her. She downed another glass of wine, then picked up the phone and dialled once more.

'Hi, Fran. I wondered if you were coming to badminton tonight?' There was an over-bright eagerness in her voice.

'Yeah, I could do; Will's seeing a client tonight.'

'Great, I'll see you there about seven-thirty.'

Physical exertion was what she needed to clear her mind, and she might even confide in Fran. Unusually, Fran beat her easily.

'You seemed distracted tonight,' Fran remarked. 'Anything up?'

Maisie had been wondering all evening if this client might be Joe.

'What time is Will finished?' she enquired, struggling to sound casual. 'Have you made plans to meet up or anything? Perhaps we could all have a drink, that would be nice.' She was aware that she was gabbling.

Fran hesitated. 'We hadn't arranged anything. He's with Mike and some community service clients; I expect they'll go across to The Red Lion afterwards. There's nothing to stop us having a drink though.'

'No, it's ok; I ought to go home and sort out my stuff for tomorrow. Bloody subject review.'

Fran nodded in sympathetic agreement. The department was in the process of being inspected, which entailed scrutiny of all their planning and assessment records; unannounced lesson observations and short-tempered senior management breathing down their necks. It was time-consuming and an unwelcome pressure.

Maisie switched off the car engine; she had deliberately parked away from the pub. She looked at her watch. It was 9.15 pm; if Will was inside, he could well be there for over an hour. It was ridiculous and pathetic, yet she couldn't bring herself to move and kept her eyes glued on the heavy pub door.

Just before ten, Will, Mike Green and a motley assortment of youngsters emerged. Straight away, she spotted Joe. *What now?* She squashed herself against the car seat, grateful that it was dark. She longed to rush over to him with a confident, *'Hi, I was just passing. Can I give you a lift?'* But that was impossible. The group walked around the side of the pub to the car park. Mike and Will had no doubt offered them a lift home. Mechanically, she followed them to St Andrew's Road, Joe's road. She'd wait for him. Despite the warmth of the evening, she was shaking with a mixture of apprehension and longing. She watched him get out of Will's car and heard his cheery farewell.

He started at first when Maisie appeared beside him, and he looked at her questioningly as she struggled to control her trembling. She ran a finger below her eyes, hoping her stupid weeping in the car hadn't smudged her mascara.

'What's the matter? What's happened? Are you alright?'

106

She couldn't speak but holding his gaze, she took his hand and pressed it against her damp cheek. She saw the flicker of a frown cross his face, but if he was taken aback by her gesture, he wasn't showing it.

'You can come in if you like.' He nodded towards the front door of his bedsit.

Maisie heard the uncertainty in his voice. 'Is that ok?' She gave a rueful smile; *was that small voice really her own?* She followed him up the stairs to his room at the front of the large, double bay house.

As he switched on a single spotlight and closed the door, she was gripped with panic. *What was he doing? What would Joe make of her attentions?* She wanted him to know how she felt about him, but the thought of scaring him off terrified her.

The room, his room, was cosy and wrapped itself around them, making her feel safe and insulated from the rest of the world; she reminded herself to cherish this moment.

'I haven't got anything to drink, sorry,' he grinned. 'I could make us a coffee, though.'

'Coffee would be great. Thank you.'

He touched her bare arm. 'I won't be long.'

She heard him run down the stairs and remembered with a smile, his stories about the Irish blokes who cremated the cabbage in the communal kitchen. Left alone, Maisie inspected his meagre possessions – a few paperbacks, an old stereo. She flipped through the small pile of LPs, Bruce Springsteen, Steve Harley and Cockney Rebel, Dire Straits, no surprises there. A single sleeping bag lay on the double bed. She ran her fingers over the crumpled pillowcase. An armchair was placed in front of the gas fire and in the corner stood a cheap table and two chairs. She sat down and waited for him.

Her chest was tight with emotion when he appeared clutching two coffee mugs. His wide grin displayed even, and unexpectedly white teeth and the sun had given his face a rich tan. He wore faded Levi's, desert boots and a crew-necked, navy jumper. He looked happy, and she was shocked to realise how important his happiness had become to her. There was a spring of energy about him; a vitality that had replaced the pent-up restlessness she'd seen before. He opened the window, allowing the warm night air to lift the floral curtains and put a Roxy Music LP on. He sat down in the other chair. His gaze was steady, but a flash of uncertainty hung between them.

'Am I forgiven?' he asked.

She nodded and pressed his hand to her cheek. Then taking his face in her hands, she bent to kiss him. A shiver of anticipation ran through her as their lips touched. He pulled her towards him. There was no awkwardness or uncertainty now. He undid her bra and lifted the white t-shirt over her head before burying his face in her soft breasts. He gave a low moan and pulled off his t-shirt, so their warm skin pressed together. Without embarrassment, she slid out of her jeans and pants and lay on the bed and watched as he wriggled out of his tight Levi's. His lean body was strong and compact, and Maisie experienced the familiar, hot ache in her groin. Joe smiled that now familiar smile, but behind it, in his eyes, she recognised desire. She allowed him to explore her body with his mouth and his hands

'You're so beautiful, Maisie.' He told her; his voice so tender that a shiver ran down her spine.

He makes me feel beautiful, she thought, ridiculously happy because, for the first time, he had used her name. He kissed her soft, inner thigh as he squeezed both buttocks rhythmically, almost hypnotically. He parted her legs and ran his tongue either side of her swollen clitoris. The effect on Maisie was electric. She had to concentrate fiercely to contain the powerful orgasm that was in danger of overwhelming her.

'I want you so much, Joe.' She wrapped her legs around him, and they moved together.

Afterwards, she lay unable to move, delighting in the throbbing aftermath of her orgasm.

108

Joe propped himself on one elbow. He entwined his fingers in her hair and kissed her on the lips.

'You are the most amazing woman. Will you stay with me tonight?'

Too emotional to speak, Maisie clung to him. They covered themselves with the sleeping bag and lay with their arms wrapped around each other.

She couldn't believe how well she had slept. She could smell his sweat; it was a sweet, erotic smell, unlike when he attacked her and had smelled stale and unwashed. She closed her eyes; it all seemed a long time ago now, and she didn't want to think about the past. But nor could she think about the future. It didn't matter; she refused to let it matter. For the moment, they wanted each other; it was as simple and as dangerously complicated as that. She stretched blissfully. It was still the Easter holidays, and she didn't have to go to work.

All morning, they lay in each other's arms and talked about anything and everything. Joe told her about his family, about his year at college and about his determination to get his life together now. She told him about her friends and her life. But even as she spoke, she was struck at how superficial and shallow her life seemed. With a surprise, she realised that she was lonely. She flirted with men, particularly with Will and even Shaun on occasion, but for years there'd been no real commitment, just times when she'd become obsessed with the current man. She so wanted it to be different with Joe. But beyond the obvious sexual desire, unexpectedly, Maisie liked him. They shared the same sense of humour, and he made her laugh out loud with his perceptive, witty remarks. There was nothing self-centred about him, and he'd seemed genuinely interested when she'd rabbited on about her life.

'How old are you – twenty?' she asked.

Joe nodded, then that smile. 'I know; don't tell me; you're actually a well preserved forty-year-old.'

'Damn, you've guessed,' she laughed. 'Come on,' she pulled him out of bed. 'It's a gorgeous day; let's go out somewhere.' She looked at her watch. 'It's nearly midday so why don't we drive out to a country pub?' *Somewhere out of town where no one knows me*, she silently added. This was the second thing that she had kept to herself.

'We don't have to go to a pub if that's difficult for you. We could have a walk if you like.'   Maisie frowned. *How could she have been so insensitive?*

He took hold of her hand. 'Just because I'm not drinking doesn't mean that you can't. Honestly, it makes no difference if someone else is drinking, and I'm just happy to be with you.'

They sat on a wooden bench beneath an ancient and abundant wisteria. Joe had an orange juice and lemonade and Maisie a white wine spritzer. Oblivious to anyone else, they sat with their thighs pressed against each other and their fingers entwined. Without speaking, they finished their drinks and walked across to the field opposite the pub. Their feet crunched on the hard chalk soil as, arms around each other, they followed an overgrown path to the edge of the sun-dappled wood where they made love once more. Maisie lay beside Joe with her head on his jacket. She watched the leaves wave gently above her head and drank in the peaceful atmosphere. She took hold of his hand.

'Will you tell me sometime what it's like for you to struggle with your drinking and the other stuff?'

Joe sat up, and the moment was shattered.

'No different or harder for me than anyone else I guess,' was all he said.

Afterwards, she dropped him back at his bedsit and drove home. Bubbling with excitement, she sang along at full volume to her favourite song, *My Guy*. Exhilarated, she wanted to yell out of the open window that she'd just made love in a beautiful wood with her secret lover. The sexual attraction she felt for Joe was further heightened by the excitement of an illicit affair.

110

The week after next was an unofficial half term at the university while the students revised for their exams. Joe and Maisie sat in her car, and she was fretting about how they could be together.

Then she sat upright, nodding to herself.

'There's a wonderful place on the island, an old boathouse we used to go to on holiday when I was young. If it's still available, we could go there for a few days. What do you think?' She tried to hide her eagerness.

With a big grin on his face, Joe pulled her into his arms. 'Yeah,' he breathed, burying his face in her hair.

She let herself into the flat. *They could go on Friday night, five days away*; she hugged herself and laughed out loud. Sally poked her head around her bedroom door.

'Where did you get to last night? I was worried.' She stopped and grinned at Maisie. 'You have a certain glow about you, my dear,' she teased. 'Anything I should know?'

'I wish. I had too much to drink and stayed over at Will and Fran's; that's all.'

It was uncomfortable lying to Sally, and she longed to tell her about Joe, about how wonderful he was and how fantastic it was to be with him. She longed to tell all her friends, even Will, but she knew it was important for both their sakes, for the moment at least, to keep him a secret. Chris's words about Joe being vulnerable, kept haunting her.

'I'm going to have a drink right now; do you fancy one?' Sally inquired as she made her way down the stairs. 'Oh, by the way, Will phoned about half an hour ago; he wanted to know what you were doing tonight?' She gave her a knowing look and Maisie was grateful that Sally had curbed her curiosity. She would confide in her soon when the time was right.

They caught the six o'clock hovercraft. As it was Friday most of their fellow passengers were dark-suited, businessmen returning to the island after the working week in London. The sea was calm, but the sky a dull, flat grey. Maisie had hoped for warm, sunny weather. She was nervous about spending time away with Joe. She scarcely knew him; she knew about him and that he could be kind and thoughtful, *but did she really know him?* Supposing he got bored when it was just the two of them.

When they arrived, Ryde looked uninviting. Maisie was anxious to get to Bembridge and pick up the key from Mrs Snowden who lived in the caravan park and still owned the boathouse. They sat upstairs on the bus. She remembered hurtling along the narrow roads as a child but, unlike the carefree anticipation of childhood, now there was anxiety. Mrs Snowden didn't recognise her, which was a relief. Either that or she was being discreet, which seemed unlikely.

A pang of nostalgia hit her as they walked across the duver wall towards the lower end of the harbour. A few yachts, catching the last of the flood tide, made their way up the narrow channel to the marina. On one side of them, several youngsters from the yacht club were racing small dinghies. While within the protection of the sea wall, parent swans escorted three young cygnets. Joe had barely spoken since they got off the bus, which added to her apprehension about the trip. Halfway across the wall, they passed a father and his young son fishing. To Maisie's delight, Joe stopped to chat as he inspected their catch and was proudly shown two small bass. She stopped worrying and slid her arm through his.

Then something occurred to her. She turned to Joe and made an apologetic face. 'Damn, I forgot to bring anything to eat.' She tutted, annoyed at her stupidity, and looked at her watch. 'The beach café shuts at seven this time of year, so we don't even have anything to drink. Sorry'

He laughed. 'You don't have to worry about me; I'm well used to going without.'

By the time they reached the boathouse, the evening had fined up. A reddish tinge in the sky promised good weather for tomorrow and made the boathouse look enchanting in the calm light.

112

'Why don't you relax and have a shower?' Joe suggested after she had shown him around. 'I fancy having a look outside before the light goes.'

The water was hot and soothing. Maisie combed her hair and had just wrapped herself in a towel when he re-appeared with a massive grin on his face.

'You look pleased with yourself.' Sliding her arms around him she, buried her face against his neck and breathed in his warmth.

'And you're supposed to be the organised one.' Joe adopted a mock Irish accent as he displayed the contents of two carrier bags at his side. 'We have, Madame,' he declared, 'one loaf of bread, half a packet of bacon - best back mind, some eggs, oh and a bottle of wine.'

'Blimey.' She unwrapped her damp arms from around his neck and took the bottle of Fitou from him in amazement. 'Where on earth did you find this lot?'

'From the woman in the caravan behind the beach. When I explained our predicament, she said she couldn't have our romantic evening spoiled because we had no food and worse still nothing to drink. We can replace the stuff tomorrow so no worries.'

'Thank you,' she whispered. She kissed him on the cheek and took the glass of wine he held out to her. 'And thanks to Mrs Caravan.' She raised her glass in salute. 'I wonder what she thought. Probably thinks we're having a dirty weekend.' She blushed, realising that's exactly what they were doing.

'Stop laughing,' she demanded and threw a cushion at Joe, who was collapsed with laughter on the sofa. She pulled on jeans and a t-shirt and towel-dried her hair. Soon, the wonderful smell of bacon frying filled the small living room. I'll buy candles tomorrow she thought and cook a proper meal.

After their impromptu supper, they took the rest of the wine out on to the ancient, wooden decked porch. Lights from the holiday flats at the top of the harbour shone across the water. The salty, night air was warm and dry as Maisie scrunched the sand on the bleached boards beneath her bare feet. The place still had the same feel of happy contentment that she had experienced as a child on holiday. But she couldn't get over the sight of Joe drinking red wine. She had managed to stop questioning him but was worried that he might slip back into his old habits. They stood with their arms around each other and listened to the raucous birds feeding in the marshes. When the light faded, they went inside and climbed into the bouncy double bed. Maisie couldn't stop giggling when Joe marvelled at the crisp white sheets. Gathering her in his arms, his hands explored the smooth, warm skin of her thighs and her buttocks. With a choke of desire, he ran his tongue over her hardening nipple. They made love unhurriedly, and Maisie experienced a new depth to her orgasm. She lay back in contentment; this was the perfect place for them.

For the rest of the week, they ate, drank, slept, and explored the island. An old, wooden dinghy was pulled up on the weedy beach in front of the boathouse, and they rowed around the harbour just enjoying being together.

'The sun's given you freckles on your nose.' Joe smiled and leaned forward on his oars to plant a kiss on her nose.

Maisie sat back; Joe was surprisingly good at rowing. He wore a cut-off, pair of Levi's and the sight of his tanned, muscular forearms and lean stomach were irresistible, and she allowed her fingers to trail over the fine hairs on his abdomen. Alone in the small boat, there was a tranquil sense of isolation. It was just the two of them with nothing and no one to bother them.

That night Maisie lay with her head resting on Joe's chest. 'What do you see in me, Joe?'

He laughed and stroked her hair. 'Don't ask me.'

Maisie poked him in the ribs. 'You know what I mean.'

'I like the way you bite your nails and don't even realise you're doing it; I like the way you clasp your hands in

114

front of you when you are nervous, and when you laugh it's infectious. I like that.'

Maisie was impressed by how much he had noticed in the short time they had been together. It became a habit, to laugh and talk in bed often late into the night. They talked not just about themselves but also about much broader issues. *Could Joe be the soul mate she'd unwittingly been seeking?* She loved the way they laughed together at the same absurdities and were comfortable enough with each other to engage in some forthright political banter. Joe had become engagingly animated when they got on to Margaret Thatcher's right-wing views. Maisie didn't agree with her politics either, but she couldn't help admiring her. She thought his outlook was narrow and told him as much.

On their last evening, they drove to the cinema in Newport to watch *Kramer v. Kramer*. Joe was much amused when Maisie was unable to stop the tears that flowed down her cheeks. Later, in bed, he kissed her soft curls and clung to her.

'I love you, Maisie,' he whispered. 'I love you so much.' He stopped. 'Please don't cry,' he told her, his voice full of concern.

Maisie sighed, daunted by the difficulties that lay ahead of them. She laid her wet cheek against his.

'I love you too, Joe; I will always love you.' The emotion hung between them.

It was a strain being back at work. Maisie kept quiet about her week away with Joe. She informed anyone who asked that she had spent the week with an old friend. But she was frequently distracted as the image of him drifted in front of her eyes or she recalled his soft low voice that would rise questioningly at the end of a sentence. His voice, his face, the touch of his hands on her body continued to haunt her in the early hours of wakefulness.

Outwardly, she carried on as usual. She played badminton with Fran and went to Pebbles on a Wednesday night as usual. A couple of times, when Sally was out for the evening, Joe came around to the flat. One night she went to his bedsit, but she felt uncomfortable and out of place although she couldn't pinpoint why. Most nights, she tossed and turned, worrying about how they were ever going to have any time to be with each other. Moving into Joe's place wasn't an option because his tenancy agreement wouldn't allow it and she and Sally had an understanding that male friends could stay over for a night or even a weekend but not long-term. If they were going to be together, they would have to find their own place.

Chapter 18
Joe

Joe went to see Mike Green. His community service had finished, but he still had to attend regular, monthly meetings for the next six months. He was also obliged to tell Mike if he changed his address. Mike had always seemed a decent bloke, so Joe decided to tell him about his relationship with Maisie.

'Maisie has changed a whole lot of things for me,' he told Mike. 'My life seems to have some purpose for once.' A light came into his eyes. 'I can start to think about the future; make some plans, you know.'

Mike nodded. 'What plans did you have in mind?'

'Learn to drive for a start; that would be good, and I've always wanted to travel, go to Thailand maybe, particularly if I can go with Maisie.'

If Mike was surprised by Joe's news, he had been well trained to conceal it. He cleared his throat before speaking.

'I have to warn you that a liaison of that kind would be frowned on by the probation service. You have several months of supervision left and, in my view, it would be premature and potentially harmful to both yourself and Miss George to become involved. It's good that you feel so positive about your future, but please take things slowly, one step at a time.'

Joe looked him steadily in the eye. 'I get what you're saying, but we're both adults and know own minds. It's important to us to be together regardless of what others may think.'

He could feel a bubble of anger begin to surface. Being told what to do did not sit well with him, and he resented the interference. His counselling sessions at Alpha House had taught him to contain his impulsive behaviour, and this was the moment to draw on that advice. If he were to lose his temper, which he was close to doing, that could have a bad outcome. Not to act in an abusive manner towards his

probation officer was one of several rules he had signed up
to.

Mike sighed audibly and rearranged the pens on his
desk. 'It's not so much a question of what others think. As
you know, I am obliged to approve your living arrangements
for the duration of your community sentence. I do have
considerable reservations about this relationship, but I am
prepared to sanction the change in living arrangements. This
will, of course, need to be closely monitored.'

Joe watched as the other man pressed his fingers
together in front of him on the desk and remained silent. Joe
was unsure what to do when, finally, Mike Green spoke.

'I have an idea which may appeal. My brother-in-law
lives on a houseboat; it's an old barge moored on the River
Hamble. He's going to work in France, in Montpelier, for a
couple of years and he's thinking about renting the barge out.'

'Sounds good,' Joe replied, 'How much do you reckon
he'll want for rent?'

'Look, you best speak to him yourself.' He wrote down
a number and handed it to Joe. 'It's his work number; there's
no phone on the boat, but that'll be ok. You can tell him that I
suggested it.'

'Thanks, I will. Maisie will be made up with this; she
loves boats.'

'Well, good luck with it. He opened his diary. 'See you
at the end of May. What about the 28th?'

Joe nodded. 'Whatever, yes that'll be fine.' He was
anxious to go and tell Maisie.

She looked shocked. 'Do you think it's such a good idea?'
she asked when he told her about his conversation with Mike
Green.

'Forget about him,' he told her impatiently. 'He's alright
with it. What do you think about the boat idea? Let's go for
it.'

Chapter 19
Maisie

Just like that, she thought. Her mind was racing; it was all so simple for Joe.

'Do you think Mike Green is likely to tell Will?' she asked.

'I shouldn't think so. Anyway, what does it matter? But you should tell him yourself if it's that important to you.'

It was true; it did matter what Will thought, and Fran and Sally and all the rest come to that. Then there was the flat; she couldn't just leave Sally in the lurch.

She avoided Joe's concerned look. 'How soon before we have to decide?'

'Look, don't worry about it; I haven't even rung the guy yet. It was just an idea; forget it.'

From the edge in his voice, she knew he was hurt by her hesitation, which helped her to make a swift decision – *to hell with other people.*

She smiled at him, anxious to make things right again. 'It sounds perfect; let's give him a ring straight away and see when we can go and see it.'

It was a big commitment, and it scared her, so she decided to phone Chris.

'I thought this was what you wanted?' Chris sounded puzzled. 'What's worrying you?'

'Oh, I don't know. It all seems to have happened so fast.'

Chris laughed. 'Plus, your nose has been put out of joint because he took the initiative – right?'

Maisie was indignant. 'You know me too well. Seriously though, it's a big step. We've kept our relationship quiet up to now. Plus, there are the practicalities of moving. I'm about to live on a 72 ft barge, for Christ's sake.'

'It sounds fun to me.' Chris was as upbeat as ever. 'I shall look forward to coming to stay. So will the girls; they'll be made up with the idea. Come on Mais, think of all the positives – romantic sunsets over the water and all that.'

Maisie smiled. She might have known that would be Chris' reaction; her friend was bold and unconventional, and nothing phased her. It was just what Maisie wanted to hear, but it failed to dispel her worries.

That evening, she decided to broach the subject with Sally, especially if she was going to have to find a new flatmate. Sally snorted into her glass when Maisie told her about their plans. But, far from being annoyed or disapproving, Sally found the idea wildly exciting.

'God, Maisie,' she screamed. 'You dark horse, that is the most fantastic news I've heard in ages. And with Joe, he's gorgeous.'

He is, thought Maisie. Initially, it had all been about the physical attraction, but now it was so much more. Tears pricked the back of her eyes. Joe was her soul mate; he was warm and funny and kind and unpredictable. She couldn't imagine life without him now, *so why did it feel so surreal?*

The two flatmates sat cross-legged on the settee with a second bottle of wine and discussed the practicalities. They agreed to ask their friends and to put cards up at their respective workplaces, advertising the flat share.

Maisie was suddenly overcome with tiredness and felt emotional. 'Do me a favour, will you? I haven't told anyone except Chris about this yet, so could you keep it to yourself for a couple of days?'

Maisie lay in bed, her mind wandering. Despite being tired, she was on overdrive as she rehearsed how to tell Will. Each time she tried, it never seemed convincing. He knew her pretty well; plus, he was straightforward when it came to his opinions. A knob of uncertainty grew; his reaction might be less encouraging than Sally's. *What would she say if he disapproved and told her to stay away from Joe?* She couldn't lose Will's friendship; he meant too much to her for that. Then there were her parents, and Richard, none of whom were likely to be thrilled at her news.

Next morning, she was feeling short-tempered from lack of sleep and still caught up in the turmoil of her nocturnal ramblings when Mike Green phoned.

'I guess Joe told you he came to see me.'

Maisie leaned on the back of a chair. A dreadful headache was making her queasy. 'He did,' she replied her voice over-bright. 'I think the idea of the barge is great. You were brilliant to think of it.'

'I hope it works out.' Mike paused. 'Look, Maisie, please take some time to consider before you make any big decisions. I know how easy it is to get carried away.'

How would he know? She thought crossly. He had always struck her as the staid and unadventurous type.

'Thanks, that's sweet of you', she told him. 'But please don't worry about me because I couldn't be happier. It's absolutely perfect for us.'

'I hope you're right.' Mike sounded embarrassed. 'But I have to remind you that Joe is still on probation until July, and I've insisted that he wait until then. I've also briefed Will Stevens as he has been involved in Joe's supervision.'

Maisie's heart sank. 'I understand, and I am going to speak to Will tonight.'

Trying to push aside any apprehension, she pushed open the door to the wine bar. As it was a Wednesday, most of the crowd would be at Pebbles, and she had decided to tell them en masse. The Will situation was awkward; she should tell him first while they were alone, but she couldn't face it.

She drank several glasses of red wine in rapid succession then blurted out, 'Did I tell you my fan-tas-tic news?' She waved a hand airily to encompass the group, so she was assured of their full attention. 'You remember Joe?' she hesitated, 'Well, we've been seeing each other and have decided to live together – on an old barge, actually,' she ended, her tone a mixture of challenge and triumph.

121

Shaun reached for the bottle and topped up his oversize glass. 'Well, well,' he muttered, stroking his beard. 'You kept that pretty quiet; I had no idea.'

Fran was silent, her face expressionless. Maisie forced herself to look at Will. In contrast, his face was creased into a frown. She longed to put her arms around him and try to explain. Surely, if he realised her sheer joy at being with Joe, then he would understand. She wanted to hold him and say sorry, but it was impossible, not tonight.

She woke late with an excruciating hangover. It was practically the end of term, thank goodness. Lectures for the students finished a couple of weeks ago, but she still had to attend a moderation meeting to look at the first-year practicals. Fran would be there too, and Maisie wondered if she'd say anything. After an hour, Maisie's concentration flagged.

'So, how do the final grades for your group compare with mid-year predictions?' Fran's tone was cool, and Maisie resented being put on the spot.

'I assumed we weren't going to comment on final grades until after moderation,' Maisie countered. She turned to Shaun. 'But I've got the figures here if you'd like to hear them.'

With some satisfaction, she informed them that apart from the couple of girls she'd already discussed with Shaun, who were struggling, the rest had achieved above predicted grades. Maisie was amazed the results were so good considering how distracted she'd been for much of the academic year. Still, she didn't want to fall out with Fran, and when they broke for lunch, she tried to be friendly.

'If we ever do manage to rent this barge you and Will must be our first visitors,' she told Fran casually.

'Actually, I doubt if I'll be here,' Fran replied, her face again impassive.

'I'm surprised Will didn't mention it to you. I'm leaving at the end of term to take up a job in Nottingham.'

122

Maisie felt a mixture of hurt and irritation. 'Christ, Fran, you never said a word.'

'No, but you have been somewhat distracted lately.'

'Maybe, but you should have told me and what about Will is he going with you?'

Fran looked her in the eye. 'No, Maisie, I'm going on my own.'

She sounded matter of fact almost confrontational, but Maisie heard her sadness.

'It hasn't been working out between us for a while now, and it's time to move on.'

She touched Fran's arm. 'Oh, Fran; I'm so sorry, and I've been blabbing on about myself. You will keep in touch, won't you?'

Fran smiled non-commitally. 'Look, it's time we were off. Why don't you come over tonight? I can cook something and tell you all about my new job.'

Maisie was relieved that Will was staying. She couldn't imagine him not being around, and Nottingham was a long way.

Next morning Will phoned her.

'I've just had an update about Joe Oliver from Mike', he informed her. 'I must say I can't believe that you could even consider a live-in relationship with him. Yet again, your naivety astounds me. He's a troubled young man and frankly in your position you should know better. I've asked Mike to reconsider his decision to sanction the proposed change in Joe's living arrangements.'

His attitude shocked Maisie. 'Now hang on,' she struggled to keep her voice level. 'What the hell gives you the right to dictate how I should conduct my life?' She was shaking. 'I can't speak to you right now, I'm too angry,' and she put the phone down. *Pompous git, how dare he?*

She agonised over whether to tell Joe about Will's intervention. It felt uncomfortable keeping things from him, and he was bound to find out sometime, but she wasn't prepared for his reaction. He paced up and down in her kitchen, kicking the furniture and shouting obscenities about Will. His face drained of colour, and he had a steely glint in his eyes. Alarmed, Maisie caught hold of his arm.

'Calm down. Will hasn't actually done anything yet and anyway it's not up to him. Mike Green will have the final say.'

Joe pulled away from her. 'Wake up, Maisie. Why do you think he's so against the idea?' He grabbed his jacket from the back of the chair and began to run up the stairs.

Maisie was in tears. 'Where are you going? Don't run off like that we need to talk. Please, Joe.'

'Sorry, Maisie but I've got to sort this out.' His voice was terse; then she heard the front door bang.

Panicked, she didn't know what to do. *Should she phone Will to warn him? Did Joe even know where to find him?* Shaken by Joe's behaviour, she decided there was nothing for it but wait and see what happened. She was reluctant to phone Will in case Joe had calmed down and changed his mind. *Besides, what would she say to Will?* Joe had decided that Will was motivated by jealousy. *Supposing he was right?* She choked back the tears. The whole situation was ghastly.

Thankfully, Sally was out at a meeting and by the time she got back, Maisie could legitimately be in bed. She couldn't face explaining why she was so upset. Up to now, Sally had been a Joe fan having only seen his caring, fun side. Maisie, however, had seen glimpses of his mood swings. She knew his history, and from a professional point of view, she knew what to expect. Nevertheless, it was disconcerting.

It was a long and restless night. She half hoped that Joe would reappear with his lopsided grin; pull her into his arms and tell her all was well. When she didn't have any contact from Will all the next day, she dared to hope that no confrontation had taken place. But there was still no sign of Joe. She would just have to be patient. He would be back in his own time.

124

Chapter 20
Joe

Joe kept walking when he left Maisie's. He ended up at the beach and sat on the pebbles hoping the sea would have a calming effect. It was a warm evening, and he lay back on the stones to look at the stars. This was his biggest test since leaving Alpha House. His brain was telling him that he needed a drink or a smoke. He thought about Maisie. *Was she worried where he'd got to or what he might have done?*

He stayed on the beach all night fighting his demons. The early sunrise made him feel worse; he hadn't eaten anything since yesterday lunchtime, and now he felt sick and anxious. He wandered along to the little café at the end of the pier where he sat with a mug of coffee and a bacon roll. He tried to distract himself with yesterday's paper that someone had left, but the cravings wouldn't leave him. This was different from sharing a bottle of wine with Maisie or convincing himself that a pint in The Apsley couldn't hurt. Still in turmoil, he wandered back towards town but trying to convince himself that he had the mental strength to get through this was a fluctuating battle. Then he spotted Mac on the other side of the road. It was such a fortuitous meeting that his anger at Will and the need for a drink just melted away.

'Hi there,' he called. 'It's great to see you again.'

'Pretty good, especially now I've bumped into you.' There was so much he wanted to share with Mac. 'Where are you headed? Perhaps I can walk with you?'

'I've got the bike over there but come on round – 25 Freshwater Grove. It'll be good to catch up.'

'Great; put the kettle on, and I'll see you in a minute.'

Mac's house was much as expected. They sat on two old-fashioned fireside chairs next to the open French windows and drank tea. To Joe's surprise, Mac produced a tin of homemade rock cakes. It was comforting to bite into the moist sponge. The rows and rows of battered, brown-backed books caught Joe's eye.

'Mind if I have a look?'

'Help yourself, though I doubt there's much that would be to your taste,' Mac replied.

You're not wrong there, thought Joe as he inspected the Greek and Latin tomes. Recognising a title that he knew; he picked out Thomas Hardy's *The Return of the Native*. Inside the cover was inscribed 'To my darling Kate, October 1923'.

'Was Kate your wife?'

Mac nodded without offering further detail and took out his pipe. 'Go on then. What's been happening in your life?'

'Well,' said Joe. 'I've finished the community service, thank God, and social services have fixed me up with a bedsit in town. You'll have to come and visit.' Then he remembered. 'You'll have to make it soon though, all being well, I'm hoping to move on to an old barge. It's a houseboat these days, and we can rent it for a couple of years.' He hoped to God that it would happen. He'd been so excited by the idea. *Fuck Will.*

Mac listened without interruption as Joe explained his relationship with Maisie.

'When Maisie talks, she always sounds as though she's smiling,' he confided. 'I just want to be with her all the time.' He half wished Mac would comment or offer some advice, but that wasn't his style, and he merely sucked on his pipe.

Joe remembered one time at Alpha House when Mac had talked about bringing up his three daughters who were now grown up with their own families.

'We taught them as far as possible what was right and what was wrong; then we stepped back and let them make their own choices.' Mac had told him.

Joe hoped that his decision to be with Maisie was the right choice for them both. Unexpectedly, he felt a responsibility for Maisie's emotions and vowed that he would never betray her or let her down.

126

When he arrived back at her flat, Maisie flung her arms around his neck and smothered his face with kisses.

'You're in a good mood', he grinned. 'I wasn't sure what sort of a reception I was going to get.'

She waved her arm, dismissively. 'All done and dusted, that's yesterday's news.' She squeezed his hand. 'We're all good; aren't we?'

By way of reply, Joe pulled her into his arms.

'I did a lot of thinking last night, and I've decided to hell with the doubters. I think the idea of living on a barge is perfect.' She clapped her hands together as she often did when she was excited. 'There's a lot we need to sort out before that, though. I've already warned Sally to look for a new flatmate, and you'll have to give notice at your bedsit I guess.'

Joe shrugged. 'No idea, I'll ask Mike Green, he'll know.

'When can we look round the barge? I want to start packing, but I don't know how much room there will be for all my stuff.'

Next morning while Maisie was at work, feeling upbeat, Joe set about contacting Mike Green to start the ball rolling. He agreed that they would cover the mooring fees from the beginning of July and keep up the maintenance on the barge, whatever that entailed. He walked slowly on his way back from the phone box. He was a take one day at a time sort of guy, and this level of responsibility felt serious. Money would be tight for a start as Maisie would have to pay rent on her flat until the end of the month.

When he arrived at her flat, he found Maisie in tears.

'What's wrong? What's happened?' He kissed her wet cheeks. 'Don't cry. I hate to see you upset.'

Between sobs and blowing her nose, she told him about the conversation she'd had with her mother.

'You'd think I was sixteen, not twenty-six. She should learn to keep her opinions to herself. I honestly thought she'd be pleased that I'd found someone who makes me so happy, but she went on and on about your problems and how we met. How can she be so judgmental when she's not even met you?'

'Maybe that's part of the problem,' Joe put in gently. 'She probably feels shut out and from what you say she's not used to that. She'll come around; I'm good at charming the older woman.' Joe tried to make light of the situation, but Maisie was having none of it.

'It's not just her. Mum was adamant that dad and Rich would think the same. Where's the support for me? Honestly, Joe, I'm so angry with her.'

Joe didn't know what to suggest other than to give it time. None of this was going to be easy. From what she said Maisie's work colleagues, while not openly opposed to the idea, were lukewarm in their response.

After his meeting with social services to sort out the tenancy on his bedsit, he found Maisie in a buoyant mood.

'As of tomorrow, I'm on holiday,' she squealed, jumping up and down and clapping her hands in her signature move. 'Three wonderful months of holiday.' She turned to Joe. 'Here; hold this a minute; there's something I want to show you. No doubt it will give you a good laugh at my expense.'

She smiled as she showed him photos of herself as a baby, sitting up in her pram with white-blond curls and a toothy smile. She pointed out her brother Richard, dark-haired and solemn.

'And look at me in this one,' she giggled. 'I was about fourteen, I think.'

Joe studied the picture of Maisie looking sexy in her school uniform. She showed him more recent photos of her parents and the farmhouse in Somerset where they now lived. He was glad he had shown him the album. He knew she wanted to make him feel more a part of her life, but for some niggling reason, he couldn't imagine future photos of the two of them together. He'd never considered how they were perceived as a couple before.

He got to his feet, hoping to shake away these obtrusive thoughts. What did that matter? He loved her, and he wanted to be with her.

Chapter 21
Will

'Do you mind if I take this?' Fran held up an old oil lamp. Her expression was tight with impatience.

Will sighed. The dark circles under her eyes signalled her exhaustion. 'Don't be silly; take whatever you need.'

She continued to stuff her belongings into cardboard boxes. Already the flat seemed alien and no longer a home for either of them. The heat was stifling, and Will crossed to the open window to get some air. Outside there was still light in the sky.

'Do you know what time you'll be off tomorrow?' His voice was flat; he wanted to ask her why she was going at all.

They had shared their lives for five years, yet now they couldn't even to talk to one another. Will felt leaden; all this was his fault. He had indulged his obsession with Maisie to the point where it dominated him. No wonder Fran sensed his withdrawal from her. He knew how much he had hurt her, but he couldn't help himself; he couldn't switch off his emotions.

Fran was brisk. 'As soon as I'm ready, I suppose. I told Mum I'd be there sometime in the afternoon. On a Saturday it shouldn't take me more than an hour and a half to drive to Peckham. Will you be here in the morning?' Her face softened. 'I could do with a hand to load up the car.'

He went over and put his arms around her thin shoulders and stroked her hair.

'I'll be here. Look, you've done enough for now; have a drink with me.' There was so much they still needed to say to each other.

She frowned and plonked down on the bed. 'OK, just a quick one. I'm nowhere near finished yet.'

Will poured two large glasses of Merlot and sat next to her. They were silent as the open windows let in the noise of passing traffic and the brash sounds of young lads off for a Friday night's clubbing.

'Are you sure this is what you want, Franny?' His face was burning, and he couldn't look at her; he was afraid she might say something he was reluctant to hear.

After a long pause, Fran spoke. 'I don't think there's much future for us, not anymore.' There were no recriminations, just sad acceptance. 'After we'd been going out for a few months I thought we'd always be together; get married and even have children.' She sounded almost apologetic. 'That was never what you wanted was it?'

It was sad, but she was right. At least he owed it to her to be honest now.

'To be truthful, I never gave it much thought,' he told her.

He had enjoyed living with her; she was easy-going, and they had a lot in common. He was trained to be sensitive to people's feelings and their hidden agendas, and yet he'd been blindly self-centred when it came to the person closest to him.

He took hold of her hand. 'I can't pretend I would feel differently if you stayed. I don't think I know what I want or where I'm heading with my life. I'm so sorry, Fran.'

She laid his hand against her warm cheek. 'Don't worry, Will; I accepted some time ago that I wasn't the love of your life. I suppose this new job pushed me into making the decision that I'd been avoiding.' She topped up their glasses. 'Let's drink to the good times. There were good times, weren't there?'

Will brushed away her tears and held her in his arms. 'Of course, there were lots and lots of them. By the way, I'm proud of you,' he added. He raised his glass. 'Here's to the new Deputy Head of Department. Good luck, Franny – you'll knock 'em dead.'

His words were cold and detached, something a colleague would say, but she didn't comment. Will was relieved. Until now, he had struggled; ashamed that on one level he wanted Fran to stay and maintain the status quo like some cosy favourite jumper. But he was grateful that they'd at last been honest with each other. Their conversation brought with it an air of finality.

Fran continued to pack. They opened another bottle and were soon giggling helplessly as they hunted in the dark garden for her gnomes. When they first moved into the flat Fran had introduced Will to her motley collection of garden gnomes. They had increased in number over the years and were lovingly cared for. Come autumn, they were brought indoors to be carefully wrapped up and stored until the spring. It was this quirkiness that had attracted him to Fran in the first place.

Once they had completed the remainder of the packing and discussed practicalities concerning the flat, it seemed natural to climb into their shared bed for the last time. Will felt relaxed and more at ease with her than he had for months. Fran was very still as they lay side-by-side in the darkness under a thin cotton sheet. She stroked his arm.

'You should tell Maisie how you feel about her, you know. Before it's too late.'

A burning resentment shot through Will's body. He didn't want to discuss Maisie with Fran. The dark walls closed in on him. Suffocating and struggling to contain an inner rage, not at Fran but at his pathetic inadequacies, he jumped out of bed and pulled on jeans and a t-shirt.

'I'll just get some air; I won't be too long.'

He let himself out into the now empty street. He walked quickly, grateful for the cool breeze; his brain was soggy with half-finished thoughts. Maisie. *Why did she have such a hold over him?* Perhaps Fran was right, and he should make it clear to Maisie how much he longed to be with her, to talk to her and to hold her. He could think of little else. He gritted his teeth in anguish reluctant to admit that, in truth, she was aware of his puppy-like infatuation and would run a mile if he opened up to her. The last thing he wanted was to ruin their friendship. He would always be her friend;

132

someone she could turn to and trust. He would have to learn to cope with the other stuff.

He walked along the deserted seafront and sat on one of the seats on the promenade. Close to despair, he gazed out at the black water. There were the beginnings of light in the sky when he arrived back at the flat. Fran's car and all her stuff were gone. She had left a note to the effect that she was sorry, but she couldn't take any more of his thoughtlessness and had decided to go straight away. She tersely wished him well for the future. He poured a large slug of Scotch and sank on the bed. *Was he that transparent, that insensitive?* It was a bleak thought.

Chapter 22
Maisie

Sally found another girl to share the flat; she was the new probationer at her school and wanted to move in at the end of August, a week before the start of the new term. Maisie agreed to pay her share of the rent until then.

The first time they visited the barge Maisie swung round to Joe; her eyes were shining with excitement.

'What's up? You're looking very serious,' she asked.

'It's in a bit of a state.' He pointed out the condition of the ancient, black timbers of the hull. 'I wouldn't have a clue about maintaining it and one of the yard hands reckons we'd have to pump the bilges every few days. I don't know about any of that stuff, Maisie.'

She took hold of his hand. 'We'll be fine. Stop worrying.' She dragged him to the stern to inspect the huge, original wheel in the wheelhouse and she ran her hand over the red and blue, scrolled paintwork on the stern. 'I think it's just wonderful', she declared.

The barge was in a mud berth in the middle of a rundown boatyard. It was bow on to a manmade shingle bank and faced a rusting corrugated iron shed which housed yachts laid up for winter. Moored either side of them were an old MFV and an old tug. Both boats were lived on, but Joe and Maisie had yet to meet their new neighbours.

Down below took Maisie by surprise; the main saloon had rugs on the floor, an ordinary, drop-leaf table and even housed a floral, three-piece suite. There were no portholes, but light came from a corrugated, plastic skylight. To keep warm in winter, there was an old, solid fuel stove. Beyond the saloon was the bedroom where there was no natural light at all.

'It's gloomy and claustrophobic in here. I like the galley part best,' Joe declared.

The galley in the bow was a triangular shape with a curved seating area around a bright red, Formica table. Much to Maisie's delight there was also an old Rayburn for cooking.

A week later it was time to move in. Maisie surveyed the mound of cardboard boxes and black sacks that contained her life to date. There were a few pieces of furniture from her parent's house, nothing much, a couple of old chairs and a bedside cabinet. She looked around the lounge. She had packed her plants, pictures and knick-knacks, and the room no longer looked like home.

It was ten thirty; Will was late. He'd promised to arrive by ten at the latest. She was about to phone when he rang the bell.

'God, you look awful. Heavy night?' and without waiting for a reply, she shouted up the stairs for Joe.

'He's just got out of the shower,' she explained. 'He won't be a minute. Did you pick up the van ok?'

Will nodded. 'I couldn't get a parking space right outside, but it's close enough. Any chance of a coffee and toast before we start? We've got the van all day, and your stuff should all fit into one run.'

Maisie tutted at him; she was anxious to get the move underway.

'Come on,' he urged. 'I need my energy to shift this lot.'

The three of them sat in Maisie's basement kitchen. It was the first occasion they'd been alone since Maisie and Joe had become a couple, and Will watched uncomfortably as Maisie struggled to keep the conversation going.

'At least we won't strain ourselves shifting Joe's stuff,' she laughed. 'It's the meagre pile at the bottom of the stairs.' It was a mean and throwaway remark. Why did she do that?

She glanced across at Joe who remained silent, head bowed, as he absently pushed toast crumbs around his empty plate. She saw Will looking at Joe as well and wondered what he was thinking. She knew he was jealous of Joe and had been shocked when he'd once asked her what would

135

happen once the novelty wore off and the age difference became an issue?

Will turned the van into the boatyard.

'Can you pull up here for a minute?' Maisie asked. 'I need to pick up the key from the office.'

'No, I'll go.' Joe insisted, and as soon as Will came to a stop, he jumped down and turned to give them a big grin. Maisie was thrilled that he regarded the boatyard as his territory.

'Hey, this is quite something,' Will told them, as he struggled up the gangplank with a box of Maisie's books. 'It's bigger than I expected. I envy you the summer on the river.'

All afternoon they ferried stuff from the van. Now and then, Joe stopped to chat to Knocker and Mo. They were two of the older boatyard hands who had kept an eye on the barge. Maisie smiled; Joe seemed so at home.

When they had finished Maisie suggested they walk up the hill to the local pub. There was just time for a quick drink before they had to drive back to town get the van back by eight.

'Next time we can row to the pub they've got a landing jetty there,' Joe told them. 'I'll have a look out for an old dinghy tomorrow. We can keep it moored on the stern then we can climb down the ladder when we want to use it.'

She linked her arm through his and smiled up at him. 'Sounds perfect.' She gave a little skip. 'I'm so excited, Joe. We're going to have such a lot of fun here. I love it already.'

In the pub, she asked Will about Fran. He was non-committal and told them with a small shrug that she had moved out yesterday. Maisie touched his hand, sensing that he didn't want to talk about it.

'I've got some holiday due; perhaps this is the moment to go somewhere far away. There are plenty of places I've always wanted to go.' He let out a sigh. 'That's if I can summon up some enthusiasm.'

Maisie couldn't think where she was when she woke. There was a faint aroma of diesel and paint. Then she remembered that they'd just spent their first night in their new home. She left Joe asleep and made her way to the galley. In the winter they would have the Rayburn alight, but for now, she filled the kettle and boiled it on the Calor gas cooker. She pulled on some jeans and ran on deck to drink her coffee. It was Sunday, so there were no boatyard workers about, just the weekenders, unloading cars, launching dinghies, and looking busy. A man from the tug next door carried a pint of milk as he came down his gangway. He smiled at her.

'Just moved in? he asked somewhat obviously. 'I'm Peter by the way. John said he was going to rent out the barge while he was away.'

She smiled. 'That's right, I'm Maisie and still in bed is Joe, my partner,' she added. 'Do you live aboard?' She nodded towards the old tug where work was evidently in progress.

'Yes, this is home, just the two cats and me. I'm sure you'll like it here; it's a great place to live. Anyway, see you later.' Waving an arm, he disappeared through a hatch.

Maisie finished her coffee and began a tour of inspection. It was a bonus to have mains electricity which came from one of the corrugated iron sheds via a loop of somewhat dangerous looking wire. Their water came from a fixed hosepipe, and she followed it to the shore to check where it connected to the mains supply.

She needed a shower after the exertions of moving yesterday. Her thoughts drifted to the bathroom in the flat, but such luxury was in the past now. She could either wash in the galley sink with water heated by an antiquated ascot or walk through the boatyard to the communal shower block. It was warm and sunny, and best not to think about what having a shower on a wet, November night would be like. As she had failed to master the vagaries of the barge's loo pumping system, she decided on the shower block. The tide

137

was up by now which made the gangplank steep. She made her way gingerly down it, clutching her shower stuff. This was mad, all of it, quite mad. She held her face up to the sun, laughing out loud.

Chapter 23
Joe

Joe knew immediately that life on the river was going to suit him. It might be different in a cold, wet winter but it was mid-summer now, and he loved the stillness of the early morning. As promised, he bought an old wooden dinghy from Knocker for £8 and Maisie had painted it up in different colours of blues and reds, using bits of old paint left lying around by the yachtsmen. Climbing down the stern ladder on such a glorious dawn morning gave him the sense of freedom that had been lacking in his life. With the river deserted he decided to row out to what the locals called the pool and practice sculling over the stern. He had watched Knocker use a long wooden sweep to scull the yard launch with such apparent ease that he was eager to acquire the skill. There was so much about this new life that he was looking forward to learning.

He loved seeing Maisie so relaxed and happy. Relishing her long summer holiday, she had set about turning the old boat into a home for them. Her eclectic collection of lamps made up for the lack of natural daylight, and she had persuaded him to put up a couple of shelves for her bits and pieces as she called them. She knew exactly where she wanted her favourite pictures to go but hanging them was another matter, and he quickly discovered that Maisie had bags of infectious enthusiasm but limited practical skills. He had laughed out loud one afternoon when she came running down from the wheelhouse to announce that she intended to grow tomato plants up there.

While Joe was busy learning about how the bilge pump worked and contemplating the frightening amount of maintenance required on the barge, Maisie explored the local area. She found an old bike dumped in the yard skip and pedalled off in search of the nearest supermarket. This turned out to be a village about three miles away, and on her first excursion, she was gone for such a long time that Joe began to worry. It turned out that she had got carried away and bought too much shopping, which meant she had to push the bike back instead of riding it. Relieved, Joe was much amused by her breathless account of her ordeal. He was beginning to realise that this was typical of the scatty side of Maisie.

As the days went by and he got to know her better, he decided that there was a lot to love. She surprised him with her natural spontaneity and was always coming up with new ideas. She was generous with her time and affection and, happily, she seemed disinterested in material possessions. Nevertheless, living with someone else required adjustment. The camaraderie of the Alpha House set up was different from this sense of responsibility that occasionally weighed heavily on his mind. Maisie had so much faith in him, and he worried that he might let her down. Maisie tended to drift around in her bubble of happiness. He was happy too; he loved his new life, but some aspects would take getting used to.

It was the day of Mac's visit and Joe spotted him walking across the top of the slip.

'Hi, come aboard; you're our first proper visitor,' he told him. 'It's about half tide now, so the gangplank is pretty level.'

'Just lead the way,' Mac replied, handing him a packet of custard creams.

'I'll show you on deck first; then you can come below and meet Maisie; she's got the kettle on.'

Joe explained how the steel sprit was used and pointed out the copper navigation light at the top of the mast before ushering him inside the wheelhouse.

'I see you're getting to grips with nautical terminology,' Mac sounded amused.

'Did you know a barge this size would have been sailed by just one a skipper and a boy? They must have been pretty tough in those days.'

He grinned at Mac as he rang the ship's bell that served as a doorbell, to alert Maisie. Mac followed him down the wide stairs into the main saloon. His eyes crinkled with delight when he saw the floral covered three-piece suite.

'Watch your head on these low beams,' Joe warned.

Maisie joined them from the galley. A little uncertainly, she held her hand out. 'Hello, you must be Mac.' She smiled, and her shining eyes held Mac's gaze of approval. 'Joe never stops talking about you,' she added. 'Why don't you show Mac the rest of our strange abode and I'll pour the tea?'

Joe showed him the massive, old Lister engine. 'The chap next door helped me to start it up the other day; it sounds amazing with the old pistons going donk.' He demonstrated with his hands.

'How long has the barge been used as a houseboat?' Mac inquired.

'About six years, I think. It's lucky for us there's some furniture. Come and see the galley; there's even an old Rayburn. Maisie reckons she's going to make bread in it when the weather is cold enough to light it.'

They carried their tea up on deck and sat in the sunshine and Joe pointed out various boats and landmarks. Mac was a good listener, and his questions showed interest without seeming intrusive. Joe didn't believe Mac would ever be judgmental and was pleased that he accepted them as a couple.

When it was time for Mac to catch his bus, Maisie kissed him on the cheek.

'Perhaps you could come over for a meal one evening soon, and we could take you across to The Jolly Sailor for a drink.'

'Great idea, we can row over there in the dinghy if you're feeling brave,' Joe added.

'Sounds good to me,' Mac replied. 'Just let me know when and I'll look forward to it.'

Afterwards, Joe and Maisie lay together on the cabin top in the late sunshine with their fingers entwined.

'I said you'd like him, didn't I?'

Maisie stretched. 'Hmm. He's a nice man. By the way, don't forget Will and Shaun and co. are coming over on Saturday.'

Joe slipped an arm around her shoulders and laid his head next to hers. 'That's cool. Whatever makes you happy.'

Chapter 24
Maisie

Maisie was slightly dreading entertaining her friends on the barge. It was difficult to imagine the whole scenario of Joe socialising with her work friends. She knew he'd do anything to please her, but he had confessed to having little in common with the Pebbles crowd, and if he felt socially inadequate, he might drink too much. She'd noticed with alarm that he was drinking more red wine during the day, claiming that he was bored, and it helped to pass the time when she was at work. If he'd been drinking all day, there the possibility that he might be drunk by the time their visitors arrived. She'd seen glimpses of the morose side of Joe when he'd been drinking, and she couldn't bear it if he were like that in front of her friends.

Then there was the situation between him and Will. Things had been ok when Will helped them move onto the barge, but there was definitely history between them. Anticipating the evening engulfed her in a cold panic. She wanted her friends to accept Joe and get to know him as the person she loved so much.

Cursing life for being so complicated, she resolved to think positively. At least she knew she could rely on Chris who cheerfully accepted anything if it made Maisie happy. Chris would like Joe; she might even flirt with him. She smiled at the thought and made her mind up to invite Chris down from Scotland before the end of the summer.

Maisie turned into the boatyard and parked the car. It was a long time since she'd entertained, and she looked forward to spending the whole afternoon cooking a big pan of chicken curry. Knocker and Mo were messing about on the slip launching a yacht, so she had to step over the thick, rusty wires attached to the ancient tractor.

Knocker, who was forever looking for an excuse to stop work, nodded towards her heavy shopping bags.

'You been buying up the co-op?' he enquired.

Maisie squinted at him in the bright sunlight and rested the bags on the ground.

'We're having a dinner party tonight.'

'Very posh. Will you require me to pipe the guests aboard?' Mo grinned at her and displayed a lot of long, yellow teeth.

She laughed. 'Well, gentlemen, I must get cooking. I wouldn't want to hold you up any further.' She pulled a wry face and lugged the shopping up the pier to the barge.

She'd driven into Southampton specially to buy spices from the Indian shop, and soon the galley was filled with the pungent aroma of coriander and cumin. She chopped loads of onions to make a paste with finely chopped ginger and garlic. Life would be easier with a blender, but she managed. It was hot down below, but she happily chopped and stirred with her transistor radio blaring alongside her. Once she'd browned the chicken portions and flung them into the sauce to cook, she could escape into the fresh air.

She made a cup of tea and took it round to the shade behind the wheelhouse. She sat on the bulwarks and watched the ever-changing scene on the river. Knocker and Mo had launched the yacht without incident and were now putting it back on a pile mooring in the middle of the river. Mo was aboard the boat and Knocker operated the yard launch. They had worked together for so long that they did not need to speak or shout instructions. Although they skived off at every opportunity, it was evident that they were a skilled team when it came to handling boats. Then, she saw Peter from next-door rowing upriver. Joe was with him. They'd been paid a few pounds to anti-foul a boat on the public hard. Maisie was pleased; it would be good for Joe to have some money of his own and he got on well with Peter.

'Blimey, Maisie,' Peter called out. 'We could smell your curry when we were by The Elephant.' He rested his oars in the rowlocks and drifted past the stern sniffing the air as he went.

'Wonderful. It smells just like The Spice of India.

144

He dropped Joe at the stern who followed Maisie into the galley.

'How many did you say were coming tonight?' he asked, lifting the lid off the big pan. She banged the back of his hand with a wooden spoon.

'Oi, hands off. Five, I think. Will, Shaun and Kay and Adrian and Laura, so there will be seven of us all together. It will seem funny without Fran.'

Joe opened the fridge. 'Good. You bought lots of beer.' He extracted two cans. 'I'll take one over to Peter. See you later.'

Maisie smiled after him. He was settling into life on the barge. *And drinking more and more, her inner voice* reminded her. He already smelled of beer, and she wondered how many cans they had already consumed.

Joe didn't come back from Peter's boat until just before the others were due to arrive.

'Be nice tonight won't you, especially to Will and don't drink too much.'

He stared at her for a moment. 'Yes, I'll be nice.' He raised his eyebrows. 'There's no need to sound like a nagging mother.'

Maisie kissed him on the lips. 'Sorry, I'm just anxious about tonight; that's all.'

Happily, the curry was a great success, and afterwards, Joe suggested that they all go over to The Jolly for a drink. Maisie leaned over the bulwarks at the stern of the barge. Her stomach ached from laughing so much. Their laughter, aided by several bottles of wine and cans of lager, started when Shaun baulked at descending the wooden ladder at the stern. Despite the millpond state of the river, it took several attempts to persuade him into the dinghy.

Maisie and the others watched, helpless with laughter, as Joe rowed the first contingent across with Shaun sat bolt upright and rigid while Kay frantically bailed out water with the aid of a plastic box. The unaccustomed extra weight caused water to seep through the gaping topsides and by the

145

time all seven were safely on the pub pontoon they had decidedly soggy feet.

It was a warm evening, and they sat outside on wooden picnic benches and drank yet more beer. When closing time came, Shaun and Kay opted to go back via the shore, so Maisie volunteered to guide the way through the boatyards. Just before they arrived back at the barge, Kay slipped her arm through Maisie's.

'I can see the attraction,' she whispered. Maisie knew that she was referring to Joe and not the magical qualities of the river.

She was exhausted by the time her head hit the pillow. It had turned out to be a memorable night; her guests seemed to have enjoyed the experience too. They had been genuinely fascinated by the barge and expressed much excitement at the whole idea of rowing to the pub. Best of all, Joe, bless him, had been relaxed and cheerful and wonderfully attentive to Kay.

For the next couple of weeks, they pottered around. The weather was hot and sunny, and they both grew tanned and healthy, revelling in their outdoor life. Life aboard became ordinary rather than extraordinary as they made friends with other liveaboards in the boatyard; rowed up the river for a picnic or across to the Jolly Sailor where they were rapidly becoming an accepted part of the Friday night scene.

Joe's mother and sister were to be their next visitors and Maisie was nervous about meeting his mother.

'What time did your mum say they were arriving?'

'Around lunchtime, I guess.'

'You did invite them for lunch, didn't you?'

Joe was exasperatingly vague as usual. 'Yep, now will you quit worrying?'

But Maisie couldn't help it. She'd not met Joe's mother, Lily before and didn't know much about her except that she taught in an infant school. As for Jess, she was fourteen and most probably a stroppy teenager. It troubled her to think that not so long ago, Joe had been in that category. *What would Lily make of her relationship with Joe?*

Maisie watched as Lily swung a pair of brown legs onto the gravel. Then Jess emerged from the passenger side; her hair, wiry like her brother's, was blown into a rat's nest. Maisie's heart lurched with affection as she spotted Joe striding across the slipway towards them. He looked tanned and fit, and she could tell from his grin that he was happy and relaxed. He stooped to pick up their bags, and as they got nearer to the barge, Maisie could hear Joe explaining to his mother about the gangplank.

'The tides on its way out now so the gangplank is quite steep. Best hold on to this rope.' He instructed.

'Thanks, you make me feel like an old woman.' Lily grumbled.

'Where's your new bird then?' Jess asked. Much amused Maisie ran up the stairs.

'Hello. It's so lovely to meet you.' She hugged them both.

Lily was a beautiful woman. Her olive skin was flawless, and her lustrous, dark hair was escaping from its clip. There was a surprising amount of voluptuous cleavage on display, and Maisie was taken aback at Lily's effortless glamour.

'Come inside. What can I get you? Cup of coffee or there's wine?'

'Oh wine, white please if you have it. That would be great. We didn't have a bad run from Bath, but it was stifling hot in the car. Here, just a few contributions.' She handed Maisie a carrier bag containing a bottle each of red and white wine, a packet of scrumptious chocolate biscuits and a big punnet of raspberries.

'That's so thoughtful of you. Thank you.' Maisie held Lily's gaze and knew that they would be friends.

When they all went below, Joe stopped to observe his sister.

'Blimey, Jess, you've grown.'

Jess ran a hand over her unruly hair and struck a pose. Unlike Joe, her body was willowy, but she had the same twinkling, brown eyes and warm smile and didn't look in the least sullen or stroppy. She wore a light blue t-shirt with a slogan declaring 'I don't like Mondays' and jeans that looked as if they'd been splattered with white paint.

Maisie opened the bottle of Chablis that she'd been saving and got out a can of lager for Joe and a coke for Jess. Meanwhile, Joe showed them around. It was quite dark below, despite the sunshine outside.

'Are you on mains electricity?' Lily asked. 'It seems odd not to be able to look out of a window, but I must say you've made it into a lovely cosy home.'

'Yeah, the electric comes from a box in the shed. It's cunning because the main cable is weighted to go up and down with the tide. Otherwise, it would either be stretched too tight or hanging in a great loop across the pier. I'll show you later,' Joe told her.

'Is that your loo?' Jess shrieked. 'How cool is that? Come and show me how to work it, Joe,' she demanded.

Joe laughed at his mother's expression. 'Don't worry; there are proper loos in the yard. You just need to take the key.'

Maisie emerged from the galley. 'It's such a beautiful sunny day I thought we could have a picnic on deck. If that's ok?'

She spread a big rug on the faded green canvas which covered the hold, and they all helped to carry up the picnic. There was a basket filled with warm bread, a big bowl of salad and another of coronation chicken, which was Joe's favourite. They balanced plates on their knees and chatted in the sunshine. Jess was fascinated by all the activity on the river, so Joe suggested he take her for a row in the dinghy. Maisie and Lily sat together and listened to Jess shrieking with laughter as she attempted to row and almost tipped Joe into the murky waters of the Hamble.

148

Lily jumped up. 'Come on; I'll give you a hand with this lot.'

They talked as they washed up but not about how Joe and Maisie met, that topic was avoided. But Lily wanted to know about Maisie's job and the practicalities of life on a houseboat. In return, she told Maisie about Jess and her plans to go to college next year to do her 'A' levels. She talked about Joe's father, Jack, and how much his death had affected Joe and how much they all missed him.

Then Joe and Jess were heard clumping overhead, so they all decided to have a walk along the riverbank towards Warsash. Although it was a weekday, this was the height of the sailing season, and a crowd of yachts were underway. Lily gazed at them wistfully.

'I'll have to find myself a rich toy boy with a big yacht,' she told them.

Joe and Jess, walking ahead both turned in unison to observe their mother.

'There's no need to look so shocked.' She peered at Joe. 'As Jess very well knows, I have met someone; his name's Paul.'

As they walked on down the footpath, she told them how she'd met Paul at French classes.

'It's early days yet, but he's kind and funny, and we get on really well,' she added, giving Jess a sharp look.

'What mum means is that he's her toy boy', Jess declared with a giggle. 'He's not exactly rich though which is a shame.'

Maisie looked at Joe; he didn't seem upset by his mother's announcement.

Lily suggested she buy them all dinner at The Jolly, so Joe borrowed a larger and more stable dinghy from Peter next door.

'It might be cold on the water, so I'd wear a jumper and flat shoes,' Joe suggested.

Lily duly appeared in a cosy 'fruit of the loom' jumper and trainers. She descended the stern ladder carefully and sat in the middle of the dinghy as instructed.

Jess followed and sat beside her, leaving Maisie to perch on the stern. The moonlight shone across the water as Joe rowed smoothly towards the lights of the pub. As they got nearer the voices of The Jolly Sailor's clientele carried towards them. Jess put her hand on Lily's knee.

'Hey, this is cool, isn't it, mum?'

Joe helped his mother on to the pontoon, and they all sat outside on a wooden picnic bench. Maisie had given Joe some money beforehand to buy a round of drinks. She smiled at Lily.

'Let's go mad and have a bottle of white wine between us?'

'Why not? Just promise me you'll get me back in the dinghy safely,' she laughed.

Joe went to the bar to get a coke for Jess, a pint of lager for himself and a bottle of house white and two glasses.

While he was gone, Lily touched Maisie's arm. 'I know it's only lager, but that will be the second one Joe's had today. I didn't know he was drinking again. How do you feel about that?'

'I know what you're saying, but I guess as long as it's just the occasional lager that's ok.' She didn't mention his increasing consumption of red wine.

Lily was a comfortable companion and showed genuine interest in their life on the barge and Maisie's job. She had an infectious laugh, and it was hard to believe that she was old enough to be Joe's mum. Maisie didn't like keeping things from her about Joe. Maybe when she got to know her better, she would feel able to confide in her. Maisie rubbed her thumb across her forehead as a thought took hold; a premonition perhaps that one day she would need Lily's strength.

Next day, Maisie drove them into town to visit the shops. She didn't much enjoy shopping as a rule, but it was

150

hard not to get swept up in Jess's dedication to the task. It would be her sixteenth birthday in a few weeks, so Maisie treated her to a pair of the latest Kickers trainers as an early present. When they returned, they left Jess sunbathing on deck while they went for a walk along the river. It was a Saturday, and Lily swooned once more over the parade of gleaming white gin palaces off to the Isle of Wight for the weekend.

By the time they left on Sunday afternoon to drive back to Bath, Maisie felt more relaxed than ever. She hugged Lily. It had been a successful visit.

A few days later, Maisie received a letter from Chris. Without a phone, it was strange to be forced to communicate in this way. She could go over to the marina and use the public phone box there, but otherwise, it was letters or nothing. Chris' husband, Greg was expecting a new posting, but this had been delayed so she wouldn't be able to come down after all. It was five months since they'd seen one another at the reunion, and she had been looking forward to showing Chris her new life on the barge and introducing her to Joe. Still, it wasn't all doom and gloom because there was a strong chance that Greg would be posted to a Portsmouth based ship. Even so, Maisie couldn't shake off her disappointment. She wished she could talk to Joe. He knew how much she had been looking forward to seeing Chris. Close to tears, she tried to reign in her emotions. *Where was Joe?* Once again, he'd left without saying where he was going. She didn't expect him to be at her beck and call, but the growing distance between them was horrible. She just wanted to be in his arms and be on the receiving end of some of his tlc. Instinctively kind, Joe always knew just what she needed. *But was that even true, anymore?*

She decided to go for a walk, but her mind was constantly on Joe. With each step, his name was on her lips. Tears ran down her cheeks as she repeated her mantra *Joe, I want Joe.* She knew she could never tell him the depth of her feelings. Suffocating him wasn't the answer, and her actions were bordering on the obsessional. *Why was she like this?* What Joe needed right now was space. If that meant distance from her, then that's how it would have to be. She would just have to trust him.

When she woke next morning, she couldn't remember, for a minute, what the row had been about, but she remembered shouting. She looked at her watch, 8.30 am. *Damn,* if the traffic was bad, she would be late for her first lecture. She frowned and rubbed her eyes; it had been another night with interrupted sleep, and she had a headache. She looked at Joe; he was sprawled across the bed fast asleep, his dark curls almost covering his face. She wouldn't wake him and risk cross-examining him about his plans for the day. Instead, she blew him a kiss and tiptoed away, her body leaden with foreboding.

By the time she arrived at the university, she was still struggling to stop crying. Today was her first meeting with the new undergraduates, and the heavy traffic meant she was now late as well as ill-prepared. With a shuddering sigh, she locked the car and half-ran across the car park; her usual buoyant self-confidence was ebbing away. It was new to her, this feeling of loss of control and she didn't like it. If Fran was still around, maybe she could have confided in her. *Or perhaps not*, she tutted. She didn't want anyone else apart from Chris to know how tricky things were between her and Joe. It was nobody else's business.

Life between them had been more relaxed when she was still on the long summer holiday. Now that she was back at work, she knew that Joe found the days dragged and he missed his mates from town. He was bored and often didn't get out of bed before midday and then he would immediately start drinking. The day before, he had reacted moodily when she got cross because he forgot to buy a refill for the Calor gas cylinder.

'Don't stress,' he'd told her. 'We don't have to cook, do we? We can get something from the café over the road. What does it matter?"

152

Her head ached, and she stared at him for a moment. 'It's alright for you,' she replied, her frustration palpable. 'I won't even be able to have a bloody cup of coffee in the morning.'

Joe had just shrugged and disappeared off to the boatyard. No doubt to chat to anyone who happened to be about. *What was happening to her?* She was so afraid of driving him away and yet that was what would happen if she were not careful. She couldn't bear to lose her lovely Joe.

'It's as if I'm afraid to be myself in case he doesn't like the real me.' She was in tears on the phone to Chris.

'I'm sure it's just teething troubles,' Chris assured her. 'It's bound to be strange, for both of you, to adjust to a different lifestyle. Give it time; you still love him, don't you?'

Maisie was silent for a moment as she pictured Joe. She couldn't help loving him; he was the first person in her life to make her feel cherished. Right from the start, he'd shown his affectionate nature. He always held her hand in public even if it was just going from the car to the front door. He rarely came to bed before midnight, unlike her, but he would visit her in bed to see how she was and tuck her in like a child. He was thoughtful too, always making her a drink if she'd had a hard day at work or thinking up outings that he knew she would enjoy. Above all, he was good company and never dull. But he was also moody and unpredictable. He wanted to live for the moment while she was more cautious. She smiled to herself, but so what, she could be impulsive at times.

'Oh, Chris, I love him so much. That doesn't stop him from driving me mad, though. Honestly, he's so laid back I could scream sometimes.'

Joe looked up as Maisie came down the stairs to the saloon. 'You look as if you need a hug. What's up?'

She swayed against him, unable to stop weeping. 'It's that bloody Eve again. God, she is so patronising. I'm sure

153

she thinks that I'm completely vacuous. I wish I didn't have to work so closely with her.'

Eve had replaced Fran in the psychology department, and Maisie secretly enjoyed playing along with this perception and was happy to remain an enigma.

Chapter 25
Joe

Joe drank a mug of strong, black coffee and wandered along to the communal shower block, hoping to shake off his lethargy. He stopped to chat to Knocker and Mo who were preparing the tractor to haul a boat out for the winter.

' I'll get the bus into town later.' He kicked at the rusty chain links with his trainer. 'I can't hang around here all day; it's doing my head in.'

Joe loathed buses. He was used to living in town where he could walk places, but he'd made up his mind to go to The Joiners. It was near the university. He liked the atmosphere there, but it was too far to walk, ten miles at least. One of these days, he would have to learn to drive instead of relying on Maisie all the time.

He had been to The Joiners twice in the last week. Outside was sunny, and he blinked as he entered the dark, smoky pub. He bought a pint out of the ten pounds had Maisie left for him. It felt like being given pocket money, but he had no alternative; perhaps something would turn up.

He joined a group of students he vaguely knew at the big, beer-stained table near the window. Cursing the bus for taking so long, he downed his pint and bought another. At closing time, the group drifted off, and Joe reluctantly got up to leave.

'We're going back to our place for a smoke; you can join us if you want. I'm Ben, by the way, and this is Rick.'

'Yeah, thanks; I've nothing else on.' Joe was pleased with the offer.

Their place turned out to be a squat in a grotty, terraced house opposite the docks. When they got into the living room, Ben introduced a sullen girl with short, blond, spiky hair who was sprawled across a worn settee and chewing her nails.

'That's Ronnie; you'd best ignore her. Once she starts, she never stops gabbing. Isn't that right babe?'

'Don't fucking babe me.' She tilted her head back to reveal a pointed chin and glared at Ben.

To Joe, she looked pale and thin, too thin, but it was hard to tell underneath the baggy cotton trousers and a loose top. She sprung to her feet.

'Want a beer? Whatever your name is,' she asked.

She looked better when she smiled. The wide mouth and full lips revealed crooked front teeth. Joe wondered how old she was. He smiled back at her.

'Yeah, that would be great, if you've got one. I'm Joe, by the way.'

He thought about this scatty, frenetic girl on the bus home. She had a pent-up restlessness that he recognised in himself and there was an air of sadness about her. He gathered from the conversation that her boyfriend had died of a heroin overdose, a few months back.

It was seven by the time Joe arrived back. Maisie would have been home for ages. In the squat, he could doss around and drink and talk with no one to hassle him about how much he was drinking. He hoped she wasn't going to start tonight. Last night's argument had unsettled him.

Most of the time, it was fantastic being with her, but it was hard sometimes to fathom what she wanted from him. He sat next to her on the settee, and she snuggled her body against him. He was relieved when she didn't ask him where he'd been or what he'd been up to all day.

'Shall we walk up to The Ship and have a drink, then we can get a Chinese takeaway on the way back?' she suggested. 'I don't feel like cooking tonight.'

By the time they arrived back, Joe was glad of the food. He'd been drinking since lunchtime and now lay on the bed in a soporific state, enjoying Maisie's attentions. Everything else was forgotten as they lost themselves in the mutual pleasure of their lovemaking.

Chapter 26
Maisie

Maisie had arranged to meet Joe in The Joiners. She sighed as she peered at the bare floorboards and scarred, wooden tables and chairs. The place was crowded and stuffy, which didn't help her tiredness. She had come straight from a heavy meeting with the external examiner and felt hot and sticky. The live band was so loud that she decided it was bad for her health, not to mention her eardrums.

Where the hell was Joe? Her usual confidence had deserted her, and she felt old and conspicuous in her work clothes. She bought half a bitter and spotted him by a grimy window. As always, the sight of him lifted her spirits until she saw that he was deep in conversation with Ronnie. His new best friend, she thought sourly. The two of them had their heads bent close together so they could hear over the noise. Joe looked up and winked at her. She clutched her drink and made her way across to them. Ben and Rick were there too, so there was nowhere to sit down, and she ended up leaning awkwardly against the windowsill behind Joe's chair.

At the end of the first set, Joe went to get more drinks, and Maisie slid into his seat. Ronnie drew deeply on a fat joint and turned towards her.

'Alright?' She squinted at Maisie.

Maisie regarded the spiky-haired girl and wondered if there was a hint of mockery behind her steady gaze. The combination of noise, heat and smoke was making her feel light-headed, and when Joe returned with the drinks, she trembled as he put his hand on the back of her neck. She turned towards him, suppressing an urge to touch his face.

'Sorry, Joe, but I must eat something'. She pulled a rueful face. 'I'll see you back home, then?' she continued. Unable to keep the questioning note from her voice, she willed him to say that he'd come with her. But she already knew what his response would be.

157

He gave a slight shrug of his shoulders. 'OK, Rick and Ben are going back to Bursledon, so I'll grab a lift with them.' He touched her face with a brush of his fingers.

Back on the barge, Maisie sat on deck. It was still warm and usually the ripples of the water glistening in the moonlight both entranced and soothed her. But tonight, she couldn't shake off a sense of unease. The cracks in their relationship were widening. She couldn't bear it, and yet Joe seemed oblivious to any problems. She bit her lip annoyed that tears were welling up. *Perhaps, he just didn't mind as much, or maybe he was ready to move on?* She knew he would never deliberately hurt her, but he had changed. He was more confident now and had begun to put the dark days of his squalid, old life behind him. She felt a huge lump in her throat and hugged her knees; *what if he didn't need her anymore?*

'Oh, Joe,' she whispered into the dark. How could she tell him that she was lonely and out of step with his evolving lifestyle? She was glad he was happy and had friends; nevertheless, a heavy weight hung in the pit of her stomach as she contemplated the future. When they were first together, she had stubbornly refused to look beyond the glorious, all-consuming pleasure. Simply being with him had made her feel alive and overflowing with happy confidence.

Maisie looked at her watch when she heard him come aboard. It was two o'clock, and she was surprised that she had managed to sleep. She reminded herself not to be possessive; *she must not ask what he'd been doing and who with*. A sob choked her as Joe, noisy and cheerfully drunk, bounced on to the bed. He drew her towards him, and as he kissed her smooth stomach desire flooded through her. He shed his Levi's and trainers, and, with a small moan, he entered her.

Afterwards, gasping with exertion and damp with sweat, they clung to each other as reality was kept at bay for a short, sweet moment. Maisie's fingers gripped his t-shirt as he buried his face in her neck and snuffled aside the blond curls.

'I do love you, Maisie.' His voice was bleary with alcohol.

As the days went on, Maisie couldn't shake off her apprehension as the emerging differences between them leapt out at her. She worried about their different interests and different set of friends.

She slid out of bed and picking up her notebook and pen she went into the galley. Writing it down, the words flowed in time to her jumbled thoughts. She knew she was obsessional, and like any strong emotion, it was almost impossible to control. She was forever analysing her life and had started to write down her worries, recording the different permutations of their relationship. She would write in the car, or the canteen at coffee break when she would scribble feverishly until satiated. Sometimes she read what she had written, allowing herself to wallow in the heightened emotions that formed such an integral part of her relationship with Joe. Over and over the different scenarios, the what-ifs floated before her. *Was Joe getting too close to that Ronnie girl?* The signs were all there. She mustn't be needy and demanding - he hated that. Joe liked her confidence. He loved the fact that she was intelligent with a good job and was an independent woman. She bit her knuckle, trying to hold back the tears. Joe would be horrified if he knew the truth; she was pathetic, acting like some lovesick teenager and worse – self-pitying. Her cheeks were wet with tears. Self-pity was so not her style, but the feelings were relentless and now proved to be overwhelming.

Anxious not to smother him she continued to go to Pebbles on Wednesdays, whenever possible. He accompanied her just the once. She smiled at the memory; it had not been a resounding success. He had grumbled because they didn't serve beer, and as soon as the conversation among the group became animated, he had clammed up and

159

slumped morosely in his chair. Maisie teased him about it afterwards.

'You looked as though you were undergoing a form of torture tonight.'

'I was if you must know. Half the films and books they were going on about I've never heard of, and they all try to score points off each other. Talk about pretentious, especially Will. He fancies the pants off you by the way.'

'Don't be daft of course he doesn't fancy me. No worries: I'm happy to go on my own if you're OK with that.'

Joe sighed. 'You don't need to ask my permission, Maisie.'

After that, he didn't want to know about any social functions that involved her friends from the university, and it was less stressful to go on her own. Now that they lived on the barge, it was a fifteen-mile drive to Pebbles, so she slipped into the habit of staying behind at work to catch up with her marking rather than going home first.

It was late November as Maisie drove back from Pebbles. It was irritating not to be able to have more than a couple of glasses of wine. She missed being able to walk back to her old flat and had a sudden pang of nostalgia for the place. She remembered, with a jolt, that it was over a year since Joe's attack. Christ, *what an anniversary.*

They were selling tickets for the Christmas party at Pebbles on 17th December, and she was struggling to decide whether to try to persuade Joe to come with her. Perhaps he would, as it was Christmas.

'God, Maisie, do I have to?' he asked when she broached the subject.

'No, you don't have to.' She didn't mean to sound so brusque. 'I thought it might be nice to go together, that's all. But it's not a big deal; I'm happy to go on my own.'

He stared at her. 'Do you mean that? I'll come if you really want me to, but I feel like a fish out of water with that lot.'

160

So, it was settled. Maisie arranged to stay the night with Shaun and Kay and intended to get extremely drunk.

The following week, while Maisie and Joe were watching their crackly old black and white television, the programme was interrupted by a news bulletin saying that John Lennon had been shot dead by some crazed bloke. He had seemed so invincible, and his pointless death brought home to them how unpredictable life could be. Maisie tossed and turned, unable to sleep that night. By morning, she had decided that life was too short and resolved to live for the moment and have fun.

But by the time the seventeenth came Maisie was both tired and emotional; it was the end of a long and stressful term. She showered, washed her hair until it gleamed and selected a short, black dress that complimented her blond hair. The liberally sprayed on Rive Gauche made her feel sexy and ready for anything. She checked her makeup one more time in the inadequate mirror. Her tiredness had miraculously vanished, and she detected a dangerous glint in her eyes. This promised to be a wild night.

Joe's eyes widened, and his mouth creased into his special smile when he saw her. 'Hey, you look fantastic.' He hesitated. 'Really sexy.'

She raised her eyebrows in a teasing manner. 'Come on then.' She pulled him up from the squashy sofa. 'If you want a lift to The Joiners.'

There were two floors at Pebbles and on party nights they cleared most of the tables out of the main bar to allow enough room for dancing. The downstairs bar was used as a seating area with tables along the back wall for the buffet. This year, the jazz band was in good spirits and effortlessly caught the mood of the regulars. Maisie kicked off her black high heels and danced with eyes closed amid the hot, excited bodies. She knew Will was watching her. She pulled him by the hand towards the centre of the dance area.

161

'Don't think you can escape by lurking back there.' She put her arms around his neck and pressed her warm body against his.

He groaned. 'Bloody hell, Maisie.' He pulled away from her. 'How much have you had to drink?'

'Not yet enough, it would seem.' She reached up on tiptoe to nuzzle his ear. 'I'm disappointed in you, Mr Stevens. I thought you fancied me.'

He stepped back, and she saw his jaw tighten. 'Come on, Maisie; I do have some pride, you know.'

She was taken aback by the coldness in his voice. 'Sorry, Will. I'm behaving like a tart, aren't I?' Her eyes filled with tears. 'God, I'm such an idiot.'

'Come on; let's get you out of here. I think we've both had enough.'

She leaned against him, furious at the stupid tears that coursed down her flushed cheeks. 'I'm supposed to be staying at Shaun's.'

'Look, I think you should give that a miss. You can stay at the flat; I think we need to talk, don't you? Don't worry; I'll kip on the sofa,' he added.

Maisie woke with a pounding headache and a mouth like a hay bale. She shivered with a mix of nausea and shame, remembering that Will had wanted to talk, but once the cold air had hit her, she was beyond sensible conversation. She had succumbed to a fit of the giggles as he pulled her dress over her head and flopped down on his bed where she remained in a stupor for the rest of the night.

She dragged herself out of bed to get a glass of water, holding on the door frame for support. Will had abandoned the sofa and was on the floor in a sleeping bag. She looked at his face. He didn't deserve to be treated so shabbily. Once again, she had taken advantage of his good nature. She was tempted to creep out, but she needed to tell him how sorry she was for her behaviour last night and at least try to explain. She clutched the glass and sat on the sofa. *What could she say? Sorry I tried to seduce you when all I can*

162

think about is Joe. None of it made sense. What the hell was she playing at?

She remembered what Richard said to her, not so long ago. It had shocked her when her brother had told her that when she was seventeen or eighteen, she had been a selfish cow. He proceeded to reel off a list of examples and finished by reminding her of her habit of laughing if someone got hurt. It was true; she did and would often attempt to explain it away by claiming that it was a nervous reaction. She knew she had a selfish streak and tended to get carried away by her impulses regardless of the effect on others. It was a sobering thought.

She sat there for some time until stiff with the cold she went to the kitchen and made coffee for them both. Will stirred when she placed the mug alongside him and smiled up at her.

'How are you this morning? You don't look too bright,' he added.

Maisie sat opposite him. She was wearing one of Will's baggy jumpers and biting her nails.

'I was pretty stupid last night, wasn't I? I'm so sorry, Will.' She moved to sit next to him on the floor and hugged her knees. 'It's just that....'

'It's OK. You don't have to explain; honestly, it's all forgotten. Now come here and give me a hug.'

He touched her cheek and stroked her hair. 'It will all work out, you know; with Joe, I mean.'

Joe wasn't there when she arrived back at about midday. She presumed he had stayed with friends from The Joiners and hoped he hadn't got too drunk which he increasingly did when things got tough. Her eyes were full of tears, and there was a familiar tightening in her throat. *Was Joe finding it tough now to be with her?* She couldn't bear the thought of losing him. So much had changed. She worried that she had been the driving force behind it all, but then it was Joe who had suggested they move on to the barge.

A letter for her lay on the galley table; she recognised Richard's writing and was surprised to see a different address at the top. With mounting alarm, she scanned the letter. Her steady, upright, and hitherto staid brother had been caught having an affair. She groaned when the letter revealed that it was with a secretary from work. 'You could have been a bit more original Rich,' she said aloud. Apparently, he was now living in a bedsit. Without a phone, she couldn't call him, and she knew he would be feeling wretched.

When Joe arrived back, she showed him the letter. 'At least he's still going to mum and dads' for Christmas. Hopefully, we can have a chat and cheer him up. He must miss the children so much. I wonder how poor Lynne is coping.'

Joe looked uncomfortable. 'Listen, Mais, don't be mad at me but I've decided to stay here for Christmas. Your parents won't want me around, especially with all this going on; it's a family time.'

She was on the verge of tears. 'Don't be silly, you must come, it's our first Christmas together, and I'd hate to spend it without you.' She hesitated, torn by loyalty to her brother. 'But not to worry, I'll stay here, and we can make our own Christmas on the barge. It'll be fun,' she finished lamely, wondering when she had turned into this pathetic, grovelling woman. *Was she really that desperate?* All her old determination seemed to have deserted her.

Maisie lay in her old, single bed at her parent's home. She could hear her mother hard at work in the kitchen. She was bound to be busy; it was Christmas Eve, and as usual, there was a great deal to do. But she couldn't shake off the blanket of gloom that pressed around her, and her brain was foggy and unfocused. She should go downstairs and help, but she couldn't bear the atmosphere with everyone tiptoeing around each other. Last Christmas had been strange enough as she struggled to come to terms with Joe's assault on her.

164

Now it was different. They all missed Lynne and the children with their noisy exuberance. Richard, although making an effort, seemed locked inside his problems. The confident lawyer with a dry sense of humour and ready wit was missing and came across as both morose and colourless. He was lonely without his wife and children, and she knew that he would be eaten away by a corrosive sense of regret and ashamed of his weakness.

She heard a tentative knock, and her mother poked her head around the bedroom door.

'Thought you might appreciate a cup of tea, dear.' She smiled fondly at her daughter.

Maisie hauled herself into an upright position and patted the quilt. 'Come and sit down, Mum. I'll get up and help when I've drunk this, promise.'

'There's no rush; you enjoy the rest.' Her mother paused for a moment. 'It's quiet without the children, isn't it? But it's good to have you both home again and back in your own rooms. It reminds me of when you and Richard were both students and home for the holidays.'

Maisie looked at her mother's face and realised that although saddened by Richard's marriage break-up and by Maisie's problems, she still found comfort in having them here. She must have missed the two of them so much after they left home. She was always busy and so contained and Maisie admired her mother's strength.

Richard left on Boxing Day, after lunch, claiming a mountain of work to be done. Maisie went the day after. Somehow, they'd all survived Christmas. But as she drove back to Hampshire, she reflected on how the old excitement and comfort of Christmas that had remained from her childhood had gone. All the George family had gone through the motions and were left with a watered-down flatness to their celebrations. Whatever happened in subsequent Christmases this year was a turning point, and she knew it would never be the same.

She wondered how things would turn out for Richard. He still lived in the one bedroomed flat and put all his energy into his legal work. There had been no contact with Lynne over the Christmas, so far as Maisie could tell, although he did speak to the children on Christmas morning. She recalled his grey face and expressionless eyes afterwards. He didn't want to talk, and Maisie had no desire to press him. All their conversations were mundane with both aware of the other's hurt and neither knowing how they could help.

She was nearly back to the boatyard now and couldn't help wondering what Joe had been doing while she was away. She struggled to curb her jealousy, but no matter how many times she reminded herself that she must trust him, she never managed it. Coming home should be a joyous occasion; instead, she felt queasy and anxious. As she drove, she found herself repeating 'Please be there Joe, please be there.'

Chapter 27
Joe

Joe groaned and closed his eyes. It was Christmas Day, and he was so hung-over it was hard to breathe. Yesterday had seemed like a good idea. The four of them, Ben, Ronnie, Rick, and himself had been drinking since eleven in the morning. He looked at Ronnie, who was curled up in a sleeping bag beside him; her white face was waxen and pinched and her small, thin body like that of an old child. He remembered walking back from The Joiners and smoking some dope and was dimly aware of her coming on to him before he crashed out on the settee.

He pulled on his jeans and groped around for his coat. All he wanted was to get out of the squat. He missed Maisie. *Why the hell hadn't he just gone to Somerset with her?* Nobody else stirred as he set off to walk the six miles back to the barge. As it was Christmas Day, there were no buses and, in any case, he wanted to walk to clear his head. The roads were quiet. A few cars passed him, and he saw the parcels on the back shelf and excited children off to visit relatives for yet more presents. Last year, he had still been at Alpha House, and in some ways, he missed the structure and routine of the place.

When he got back, the boatyard was deserted, and the barge seemed cold and unwelcoming without Maisie. He set the bilge pump going and decided to go out. Despite his long walk home, he was still restless and full of pent-up energy, so he walked along the riverbank to the next boatyard where thin plumes of smoke from the chimneys on deck indicated that other houseboat dwellers were in residence. Somehow this made him feel less alone. He carried on under the motorway bridge until he came to the woods. No yachts were moored here; it was just the quiet, peaceful river. He came to a small area of beach and sat on a fallen tree stump to smoke a roll-up.

He was glad he hadn't had sex with Ronnie. Beneath the blasé attitude, she was vulnerable, and he didn't want that kind of complication. Nor could he ignore his feelings for Maisie. He loved her, and she gave some purpose to his life. Although they argued a lot of the time surely, that was superficial, and they could get beyond the petty squabbles. A lot of it was his fault. Time and again as soon as it got tough, he slid away from responsibility and cocooned himself in selfish lethargy. They had taught him at Alpha House to list in his mind all the positives going for him. Well, Maisie was at the top of the list, as was the barge. Living there was great, and if he put in the effort, he could make it even better. He resolved to stop drifting and for once in his life be pro-active.

It was cold and growing dark as he walked home but, buoyed up by a new enthusiasm, he scarcely noticed. Back aboard, he lit the Rayburn in the galley and the coal stove in the main saloon. Once they got going, it soon warmed up. He lit the oil lamps for a change, instead of the harsh, single, electric bulb and Maisie's photos and ornaments were soon bathed in a warm orange glow. He had never taken much notice of them before, but this was their home, their own special place, and he wanted to make everything alright between them. She'd be home the day after tomorrow; he'd make it cosy and welcoming for her.

Chapter 28
Maisie

Joe slept beside her; she lay still, but her mind raced, and she couldn't keep at bay the sadness and resentment that yet again he'd come home drunk. She was jealous of Ronnie and resentful of Joe's new life, which increasingly didn't seem to include her.

In the morning, she was still annoyed about Joe's drinking and could feel herself building up for a row. Despite knowing that it was a very bad idea, she couldn't let it go. If something was on her mind, she had to get it out in the open. She had always been the same, and often it didn't end well. She got out of bed and stomped around, her mood blackening.

'For god's sake. What's up with you?' Joe muttered.

That was enough to give full vent to her pent-up feelings, and she was soon shouting, virtually screaming at him. It was all so wrong, but she couldn't stop. When Joe told her to lighten up and then to piss off, she grabbed her bag and car keys and stormed out. It was the first time that she had not kissed him goodbye.

Feeling tearful and dithery, she drove to the university. Thankfully, she only had one lecture that morning and then she was free. It was the last thing she felt like doing, but she wasn't going to let her students or her colleagues down. Come midday she was at a loss. Still upset and still angry with Joe, she pondered her choices. Staying away and having no contact with him felt as if she was trying to punish him. But he probably won't even notice I'm not there, she thought sadly. She drove to the seafront where the water had its usual calming effect.

Joe apparently wasn't expecting her back just yet, and when she ran down the stairs, he seemed flustered.

'Joe?' she asked, tilting her head to one side.

'Just tidying up a few things,' he mumbled.

169

In the galley, she noticed him push something hurriedly into a cupboard. Inside was a half-empty vodka bottle and a glass.

'Why were you trying to hide it from me, Joe?' There was no anger or shouting this time.

'Because I knew that you'd give me a hard time.' He wasn't apologetic just matter of fact.

'Why can't you tell me if you're finding it hard? Why lie to me?'

'I didn't lie,' he protested.

'It amounts to the same thing. I can understand you having a lapse, but you will never talk about it, and hiding spirits makes me feel that I can't trust you. That's a big thing for me, Joe.'

Joe didn't respond, and her sadness was replaced by irritation. 'Thanks, that's helpful,' her sarcasm was obvious. 'Oh, suit yourself. I'm exhausted. I'm going to get some sleep.'

She woke a few hours later feeling queasy and muzzy headed. To her relief, Joe was still there. It took considerable restraint not to cross-examine him. *How long have you been drinking vodka again? Have you hidden your drinking from me before yesterday? Why couldn't you have talked to me if you were struggling with it?* But of course, she couldn't say these things. Instead, she found herself on constant alert, listening for the sound of him opening a bottle or the chink of a glass and surreptitiously trying to smell if there were signs of alcohol on his breath. Once or twice, her suspicions were confirmed, but Joe always had some excuse. She hated herself for being on his case, and she hated his weakness.

In desperation, she phoned Chris. 'I've told him so many times that it's not the fact that he's finding it hard to control his drinking, but it's the secretiveness.'

'I've known you a long time, so I'm going to be honest with you.' Chris told her. 'You want to control everything, but it's not always possible. Joe is his own man; he has to do it for himself. Give him some space to find his own way of coping; otherwise, I'm afraid you will lose him.'

'I know what I should do, but it's easier said than done. If I can't trust him to tell me the truth about his drinking, then I start doubting whether I can trust him about anything. It's just horrible to feel like this.' Her voice wavered with emotion.

'I know', Chris told her kindly. 'I wish I didn't live so damn far away. Why don't you go away for a few days? Give yourselves a bit of space. It might help.'

Although Chris was right, it didn't stop Maisie from agonising over where she could go. She couldn't face going back to her parents, and her brother had his own issues. There was always Will, but she didn't want him to know about her problems with Joe. There was no one else she knew well enough then she remembered Sally, her old flatmate.

'Sally's not back yet, but she shouldn't be more than an hour,' the girl told her when she explained who she was. 'But you're welcome to come in and wait.'

She showed Maisie into the lounge and left her alone, explaining that she had to get ready for a date. It was strange to be in the once familiar room. It looked quite different, and Maisie felt out of place.

'Of course, you can stay,' Sally told her. 'It will have to be the sofa though.'

She grabbed Maisie by the hand, and they went down to the kitchen and produced a bottle of wine. Halfway down the second bottle, Maisie's emotions got the better of her, and she started to sob uncontrollably.

'Right, bedtime for you,' Sally declared. She dug out spare bedding and tucked her up on the sofa with a large box of tissues.

Maisie drew a deep, juddering breath of despair. She had lain awake for much of the night. Sally thought much the same as Chris that she needed to be less controlling and more supportive. But in her darkest thoughts, breaking up with Joe was beginning to feel inevitable. For days now she had silently repeated his name unable to focus beyond her desperate longing to recapture their closeness. She dug her nails into the palm of her hand as her throat tightened and her heart ached, physically ached with longing for his presence. She wanted him to love her, to need her, yet he was slipping away from her, and she couldn't bear it.

Sally appeared with a towel and a cup of coffee. 'Have a shower; then I'll make us some breakfast,' she instructed.

Maisie let the warm water flow over her. It made her feel calmer, but she had no idea what she was going to do. She regretted flouncing off like that and was unsure what sort of reception she would get from Joe. She couldn't bear it if he were cold and distant towards her. She rough-dried her somewhat tousled hair; wound the towel around her and padded down to the kitchen. Joe was sat at the table with Sally.

'Look who's here?' Sally had a big grin on her face. She poured them both a coffee and disappeared upstairs ostensibly to have a shower.

'How did you know I was here?'

'I didn't; it was just a hunch. I got a lift with that guy on the motorboat. I'm so sorry, Maisie. I've been such a stupid sod.'

There was so much sadness in his eyes that Maisie gave him a small reassuring smile. He took her hands and held them up to his face.

'Come home, Maisie. I can't bear it without you there.'

She clenched her teeth. *Would anything change if she went back?*

'I want to be with you, Joe, more than you know but, and it's a big but, there can be no lying to me about your drinking. Is that understood?' *Why did she have to sound like some schoolteacher reprimanding her students?*

'I get it about the trust issue, and I'm sorry that I was so weak. Give me another chance?'

172

Maisie peered at her watch; her head ached, and she would be late for work; it was an important session for her second-year group who were finalising their third-year options. She struggled to summon the energy to get out of bed. She put her hand across and touched Joe's arm. At least he was still here but for how much longer. Things had improved since her huffy moment, as Joe referred to it, but the cracks and uncertainties were still there. Suppressing an agonised howl, she swung her legs out of bed.

'Coffee?'

Joe pulled her around to face him. 'Please come with us, Maisie. It'll be great; just what we need.'

Why couldn't he have said come with me? She turned away, shaking her head as the sadness she saw in his eyes made the stupid tears return.

'I can't Joe; I can't; you know I can't,' she sobbed, her head in her hands. *Why couldn't she stay in control? Why didn't he love her enough?* Her heart knew that he was already reconciled to her staying behind; he had moved on, but neither of them could bring themselves to acknowledge this. She pushed away a strand of hair that clung damply to her tear-streaked face.

'God, I hate this.' She sniffed and attempted a smile. 'Pass me a tissue. I've got to go to work. Can we talk tonight?'

As she walked down the gangplank to her car Maisie was hit by such exhaustion it was a struggle to lift one leg in front of the other. Last night, Joe had bounded down the stairs to the saloon and announced that they were off to Greece. They included Ronnie, a couple of mates from the pub and Maisie. He wanted her to go with him, and she believed him. But he expected her just to give up her job and go. He provided an easy solution to all her objections. *What would they do with the barge?* They couldn't leave it unattended for months. *What about the cat? What about, what about, what a bloody bout* screamed around her head.

Why couldn't he understand her reluctance? He held her close, and she breathed in his warm, familiar smell.

'Come on, Mais; let's go for it.'

Go for it. Maisie sighed; that used to be her motto, and she'd been proud of her spontaneity. But it wasn't this that held her back; it was a deep-rooted, conviction that it was already too late for them, and it broke her heart. She was struggling to come to terms with this herself, and it was even harder to explain to Joe. In any case, it wouldn't alter the way he and Ronnie were with each other, the shared jokes, the eye contact held for just that little bit too long. They were tactile with each other, and before her eyes, they had become a couple. They were right for each other. Ronnie brought him alive again. He needed to be with someone his own age. Oh, she could rationalise it alright what she couldn't do was bear it.

Chapter 29
Joe

Joe couldn't stop agonising about Maisie. He just couldn't understand why she wouldn't go with him to Greece. He knew she loved him, and her decision didn't make any sense. He couldn't bear the idea of life without her, but he also knew that he couldn't stay. *Why couldn't she see that?* He was treading water just to get through each day, as it was, and Alpha House had taught him to recognise a potential flashpoint which could trigger his addiction. He was drinking too much again, and he daren't risk it; his only choice was to get away. He adored Maisie; they were good in bed, incredibly good, and she constantly surprised him, but there was an aspect to their relationship, which lurked at the back of his mind. 'Like inhaling cotton wool,' he had answered when Stu and Andy asked him how life was going. Afterwards, he had felt disloyal towards Maisie, but that didn't stop it being true.

It hurt more than Joe could have imagined when Maisie had gently told him that their relationship had run its course, and perhaps she was right. He found it hard to believe that she was giving up on them so easily. *Didn't she want to fight for him?* She kept insisting that she didn't want him to stay and was fine about him going. *Did she really mean that?* A heavy sadness enveloped him. Maisie was warm-hearted and wise; she was intuitive about people's feelings he'd seen as much many times. She had helped him to escape the half-life that he'd slipped into and understood him better than anyone ever had.

His brain was so muddled by these conflicting emotions. He couldn't escape the fact that he did feel suffocated at times. He kept things from her as well and never discussed his fears about his mental state with her. He told himself this was to protect her, but instinctively he craved some independence and autonomy. That didn't seem like the basis for a healthy relationship. *Why was life so*

175

complicated? Perhaps the wayward and unpredictable Ronnie was what he needed? Besides, once Ronnie had made up her mind, there was no stopping her.

After a lot of tears and anguish, he and Maisie had eventually agreed that they both needed some space to work things out, so Joe had taken himself off to stay in the squat with Ronnie. He'd been there for two days now and Ronnie, as usual, was prattling on about nothing of interest. Joe couldn't think straight; he needed to be on his own for a while so ignoring Ronnie's protests, he ran down to the street. With a shock, he saw that Maisie's car was parked on the other side of the road. *What was going on?*

'Jesus, Maisie. What are you doing here?' He opened the passenger door of her car and slid in beside her.

'Hey.' He gently lifted her head from where it rested on the steering wheel. Her face was ravaged with weeping, and her body shook with uncontrollable sobs so that she was unable to speak. He ran his thumb under her puffy eyes to wipe away the flowing tears and pulled her into his arms.

'Maisie don't. Joe's here. Don't be upset.' For a while, he just held her until the trembling subsided. She sat back up and blew her nose loudly on a piece of kitchen roll.

'I can't bear you seeing me like this. I'm so sorry, Joe. I just wanted to be near you. You weren't supposed to see me.'

'I don't have to go away, you know. I'm not going to leave you like this, Maisie. Please stop crying.' He could feel her juddering sobs against his chest. 'Besides, it's not like it's forever. It's just a trip, and I'll be back before you know it.'

She put her hand on his cheek. 'Oh, bless you, Joe. Hard as this is, I think we both know that it's not about you going travelling. It goes so much deeper than that. Of course, you must go. You need to go. And after this trip, there will be more travels, more adventures. You've got all your life to live, and that's wonderful. I will always, always love you, Joe. I've loved our time together and all the fun we've had living on the barge, but it's time to move on.'

176

They sat in silence. Joe didn't trust himself to speak.

'I don't want to move on without you. We can sort this out I know we can. Please, Maisie don't give up on me.' *Did he really believe that? He just didn't know any more.*

Maisie shook her head slowly and climbed out of the car. 'Come on, give me a big hug and get back inside and sort Ronnie out.'

Joe saw her sad attempt at a smile before they clung to one another. He held her hands against his chest. 'I'll be there for you, always.'

Joe made his way back to Ronnie's flat. He didn't tell her about seeing Maisie. After a restless night, Joe's emotions were still churning, but a lot of what Maisie had said made sense. He was still young, and it was in his nature to be impulsive. Above all, he needed a change in his life to keep his demons at bay.

Forgetting a torch was stupid. By the time Joe and Ronnie stepped off the ferry from Dover, it was already dusk, and they argued about the best way out of Ostend. Joe dug out their one and only map and Ronnie, who happily confessed to being hopeless with maps, peered at it half-heartedly.

'What does it matter if we don't know exactly where we're going?' she told him. 'South to the sun and a free and easy life; that's the general idea.'

They got a lift to a small Belgian town. They hadn't brought a tent, as it would be too heavy to carry, so they set about finding somewhere to kip. It had begun to drizzle. Without street lighting and with no torch, it was difficult to make out their surroundings, and they ended up crawling under a lorry which was parked on some waste ground.

'I'm not sleeping here.' Ronnie sounded tired and irritable. 'Suppose the driver comes back while we're asleep and drives off.'

'Please yourself, but it'll do for me. I'm knackered.' Joe began to arrange his sleeping bag on the ground.

Opposite was a row of small, terraced houses. In the middle of the night, they heard a sudden commotion as cars pulled up and people emerged from their homes on to the dark street. Unseen, they watched as a small coffin was unloaded from a large, black car and carried into one of the houses.

'What's going on? I don't like this, Joe.' Ronnie clung on to his hand.

The guy who picked them up next morning told them that a coach full of local school children had crashed on its way to Austria. What they had witnessed was the return of a dead child. It was a difficult start to their trip.

The guy took them to Frankfurt where they treated themselves to a glass of German beer.

'Where do you reckon, we can sleep tonight, Joe?'

For all her previous bravado, she looked worryingly young and vulnerable. He shrugged, not welcoming the responsibility for planning such matters.

'Let's just start walking out of town and see what happens,' he told her.

Bed that night was under a bridge near the autobahn; it was cold and bleak amidst the litter and graffiti and reminded Joe of dismal days living rough before he met Maisie. He suppressed a sudden longing to be cuddled up with her on the barge.

After a restless night Ronnie sat up and rubbed her eyes.

'I'm not doing that again' She glared at him, her eyes blazing with indignation.

In what way is this my fault? Nevertheless, Joe put his arm round her. 'I think there's a youth hostel in Munich. Let's try to get as far as there tonight?'

It took two lifts to get there and between lifts they managed to have a wash of sorts in the public toilets. But when they walked into the hostel grounds their spirits lifted. The place was teeming with young people of different nationalities who lay on the grass playing guitars and talking.

The whole place was semi-organised chaos and alive with laughter.

Next morning, after a shower and fried eggs, Joe went to find Ronnie. She was sat on the gras having an animated discussion with a couple of American guys.

'I think we should get going this morning,' Joe told her.

'What's the rush? I like it here.'

'I guess it's tempting to stay for a couple of days but think of that Greek sun. We could be in Salzburg this evening, lifts permitting.'

Ronnie shrugged and jumped up. 'Fair enough, see you guys. I guess I should grab my stuff.'

The sun was shining in Salzburg and they sat on the riverbank eating bread and cheese.

'Just look at that view.'

'I know,' Ronnie slipped her arm through his. 'It's quite romantic, isn't it?'

Joe closed his eyes. *I wish Maisie was here to share this moment.*

Ronnie hacked at her lump of cheese with a plastic knife. 'I wish to hell we'd remembered to bring a sharp knife. This is ridiculous.'

When they had finished eating Joe pulled Ronnie to her feet. 'Come on, you. We better find the hostel.'

Unlike Munich, this hostel there was run on military lines by a large and sweating *fraulein*.

'Definitely SS in a former life,' Ronnie declared after she was reprimanded for putting her rucksack down on the bed.

Despite the magnificence of Salzburg, they weren't sorry to leave the hostel. At the nearest point to the autobahn, they started hitching.

Joe consulted the map. 'Next bit should be interesting; it looks as if once we get to a place called Badgastein, all the cars have to be loaded onto a train to take them through a tunnel under the Alps.'

Emerging from the tunnel, they were met with dramatic scenery. 'Look, Joe,' Ronnie gasped. 'There's snow on the mountains.'

Half-listening, he was more concerned about the chance of a lift in this remote place.

To his relief, a car pulled up, and the Yugoslavian businessman told them that he was going to Rijeka on the Adriatic coast. It was a fantastic lift, and they clambered in, excited to get going again. The driver, anxious to practise his English, even bought them lunch at Llubliana on the way.

Rijeka was mesmerising with its faded Italianate glamour, and at sunset, the beautiful Venetian buildings were reflected in the golden waters of the harbour. On the strength of the free lunch and long lift, they decided to treat themselves to a night in a small, cheap hotel. Joe looked at the double bed. It felt like a turning point in their relationship. The trip had brought him and Ronnie much closer. She made him laugh and the more comfortable he felt with her, the more his desire grew. So far, the hostels had been single-sex dormitories but tonight they would be sharing a bed. Back at Christmas time, he'd decided not to sleep with Ronnie. He quite often stayed over at the squat and sometimes they shared a bed. He'd explained to Ronnie that his decision was out of respect for Maisie, and she seemed to have accepted the situation. But he could feel things changing as an array of conflicting emotions danced in his head.

After a few initial whinges, Ronnie had turned out to be a good travelling companion. She was deceptively tough and uncomplaining and appealingly eager to see new places and meet new people. *But she wasn't Maisie.* He was surprised just how much he missed her. She was on his mind all the time; wondering what she was doing and how she was getting on. Several times he had nearly called Ronnie by her name. *He should be here with Maisie.*

Ronnie emerged from the shower wrapped in a white towel, which emphasised her childlike body. *It was hard to*

180

believe that she was twenty. She smiled and looked down at the floor as she let the damp towel fall to reveal small breasts and slim hips. Her face was a mixture of challenge and vulnerability. Joe lifted her pointed chin and kissed her on the lips. Then peeling off his t-shirt, he pulled her warm, damp body against his. She reached for the metal button of his jeans and without hesitation, knelt down. Joe groaned with pleasure and pulled away. But, insistent, she pulled him back onto the bed. He curled against her back and, with her still damp hair against his cheek, he pushed himself inside her. Afterwards, they lay still, locked together until, eventually, Ronnie rolled over; she was smiling, but tears glistened on her cheeks.

'Hello, you,' she said softly.

To his shame, all he could think about was whether she was on the pill. *Surely, she was?* Joe screwed up his eyes, his whole body tensed. Ashamed by his lack of control, he couldn't believe how easily he had succumbed. Now he felt guilty about Ronnie as well as Maisie. *This was all wrong he had to get home to Maisie and sort things out, but he couldn't just abandon Ronnie.* Feeling wretched he fell into a fitful sleep.

After a breakfast of fresh, white rolls and strong coffee, they set off for Split. They didn't have to wait long as a silent but smiling farmer picked them up in his truck, and they bumped along the rutted coast road.

Ronnie had gone off to buy paracetamol, so Joe waited on a bench on the quayside. The hot sun was on his back, and he was enjoying the solitude. Palm trees were dotted at regular intervals along the promenade; tall, faded buildings stretched up the hillside; their reflection was giving the water a yellow tinge. Several white painted, wooden boats lay alongside the stone quay, and on one a golden, flax mainsail flapped in the evening breeze. It was a tranquil scene, and Joe felt himself relax. The smells of the harbour and the music from the small, street café behind him were both exotic and enticing, and he looked forward to exploring the back streets. When Ronnie returned, he was glad to see her.

'Come on; let's find somewhere cheap to eat.' He put his arm around her thin shoulders, and they strolled over the small bridge towards the old town. After splashing out on a litre of local wine they wandered in mellow fashion looking for a suitable place to spend the night.

'There's no hostel here and I don't think we should pay for another room. Do you?' Joe asked.

'I guess we could try the beach,' Ronnie suggested.

So, they spent an uncomfortable night sleeping on the rocks. Yugoslavia, they discovered was not blessed with long, sandy beaches and although the sea was clear and warm, the coast was rocky. Joe woke to find the hot sun beating down on his sleeping bag and decided to attempt to wash in the sea. He let out a yell as the spines of a sea urchin drove into the soft, pink sole of his foot.

'Come here,' Ronnie laughed. She took a pair of tweezers from the rucksack and pulled at the black spines.

'Will you stop laughing? It bloody hurts. Do you think they're poisonous?' Joe asked.

'I have no idea. Come on; I'm sure you'll live.' She pulled him to his feet. 'Let's find some breakfast. I'm starving.' Despite her slim frame, she was forever hungry.

In the village, they found a small shop where you could buy pots of thick, goat's milk yoghurt and a small, soft round roll for a few *dinari*. Ronnie scooped up the thick, yellow skin from the top of the yoghurt.

'This is gorgeous.' She leaned back on the slatted, wooden chair. 'Do you think we'll get as far as Dubrovnik today?'

'Hope so; it sounds a pretty interesting place.'

In Dubrovnik, they met up with other hitchers. It was the first company they had had since the hostel in Salzburg. A group of them sat by the fountain in the centre of the beautiful, old city for hours on end. They drank the cheap wine and talked endlessly as they munched on grey bread and tangy, soft cheese.

One evening, they started talking to a local man in a bar who said they could sleep on his boat in the harbour for a few nights. He also warned them not to travel too close to Albania by road, so they decided to get a ferry to Corfu and try the youth hostel there.

Arriving at the harbour in Corfu, they caught a ramshackle old bus and walked down a dusty track to a small, isolated hamlet. The few small houses were dominated by a breath-taking old manor house which was now used as a hostel. Yannis, a friendly, laid-back Greek, greeted them and explained that they would be expected to take turns preparing the evening meal and that the water was turned off during siesta time.

'Will there be enough food for us tonight?' Joe inquired. 'I guess we're a bit late.'

Yannis shrugged. 'You can get omelette and chips or maybe fresh fish over there.' He pointed out a small taverna.

After showering, they made their way to the tiny taverna. They were soon joined by a few of the locals as well as half a dozen young Greek men who walked the dusty track in their brilliant white shirts to drink ouzo and kumquat and to dance on the dusty, beaten earth. It was a heady, sexually charged atmosphere that Joe found both exhilarating and unnerving.

Next morning, after a breakfast of yoghourt and fresh peaches Yannis announced that the minibus to the beach was about to depart. Before long, they were scrambling down the path from the road and through the olive trees, with the heady scent of thyme in their nostrils. Once they reached the beach, they plodded across the burning sand towards the dunes where they could see people with sleeping bags lying around and chatting. Somewhat tentatively, they dumped their rucksack and undid their roll mats before charging, with whoops of delight, into the warm and crystal-clear Ionian

Sea. Joe noticed Ronnie stop to talk to a guy who was splayed out in the shallow water.

'Who was that?'

She smiled teasingly. 'That is my new friend, Peeve. Isn't he magnificent?'

Joe raised his eyebrows. He was in no hurry to agree with her description. Peeve was tall and lean with long brown hair and a deep tan. He was wearing tight light blue bathers that hid nothing. Not that it mattered to Joe; he didn't want or expect commitment from Ronnie.

'Actually, he's a fascinating guy. He's doing criminology at Trinity College Dublin, and he's been here for ages. Lucky sod.'

Peeve introduced them to some of the other beach dwellers, and they set about organising their little place in the dunes.

'Come on,' Ronnie tugged him up. 'Let's explore the rocky bit over there. I've got to get back in the water it's so bloody hot.'

Ronnie was an unexpectedly strong swimmer and was soon diving down to explore the seabed. One of the others lent her his face mask, and when she surfaced, she was ecstatic.

'Joe, come and have a go. It's just awesome down there. We've got to get one of these.' She tugged the mask onto the top of her tousled hair.

Afterwards, they lay on their towels to dry off, listening to the languid conversations around them. Ronnie showed no signs of shyness and soon joined in.

'What's up with your face?' she asked the guy nearest to them.

'Mosi bites. They eat me alive. Look.' He pointed to his swollen eyelid. 'Last night, I zipped my sleeping bag right up to my ears. I nearly died of the heat and still the bastards got me.'

Joe watched as Ronnie squatted on her haunches and chatted away. He lay back looking at the cloudless sky and once again his thoughts drifted unbidden to Maisie.

Mid-afternoon when the sun was at its hottest the group wandered up the sandy steps to the cool terrace of the taverna. Peeve explained that it mainly catered for a handful of Germans from the small campsite behind the beach.

'The old boy is pretty laid back and lets us get away with sharing a Greek salad and some bread.' He told them.

Joe noticed that the ever-hungry Ronnie was eying up some pizza and cold chips that a party of Germans had left. He laughed out loud for before they were half-way down the steps, she had whisked the leftovers to their table where they were swiftly devoured. Observing this, another customer ordered chips all round for them, amidst heartfelt thanks and laughter.

After four or five days on the beach, the desire for cool sheets and a shower drove them back to the hostel for a few days. The deal was that they make their way back up to the road to coincide with Yannis dropping people off. For a month it was an idyllic lifestyle, but Joe knew it was time to move on. Peeve had already left, which changed the dynamic on the beach.

'We can get a ferry to Igoumenitsa on the mainland,' he told Ronnie. 'We can't stay here all summer.'

Ronnie pulled a face. 'Why do we have to keep moving all the time. I love it here.'

Joe sat down on the hot sand beside her and put his arm around her. 'I do too but we need to think about how long our money will last. I really want to get to see Athens and after that maybe Italy on our way home.'

Ronnie grinned at him. 'OK, Mr Sensible.'

Next night they ended up sleeping on the dirty town beach in Igoumenitsa. After much tossing and turning, Ronnie sat up.

'This place is horrible. It's swarming with mosies.'

Joe stood up and looked along the dark beach. 'We could try moving to a less weedy bit, I suppose.'

Tired and grumpy from lack of sleep, they struggled out of their sleeping bags as soon as it got light. Ronnie was pacing around picking stuff up and throwing it back down onto the sand.

'What's up?'

'I can't find my jumper. I must have dropped it when we moved in the night.' She peered along the beach. 'I think that's it,' and she trudged off to pick it up. They both stared helplessly as a Greek on a bicycle picked it up and rode off.

'Come back. That's my bloody jumper,' Ronnie shrieked at him, but it proved futile, and she sat back on the sand disconsolate.

'Bloody hell, Joe.' She aimed a kick in the small of his back. 'It was your idea to only bring one rucksack.'

It was true. Joe reasoned that people would be reluctant to pick them up if they carried too much stuff, so they had rationed themselves to just one backpack. In practice, it was too heavy for Ronnie, so she carried plastic bags containing bits of food and so on.

'Come on. Let's get out of this hole,' Joe put a comforting arm around her.

The ride to Athens was uneventful. At times, the Greek roads petered out to become no more than a dirt track. One driver sped at an alarming rate through the dusty villages causing children, dogs, and chickens to scatter as he blasted his horn. Ronnie clasped Joe's hand so hard it was painful. The driver dropped them by a park in Athens, and they wandered along the wide pavement, unsure what to do next.

'Bloody hell. It's Peeve.' Ronnie yelled across the road, and he came loping across to meet them with a massive grin on his face.

'I'm staying at the hostel. It's a brilliant place. Come on; I'll show you.'

On the way, Ronnie swore loudly. 'Fucking hell! My sandal's broken.' She held the broken strap up for them to see.

They collectively agreed that the sandals had indeed had it, so she stuffed them into the nearest bin and proceeded in bare feet. Rather uncharitably, Joe and Peeve laughed as she hopped from shadow to shadow.

'It's alright for you,' she moaned. 'You could fry an egg on these pavements, and it's killing my feet.'

At the hostel, they were greeted by a lanky old, guy with a hook nose who showed them to their dormitory. It was hot and airless on the fourth floor, but it had its compensations as he showed them an outside door which overlooked an open-air cinema. In adjoining beds, they unpacked their stuff. Ronnie didn't have much in the way of clothes left, but she didn't appear to mind. She had left England with one pair of jeans, but after the zip broke in Germany, she unceremoniously binned them, and after losing her jumper she was left with just the cotton dress she was wearing.

Athens in August was unbearably hot, and after a few days, Joe was keen to start heading for home. Constantly at the back of his mind was the urge to get back to Maisie and sort things out. He heaved the rucksack on to his shoulders.

'Come on; time to go,' he told Ronnie.

Ronnie raised her eyebrows. 'Go where? Why?'

How could he explain his decision to Ronnie? He could feel the tension between them and with it a disturbing restlessness.

Piraeus was noisy and smelly, but they managed to secure a cheap, outside ticket on an overnight ferry. As it grew dark, the bright, deck lights illuminated the motley assortment of travellers, who settled themselves for the night. Joe and Ronnie arranged their sleeping bags on the metal deck and ate the ubiquitous bread and cheese. As the ferry prepared to cast off, without warning, the lights were extinguished, and the cramped area was plunged into cheerful pandemonium. Gradually, order was established, and the deck passengers drifted off to sleep under a velvet Aegean sky.

In the middle of the night, Joe shot out of his sleeping bag and cursed yet again at the absence of a torch. 'Are you alright? What the hell's going on?'

Ronnie was groaning and gasping for breath. Someone shone a torch.

'Christ, are you ok? I didn't see you in the dark.'

Joe recognised the cyclist they'd chatted to earlier. He'd brought his bike on the ferry and was returning from cycling in South America. He leaned against a bollard and clutched his head.

'Jesus, I only got up to have a pee. Are you sure you're alright?'

Ronnie, who was still winded and unable to speak, nodded. Joe discovered that on his way back from the loo, the cyclist had jumped over him, thinking it was a clear space. His heavy boots had landed in the middle of Ronnie's stomach.

'Otherwise, an uneventful journey,' Ronnie joked as they walked down the gangway and on to Italian soil. Italy was a whole different ball game. Straight away, people warned them not to sleep rough.

'*Pistoleri, bandito,*' a woman whispered.

Her warning spooked Ronnie, so they paid out for a room and spent a chaste night on a high, hard bed dominated by a large crucifix and a portrait of the Madonna and Child.

Next day, they walked beyond the town until they were beside sun baked fields. They waited a couple of hours and eventually two Italian businessmen, on their way to Naples, stopped for them. They were friendly enough and even bought them lunch at a magnificent, old restaurant, miles from anywhere. They persuaded them to try raw razor shellfish that writhed when they squeezed lemon juice on them. To follow, they had a fluffy omelette with piping hot, fat chips. The wine flowed, and they ended up with three

188

liqueurs to try; one had coffee beans floating in it much to Ronnie's delight.

When they climbed into the car again, Joe felt light-headed and soporific. That was until Ronnie's

scream cut through the thick, mid-afternoon air.

'Joe, come on you bloody idiot.' She tugged wildly at his arm.

He fell sideways through the car door as the two of them rolled down the dusty bank at the side of the road. The car sped off, a yellow cloud of dust in its wake. Joe lay on his back and gazed at the cloudless sky.

'You're pissed,' she sobbed, rubbing her knee.

Bemused, he sat up. Five minutes ago, he had been pleasantly mellow. Thank God she'd dragged the rucksack out of the car as well.

'Couldn't you see what was happening? They deliberately got you drunk so that you couldn't help me. Bastard.' She began punching him wildly.

Joe fended her off. He rubbed his eyes and blearily tried to piece together what was wrong as he held her in his arms until the sobs subsided. He wiped away her tears.

'What happened?'

'The one in the back tried it on with me. His hands were all over me. I couldn't hold him off; he was too strong.' A shudder travelled through her slender body. 'Didn't you think it odd when they suggested that you sit in the front?' She demanded, pulling away from him.

'Shit, Ronnie. I'm so sorry. Come on let's get out of here.'

They tramped along the dusty road. Joe looked at the dried-up soil of southern Italy; there were just a few dust-stained olive trees and scrubby bushes. *God knows where they were.*

'I told you not to drink anymore; they wanted to get you pissed.' She turned to face him; her dirt-streaked face was small and pinched with worry beneath her spiky, bleached hair.

Joe slid the rucksack off his shoulders and pulled her towards him. With his thumb, he wiped away a damp streak beneath her eye. He couldn't help responding as she wriggled closer and pressed against him. She tilted her chin towards him.

'It's ok; you're forgiven. It wasn't your fault.' She peeled off her dress. She never wore underclothes of any description and now lay back naked on the dusty verge. He groaned at the sight of her. She caught his hand and pulled him down beside her, and he began to run his hands over her arching body.

Afterwards, he lay beside her, sweat-drenched in the hot sun. Ronnie sat up and picked bits of dried grass from her hair.

'God, just look at me; I'm filthy.' She grinned at him accusingly and not bothering to dress she rolled a joint, leaving Joe to contemplate what to do next.

He tugged on his jeans and black T-shirt and inspected the surrounding countryside.

'Looks like a bigger road on the other side of that field. Siesta time must be over by now, so with luck, there might be the odd passing car.'

Ronnie dragged the grubby dress over her head. 'Whatever,' she replied, her voice lazily mellow.

Joe was excited to reach Rome. Tired and emotional, they wandered into a bar where one of the locals engaged them in conversation. By the end of the night, he had offered them a room in his flat which they gratefully accepted.

Joe woke instantly as Ronnie gripped his arm.

'Who the fuck's that?' she whispered.

He sat up as the bedroom door burst open, and a man stood at the foot of the bed. He shouted in Italian, and when Joe spoke to him in English, he produced a flick knife. Ronnie leapt out of bed and pulled on her dress. Joe had no idea what was happening, and the guy they'd met earlier seemed to have disappeared.

'It's alright mate. Misunderstanding.' He tried to keep calm as the guy paced around the room, still shouting. They stuffed their belongings into the rucksack and were soon shivering on the pavement outside. It was the middle of the night. Joe's head ached, and his stomach heaved.

'I fucking hate Rome; I don't want to stay here, Joe,' Ronnie pleaded.

He sighed. 'We only arrived last night.' Rome would be a good place to hang out for a while, but she was adamant; the incident with the flick knife had scared them both.

'Come on; we might as well walk out of town and start hitching.' Reluctantly, he picked up the heavy rucksack and Ronnie trudged after him.

Tempers improved later when a glinting black Jensen purred to a stop and whisked them to a small town near Milan. But Joe had had enough now. Enough sun, enough uncertainty and enough of feeling responsible for Ronnie. He just wanted to be back home, back with his Maisie and their life together. *What an idiot he'd been for throwing it all away on a whim.*

He was concerned about Ronnie; she had been quiet all day and was slumped forward hugging her knees.

'You alright? You've gone really white.'

Her face creased with pain, and she shook her head. 'I thought it was just period pains, but it's never been this bad before. I've taken three paracetamols, but they didn't do any good.'

Before he could answer, she threw up and curled on the grass verge clutching her stomach. She looked so small and vulnerable.

'Take it easy.' He lifted her to her feet. 'We'll get you to a hospital and have you checked out.'

The hospital was in a beautiful setting with lush, tree-covered mountains surrounding the small town. But Joe's mind was on Ronnie as he wandered the narrow streets.

They had confiscated her passport at the hospital, and no one spoke English. When he visited the previous afternoon, he had found her tearful and frightened.

'They want to operate, Joe. I couldn't understand what they were saying, and the doctor drew a diagram in biro on the sheet to try to explain. They kept talking about lire. They know we can't pay, don't they? I can't seem to get through to them. I kept saying *no molti lira, no molti lira* or whatever.'

'Hey, it's ok,' he replied, taking her in his arms. 'It'll be ok. I promise.'

But by this time Ronnie was distraught and her noisy sobs so alarmed the staff that they sent for one of the doctor's wives who spoke English. She explained to Ronnie that the doctors suspected an ovarian cyst. Ronnie was adamant there was no way she was going to have an operation in a foreign hospital, so they gave her antibiotics, returned her passport and much to Joe's relief, discharged her.

Despite the beauty of the Italian town, it had been a tense time and they were both glad to move on. A Swiss guy picked them up, but he was a crazy driver who drove around the hairpin bends like a lunatic.

Ronnie shrieked in fear. 'We'll have to get out, Joe. Tell him to stop,' she insisted.

'Don't be daft, we're in the middle of nowhere.'

'I don't care,' Ronnie told him, and proceeded to scream at the driver to stop.

There was no alternative that night but to sleep in a hay barn. Ronnie laughed as she picked hay out of her hair. 'God, what an itchy night.'

'I have no idea why you think that funny,' Joe responded.

By the following evening, satiated by hot, sun-scorched days, they scampered like children, revelling in the pleasure of damp grass in a rainy Belgian park.

'People are never satisfied, are they?' Ronnie squished rainwater through her toes. 'We long for sunshine, and when we've had enough of that, we're longing for cool rain.'

As they boarded the ferry for Dover, she was still barefoot and still wearing the pale blue, cotton dress. Joe watched her fondly as she rubbed at a dirt smear on her leg. Neither of them could bear to be below; it was too claustrophobic after all the fresh air. They didn't talk much, and Joe was aware that they hadn't discussed what would happen when they got back to England.

He suddenly felt overwhelmingly tired and lay on the deck, his head resting on the lumpy rucksack.

He was in the middle of a nightmare, but he couldn't wake himself out of it. He is in a sewer tunnel. It's dark, and he keeps slipping. He can see a light at the end, but the walls close in on him, and the putrid smell suffocates. With mounting panic, he pushes against the slimed brickwork. A searing pain strikes his chest as he struggles to breathe. The light begins to grow larger, then more distant. He wipes the beads of sweat from his eyes as a rushing noise fills his ears. He can't think straight and struggles to escape the claustrophobic atmosphere, to breath clean air and let bright light fill his eyes, yet part of him feels at home in this dark world. It is familiar, and there is an intangible sense of belonging.

He woke with a start, but the dream remained disturbingly real.

Chapter 30
Maisie

It was two weeks now since Joe had left. Every night since, she had either tossed around unable to sleep or, had drifted into a stupor and been plagued with these disturbing dreams. She didn't know which were worse the horrible dreams or the endless going over and over what had gone wrong between her and Joe. Often when she woke from a nightmare, she could only remember snippets, but tonight's offering had been particularly vivid.

In the dream she didn't know she was, but she didn't like the look of the scruffy group of men sitting on the bench beside the phone box. No one else was around which was not surprising as it was the early hours of the morning. *Why was she here?* She had a vague idea that she was in danger but was reluctant to hurry away. The men stared back at her, mildly curious.

She spread her palms. 'What am I going to do? I don't know what to do.' The words choked in her throat, and she could hear her noisy sobs.

'What's up, love? Don't be upsetting yourself so.'

The comfort of his soft Irish accent washed over her, and soon the four strangers were giving her advice. All the emotion flowed out as she told them how bereft she felt since Joe left. *Her lovely Joe, why had he left her?* As the words spilt out, they became more random. Bizarrely, she started coming out with a load of religious twaddle.

'Pray to God; pray for me. God takes care; he will care for me.' This was repeated in a loud monotone until one by one the men, bored by this nutter, wandered off.

Overcome with fatigue after her outburst, Maisie looked around. Just beyond the phone box was a circular area surrounded by a low concrete wall. Blue, plastic covered mattresses covered the ground, and a semi-conscious young man with long matted hair was already

194

in residence. She climbed on to a mattress and sank down; she lay her head on the low wall, allowing her blond hair to splay across the concrete. A black car pulled up by the phone box and some men, smartly dressed in suits and white shirts, got out. They were obviously looking for someone and had an air of menace about them, drug dealers possibly. It was a struggle to focus. Then, one of them spotted her hair. She sat up, her throat tightening with fear. With a jolt, she realised that she was in bed on the barge. Shaking, she scrabbled for the bedside light. She pulled the quilt around her and bit her lip to stop the tears.

On other nights, sleep wouldn't come at all. If she had been different towards Joe, more relaxed, more fun … on and on her brain whirled until, unable to switch off, exasperation set in. On too many nights she lay in the double bed too exhausted to move for what amounted to hours of total inactivity.

She peered at the bedside clock, 3.45 a.m. It would be light soon. It was Saturday, and the prospect of a lonely weekend stretched before her. The miserable self-pity wouldn't leave her; she lay back on the pillow and closed her eyes.

She must have drifted back to sleep when she heard footsteps on deck and the clang of the ship's bell that served as a doorbell. She looked at her watch. It was ten o'clock; still weary, she pulled on jeans and a t-shirt and pushed open the door.

'Will?' She stared at him in surprise. 'You've had your hair cut.' She frowned at him accusingly. The familiar flop of fair hair had gone. It was cut short on top and looked darker, which made him look older.

He grinned at her and blinked in the bright sunlight. 'Thought you might like some company. We haven't seen you at Pebbles for weeks.'

He followed her down below to the galley. Maisie filled the battered, red, enamel kettle and placed it on the Calor gas cooker. Will produced juicy bacon rolls from a

195

paper bag concealed in his coat pocket and they sat together at the small galley table and devoured the rolls washed down with big mugs of coffee. As they chatted inconsequentially about mutual friends, Maisie's spirits rose. It was good to have someone else here. Joe wasn't mentioned. Then Will covered her hand with his.

'OK. How are you really?'

The intensity of his gaze made her look away, irritated that her eyes were brimming with tears yet again.

'It just seems so pointless, Will; my life seems pointless. Truth is, I don't feel there is much left of me inside. Sorry,' she attempted a grin. 'That sounds rather melodramatic, doesn't it?'

He shrugged. 'You're bound to feel a bit empty.'

She leaned her head back and sighed. *She was doing a lot of sighing these days; it was time she got a grip.* Deep in thought, she stirred her coffee.

'I don't want to do anything, and I don't seem to have an opinion about anything; hard to believe I know.' She paused for a moment and stared at the swirling coffee. 'I feel so lonely, and I miss him so much. Shit, sorry.' She scowled and tried to wipe away the tears with the back of her hand. 'What is the matter with me?'

He stood up and pulled her to her feet. 'Come on; you need to get out of here.'

She shook her head. 'I don't know Will; I honestly don't feel up to it. Besides, I'd be pretty dismal company.'

But Will insisted. They drove in his car to a pretty country pub. Maisie as always was surprised at how fast he drove; she felt safe enough with him, but it was out of character somehow. He parked the car, but instead of going inside, he led her along a footpath and up a steep, stony track. They stood at the top to look at the view. A gentle breeze ruffled her hair, and she was surprised to find herself laughing. They followed the circular walk until they arrived back at the pub.

196

'Thank god for that, I'm starving,' she declared. It was a relief to feel physically tired instead of the numbing, emotional drain of the last two weeks.

They sat, warmed by the sun, on the pub benches. In front of them, large, white, soup bowls were brimming with delicious, homemade soup served with a massive chunk of warm, crusty bread.

'Thank you.' She smiled, overcome with a wave of tenderness for him.

'It was just what you needed,' he replied. 'I know.'

Afterwards, he dropped her at the boatyard.

'Coming in?' she enquired.

'No, I'd better be off. He bent down and kissed her cheek. 'Keep in touch, you hear?'

Maisie nodded and hugged him.

After he had driven off, she sat crossed-legged on the warm, canvas-topped hatch cover and inspected her tanned knees. The sunny afternoon with Will had lifted her mood, and she scribbled a "To-do list" in the notebook on her lap.

Her priority was to give up the tenancy on the barge and find somewhere else to live. It helped to have all the paperwork in her name. During one of many sleep-deprived nights, she had toyed with the idea of staying on the barge on her own. In the eight months that they had lived on the river, she had come to love the community of boat dwellers each with their histories and concerns. Eddie on the MFV next door was an ex-lorry driver; he was often grumpy and taciturn but would do anything for you as long as it was between April and November that is. During the winter months, Eddie would hibernate but come April he emerged with a quickness of foot and began to chuck things out and re-order his life on board. Then there was Peter, the scruffy mechanic who always smelled of diesel but had an enigmatic appeal. Living aboard meant adopting an unconventional lifestyle which brought its pitfalls, as well as freedoms, and Maisie doubted that she was strong enough on her own. She certainly wasn't practical enough.

197

She abandoned her list after the first item and watched the still water. It was in limbo like her and waiting for the evening tide to begin its ebb. *What was she waiting for?* Her teeth ground together as the familiar lump barged its way once more to her throat and her eyes filled with tears. Since Joe had left, the way of life that she'd become used to had ebbed away, and she was wallowing in the muddy waters of self-pity. It wasn't just living on the barge; she didn't want to live anywhere on her own. Neither could she go back to flat sharing with other girls; she couldn't bear that.

Her chest ached in an entirely physical way. *She wanted Joe; she just wanted Joe.* This triggered the usual torrent of questions. *Where was he now? What mood was he in? Would it be the bubbling charm, which signalled one of the up moods? Or the morose cloud that had hung over the last few weeks they'd been together?* Her mind raced, and once the questions started, she couldn't stop. *How was his relationship with Ronnie? Had they quarrelled? Were they even still travelling together?*

She stood up to clear her head and walked to the stern of the barge where the old dinghy still lay. It reminded her so sharply of Joe that she couldn't help smiling. She undid the painter and climbed down the wooden ladder. She enjoyed rowing and, when no one was watching, had attempted to teach herself to scull. There was a pool in the river where no boats were moored. When she reached the centre, she shipped her oars, one pink and one pastel blue and drifted downstream as the ebb tide gathered momentum. It was so peaceful; she would miss that, but it also increased her growing sense of loneliness and isolation. She drifted past the first bend in the river and had to pull hard on the oars to get back. She was out of breath by the time she climbed back aboard the barge and energised by the exercise. Her head felt clearer, knowing that she had reached a decision.

The long summer vacation lay ahead, and she needed a holiday. The problem was she had no one to go with and couldn't face going away on her own. Maybe Will could take a couple of weeks off that would be ideal. She didn't know why it hadn't occurred to her before.

Fired up by the whole idea she jumped straight in the car and drove the twelve miles to his flat in Portsmouth. There was no response to her urgent bell ringing. Disappointed, she tried The Joiners; he sometimes went there if a decent blues band was playing. *Where the hell was he?* She drove back to Oxford Avenue and waited. There comes a moment in waiting when you cannot believe you will ever see the waited-for person again. Maisie had just reached that point when Will appeared on his bike. She clambered out of the car and spilt out her idea.

'Sorry, Maisie but I can't just take time off. I've got a stack of clients at the moment, and I decided to work through the school holiday period so the others in the office with children can take their holidays.'

She stared at him. He'd dismissed the idea of a holiday together and hadn't even hugged her to let her down gently.

'Oh, not to worry, it was just a mad impulse.' She was determined to hide her disappointment. 'Got time for a quick drink now?'

'Fraid not, I only popped back for a shower. I'm meeting up with a work colleague in half an hour.' He picked up a towel from the bed. 'There's some wine in the fridge; help yourself if you want while I get ready.'

She stood up. *Did her stunned embarrassment show?*

'No, it's OK. I haven't eaten yet, so I'll head on home. Have a good time.'

She attempted a thin smile and closed the front door behind her. She was shocked by how much it mattered that Will didn't want to go on holiday with her. She didn't buy the stuff about work commitments; surely, most courts have a quiet time in the summer. *And just who was this mystery work colleague?* It was weeks since Fran had left so it wasn't surprising that he would want to find a new woman. She just hadn't considered the prospect before.

She drove back to the river and cursing the lack of a telephone on the barge she stopped off at the public call box in the nearby marina.

'Hi, Chris,' but she could tell from the background asides this wasn't a good time to call her friend. 'I just wanted a chat, but it can wait. I can see you're busy.' She struggled to appear light-hearted and hide any hint of resentment. Nevertheless, she knew it was there. Chris was always in a rush these days. Maisie knew she was being unreasonable, yet deep down, she expected her friend's undivided attention.

'Sorry, it's mad here, and I'm already late for the kids swimming lesson. I'll call you after nine when I've put them to bed. Oh shit, I forgot, I can't phone you can I.' She laughed. 'Well, never mind, you can phone me. Anyway, must go, speak to you soon. Bye.'

Maisie took no pleasure from the warm June evening as she trudged across the gravel back to her car. She conducted an inner dialogue about what she needed to tell Chris. She was acutely aware of her loneliness to the point where every action, even just walking and putting one foot in front of the other, became deliberate and effortful. With each small movement, she had to remind herself to breathe. *Why am I so bad at being on my own?* She'd survived broken relationships in the past, been on her own before, lots of times, but she had never experienced this crushing loneliness.

It was no good; she couldn't face going back to the barge. She mentally went through her friends. *Who could she go and see? Not Will, not Shaun and Kay who were still in France and not Fran.* Maisie felt guilty about Fran. She hadn't exactly been the loyal friend, and since Fran had moved, they hadn't spoken.

'Oh god, this is horrible.' She sat in the driver's seat and spoke into the empty space. 'I haven't any friends

200

except for Joe and Will. I want Joe and Will. I am pathetic,' she sobbed.

She drove back to Will's and sat outside in the car. She didn't care that he wasn't there; just to be nearby made her feel closer to him. She jumped when the passenger door opened; she hadn't noticed that it had grown dark. Will slid into the seat beside her.

'Maisie, what on earth are you doing here? What's the matter? What's happened?

She was so relieved to hear his voice. 'Nothing's the matter,' she told him between heaving sobs. 'I just needed to see you. I'm sorry,' she finished, her voice almost inaudible.

In Will's flat, she still couldn't stop crying. They drank a bottle of red wine, and she tried to explain why she was so upset. She blew her nose yet again.

'I'm stupid and pathetic, that's all.' She couldn't tell him that coming here had been the last resort. But if she was honest, it was the only place she wanted to be right now, here with Will. She put out her hand and linked her fingers with his.

'I'm so glad you're here, Will.'

'You don't have to be on your own.' He held her in his arms, and she started to relax.

Next morning, as she snuggled up to Will, she was thankful that he hadn't tried to make love to her. She had enjoyed a good night's sleep, and for the first time since Joe left, she was keen to be up and about and get on with the day. She made coffee and toast and climbed back into bed.

'How about we pick up some of your things from the barge, and you stay here for as long as you want?' Will suggested.

'Sorry I didn't get back to you sooner,' she told Chris. 'But everything's fine right now.'

'That's good; I was worried when you sounded so down. Come on, then, what's changed?'

'I've been staying with Will for a couple of weeks that's all, and it's great. He's been wonderful.'

'Well, I always knew he fancied you.' Chris told her. 'Persistence paid off then.'

'Don't be such an old cynic. I'm happy to be with him, and it's all good, especially the sex; this will make you jealous; it's great sex.' She knew Chris had always thought Will to be dull and staid. 'You'd be surprised, my dear,' she laughed, but she knew it would be disloyal to discuss him like that even if it was with her best friend.

'No doubt,' Chris told her wryly. 'But I'm happy for you and remember if he is the right man, you will cherish him; won't you?'

Afterwards, Maisie puzzled over this last remark. *What did Chris mean?* Cherish was such an old-fashioned word. If it meant the same as love and adore well, she'd done that with Joe. She wondered for the hundredth time where he was now. She still missed him so much despite the contentment she had found with Will. Yet by moving in with Will, she had taken a step away from Joe. With Will's help, she would cope, and for the first time in ages, she could see a future that didn't scare her.

She heard Will's key in the lock, and her spirits rose. She smiled; he had that effect on her, and she was always glad to see him. He had the happy knack of making her feel included in his life where she was warm and safe. He threw his briefcase on the settee and bent to kiss her.

'You smell of summer,' she told him, locking her hands behind his neck for a moment. 'Hey, it's not fair; you're going brown.' The new haircut suited him, and his face seemed leaner and more defined.

'One of the many advantages of cycling to work', he told her. 'The minute I'm in the saddle, I can relax and leave any tensions behind me. You should try it.'

'I haven't ridden a bike since I was fifteen. Besides, I enjoy my drive to work', she retorted. 'I can listen to the

202

radio, and I can speculate about the other drivers. Plus, it gives me a chance to think about the day ahead.'

She handed Will a cold beer. 'I've made a chilli for supper.' She saw him hesitate and made a face at him. 'What? So, you don't like my chilli now?'

He laughed. 'I wouldn't be brave enough to tell you even if it were true. No, it's nothing to do with your wonderful cooking. I wondered if you fancied going to Pebbles tonight. I expect Shaun, and some of the others will be there. It would be good to catch up with them again.'

Maisie sipped her wine. It was ages since she'd been to Pebbles. She'd only been a couple to times since the Christmas party. She remembered, with a pang, how confused and unhappy she'd been at the time about her relationship with Joe. Her memories of Pebbles belonged to a different part of her life. A time when Will was still with Fran and when she was still single, and life hadn't been this awful emotional roller coaster. Before Joe, her world had often been predictable and in hindsight mundane at times. *Was this what life would be like with Will?* She shook off the thought. Will wasn't dull; he was lovely; he was kind and good-humoured and a good conversationalist. People enjoyed his company. He didn't have that dangerous edge or the spark of wickedness that made Joe so exciting. But she didn't want that anymore. She sighed. *Look where it had got her.*

Will reappeared. He had changed out of his work clothes. 'What about it then? Are we going to Pebbles? I could do with a night out.'

Maisie made a quick decision. 'Why not? It's about time we went public. I don't think any of them even knows I'm staying here. It'll give them something to talk about if nothing else.'

'Yes, then?' He looked at her carefully to check that she was happy with the idea.

203

She smiled at him. 'Yes, definitely; give me five minutes to change into my jeans. We'll have the chilli tomorrow.'

It was a warm evening, so they decided to walk. She had a job to keep up with Will's long strides. It was dark inside the bar after the low sunshine outside. They went through to the garden where they found Shaun, accompanied, for once, by Kay. Next to her was the dreaded Eve, who had taken Fran's job, plus her boyfriend. They were sat at a small, wooden table and were deep in conversation. Maisie hesitated; they looked so intimate the four of them that she was uncertain about interrupting them. But she needn't have worried. As soon as Shaun saw them, he leapt up and gave her a big bear hug. His beard tickled her cheek. When he released her Will slid his arm around her shoulders. Maisie followed Shaun's gaze. She willed him not to comment and bless him he merely smiled and pulled a mock poker face of surprise behind his hand, which made her laugh. Will went to the bar to order a bottle, and she slid on to the bench next to Kay. After a couple of glasses, she felt more like her old self. It seemed natural to be here with Will, and the others apparently agreed. It was a happy and relaxed evening, and as they made their way home, a warm glow of affection for Will swept over her.

'Thank you. Tonight, was such a good idea.'

They lay on their backs in companionable silence.

'I ought to go to the boatyard and check the barge out tomorrow. I hope the bilge pump hasn't packed up; otherwise, I'm in trouble,' Maisie told him.

'Peter will keep an eye on her and let you know if there's a problem, but if you can wait until after work, I'll come with you.' Will reached across and took her hand. 'How about you make it a permanent thing, living here?' He paused when she didn't reply. 'How much notice do you need to give Mike's brother?'

'Four weeks.'

'Don't you think it would be good to get it all done and dusted before you start back at work.' He propped himself on one elbow and was looking at her expectantly.

After an obvious hesitation, she smiled. 'You have the best ideas, Mr Stevens,' she whispered and pressed her face against his warm chest. 'Thank you.'

Wandering around the barge next evening, she gathered together the last of her possessions. There was scant evidence of Joe ever having lived there. He had taken most of his meagre belongings with him when he went travelling, but there were still a few of his bits and pieces left. She couldn't bear to ditch them in the yard tidy bin, but neither did it seem right to take them with her to Will's. She picked up Joe's old navy jumper and held it to her face. It might once have smelled of Joe, but it didn't any longer. He was gone she reminded herself. It was a bleak prospect, and she bit her lip to keep back the tears. She stuffed the jumper into a black sack along with a couple of books that Mac had leant Joe. But apart from the Bruce Springsteen tape, she'd given Joe last Christmas that was all he owned in life. She ran up the stairs to the deck. Will was having a beer in Peter's cockpit. It was a sunny evening, and they looked peaceful as they chatted away. She waved.

'Two minutes,' she called. 'After that, I think I need to buy the two of you a pint in The Jolly.'

This suggestion was met with nods of approval, so she went below for a final inspection. She ran her hand along the rail of the old, solid fuel Rayburn. It was cold and lifeless now, but she remembered the cosy heat of last winter. When they had first moved aboard, she had grand plans to bake bread and do the whole domestic earth-mother bit but that never happened. She sat down at the red table. She and Joe had chatted, argued, and sulked at that table. Then, forcing herself into practical mode, she checked that the electric water heater was switched off and the food cupboard empty and returned to the main saloon. It looked bare now the shelves were cleared of all her books and knick-knacks. Only

205

the three-seater, floral-covered settee remained. She didn't go into the bedroom. She'd checked in there before and knew it would make only her feel sad and sorry for herself.

It was such a beautiful evening on the river, and she was determined to be a cheerful companion for Will and Peter. They decided to go to the pub in Peter's dinghy. Maisie's brightly painted craft was still moored at the stern of the barge, but it leaked with three aboard.

'Could you do me a favour?' she asked Peter. 'Could you pull my dinghy up into the boat shed at low water? I don't suppose I'll have much use for it anymore.'

He smiled at her. 'Yeah, no probs I can do that.' He rowed across to the pub's mooring pontoon, and they sat outside on a wooden bench. For once, all three of them were silent.

Will squeezed Maisie's knee. 'We can visit lots, you know.'

But they never did return to the boatyard. Maisie heard later that a couple with two small children had bought the barge and to go back would be too painful.

Hearing Will's key in the lock always lifted her spirits. She put her arms around his neck.

'You're looking pleased with yourself. What have you been up to?'

'How do two weeks sailing in the Ionian grab you?'

'How come?'

'Well, Greg at work and his wife had booked the trip with another couple. But they've had to pull out because their son is ill, and Greg asked me if we were interested.'

Shamefully, all Maisie could think about was Joe. He was in Greece, and this felt like a way of being closer to him.

'Sounds wonderful. When is it?' Her manner was over-bright as she struggled to shut down her longing for Joe which stubbornly refused to lessen.

Will raised his eyebrows. 'That's one of the difficulties because it's next week. Shouldn't be a problem, should it? You're on holiday, and I've tentatively arranged cover.'

'I guess not, but I don't know anything about sailing. Knowing me, I'll probably get seasick and what about this other couple, Greg and whatever his wife is called? We might not get on with them, and it's pretty intimate sharing a small boat with strangers.'

'Greg's a good guy; you'll like him. I've not met Gilly. She's an interior designer apparently.' He laughed. 'Don't pull that face. I'm sure it'll all be fine.'

Maisie sat in the cockpit of the yacht. Will had been right about Greg; he was lovely and Gilly, although irritatingly scatty, was a laugh especially when she'd had a couple of gin and tonics. Will always saw the best in people; she liked that.

The temperature was in the mid-thirties, and the slight breeze on the back of her neck was a welcome relief. Her legs tingled with the heat, and from time to time, she used the deck shower to hose them off. Several times she had tried reading her book, but her mind kept drifting to Joe. She ached to be with him, yet her brain gnashed and wailed at the thought of the wretched Ronnie. At least the good-looking Spanish guy on the next boat was a welcome distraction.

Next day they prepared to set sail. It was a bit of a hassle getting the food aboard as Will had proved unexpectedly reluctant to embrace the local Greek fare and insisted on buying whatever tinned food was available in the little supermarket. Maisie gritted her teeth. *It was too hot for this.*

'Just try it, you never know. Besides, nobody else wants that stuff.'

Eventually, they left the bustle of Levkas quay behind. There wasn't enough wind to sail so they motored, taking

207

turns to steer. Will picked it up quickly, and when they arrived in Aberlike Bay on the little island of Meganissi, he confidently followed Greg's instructions to let go the anchor.

It was a luxury for Maisie to have time to enjoy her surroundings. Fascinated, she watched the changing mood of the sliding, metallic sea when the calm of the morning gave way to a sparkled ripple as the afternoon breeze set in. It was beautiful, yet despite the company of Will and the others, a blanket of loneliness descended as her longing for Joe grew stronger each day. She wanted to share the magic with him; no one else.

Being moored in the bay was great for people watching and observing the different nationalities at play. One of Maisie's favourite things was going in the dinghy with Will. He was a strong rower and tolerated her desire to be nosy. The Italians were boisterous and full of fun. The slim, tanned youngsters swam like fishes then come evening they would shower copiously on their swimming platform and change into impossibly white T-shirts before trooping off to the taverna to eat. Maisie was aghast at the vast quantity of food set out on the long table and to see the daddy figure and his, no doubt, big wallet, preside over ceremonies with evident pride.

Then, there were the Dutch, smiley and boring with a couple of tolerant, adolescent children in tow. Unusually, according to Greg, there was an American couple who were always busy, busy, busy even in the heat of the day. Greece wakes slowly and late in holiday mode, but these Americans breakfasted in the cockpit soon after seven and their day continued in a fashion of getting jobs done.

The man aboard a small yacht moored next to them caught Maisie's attention mostly because he was tanned and lean. Will, seeing a French flag, asked him in embarrassing French if he was French. *Suisse* was the single word reply. Maybe he didn't indulge in long conversations or didn't speak much English or both.

On the third morning, he engaged in conversation with Will. His English was in fact good, and Maisie learned that he lived aboard all year round. It seemed a solitary life, especially when he described Meganissi in the winter.

Maisie's imagination took over. *Was he hiding from some unwelcome truth? Did he have a wife and children that he'd left behind or perhaps he was a spy in between jobs?* Perhaps she would persuade Greg and Gilly to invite him aboard their boat for a drink. He'd no doubt have some good stories to tell, and he held a certain mystery which was appealing.

Next day, there was a small excitement. One of the boats with a French couple aboard reported a rat on board and said they had been keeping watch for it in the cockpit since early morning. At about ten, they prepared to leave, but when they lifted the lid on the chain locker to pull in the anchor, lo and behold, ratty had taken up residence. Much commotion followed, and Mr Suisse rowed over to advise them. It wasn't at all clear what the advice entailed, but Greg resolved to concoct some rat defences for their boat next night. Apparently, the rats could swim from the shore and climb up the mooring lines, which was most nimble and enterprising in Maisie's view. She didn't much mind live rats but hated the idea of a festering, smelly dead one.

Next morning, they made a dawn start as they had a long passage ahead. Few yachts ever visited the isolated harbour at Marathopoulis put off by the rocky entrance. The harbour breakwater had collapsed during a winter gale. It was also a lee shore; this worried Greg, but they crept in and managed to squeeze alongside a fishing boat at the end of the quay.

After lunch, Greg and Gilly went off to explore leaving Will and Maisie to sunbathe. Not long after they'd gone a battered, red car pulled up with an older man and four younger ones. The old *babas* was Greek, but the others were talking a language that Maisie didn't recognise. Greg, it seemed, had unwittingly moored in their customary afternoon swimming spot. Maisie smiled as they proceeded to swim around the yacht. Then the old boy cheekily climbed on their stainless-steel pulpit to dive off.

As he dived, his feet slipped, and Maisie was worried that he would hurt himself. Then he came along the side deck to where they were sitting in the cockpit and accepted Will's offer of a beer. He told them in passable English that he was a blacksmith and pointed out a workshop across the harbour. He was small and wiry and claimed to be fifty-four but looked ten years older. He wore a pair of black underpants and had an interesting line in conversation.

He asked lots of questions, as is the Greek way, but Maisie was alarmed when he barked at Will, 'Why? Why you do this? Why you come to Greece? Why you fuck this woman?'

Will merely smiled in his tolerant way, but Maisie found the man unnerving. It transpired that he was anti-British and even more anti when it came to Americans. He lived alone he told them but had a son who lived in Argos. He spoke with passion about Greek history and culture and told them about Epidavros – urging them to visit. He banged his chest theatrically at this point saying that anyone who went there would feel calm and good in their heart. He'd learnt English, he said, by watching lots of films at the cinema. One of the lads passed him a big, fat spliff and he sat on the cabin top to smoke it. Soon his manner became more suggestive, and he made sly remarks about Maisie's figure and leered at her breasts which made her feel uncomfortable. Will went in the water for a swim and Babilis, as he was called, joined him. He swam up to Will and splashed him aggressively in the face. Apart from the young lads, there was no one else about, and Greg and Gilly could be ages yet. If it turned unpleasant, Maisie hoped the younger men would

210

help. Urgently, she beckoned to Will to come out of the water. Unhurriedly, he began to climb the stern ladder. *Why could he never see what was happening?*

'What's up?'

'He scares me, Will', she whispered. 'Let's go down below and shut the door. He might get the hint then.'

Thankfully, after a while, the lads drifted away, and Babilis crashed out in his car to snore the afternoon away. When Will and Maisie went ashore later, they passed his chaotic and ramshackle workshop. He had invited them to drink coffee with him and if he hadn't been so threatening it might have been interesting, but she was glad that he wasn't there and relieved that they were moving on next day. His behaviour had unnerved her, and she had felt vulnerable.

Lazy days in the Greek sunshine were helping Maisie to unwind but living on a yacht with three other people was claustrophobic. Little irritations sprang up, and she found herself comparing Will unfavourably with Joe. He was forever cleaning, wiping surfaces then wiping again and was clearly a perfectionist. She knew he found her slapdash at times and he was yet to discover that she was happy to sleep between greying sheets for weeks on end and that cleanliness didn't much bother her. Maddeningly, he also failed to pick up on social cues and never seemed to notice when people didn't want to engage in conversation. This surprised her given his job as a probation officer. These new insights into Will's character made her worry about going home. Will expected her to go back to his flat, but she couldn't shake off her doubts about their relationship in the long term.

The flight from Greece was delayed for three hours and by the time they'd struggled back to Portsmouth on the train they were both tired and irritable. Will had to be back at work the next day, so he took himself off to his study to catch up with some paperwork. Maisie wandered listlessly around the flat; she didn't intend to spend the summer cooped up inside. She longed for the river where there was always something to do and someone to chat to but that would only

211

stir up memories. As her mother was fond of saying, it's always a mistake to go back. She had several weeks of holiday left and hated the idea of returning to work. Although she loved her job, it wasn't the same in the department since Eve had arrived and she was seriously considering looking for another post. Maybe she should move away altogether as Fran had done. Perhaps she could go abroad and do voluntary service, but at heart, she knew that it wasn't for her. Even the idea of moving somewhere in England had lost its appeal. She wasn't independent like Fran, and she needed her friends.

Chapter 31
Joe

Joe sat on the edge of the bed and gazed out over the Sussex countryside. He could see across to the Ouse valley on the other side of the main road. Already, cars had dipped headlights on. It had been a day of leaden skies, windless and depressing. Lying on the burning sand of Agios Georgios beach was becoming a distant memory. The clocks went back the next day; that meant longer dark nights.

He sighed and stretched his legs. He could feel that beat of restlessness settling in again. He and Ronnie should talk about what they were going to do, but he'd been putting it off. They couldn't stay at Hill Farm Cottage much longer. Celia and Paddy had been great to let them stay, but they were both out at work all day, and without a car, Joe felt isolated, which in turn made him moody. A couple of times, he had walked the quarter of a mile down the rough track to the main road and caught the bus to Newhaven where he had sat in a bar by the harbour and attempted to chat to a couple of local fishermen. It had not been an uplifting experience.

It was his turn to cook tonight, so he made a start on a chilli con carne; it was something easy that he didn't have to think about. He was glad to be occupied and for a time was happy chopping onions and garlic. For good measure, he sloshed in some red wine and left the sauce to simmer. He heard John's car bumping its way up the lane and wasn't surprised to see Ronnie with them. John gave him a wave.

'Picked this one up on the way back from Lewes', he grinned, tossing his head in Ronnie's direction.

Joe couldn't be bothered to ask where she'd been all day. At least he could look forward to chatting to Celia and John about their day and sinking a few bottles of their red wine. Soon after eleven, Celia and John disappeared up to bed. Ronnie stretched out on the settee and put her feet in Joe's lap. The wine had made her relaxed and mellow, and there was less tension between them.

'I've done a lot of thinking today,' she began. Uncertainly, she looked down at her glass and twiddled it between her hands. 'I've decided to go to Spain,' she told him bluntly. 'As soon as I can get some money together.'

Joe sat forward and shook her off. 'Spain? Who the hell with?' He looked at her questioningly. 'Spain?'

Ronnie leant over and took a drag on his roll-up, her eyes squinting at him through the smoke.

'There's this mate of mine from Art College. She's been working as a waitress in this place in Brighton, but now she's got a job in a bar in Spain. She reckons there'd be a job in it for me as well.'

Joe didn't ask her how she knew all this. It was evident that she'd been planning it. They sat in silence, and he found himself staring at her. He often stared at people when he was thinking deeply. He poured them both another glass of wine and Ronnie expanded on her plans for Spain.

They ended up talking for hours, something they'd not done in a while, and it became clear that they both wanted different things. Listening to Ronnie, he felt ready to start taking life more seriously and do some growing up. Perhaps he could get back to his graphic design stuff and even get a place of his own. The restlessness, interspersed with lethargy, still lurked but he was surprised to find that he was keen to get going with his fresh start.

He pulled Ronnie closer and gave her a big hug. 'I think Spain's a good idea for you. When do you reckon you'll go?'

'I might go down to Brighton pretty soon if that's ok with you. My mate can put me up, and I'll find a bar job or whatever until we've enough for the ferry fare.'

Joe went to bed, his head spinning with plans. But he couldn't sleep, and the ideas and the energy faded away. He envied Ronnie the certainty of her next step while he only had some vague notions washing around his head. He had no idea where to go from here and once Ronnie went to Brighton he'd have to move on. It was a long time since he'd

214

been on his own. He was back to square one and plagued by the idea that he was twenty-two now with bugger all to show for it.

Ronnie glared at him. 'What's up? You've been bloody morose for days. Even John and Celia are fed up with you. I thought you were ok about me going to Spain.'

'It's not always about you, you know.' He walked off up the lane beside the farm. He didn't even have the energy for a row and just kept walking.

He and Ronnie were finished, so he wasn't leaving anything behind. He was used to sleeping rough; he'd done it before, and he knew his way around the system when it came to blagging an extra night in a hostel and where to go for free food. None of it held the slightest appeal, but there wasn't much choice. He wondered if Maisie was still living on the barge; it was a sweet thought to turn up with a cheery smile. *Hi gorgeous, I'm back. Did you miss me?* He groaned aloud. What a ridiculous notion, there was no way he could mess her up any more than he had already. He didn't have the energy for all that stuff, and it was as much as he could do right now to put one foot in front of the other.

After a few uncomfortable nights sleeping in the shelters on Brighton seafront, he decided to go back to Bath for a while. It was November and too cold to sleep outside for much longer. He was scared that he was going to revert to the stinking wreck he'd been at nineteen. There was no way that he could let that happen.

He knew all too well that there was no glamour or excitement in being homeless, just the sheer tedium of attempting to survive. He'd already got a bladder infection as well as conjunctivitis and an overwhelming despair that nothing could alleviate. He lay on the narrow, iron bed. At least he had a bed in the hostel for tonight. He tried to make plans to get to Bath, but he couldn't think straight. The guy in the next bed was snoring; it wasn't so much the noise but the irregularity that disturbed Joe. He would stop breathing for

215

several minutes, then his whole body jerked, and the snoring would resume. Exasperated, Joe got up from the bed and leaned across.

'For fuck's sake, mate. Your snoring is doing my fucking head in.' Joe expected some angry response, but the guy just grunted and rolled over on to his side. Thankfully, the snoring stopped, and after a few minutes, he sat up.

'Fancy a smoke? I'm Billy by the way. I'll never get back to sleep now, no thanks to you.' He handed Joe a thin roll-up. 'How did you end up here?'

Joe told him about his plans to go to Bath in the morning and stay at his mum's.

'How's that going to solve anything? Believe me, mate; going back's not the answer.'

'I guess I've run out of options and it's a different ball game in winter. What about you? You planning to sleep rough over the winter?'

Billy was silent. 'Who knows,' he said eventually.

Next morning, after two thick slices of white bread spread with marg and a cup of strong tea, Joe collected up his stuff. He walked up the hill past the station, and once he was on the A27, he started hitching. *Anything heading west would do.* He walked for a mile or so, but the rain was torrential. The crepe sole of his desert boots had parted company with the rest, and his feet were cold and soggy. Already he could feel blisters. He should have scrounged a pair of socks at the hostel. His dark curls were plastered to his forehead in the wet, and he was beyond miserable. But it was either stick it out and try to get to Bath or turn back and spend another night, cold and wet, in the seafront shelter. His jeans would take forever to dry out in this weather, and he'd have to chuck the shoes as they'd had it. That would mean a visit to the Sally Army hostel to see if they could fix him up with a new pair. Just then, a Morris Minor pulled up, and the passenger door swung open. Joe jogged the few steps and peered in. He was surprised to see a girl on her own. She smiled at him.

216

'Where are you heading? I'm going as far as Arundel if that helps.'

'Arundel would be great,' Joe replied as he slid into the seat beside her. She told him she was a student in Brighton and was off to see her parents in Arundel for Sunday lunch.

'Do you often pick up hitchers when you're on your own?' Joe inquired.

'I know I shouldn't, but if the person looks ok, I sometimes stop. And you did look a bit bedraggled.'

The car had an efficient heater, and he began to warm up. He'd had a shower in the hostel that morning, but he'd not washed his clothes for weeks. He shuffled his feet inside the sodden shoes wondering if he smelled. But the girl was polite enough not to say anything and chatted away obviously glad of the company.

After Arundel, a lorry stopped for him. It was empty, and the driver was on his way to pick up a load of cauliflowers from the docks in Portsmouth. He didn't speak except to pass him the odd fag, which was gratefully received. As they neared Portsmouth, Joe was nostalgic for the place and apprehensive at the same time. *Where Maisie was now? Had she stayed on the barge or moved back to the city to be nearer to her friends and her job at the university?* It had been great when they were first together. She was always laughing back then. He missed her laugh and her ready smile. It would be so good to see her again, but that wasn't fair to her. He knew how hurt she'd been when he took off with Ronnie. Long before that in truth, when he'd begun to withdraw emotionally from her, hemmed in by the demands of domesticity.

He asked the lorry driver to drop him off before he turned down towards the docks; that way, he could avoid Portsmouth altogether. He took off his rucksack and sat on a wall outside a chemist's shop. He re-lit the butt end of a cigarette that the driver had given him and tried to decide what to do next. It was gone two o'clock and would be dark in a couple of hours. He still had a long way to go, and unless he got a long lift, he wasn't going to reach Bath today. Hitching after dark was impossible. Maybe he'd stop off in Southampton. There might be some old mates still around who wouldn't mind if he crashed on their floor for a night.

Portsmouth to Southampton was twenty miles or so, and he didn't have to wait long. The driver looked in his fifties; it was hard to tell, and despite the cold weather he only wore a white shirt; his jacket was slung across the back seat. Joe hesitated before getting in the car somewhat suspicious of the guy's motives, but he turned out to be ok and dropped him at the city centre. Joe walked down to Ben's old place opposite the docks. He had no idea if he still lived there, it was worth a try. But the girl who answered the door said she didn't know where Ben was and hadn't seen him since the summer.

Joe had no option but to find somewhere to sleep rough for the night. He wandered back towards the centre and sat in the foyer of the cinema until they kicked him out. He tried to remember his way around Southampton from the time he used to hang out with Ronnie and her mates. He hadn't eaten anything since the bread and marg this morning, so he went down the lane behind the hotel in the Bargate. Maybe he'd find something chucked in the tidy bin. He dug his torch out. That was the one thing he'd never be without now. It made it easier to find the best place to kip or spot half a pasty chucked in the bin. He nicked the batteries, usually from Smiths. They were on a stand near the busy checkout and easy to slip into your pocket. Joe rarely stole food and never cigarettes, but batteries were his comfort blanket. The hotel bin was a no go on this occasion as two bar staff were outside having a smoke in their break.

He decided to head back to the centre and start begging. This wasn't a bad time to catch the office workers having a sneaky drink in the pub before heading home for the evening. He found a place to sit outside one of the big chain pubs. By nine o'clock he had enough for a bacon roll and a coffee from the van at the top of the precinct.

Chapter 32
Maisie

Maisie looked up from her marking distracted by the low spring sunshine that sent shafts of golden light through the lounge window. She loved this place. In Will's flat, there had been too many reminders of Fran, and it had never felt like home. She opened the window; the vanilla scent of clematis that rampaged over the old trellis wafted into the room, and she could hear the lusty song of the blackbirds.

The owner of Normandy Cottage was a wealthy American who used the place during the sailing season. He was due back for the start of Cowes week, and Maisie and Will had taken the place on a six-month furnished let. She heard the throaty sound of Will's old MG turn into the drive and went out to meet him. He'd bought the car from his friend Mike, convincing him that with another baby on the way it wasn't the car for a family man. Will eased his long legs from the driver's seat.

'You look happy.'

She smiled up at him. 'Who wouldn't be? It's such a beautiful afternoon.'

They walked round to the back door where an ancient, wooden table and bench stood on the old, brick tiled yard.

'It won't be long before we can eat out here in the evenings or have friends over for an alfresco Sunday lunch.' She linked her arm through his. 'Just look at that view.'

The back of the cottage looked out on to a beautiful, old meadow.

'I think I saw a hare over there this morning.'

She ran up the wooden stairs leading to what the agent had described as the deck. It had a ship-like rail and wooden flooring, and from here the views were breath-taking. On one side, beyond the meadow, lay the salt marshes and beyond that, the waters of the Solent. On the other side, you could see across to the entrance of the Lymington River. Even at this time of the year, at weekends, scores of boats could be

219

seen coming around 'Jack-in-the-basket' which marked the entrance to the river. Today, there were fishing boats; car ferries to the Isle of Wight; the occasional hardy yachtsman and dinghy sailors from the yacht club out for winter racing. Maisie leaned on the rail with the low sun glinting on her hair.

'This will be a fantastic spot to work when the weather's warm enough.'

Will joined her on the deck, and for a time they stood silently enjoying their little world.

'Let's go inside and have a drink. I've got some news,' Will announced.

She curled her legs under her on the squashy, old, leather sofa. 'Come on then; don't keep me in suspense.'

Will poured them both a gin and tonic and sank down beside her. 'Well, a guy at work is moving back to Cornwall to be nearer to his parents. That leaves a vacancy for the senior post, and he's hinted to me that it might be a good move for me to apply.'

'Wow. I'm impressed. Do you think you stand a chance?'

'I don't see why not.' He poked her in the ribs. 'O ye of little faith. Seriously though, the extra money will help if we want to put down a deposit for a mortgage. How do you fancy our own place?'

Alarm clanged in Maisie's head. *I don't want this. Why can't we just live in the moment?* She struggled to speak. He was expecting an answer, and she didn't want to hurt him. Instead, forcing a smile, she went into the kitchen to start the supper.

She had a restless night. Last night's conversation had thrown her. She didn't like being forced into thinking about their future together. They had to leave the cottage in July, but she needed to take it day by day. *If Will got his promotion, would he expect more of a commitment from her, marriage even?* She wasn't ready. Commitment to Will would be like finally severing herself from Joe, and she couldn't do it. Yet she owed it to Will to give him an answer.

Anxious to avoid waking Will, she slid out of bed; she pulled on her jeans, grabbed Will's sweatshirt, and padded downstairs. She needed some time on her own. She made a mug of tea and curled up in the armchair. She sniffed the sleeve of the sweatshirt; it smelt of clean washing. When Joe had left, she had found an old pair of his Levi's – they smelt of cigarettes and pubs and sex. She had held them to her face as she lay in bed at night and sobbed. She couldn't marry Will; it wouldn't be fair to him.

Even now, she spent too much of her time wondering where Joe was. She couldn't help it. The last she'd heard from him was a postcard from Florence six months ago. She had endured six months of this stupid agonising. Lily had her address, she'd made sure of that, but it was up to Joe to contact her. Maybe Lily had told him that she was with Will now and he'd decided it was best to let go.

The creaking floorboards told her that Will was up and about, so she made him a coffee. He didn't mention the new job.

It was May before Will mentioned it again.

'When did you say your term ends?' he asked one evening.

'End of June or thereabouts – why?' She was surprised that he was drinking Scotch instead of his usual wine.

'We'll have to move out of here before then. It makes sense to start looking soon. I don't know about you, but I'm fed up with all the travelling. I'd be happy to move back to Portsmouth. What do you think?'

She was aware of his penetrating gaze but said nothing.

'I guess it's about time I got a foot on the mortgage ladder and with the new job I can afford it, but I want you there with me. I want us to get married and buy a place of

221

our own.' He walked over to the window and stared out at the garden. 'Say something; talk to me, Maisie.'

But she couldn't look at him. She stared down at the carpet, her hair covering her face.

'I'm scared, Will; all this frightens me. It's such a big commitment. You know what I'm like and I'm worried I'll let you down.'

He cupped her chin in his hand and raised her head to look at him. He was smiling. 'I think that's a risk I'm prepared to take; besides, I'm good at handling you, remember.'

She pulled a face at him.

'Seriously, Maisie, I don't care about the risks. All marriages are a risk, but I want us to be together, and I'm not going to lose you this time.'

The trap door banged shut, and there she was. Bereft at losing Joe; mired with guilt for being dishonest with Will and feeling wretched.

The house they bought was near her old flat. It looked like a typical two up two down but had a third bedroom in the attic and a reasonably sized garden. Will was keen to knock the small lounge and dining room into one through room, but Maisie found it difficult to summon up much enthusiasm. *Maybe she'd feel differently after they came back from holiday?* She couldn't bring herself to think of it as a honeymoon. They had set the wedding date for a Saturday in the middle of July while they would still be living in the cottage, which would be the perfect place for the reception.

'So, who are we going to invite?' Will enquired.

She frowned, thinking about the pile of exam scripts that were spread out on the table in front of her, but Will looked so eager.

'Ok. Let's open a bottle, and we can make a list.' Surprised that the idea excited her, she extracted a clean sheet of paper from the pile. 'There's family, obviously. Just immediate family?' She looked questioningly at Will.

'Oh god yes, we don't want sundry aunts and uncles or cousins we hardly recognise.'

'Good, that's agreed then. Same goes for friends; I fancy a small do with just the people we are close to.'

She began her list and wrote mum and dad, Richard, and Steph, who was her brother's new girlfriend. She looked up with a big grin on her face.

'I hope Rich and Steph will be able to keep their hands off one another. Do you remember when they stayed the weekend with us?'

'Indeed, I do. They must have been at it for hours, and I swear he had his hand in her knickers in the restaurant.'

Maisie laughed. 'I know; I can't believe how much he's changed since he split up with Lynne. He used to be so strait-laced, and now he's lost all his sexual inhibitions. It's not just Steph either; he was just the same with the previous one. I think it's sweet in a weird way. I hope it lasts with Steph; she's good fun.'

She chewed her pen for a few minutes before returning to the business of composing the guest list. She added Jocelyn and Simon to the list. They were Will's parents. She had met them a couple of times and was surprised at how posh they were. Their old, thatched cottage had once been a bakery and was in a village near Winchester. Jocelyn reflected the county image. She was slim and smartly dressed, with a powdered complexion and tightly waved dark blond hair. Simon Stevens was a retired RAF officer. Maisie couldn't remember his exact rank, but she knew it was high up. Then there were Rachel and Suzanna, Will's younger sisters. They were spoilt rotten, but despite the plummy accents they were fun to have around. Next, she wrote down Chris, who was her oldest and closest friend and her family then she added Shaun and Kay from work. She paused for a moment, tapping her pen on the table.

'I know, Sally, my old flatmate and her new bloke. I'd love them to come. Here.' She slid the list across to him. 'See what you think. Anyone special you want to invite?'

Will read down the list. 'I'm not sure if they'd be able to come up from Devon, but I'd like to invite Mike Green and his wife.'

'Good idea, it will be nice to see him again.' She added their names to the list. 'I make that about eighteen, give or take a few offspring. Anyone else we've forgotten?'

They fell silent, and Maisie guessed that he was thinking about Fran. It would be great to see her, but it was an awkward situation. It was the same with Lily; Maisie hadn't seen much of her since she split up with Joe, but there was still a bond of friendship between them. Maisie kept thinking of other people to invite then remembering that they were friends from when she was with Joe and were not Will's friends. There was Mac, for instance, dear old Mac, and Peter and Eddie from the boatyard. She wanted to share her day with all those people. Close to tears, she finished her wine and stood up.

'I think I'll have a walk. You don't mind, do you? Just as far as the sea wall. It's such a beautiful evening.'

She walked down the lane from Normandy Cottage. Two male blackbirds were singing across the rooftops, marking out their territories. She stooped to smell the heavy lilac blooms. She would miss this place. Where the lane swung right towards the main road, she turned left and climbed over the stile. The path towards the sea led across the salt marshes and consisted of a series of wooden walkways with tall grasses either side. Maisie brushed away the cloud of midges that danced in front of her. When she arrived at the sea wall, she gasped with pleasure. The sun was setting, and the Solent shimmered a bright orange gold. She eased herself up on top of the flint wall and breathed in the salty air. Two or three fishing boats and a few yachts were making their way back to harbour before nightfall, but the foreshore was deserted.

She attempted to marshal her thoughts. Writing the guest list had made the whole wedding thing seem more real. She shouldn't be having doubts, but the guilt remained. She

224

adored Will; he was kind and funny, and she wanted to be with him. But she knew she didn't love him in the all-consuming way that she loved Joe. Will loved her; she was sure of that, but there was an imbalance in their relationship. She jumped down from the wall, her mind in turmoil. Perhaps lots of women experienced uncertainty before their wedding, and Will would be devastated if she told him she didn't want to go through with it. *Why couldn't they have gone on living together and take one step at a time as they had been doing?* Marriage was such a big and irrevocable decision.

Back at the cottage, she found him whisking up cheese omelettes for supper.

'Hungry?' he enquired.

She buried her face against his broad back. 'Now you come to mention it; it must be all that sea air,' she replied.

'You smell of coffee' he teased. 'Coffee and shampoo'.

The next few weeks were chaotic, leaving little time for reflection. Having exchanged contracts on the new house, they turned their attention to carpets and curtains. Then they had to start packing up their things from the cottage and amidst all this Maisie was rushed off her feet at work. There were moderation meetings to attend and course materials to be written for the next term as well as interviewing new students.

They drove over to Pebbles on the Wednesday before the wedding.

'Come on, then. Tell us about the honeymoon.' Kay demanded.

'We've bought return flights from Gatwick to Athens, but that's as far as the planning goes,' Maisie replied. 'We're going to get a ferry from there to one of the islands in the Cyclades to start with.'

'So where will you stay if you've nowhere booked?'

'We're taking a small tent. There are a few campsites, but we won't stay in the same place. You can hop between the islands on the ferries, and we intend to see as much as we can in three weeks,' Will told her.

'Not exactly romantic though, is it?' Kay raised her eyebrows at him. 'Not the height of luxury our Maisie deserves.'

'Well, I think it's romantic,' Maisie replied. 'Sun, sand and no hassles, what more could we want?' She drained her glass and smiled. 'See you on Saturday then.'

Next morning, Maisie bought lots of treats from the deli in Lymington, and they enjoyed a long and leisurely meal. Will raised his glass.

'Our last night in Normandy Cottage.' He took a slug of wine. 'And here's to our new home and to married life.'

'Don't have any more wine; you're growing sentimental in your old age.' She laughed as she swirled around, clutching her glass. *Completion day tomorrow and we pick up the keys.* Her heart pounded with anxiety. They were going to move in the boxed-up belongings, but there wouldn't be any time for unpacking as they were booked on a flight to Athens straight after the reception. Maisie's mind whirled with the sheer logistics of it all. Thankfully, Chris would be down on Saturday morning. She could do with some moral support.

'You look beautiful', Chris declared. 'Like a beautiful sixteen-year-old.'

Chris' parents had suggested that Maisie got ready at their house as they'd already moved out of the cottage and the new house was empty except for the cardboard boxes.

'This is pretty.' Chris helped to pin a simple veil attached to a white band decorated with freesias. This was no easy task amidst Maisie's clouds of pale gold hair.

'I bet Will looks the business in a suit,' Chris continued. 'I love to see a man in a nice suit. Very sexy.'

'Are you two ready up there?' Maisie's mother called from downstairs.

Chris's dad had offered to drive them all to the register office. Maisie's mouth was dry, and her heart was racing. But nerves soon turned to amusement thanks to her father.

'Dad, what are you doing?' She clung to his arm as he began hopping on one foot.

'Stone in my shoe.' He grinned at her and proceeded to remove one shoe, which he shook vigorously to remove the offending stone.

As they came into the room, people were turning and smiling at her. *What am I doing?* She took her place next to Will at the front. They'd decided against having bridesmaids or a best man; too much hassle they agreed. Maisie's father was in charge of the ring, and when the time came, he flicked it out of his pocket with such gusto that it rolled ceremoniously across the thick green carpet. The guests watched mesmerised in case it disappeared beneath a piece of furniture, and there was a collective sigh of relief when it circled and came to a stop at Will's feet. He scooped it up with a chuckle which made everyone laugh.

They had hired Pebbles to cater for the reception. The owners knew them well, and when they arrived back at the cottage a scrumptious buffet had been laid out. But Maisie wasn't hungry, and it was all becoming a blur. She kept trying to remind herself to enjoy the day.

Her brother came up and gave her a big hug. 'You looked beautiful, and the ceremony was perfect; it was special without too much fuss.'

'Thanks, Rich; trust Dad to keep everyone amused.'

He smiled. 'Sorry, you haven't met Susie before, have you?'

Richard's new girlfriend kissed Maisie. 'Thank you so much for inviting me.'

Maisie took her arm. She couldn't keep up with Richard. *Whatever happened to Steph?*

'Let's get some more wine,' she laughed. 'Tell me all about yourself. What do you do, Susie?'

227

'I'm an interpreter. It's mostly police work for the Chinese community.'

Maisie was intrigued. 'How come?'

'My father was a diplomat with the Foreign Office, and I was brought up in Hong Kong,' Susie explained.

When Richard returned, Maisie drifted off to circulate with their guests. Harnessing her natural nosiness, she discovered that Will's youngest sister Rachel had just finished her 'A' levels and was off to Cornwall the following day with a bunch of surfing friends. Suzanna had another year to go before her finals at Bristol where she was studying Maths.

'Bright girl, your sister,' Maisie told Will later.

In lieu of a best man, Chris, emboldened by several glasses of Chablis, stood up and regaled them with some risqué titbits from Maisie's past. She turned to Will.

'You jolly well look after this woman, you hear,' she demanded. They all laughed and raised their glasses in a toast.

A wall of hot air engulfed them as they emerged from Athens airport. It was six-thirty and barely light. There was an enormous queue for the bus, so they got a taxi to Piraeus.

'God. It's hot,' Will complained. 'I think we should make sure we can get on a ferry before we have breakfast. I've never seen so many people.'

Maisie, who was both tired and starving hungry, tried not to show her irritation. *Why did he always have to be so cautious?*

Without too much trouble they bought tickets for a ferry to Paros.

'Come on, let's head for that bench. At least it's in the shade.' Maisie pushed her way through the throng of backpackers and dumped her rucksack. 'If you look after this lot, I'll go below and get a cold drink and a sandwich or something.'

Shaking off her grumpy mood was hard. They'd been travelling for hours and now had another six hours on the ferry. She longed to lay down on the bench and sleep, but there wasn't room.

When they eventually arrived at Paros, they were thrust into pandemonium as motorbikes weaved precariously between the backpackers and cars unloading from the ferry. Maisie hitched her backpack into a more comfortable position. She'd have to get used to carrying it. Someone grabbed her arm, and she spun round to see a wrinkled Greek guy.

'*Domatia, domatia*,' he shouted above the noise.

'Just ignore him.' Will looked anxious.

'What about that?' Maisie pointed to a minibus advertising Koula Camping.

They paid for one night, and the guy at reception handed them a loo roll. They wandered across the parched, beaten earth in search of a suitable space. Will started fussing about where to pitch their tent.

'If we have it facing this way, we won't get too much sun on the tent in the mornings.' He kicked away a few of the larger stones and, with admirable efficiency, erected their little blue and red tent. Straightening up, he looked at his watch.

'It's nearly two now; let's leave this lot and find a decent taverna for some lunch. I don't know about you, but I'm bloody starving.'

Maisie perked up at this. 'Oh, yes. I'd like that.'

'What about all our bags? Will it be ok to leave them?'

'Stop worrying about everything. We'll take the passports and money, but the rest will be safe. It's different from England where you can't leave anything unlocked.'

The campsite was beside the scruffy, town beach. It was siesta time, and the beach was crowded with locals and children enjoying the clear water. They found the least touristy looking taverna and ordered a Greek salad and two cold beers. Then, as the effects of their travelling kicked in, they made their way back to the tent for a sleep.

When Maisie woke up, Will had disappeared. She stretched, feeling sticky and uncomfortable. By now, it was evening, and the camp was beginning to come to life. In the nearest two tents, a group of Italian boys were getting ready for the night ahead. With much loud banter, conducted in their melodic Italian accents, they went back and forth to the shower block, hanging up towels and endlessly combing their sleek, black hair.

Maisie had begun to wonder where on earth Will had got to when he appeared with his beach towel slung over his shoulder.

'I've just been for a quick swim to freshen up,' he told her. 'You were flat out, so I decided to leave you. Had a good rest?'

She nodded and bent to pick up her towel and wash bag. She would have liked a swim herself, and he made her feel like some toddler needing an afternoon nap. *No, that was unfair.*

She smiled at him. 'I'm going to try the showers. Then let's walk into town.'

Maisie let the cool water run down her back. With the prospect of a few weeks in the sun, drinking cold beer and eating lots of lovely food, she resolved to cheer up. She wrapped her big beach towel around her, slipped on flip-flops and weaved her way through the maze of tents. Will was lying on top of his sleeping bag, reading a paperback. She rubbed her hair dry and pulled a comb through it before the curls took over and then changed into a clean white t-shirt and denim skirt. Despite the cold shower, she was already hot again, and the denim seemed thick.

It was gone eight, but the scruffy town beach was still crowded with families and groups of youngsters. Maisie grabbed hold of Will's arm. It was a nightmare crossing the road as a stream of mopeds zipped back and forth.

230

'It looks a bit precarious; they don't seem to bother with crash helmets.' Will remarked.

'It looks like fun to me.' Maisie smiled at the sight of the bronzed young Greeks dressed in shorts and T-shirts. They had to step out of the way of one scooter with two adults and two children all on the one bike.

In a beachside bar, they treated themselves to ouzo with lots of ice before wandering up the back streets in search of a taverna that was away from the touristy area. In a narrow street, they came across the tables and chairs of Georgios Taverna spread across the road.

'This looks hopeful; it seems to be mostly Greeks eating here. What do you think?' Will asked.

There was no menu, but the smiling waiter beckoned to them before Maisie had a chance to agree.

'Come, come with me. I show you our Greek kitchen. Very good,' he declared.

They followed him into the back of the taverna, where he reeled off what was on offer. There were large metal trays of moussaka and pasticcio, its pasta equivalent; next, he lifted the lids of giant saucepans containing chicken in lemon sauce; lamb kleftiko, a type of stew and meatballs in tomato sauce.

'Or you can have something from the grill. Very good pork chops, chicken souvlaki, whatever you like,' the waiter finished.

Maisie sighed with delight as she breathed in the pungent aromas. They decided to share a moussaka as well as the lamb and ordered a Greek salad to go with it plus a litre of white wine that arrived in a red metal jug.

'This is just delicious.' Maisie licked her fingers. 'I'm stuffed, and more than a little pissed,' she laughed.

Georgios was a popular place and, although it was after eleven, more hopeful diners arrived. They were never turned away. Instead, waiters appeared carrying more tables over the heads of their customers, which they set up further along the street.

231

It was after midnight when they wandered back to
Koula Camping. The place was beginning to come to life as
youngsters of all nationalities laughed and called to each
other. Some had guitars and sang while their friends sat on
rush mats on the hard ground, drinking beer and smoking.
Will lit a coil to keep away the mosquitoes, and they
stretched out on top of their sleeping bags. He took hold of
her hand.

'This place has a real buzz about it.'

'I know, and I just love it.' Maisie grinned.

It wasn't the most romantic of venues for the first night
of their honeymoon. Neither of them had expected the
campsites to be so crowded and it wasn't until nearly dawn
that Will pulled her into his arms. Aware of the three young
Greeks in the next tent, they tried to be as quiet as possible,
which added to the intensity of their lovemaking. Maisie
climaxed fiercely and clung to Will as the throbbing
aftermath of her orgasm subsided. She buried her face in his
neck, ashamed. *How could she have been thinking about
Joe?*

Over the next few days, they explored the island. They
hired a local boat and motored to a beautiful beach across the
bay. The following day they rented a car and drove out to
explore the windy side of the island where the beaches were
full of young surfers. Then to the north with picturesque,
little harbours where a more upmarket holiday crowd sipped
cocktails all afternoon in the numerous waterfront bars.

After four days, they decided to move on to the nearby
island of Naxos. Feeling like old hands who knew the ropes,
they jumped straight on a minibus going to Plakka Camping.
This was less manic than the Paros site and was set back
from the vast and beautiful expanse of sandy beach at Agios
Anna. The woven bamboo canopy overhead offered plenty
of shade and creaked peaceful in the afternoon breeze.
Plakka was more isolated and had its own taverna run by the
wife and mother of the owner. Each morning they prepared

simple but delicious dishes, which were served throughout the day. Will's favourite was the *briam*, the Greek equivalent of ratatouille. But for Maisie, the highlight was breakfast, which consisted of a large glass dish piled high with the thickest, creamiest yoghurt topped with lashings of juicy, fresh peach.

Their days assumed a pattern. A cool shower was followed by breakfast then they spent the mornings on the beach, swimming in the sparkling water, sunbathing and reading. Each day, a tanned, fair-haired boy came along the beach selling delicious doughnuts and sometimes there was an old man on a donkey laden with baskets of grapes and watermelon. In the afternoons, they slept. It was too hot to do anything else.

On their last evening, they went into town in the minibus. They chose a glitzy bar where the swinging seats were piled high with squashy cushions. Maisie sipped her watermelon cocktail and gazed up at the velvet, starry sky. Then they wandered past the ferry port where they were assailed by brightly lit shops, offering gold and silver jewellery or bowls carved from the ubiquitous olive wood.

'What do you think we should do about eating tonight?' Will asked. 'I don't know about you, but I fancy gyros and eating it as we go along.'

Maisie looked at her watch; they had to be back to meet the minibus at ten. Her face broke into a broad grin, and she linked her arm through his.

'I saw a place selling chocolate pancakes by the harbour. Let's have one of those as well.'

Next morning, they needed to be at the harbour by eight to get the ferry to their last stop, the much smaller island of Koufonisia. Yannis, the campsite owner, had booked a taxi for them. Maisie knelt on the dusty ground her head bent in concentration. You had to be meticulous, she had discovered, to repack a rucksack. She had dreamed about Joe again last night and was struggling to shake off the image. Tanned and lean he had been frolicking in the sea with a beautiful girl. It wasn't Ronnie, *and it wasn't me either*, she thought glumly. She closed her eyes overwhelmed with longing to feel Joe's warm body beside her and to touch his face. A wave of disloyalty swept over her.

'You about ready? It's almost seven.' Will swung his rucksack up on his back.

Her mood lifted as she was swept up in the practicalities of buying tickets and food for the journey. *Skopelitis* was a much smaller ferry, enabling it to get closer inshore and they spent much of the journey hanging on the deck rail and marvelling at the Greek landscape. The boat stopped off at several islands; Iraklia, Shinoussa, Amorgos - Maisie loved the names which were so full of history and mystery.

Koufonissia was a delight; further south it was even hotter than Naxos and Paros. As they trudged over the blistering white sand, they passed several beautiful naked girls stretched out asleep on rush mats. Maisie was struck once again by how safe it was in Greece. In the ramshackle taverna, the clientele looked more akin to old-fashioned hippies than the typical backpacking crowd. One guy caught Maisie's attention. He had long, fair hair and was dressed in loose white trousers and a white, embroidered kaftan. A blond little girl danced beside him, and a beautiful, dark-haired woman held his hand. They were all barefoot and looked so happy and at ease that Maisie envied them.

That night Will made love to her with a rough urgency. She wondered if he had somehow picked up on her earlier mood and suppressed feelings for Joe. *Or even that she secretly found him a dull companion and longed for excitement; but was that even true any longer?*

Maisie decided to take a break from unpacking boxes as the reality of being back in England was sinking in. She sat on the sturdiest looking box and sipped her coffee. They had so little furniture between them, which made the place seem bare. Even Will's antique Pembroke table and chairs plus a

234

dilapidated leather armchair were still at his parent's house. All she had acquired were a collection of lamps and cushions. They'd bought a new corner settee, which was being delivered on Saturday and the previous owner had sold them a gas cooker and fridge. Her parents had offered to buy them a new double bed as a wedding present, but they hadn't had time to choose one yet and had been sleeping on a blow-up mattress borrowed from Shaun.

Will had gone straight back to work the day after they arrived home. Maisie inspected her bare legs; her tan was fading after only five days. Greece seemed a distant memory but at least she still had several weeks before being sucked into the new academic term and she certainly wouldn't miss the daily commute from Lymington.

She abandoned the unpacking for the moment and climbed the narrow stairs. The house was a strange configuration with two storeys at the front and three at the back. Maisie looked out of the window in the small attic bedroom. She could see a little boy playing in the garden next door. Their own garden had a patch of grass that needed cutting and an old shed at the bottom. She looked forward to doing a bit of gardening. At Normandy Cottage a gardener came and cut the grass and kept it tidy for the owner and this was the first time that she had her own bit of land. They had decided to sleep in the smaller back bedroom; it seemed cosier and looked out onto the garden and the two large sycamore trees at the end. The woman next door came to hang some washing out. She saw Maisie and gave a smile and a wave. This gave Maisie a sense of belonging and galvanised her into action. She made short work of unpacking the remaining boxes and propped her treasured photos on various mantelpieces and window ledges which made the house look more like a home.

After supper Maisie a call on the new landline made her jump. After the call she replaced the receiver with a frown.

'What's up?' Will asked. 'Who was that on the phone?'

'Hmmm?' Her mind was elsewhere. 'Oh, that was Lily. She's had a postcard from Ronnie to say that she's coming back from Spain.'

Will raised his eyebrows. 'That's a surprise. I thought she was pretty settled out there.'

'Seems not.' Maisie paused to consider Ronnie's return. After all, it was Ronnie who had taken her beloved Joe away from her. This wasn't strictly true or fair to Ronnie because when they left England, they had both tried to persuade Maisie to go with them on their trip to Europe. But she had been scared. Scared to leave the security of her lecturing job plus she knew deep down that she'd already lost Joe. Sadly, what had been so exciting in the beginning had just fizzled out. She had never managed to put her finger on the reason why this had happened. Maybe she hadn't been enough to keep him interested.

'Why is she telling you now?' Will enquired.

Maisie gave him a rueful smile. 'Ah, that's easy. Ronnie has just rung her to say that she's been given a council flat.' She paused. 'Ronnie's back in Southampton.'

'Blimey.' He downed a slug of Scotch. 'How did she swing that?'

'Oh, I don't imagine it's so hard when you have a child.' She sounded harsh and was close to tears. *Could the child be Joe's?*

Next morning, she rang Lily. She wanted Ronnie's address and used some pretext about having some clothes she might find useful. She wrote down the address and after lunch drove to Southampton. She parked her car outside the block of flats – Ronnie was on the first floor. She pressed the doorbell wondering what on earth she was going to say; Ronnie would no doubt be curious as to why she was on her doorstep. It was some time before Ronnie came to the door, and Maisie was shocked at how pale and thin she was.

Ronnie frowned at her. 'What are you doing here? Is it Joe? Has something happened to Joe?' She spoke rapidly, her voice showing concern.

Maisie put her hand on Ronnie's arm. 'No, no, you're alright. It's nothing like that. Lily told me you were back, and I thought I'd pop round and see how you were.'

Ronnie opened the door wider. 'Do you want to come in? Have a coffee or something?'

'Yeah, if you've got time, that would be good.'

Maisie followed Ronnie down the corridor and into the lounge. A grubby toddler, pale and skinny like Ronnie, was standing by a low glass-topped table. She had wispy light brown hair and a runny nose. Her mouth and nose were smudged with black, and Maisie watched as she dipped her fingers into the overflowing metal ashtray and smeared her face with cigarette ash.

Ronnie grabbed the child and swung her into the air. 'God, you mucky little oik. Let's get you cleaned up.' She disappeared into the kitchen and returned with three mugs of coffee.

'Laurie's here,' she told Maisie. 'You remember him from the boatyard? He used to live further up the river under the railway bridge.'

Maisie heard the lavatory chain, and Laurie appeared. She did remember him but couldn't work out why he was here in Ronnie's flat. He put his coffee mug down on the table, sank into one of the two old armchairs, and proceeded to make a roll-up. The child pottered over and stood solemnly watching him at work.

'What's her name?' Maisie asked.

'Samantha,' Ronnie told her.

Maisie longed to ask who her father was, but that was out of the question, and Ronnie obviously wasn't going to be forthcoming.

'How old is she?' Maisie persisted, although she already knew the answer.

'Fourteen months aren't you, Sam?' She drew the child on to her lap.

The three of them chatted for a few more minutes, and Maisie and Laurie reminisced about life on the river. Then, she finished her coffee and stood up to go.

'Do you ever hear or see anything of Joe?' she found herself saying.

Ronnie shook her head. 'No, last I heard he was dossing in Brighton.'

Maisie's heart was beating fast. *Perhaps it meant he wasn't the child's father*. She didn't think she could bear it if he were.

She forced a smile. 'I got married to Will. Did you know?'

Ronnie shook her head, seemingly disinterested. Or maybe she doesn't have the energy, thought Maisie. She stood up.

'Thanks for the coffee' she told Ronnie. 'And it was lovely to meet you.' She patted the little girl on the head. 'Bye, Laurie', she called from the front door. 'It was nice to see you again.'

When she was back in her car, it dawned on her. Embarrassment flooded over her. *Oh, God,* she groaned. *You stupid woman.* It was obvious why Laurie had been at the flat. No wonder they'd taken so long to open the door. She'd interrupted them. Lily had once hinted that Ronnie had made ends meet when she was living in Spain by working as a prostitute. Maisie was angry with herself for being so naive. No wonder the poor kid was filthy dirty; she'd no doubt been left to her own devices. Not for the first time, she hated Ronnie. She decided not to mention to Will that she'd been to see her. She started the car. *Yuk! Laurie was twice Ronnie's age.*

Chapter 33
Ronnie

Ronnie had paid the young girl upstairs a couple of quid to babysit. Usually, she had a reciprocal arrangement with her mate Sharon. They took it in turns to look after the kids while the other was working, but Sharon was in hospital with pneumonia, and her mum had taken the children back with her.

Ronnie stood in the ladies' loo staring in the mirror. She had dark circles beneath her eyes and looked gaunt. Without someone to mind Sam regularly, it would be complicated, and money was tight. She was in a dilemma. She preferred working through word of mouth. It was safer that way. She sighed and applied some bright red lipstick which made her look even more washed out and slightly scary. She hoisted up her boobs and pulled the stretch silver top down as far it would go. Not that it made much difference; she'd always had a boyish figure, and since having Sam, her boobs were almost non-existent. But the punters didn't seem to mind, and she was never short of offers. When she returned to the bar, two blokes were standing by the jukebox.

'You seen those two before?' she asked the barmaid.' Her voice almost drowned out by the thumping sounds of *Come On Eileen*.

'You're wasting your time there, love. I know the blond one, that's Justin. He works at Zenwin over the road, and he's gay.'

Ronnie raised her eyebrows. 'Oh well,' she sighed. 'Just my luck.'

Soon after ten, Justin's companion left. There wasn't much prospect of finding a punter, so she decided to get chatting to Justin in the hope he might buy her a drink. She moved along to stand next to him at the bar.

'I hear you work at Zenwin. Is that the double-glazing outfit?' He was tall, and she found herself smiling up at him.

He looked taken aback. 'That's right. I don't work full time, though; I just do a couple of shifts a week.'

'What do you do the rest of the time?' she persisted.

'I'm in my last year at uni.'

'Yeah.' She hesitated as if to say well go on then.

He pulled a face. 'You're full of questions. I'm doing graphic design if you must know which is only marginally more interesting than flogging double glazing.'

Ronnie immediately thought of Joe. 'I've got a friend who did graphic design. He never took it up after he left college, though. What's the double-glazing stuff like? Do you have to knock on people's doors?'

'I've done a bit of that; we get taken out in teams in the minibus and have to work a certain area, but most days I'm on the phones, cold calling.'

'God, how do you stick it? I'd rather poke pins in my eyes,' she declared and surreptitiously moved her empty glass in his direction.

He laughed. 'Go on, then; what do you want to drink?'

She ordered a vodka and orange, and that was the beginning of their friendship. They quickly established that she knew he was gay, and he knew she was a hooker. Having cleared the air, they found they could chat easily and shared a love of the Bee Gees and a deep loathing for Margaret Thatcher who had just been elected for a second term.

Sometimes, Justin visited Ronnie at the flat and would start tidying the place, tutting as he waded into the perennial pile of washing up. Sam adored him, and he was endlessly patient with her and would draw cartoon animals to keep her amused. They never discussed the details of how she earned her money, but one day he arrived unexpectedly and bumped into one of her regulars on the stairs.

'Don't look so disapproving,' she pleaded. 'Needs must.'

'Come and work at Zenwin,' he blurted out. 'I'm sure I could get you in on some shifts. You'd be good at it,' he added.

She snorted at him.

240

'Think about it,' he told her.

After he'd gone, she did think about it. Justin had told her that there was a whole crowd of them on the phones and it could be a laugh. Sam was getting older and getting increasingly curious; she couldn't have punters at the flat for much longer.

Her first shift at Zenwin was from four until eight in the evening. The room was hot and stuffy with fourteen of them crammed in. It was a pity that Justin wasn't working, but he had exams. She was given a script and told she must stick to it and that there would be a ten-minute comfort break but otherwise she mustn't leave her seat. She had a list in front of her of at least fifty numbers to get through. The basic money was pathetic, but if she managed to get a lead, they paid commission and a further bonus if the lead sold.

On one side of her was a monosyllabic Goth girl and on the other a boy with such a heavy foreign accent that Ronnie had to stop herself laughing when he was going through the scripted spiel. *How would he get any leads? No one would be able to understand a word he said.* People's reactions to receiving her call were interesting. Some put the phone down without saying a word. Some gave her a brief ear bashing about wasting their time. She couldn't blame them, and after twenty similar responses, she wondered how the company ever sold anything. The windows weren't cheap, but she supposed the bosses must think it worthwhile to have all these shifts of people operating the phones. The occasional person was friendly; one woman said she was in the middle of watching Coronation Street and proceeded to describe in minute detail what was happening on the screen.

'People are lonely I guess,' Justin replied when she recounted the story later in the pub. 'How did you do? Any leads?' He looked hopeful, but she shook her head.

'No, but Goth girl next to me got two,' she replied.

Ronnie decided she'd do some more shifts. Sharon would be back after the weekend, and she'd have Sam. This evening, she'd had to pay for a sitter, and if she didn't get any commission, it wasn't worth it.

Next shift, however, she was in luck. A man answered. Yes, he was the householder he told her. No, he didn't have double-glazing but joy upon joy he had recently moved in and was thinking about putting some in. Ronnie was thrilled to have her name up on the leads board at the end of the shift. It was nerve-wracking waiting to see if the lead sold, but the guy went for the whole front of the house. She couldn't wait for payday at the end of the month when she'd be able to buy Sam some new clothes and make the last payment on the television.

Ronnie slid out of bed. If she could avoid waking Sam, she would have some peace. Sam was splayed diagonally across the bed. Ronnie smiled at the sight of her in her favourite pink Barbie pyjamas with her wispy hair spread over the pillow. She pulled the duvet over her daughter and went into the kitchen to make a coffee. She'd done four evening shifts at Zenwin last week, and it was better than she'd expected plus she was developing the art of persuasion without being too pushy. This week she'd booked in for some morning shifts as well. Sharon had agreed to look after Sam. She was going to take her to toddler group with her little boy Daniel then give them both some lunch by which time Ronnie would be back to collect her.

She gazed out of the small kitchen window. Groups of school kids were trooping across the muddy green on their way to school. She wondered what Sam would make of the toddler group. She felt guilty because she'd never taken her to anything like that. Apart from the odd coffee at Sharon's when Sam played with Daniel, she wasn't used to mixing with other children. Still, she was a self-contained child; she'd be alright, Ronnie assured herself.

As promised, Sharon picked Sam up just before ten. Daniel was her third child, and she still had a double buggy, so she strapped Sam alongside him.

'Wave goodbye to Mummy,' she instructed Sam.

242

It was a different crowd during the daytime. Her usual evening shift mostly consisted of students, but the ten to one o'clock shift was a motley assortment. There were a lot of older women including a pair of blousy old tarts who delighted in coming out with outrageous remarks to the hapless person on the other end of the phone. They were also pleasingly skilled at winding up the sour-faced and bitchy supervisor. She was the opposite of the guy who ran the room in the evenings. Ronnie liked him. He knew your name and kept up the pace through cheerful encouragement and making it a big deal when anyone reached their target. He would get them all to give a big clap and often handed out small prizes like a Mars bar. This Liz woman didn't have a clue about how to motivate the staff and barked orders in a bad-tempered voice that created a miserable atmosphere.

As the weeks went by, Ronnie adjusted to a more normal existence and appreciated the regular money. Already, she'd clocked up a few leads and had an extra £20 bonus to come on Friday. Sam had talked non-stop about the toddler group, and when she had her afternoon sleep, Ronnie had some time to herself. She hadn't had a punter for three weeks now. Her regulars had been supportive when she told them she was giving up to flog double glazing and she certainly didn't miss the late nights after the pubs chucked out.

Several weeks later, Ronnie was tidying the phone room. It had been a stressful shift with no leads. That meant no bonuses next week for her or anyone else. She knew this meant that several of them, hacked off with no leads, would jack it in and she would have to recruit more staff. When the area manager had asked her to run the daytime shift, she had been chuffed. The blousy tarts had proved to be a big asset if you kept them on side and, without the poisonous Liz, spirits in the room were upbeat.

Ronnie flung cardboard coffee cups into the bin and emptied the ashtrays. If she had to manage on just the basic wage next week with no bonus, she'd have to forget Sam's new shoes yet again. Still, now she was assistant manager, she was on a better basic rate and a higher bonus if the team did well. She'd tried all sorts this week, big smiley face charts to motivate, Mars bar rewards and even the promise of a bottle of wine. For most of them, even the students, the bonus made the difference between just getting by and having money to go to the union bar on a Friday night. They had stuck at it, and it was depressing to report a big fat zero for the sales boys to follow up. She picked up her coat and locked the room.

'What a shitty week, I'm glad it's Friday', she remarked to the receptionist.

'Not to worry, love; March is always dead in this game. It will pick up over Easter when the weather gets warmer; it always does.'

Ronnie smiled, 'I hope you're right. See you on Monday. Have a good weekend.'

She shut the front door behind her. It was such a pat phrase, especially as she knew that the woman looked after her elderly mother. Nice weekends probably hadn't figured in her world for a long time.

'Bloody hell', she murmured. Across the road, in the doorway of the new wine bar, was Joe, rolling a cigarette. She hadn't seen him since they split in Brighton before Sam was born. She and Sam were doing ok and for the first time in a long while her life was more settled. She couldn't say she was wildly happy but at least she could envisage a future. *Did she want to get involved with Joe again?* When they had been together, she had tried to keep things light and had never told him the truth about how much she loved him. She had always known that she came second to Maisie in Joe's affections, and she was scared of the hurt of being knocked back.

He looked as though he was living rough and was wearing a torn and filthy dirty parka jacket and a black, woolly hat. Even from across the road, she could tell that his springy curls were greasy and matted. Aware that he was

244

watching her, she grinned at him and crossed over the busy road.

'Hello, stranger.' She touched his arm. 'What are you doing here?'

He put a hand up to brush a stray lock of hair from her face. 'You're looking good, Ronnie. Longer hair suits you.'

She looked at his shaking hands, and an involuntary sigh escaped from her lips. 'Are you living back in Southampton?' she persisted.

'Could be, no plans as such; you know me'.

She bought him a coffee and a sandwich.

'Look, I need to be somewhere'. She glanced at her watch; she should have picked up Sam an hour ago. 'Have you got anywhere to stay?' *Why did she ask that? She knew the answer would be no and for lots of reasons, emotional and financial, it wasn't a good idea to let him back into her life.*

'Not as yet.' He looked up at her from under his long lashes — *God, how she remembered those liquid brown eyes.*

'You can doss at my place for a couple of nights - no more', she declared sternly. 'And you're on the couch; deal?'

He grinned at her, and she knew for sure that this had been no chance encounter. They crossed the green to her block. She would have to tell him about Sam. Ronnie wondered, not for the first time if her daughter could be Joe's child. When they'd split, she'd not known she was pregnant? It was only after she'd worked in Spain for a couple of months that it dawned on her. But Sam looked nothing like Joe.

She paused at the front door. 'I've got a little girl,' she blurted out. 'A neighbour looks after her when I'm at work. She's fifteen months now. I had her when I was in Spain,' she added hastily.

Joe's face remained expressionless. Then Sharon answered the door, and Ronnie swept Sam into her arms.

'I'm so sorry,' she told Sharon. 'Blame him,' she nodded towards Joe.

Once inside her flat, Joe sank on to the couch. He didn't speak for the rest of the afternoon but just sat and stared at the table. Sam attempted to engage him in her little games; she passed bits of Lego to him and patted his knee, but it was as if she were invisible. It didn't seem to have occurred to him that he could be her father.

Ronnie was worried about being late for the Friday management meeting and gave herself stitch walking so fast. It took twenty minutes to get her breath back. She was unlikely to be kept on after the end of the month. Selling was an unforgiving business and, whatever way you looked at them, sales figures from leads made by her team were down yet again.

'I got you a coffee.' Justin handed her a large cardboard cup of frothy, milky coffee. She didn't have the heart to tell him she couldn't stand it like that - only a double espresso would lift her mood.

'What's up?' Justin slid into the seat beside her. 'Is that old mate of yours still stopping with you?'

She nodded. 'I'm worried about him, to be honest. He just sits staring into space all day. It's not like him at all. Usually, he hates to stay in and likes to be out and about meeting new people. I've suggested we go for a drink or meet up with some of my mates, but he says they'd talk about him behind his back. I told him not to be stupid and that they'd like him, but he just stared at me. He's not sleeping either; he paces around the lounge half the night, and he keeps opening the window so he can keep watch on the street. He just stands there for ages.'

'You're not back together as a couple, then?' Justin asked.

'Good God. That's never going to happen. Besides, he stinks; I don't think he's washed for weeks.'

Ronnie felt disloyal to Joe. She remembered all too well the handsome, vibrant Joe that she'd travelled around Europe with, and she ached at the memory of their uninhibited lovemaking.

'What will he do?' Justin ventured. 'Has he got any plans?'

'Joe doesn't do plans. I wondered if I should contact social services to see if there are any hostels where he could get a place.' She hesitated; the idea had kept her awake much of last night. *She couldn't do that to Joe, but what was the alternative?*

When she arrived back at the flat Joe was chucking saucepans and tins of food out of the cupboards. She watched him from the doorway as banged his forehead with the heel of his hand. She sat Sam in front of the TV with a biscuit and went back into the kitchen

'What's up; have you lost something?' Her voice was full of unnatural cheer.

'Where's the kettle? I can't find the kettle, and the coffee's not there either. They've been moving stuff. You won't be able to find a bloody thing I'm telling you.'

He was more animated than he'd been for weeks, but Ronnie saw that the kettle, although admittedly in a different place, was in full view on the other side of the room. She handed it to him.

'Here, you silly sod. I moved it so Sam couldn't reach it and I used the last of the coffee this morning. Sorry, I meant to tell you.'

With a shrug, he went into the lounge and resumed his place at the window. Ronnie decided it was best not to ask if he was looking for someone. It was obvious that he was.

'Does my voice sound ok to you?' Joe turned to face her.

'What do you mean, ok? It sounds the same as it always does. Why?'

He peered at her through narrowed eyes. 'When I talk, it sounds all wrong - in here.' He thumped his forehead

247

again. 'It doesn't sound like me, and sometimes the words are all jumbled up. Does it sound like that to you?' He grew louder and more agitated.

She shook her head. Her heart thumped. *Oh shit.* She'd have to contact someone; his mental state was all over the place.

She heard him up and about early next day and struggled out of bed to investigate. He was sat cross-legged on the floor in front of the coffee table surrounded by paper torn from Sam's colouring book. Her crayons and every pen and pencil Ronnie possessed were carefully arranged on the table, and he had stuck his drawings all over the walls.

Ronnie rubbed her eyes. 'What are you up to?'

Joe's eyes glinted with excitement. 'You don't need to worry about me anymore. I've had the best idea.' He swung his arm to demonstrate his work. 'Good, aren't they? I'm going to sell them. Make shed loads of money. I've got a talent for this. I'm going to be known worldwide soon.'

Maisie was at a loss. 'Ok,' she said slowly, beginning to gather up some of the half-finished pictures. But Joe stopped her.

'No, leave it. Don't touch anything I'm going to have an exhibition.'

Maisie frowned. 'In my lounge?'

She dropped Sam off, and all through her shift, worried about what might be going on.

When she arrived home, she found three bemused strangers sat on the settee with Joe trying to persuade them to buy his pictures. She'd never seen him so full of energy and zeal. He spoke rapidly, expansively, and repetitively, oblivious to any awkwardness.

For the next few days things didn't improve and Ronnie was exhausted. Joe hadn't sleep for days, and she could hear him pacing. He claimed he didn't have time to eat and talked non-stop about his grand plan for fame and fortune. It was uncomfortable to witness.

248

When she came home from work, she couldn't think what the noise was. She found Joe curled around the basin in the bathroom; he was howling in anguish. She stroked his back and spoke gently, but nothing would stop the tormented sound. She ran upstairs to Sharon's flat to make sure she could look after Sam then phoned her doctor. Within half an hour, an emergency psychiatric team were in her flat assessing Joe. They gave him some strong anti-psychotic drugs and arranged for him to become an outpatient at a psychiatric clinic.

Ronnie was glad they didn't admit him to a hospital, but he wasn't easy to live with, and she was never happy about leaving Sam alone with him. Once his medication kicked in the delusional stuff lessened, but he was depressed and still refused to leave the flat. Then he stopped taking his pills and began talking to himself sometimes muttering in a repetitive drone and at other times shouting with such anger that it made Sam cry. He constantly complained that people were spying on him from the green opposite or that they'd moved his stuff. It got to the point after he had taken up his surveillance position at the lounge window for ten solid hours that Ronnie gave in and called the clinic.

She left Sam with Sharon and went with Joe to Sturt Priory psychiatric hospital where he had more tests. He was admitted to a ward that night because he refused to answer their questions or to take any medication. As a result, the hospital authorities put steps in place to have him sectioned. Ronnie was horrified. She demanded to speak to the doctor in charge who told her that under the recent Mental Health Act, they could detain him for twenty-four hours to be appropriately assessed. And if they decided to put a section order in place that would be extended to twenty-eight days.

Chapter 34
Lily

It was ten o'clock at night when the phone rang. She presumed it was Jess to let her know that she would be late home and was shocked when it was Ronnie with the news about Joe. It was too late to do anything now she'd have to wait until the morning. She phoned Paul and was relieved that he was at home. It was his squash night, and he often went for a drink afterwards.

'I'll come straight over', he told her. Lily could hear his tenderness and was comforted that she didn't have to face this alone.

When he arrived, he made her a mug of hot chocolate and sat on the bed while she recounted what Ronnie had told her. For a long time, Joe had been unpredictable and could be moody, but she'd never expected this. She didn't know a lot about psychiatric care, but it sounded serious if they had sectioned him. When Jess arrived home, Lily gently told her about Joe. Jess was eighteen now and no longer a child; she deserved to be told the truth.

She arranged for Jess to stay at her friend's parents' house for a couple of days then drove down to the hospital. It was a two-hour drive to Romsey, and it was difficult to concentrate in her preoccupied state. She wished Paul had come with her, but he couldn't get the time off work at such short notice.

When she finally arrived at the hospital and found Joe's ward it broke her heart to see him in such an uncared for and lifeless state. *Where was her bright, funny, caring son?* The doctor explained his condition and, suddenly, Joe's dramatic mood swings made sense. *Should she have spotted the signs earlier and got him help when he was a disturbed teenager? Would it have made a difference to his condition now?* Her son lay on his back and stared at the ceiling, making it almost impossible to communicate with him. She had no choice but to return home but promised him that she

250

would be back on Saturday, which was in two days. When she got home, she knew she must phone Maisie.

'It's Joe; isn't it?' Lily could hear the emotion and fear in Maisie's voice.

'It's not good, Maisie. Ronnie has been wonderful with him, but she didn't have any choice. He needed professional help.'

'Do you have any idea what triggered it?' Maisie asked.

'We don't know. He went for days without any sleep, and he'd hardly eaten. He was convinced people were watching him and waiting for him outside the house. He became more and more paranoid and wouldn't listen to anyone until his stress escalated, and it all became too much for him.' Her voice grew small and distant. 'I'm frightened for him, Maisie. I should have realised he was ill.'

'None of this is your fault,' Maisie told her. 'You've always been there for Joe. Where is he now?' 'Will they let him have visitors?'

There was another pause.

'You'll have to ask Joe. He's in Wessex ward at Sturt Priory near Romsey. But he doesn't want to see anyone. I'm so sorry.'

At next visit, there was no change in Joe's mood, so she asked to speak to the doctor in charge. He was pleasant and reassuring in a vague way, but he couldn't tell her much. He explained their reasons for sectioning Joe and told her that various tests were underway.

She visited every Saturday after that. Paul drove her to the hospital, and once Jess accompanied her to see Joe. Lily noticed that while Jess was there, Joe made more eye contact, and although he hardly spoke, he did listen. Jess had been sweet with him and had chattered on about what was happening in her life. But she had found it upsetting to see her brother like that, and she hadn't asked to come again which was probably for the best especially as she was in the middle of her 'A' level exams.

251

It was a comfort to know that Joe was allowing Ronnie to visit. She often went in the afternoons when her shift was over and regularly phoned Lily with updates.

'The visits wipe me out if I'm honest,' Ronnie confessed. 'I never know what to expect. Generally, he's depressed and uncommunicative, but at times he rambles on about being kidnapped and kept there against his will.'

'Has he seen Maisie?' Lily asked.

'Not that I know of. I can't understand why she is staying away.'

The following weekend Lily found him more aware of his surroundings.

'They put me in a locked room, Mum. They pushed my face down on the bed and held me so I couldn't breathe. Then they injected a sedative in my bum. Can they do that?'

His speech was slow and slurred, and she guessed that he was still on sedatives. She looked at him sat cross-legged on the high bed as unchecked tears ran down his face. She held him close for a moment, but he didn't react.

When his consultant diagnosed bipolar disorder, he was prescribed lithium. This had a stabilising effect, and he no longer experienced such extreme mood swings. But he hated it on the ward. Once the twenty-eight days were up, he became a voluntary patient and was determined to discharge himself. In despair, Lily tried to persuade him to go back home with her, but he refused even to discuss it.

Chapter 35
Maisie

When Lily told her about Joe, her first reaction was to ring Tim, an old friend from university. He was now a GP, but he'd done a stint at a psychiatric hospital in Bath. Maybe he could tell her something about Sturt Priory. But he was discouragingly gloomy as he outlined how ineffectual and chaotic it was.

'To be honest, Maisie, I wouldn't put a dog there, but I guess there was no other choice.'

'Does he have to stay there? Can't he be looked after at home?' *Or with us; Will and I could look after him; we can help him.* Her mind whirled in desperation.

'There's no way they'll let him out in his current state. From what you've told me it seems all he wants is to get out of there and try to kill himself. He sounds pretty determined.'

Maisie found Lily's number and phoned her. She felt so helpless, and the pain of Joe's situation was unbearable. Listening to Lily's description was one of the hardest things she'd ever had to do.

'He's in a terrible state. Not just mentally, he won't wash, and I can't get him to talk. He just lies there in a fetid heap and the smell's awful,' she added.

Maisie was shocked, remembering her vivid and disturbing dream. 'Don't the nurses do anything?'

'That's one of the worst aspects. Apparently, it's hospital policy to encourage the patients to look after themselves. It's supposed to be good therapy, and they won't intervene if that's the way Joe chooses to be.'

Cynically, Maisie couldn't help wondering if laziness was the more obvious motive for the staff. As soon as Lily rang off, Maisie found the number of the hospital from directory inquiries. She was put through to the ward and asked if she could speak to Joe. She hadn't expected that he would talk to her.

'Hello.' His voice was thick and dulled, but snatches of their old closeness remained. Without emotion, Joe described his determination to end the life that had become so painful. Desperate, awful words flowed between them and all the while she could hear the noise and chaos that was a permanent feature of the ward.

Every day after that they talked on the phone for hours. Once, he phoned her, which was encouraging. He ended that conversation saying it was nice to talk to an intelligent person for a change.

'Does that mean I'm beginning to get through to him?' Maisie asked Will.

They discussed the possibility of Joe coming to stay with them when the doctor agreed to release him. Will, despite his reservations, had agreed and Maisie clung to the belief that between them they could help Joe; she was sure of it.

But Joe dismissed the idea; nor would he allow her to visit. Maisie experienced a shaming mix of hurt and relief. She was scared of seeing him in that state, and she felt a coward.

Then she heard from Lily that Joe had disappeared. He didn't go back to Ronnie's to collect his stuff, but she discovered from the receptionist at the surgery that he was living in a hostel in Portsmouth and was drinking again.

Chapter 36
Joe

To finally have a diagnosis was a relief to Joe. Bipolar disorder they called it, the new term for manic depression. When he'd been taking amphetamines, he'd felt full of confidence and restless energy. In that state, he didn't need to eat, or sleep and his head buzzed with grandiose ideas. Other times he felt like that without any drugs and found that hard to understand. He now recognised that this behaviour was caused by a manic episode. It also explained his paranoia. Those times when he panicked if someone walked past him in the street and looked at him and he would be convinced that they'd got it in for him. He had bipolar to thank for that.

When he came out of Sturt Priory, he decided to go back to Brighton. He knew a few people he might be able to doss with. Somehow, he had to survive the winter. Some nights he had no choice but to sleep rough, often under the pier or in one of the seafront shelters. Other times he was luckier and either slept on the floor at friends' places or got a bed at the night shelter.

For the last month, he had been living in a squat with a group of hippies. They smoked pot, but Joe had never seen them touch the harder stuff and they were easy company. Jake and Jonah were brothers, and both were charming and unreliable in equal measures. With them was Anna who had known them for years. She seemed quite content to divide her affections between them as the mood took her. Tilly had recently joined the threesome and was besotted with Jonah and his brooding dark looks. When the landlord of the squat evicted them, they pooled what money they had and bought a beaten-up old camper van. They were off to Morocco, they said, and did Joe want to tag along.

Three days later they piled their meagre possessions into the van and headed for Dover. The rusty vehicle belched out black smoke, and Joe doubted that they'd reach Dover let alone Morocco. Taking it in turns, Jake and Jonah drove through the French countryside towards Paris. When they were hungry, they picked apples and cherries from the fields and Anna often successfully blagged food from the farm cottages. If they stopped in a town, they rummaged in bins behind the restaurants which reminded Joe of sleeping rough in Southampton. It was June and warm enough to sleep out under the stars which was more harmonious than squashing into the van. Joe had run out of his medication, but he felt ok.

When they reached Toulouse, the road ran alongside the canal.

'Can we park up here for a bit?' Joe had spotted some wooden canal barges with people living aboard. The terracotta pots stuffed full of red geraniums and colourful arrays of washing that flapped in the breeze were a poignant reminder of Maisie. The others weren't in any hurry, so he walked further along the bank. The sun glinted through the straight rows of plane trees either side of the canal and was reflected in the water below. It was a tranquil scene. There were several men fishing, and Joe squatted beside one of the older men. With a mixture of inadequate school French and a lot of gestures, he managed a conversation of sorts. When he stood up to go the Frenchman picked a fish out of his bucket, wrapped it in newspaper and handed it to Joe.

'Enjoy, my friend,' he said with a broad smile.

Joe returned to the van and proudly displayed his gift. They had no idea what kind of fish it was; although Anna, whose father was an angler, declared that it must be a freshwater fish. Joe took on the task of gutting it, and Anna volunteered to fry it up. Tilly wouldn't touch it, but the rest of them wolfed it down with lots of French bread. Before leaving Toulouse, they replenished food stocks with a mixture of scrounging and legitimate purchases and washed in the public toilets. Then it was off to find a field outside of the city to sleep for the night.

The next stage of their journey took them to Andorra. The place was unchanged in the four years since Joe's previous visit with Stu. There were more modern buildings in the capital itself but the impact of the place, with its villages nestled at the foot of the mountains, still had a magical quality. Jonah discovered that there was duty-free shopping in Andorra, so he washed up in a local hotel for a couple of nights and stocked up on cigarettes.

Then it was off to Barcelona. The girls wanted to sunbathe on the warm sands, so they agreed to spend a couple of days there to chill out. Anna disappeared with a bloke she met in a beach bar, and when she didn't show up for a week, Joe was concerned. But neither Jonah nor Jake even commented on her absence and Tilly, delighted to have the field clear, latched on to Jonah at every opportunity. Joe was forced to look away from the sight of her bronzed, slim body draped over Jonah.

When Anna reappeared, they continued their journey down the coast to Gibraltar.

'God, this is a nightmare. It's worse than in Paris. Where are all these cars going?' Joe complained. 'I'm sure they just drive around in circles to show off.'

Main Street was crammed with taxis and big flashy convertibles driven by white-shirted and bejewelled young men. They found somewhere to park, and Joe went off to explore while the others went to the nearest pub. Gib was very English with smoky pubs with names like The Old Bull and Bush. Several fish and chip shops were advertising the best fish and chips outside of Yorkshire and there were even red telephone boxes.

Joe was still chuckling when he joined the others for a pint.

'Well, that was a culture shock. The policemen look just like English cops, and I asked one of them the time. "Fuck off", he replies.'

While Joe finished his drink, Anna went off to find out about ferry tickets to Ceuta in Morocco. They could afford the foot passenger price but not for the van, so they had no alternative but to stay in Gib and try to earn enough between them for the fare.

Anna and Tilly had no trouble finding work. The open-air café in the big plaza square was always looking for waitresses. The owner knew how to attract the male clientele and dressed his waitresses in frilly gingham miniskirts and low-cut blouses. The serving hatch was deliberately high, so they had to reach up to collect the orders, and they were instructed to bend over and wipe the tables at every opportunity. This tactic ensured that the tables were fully occupied throughout the day. Anna flirted outrageously anxious to maximise her tips and Tilly, with her long legs and shy smile, received her fair share.

After a hot day trudging around in search of work, Jonah and Jake were offered a few shifts as kitchen porter and washer up in a hotel, and Joe persuaded one of the Gibraltarian taxi drivers to let him cover his shifts for a couple of days. He decided not to mention that he didn't actually have a driving licence. Airport runs were the most lucrative and Joe liked to chat to the English holidaymakers.

Anna was counting the money. 'We've got enough for the ferry now, guys,' she informed them. 'I can't wait to get to Morocco.'

Africa, after the mock Englishness of Gib, took their breath away. They drove straight to Tangier and left the van on a piece of waste ground outside the city walls and headed to the medina. Many of the houses were painted white and blue, and in some of the narrow alleys, they were all pale blue, which gave the place a mystical air. In the market square, the girls, feeling conspicuous in their denim shorts, bought flowing Indian cotton dresses. Joe bought a bag of juicy, sweet oranges, and they sat in the afternoon sun outside the mosque to eat them.

Next day, they reached Marrakech. Wandering through the maze of souks in the medina blew them away. They were constantly accosted by Arabs in long cloaks, desperate to sell their goods. By mutual consent, they stayed as a group and even then, got hopelessly lost. This acted as a signal to the scruffy street urchins who pestered them as soon as they showed any uncertainty about which way to go.

'Big square, big square, this way, come with me.'

Inevitably, they would expect money as a reward for their services. Anna developed the knack of studiously ignoring them, but it wasn't easy. They wandered around the different souks. In the slipper souk, there were rows and rows of identical slippers. Then came the blacksmith quarter where the sound of hammer on metal was deafening. In the leather souk Jake, whose trainers were full of holes, bought a pair of leather flip-flops. The smell of the nearby tanneries was overpowering, so they made their way out of the alleys and into the huge square. There was stall after stall selling fresh oranges, colourful and pungent spices, and dates and in the middle of the square were storytellers, snake charmers and musicians. It was crowded with tourists amidst heavily laden donkeys and gnarled old Arabs who pushed ancient wooden handcarts to re-stock the stalls and remove the piles of rubbish. Just off the square, and overlooked by the towering mosque, were the food stalls. Each stall had set out wooden tables and benches beneath canvas awnings. Giant tagines gave off enticing smells of chicken and fish. There wasn't much left from their earnings in Gib, so they opted for the cheapest on offer. For a few dirhams, they joined the Moroccan men at a stall selling hardboiled eggs inside a baguette. It was filling and tasty and afterwards, the owner poured them a glass of complementary mint tea.

By the time they had finished, it was dark, so they made their way back through the souks to the van. They had expected the souks to be lively until midnight, but at nine o'clock they were shutting up for the night. When they reached the entrance to the slipper souk, which was the only way back they knew, an ancient Arab was struggling to lock the heavy wooden door. None of them had realised that the souks were locked overnight. They retraced their steps to find an alternative way out. The place was by now deserted, and a distraught Tilly clung to Jonah. Without the normal landmarks to guide them, they went around in circles until their feet were blistered and they had no choice but to ask for directions to the gate that lead out of the medina. A boy of about seventeen, barefoot with dirty jeans, showed them the way, but when they arrived at the gate, he demanded an extortionate amount of money. Even with three men in the group, his insistence was intimidating. This incensed Anna, who spoke quite good French. She hammered on the nearest door and told the startled woman who answered that this lad had tried to rip them off. Fortunately, it had the desired effect and, after the woman gave him a mouthful in Arabic, he slunk away into a dark alley.

It didn't feel safe to sleep in the open, so the girls slept in the van. It had been blisteringly hot in the daytime, but the proximity of the Atlas Mountains made it cold at night.

They were woken by the call to prayer from the mosque. Joe lay on his back on the sandy patch of grass and gazed up into the cloudless sky. He loved Morocco and Marrakech in particular. It was so different and so vibrant that he couldn't wait to explore further.

The five of them managed to eke out an existence in Marrakech for a month when Jonah and Jake received bad news. When they phoned their mother with their regular update, they discovered that she had frantically been trying to get a message to them. Their younger sister had been seriously injured in a road accident, and they needed to get back to England. Their mother sent a money order via the British embassy with enough money for their flights home. Tilly decided to return with them and arranged for her father to send money for her ticket. This left Joe and Anna and the camper van. They both felt flat and restless without the other three and decided to sell the van. Anna had already got to know a bloke she liked in another group of hippies and went off with them to Fez.

On his own, Joe felt adrift, and for company, he started to hang around with a couple of Australian guys. He had seen them begging on the road leading to the big square.

They let him sleep on the floor in the squalid room they shared at the back of a derelict house just outside the Medina. Joe knew this was dangerous territory for him, as both men were heroin users who stole to fund their habit. He mustn't become trapped. He knew he should get away and back to England, but he didn't have the energy. This acknowledgement of his weakness sent him into a spiral of depression, and he lay in the darkened room for days on end. He steered clear of heroin aware of how it might affect his mental state, but that didn't stop him from endlessly smoking pot. He became convinced that he was being watched whenever he left the house. One evening, when he'd ventured into the square, he got into a fight with an old Arab who pulled a knife from the pocket of his cloak. Men from one of the cafes rushed out to separate them, and Joe ended up face down on the ground being kicked in the ribs.

When he came to, he expected to find himself locked up in some jail. But instead, he was in a high metal bed with clean white sheets. An American nurse came to bandage his ribs and smiled brightly at him.

'Hi, so you are finally awake. Welcome to St Joseph's.'

Joe's head and ribs ached. He rubbed his eyes. He couldn't remember what had happened or where he was. But each day he became more alert and began to question where he was. From what he could make out this was a small American hospital. Nobody seemed concerned about how Joe's treatment would be funded.

'The good Lord will provide' was the stock response. There was a great deal of talk about the good Lord. Joe often saw a middle-aged man dressed in a smart suit hold his hands over one of the sick patients and intone volubly beseeching God to save this sinner. Any staff within earshot would respond with hallelujah, praise the Lord. Joe wondered if he was considered a sinner too.

After ten days, Joe's ribs were no longer bruised and sore, but there was no suggestion of him leaving. Instead, he was encouraged to help with the other patients and to spend any free time at their prayer meetings. At first, it didn't bother him. He had a comfortable bed and regular meals and let the religious stuff drift over him. The messages to repent of his sins and give himself to God's service were relentless, and Joe became familiar with the loud, repetitive language. He found it beguiling and began to repeat some of the stock phrases to the other patients. There was security in its familiarity, but at times he noticed that the joy was forced and insincere, particularly by Pastor Arbuthnot, the man in the suit.

Joe grew increasingly bored within the confines of the hospital and decided to move on and head back to England. He stared into the steely blue eyes of Pastor Arbuthnot and was treated to a tirade of abuse about his ingratitude and how he had chosen to forsake God.

That night his bedroom door was locked, and no food was forthcoming. He had got the message and knew it was time to clear out. As soon as he was sure everyone was asleep, he wrapped a blanket around the chair to deaden the noise and smashed the glass in the window. Then grabbing his backpack, he climbed on to the flat roof and scrambled down to the ground. He found safety in an all-night bar and sat cross-legged on the street outside until daybreak. Then he walked along the main road and headed out of Marrakech. After several miles in the blistering heat, a rickety, wooden-sided truck stopped and took him as far as Casablanca. From there he got lifts until he reached Ceuta and the ferry back to Gib.

He was near to starving and exhausted, and now there was the problem of boarding the ferry without a ticket. He found a public washroom and cleaned himself up to make himself look more respectable and persuaded an English couple to take him as a passenger in their car.

When he arrived in Gib, he was daunted by the prospect of the thousands of miles still to go back to England. But his luck changed. There was a beautiful yacht

moored alongside the quay wall in the harbour, and he
started chatting to the crew.

'We're delivering the boat from Majorca to Scotland
where she'll be sold', the skipper told him. 'One of the lads
has had to fly home because his girlfriend is pregnant, so we
need someone to replace him.'

Joe told him about his time living on the barge, and the
skipper agreed to take him on and three days later, after
stocking up with trolley loads of food from the supermarket
in Main Street, they set sail.

Joe soon got the hang of steering and following a
compass course and found the night watches peaceful. He
had never experienced such a mass of stars in a sky
unpolluted by light. In the daytime, he spotted turtles that
basked just below the surface and one sultry afternoon flying
fish landed on the deck. There were four of them on board,
the skipper and his girlfriend who did all the cooking and an
American guy who was working his way around Europe.
They sailed up the Portuguese coast round Cape Finisterre
and into the Bay of Biscay. It was October by now, and the
skipper warned of the likelihood of autumnal gales. *He's not
wrong there*; Joe thought sombrely as the yacht bucked in the
heaving seas. They all had to wear a harness on watch in
case they were swept overboard by one of the huge Biscay
rollers. It was impossible to get a proper meal, and Joe was
starving hungry, so he decided to grab some cereal. He
strapped himself into the small galley and painstakingly got
the bowl and a spoon; he got the milk from the fridge and,
despite slopping it, managed to pour it over the cereal. His
mistake was to let go of the bowl while he reached for the
sugar, but at that moment, the boat pitched heavily and the
whole lot upturned in the sink.

The Biscay gale lasted for thirty-six hours, followed by
an even fiercer storm. They were all thankful that they were
in such a seaworthy boat, and eventually, they reached the
English Channel and made for Newlyn. They had been
eleven days at sea, so the skipper treated them all to a hot

shower in one of the hotels, and that first meal ashore of fish and chips was heaven. But it was soon back to reality for Joe and the question of where to go next?

His mother hugged him fiercely when he turned up on her doorstep. 'You look well. How're things?' she inquired.

'I'm ok. Feeling pretty positive, I guess. How's Jess?' The last time he had seen her was when she visited him in Sturt Priory.

'She's great and having a wild time at university. I can't believe that she's already in her final year. You've just missed her. She went back for the start of the new term a couple of weeks ago.'

'Things still all good with Paul?' It was strange to be asking his mum about her love life.

Lily nodded, and then she reached out and took Joe's hand. 'I'm very happy, Joe. But he'll be home from work in an hour, so you can see for yourself.'

With his mother and Paul out at work in the daytime, it was peaceful with plenty of opportunities to think about his future. He didn't tell them much about Morocco. He described the colour and excitement of Marrakech but left out his experience with the American evangelical group.

After a couple of weeks, Joe decided to move on.

'Where do you think you will go?' Lily smiled at him, but he could tell that she was struggling to hide her disappointment.

'I think I'll go back to Portsmouth. There are a few boatyards in the area where I might pick up some work.'

'If that's what you want, but you know you can stay here for as long as you like. We've both enjoyed having you home.'

Joe put his arm around her shoulders. 'I know, mum. It's been great for me too. You don't need to worry about me; I'm good at the moment, and that's without my medication.'

After a few unsuccessful attempts, he found a job at a small boatyard on Hayling Island. By day, he kept the yard tidy and made endless cups of tea for the other yard hands. At night, he slept in an old, corrugated iron shed, which had at one time been the paint store. Lily had given him enough money to tide him over for a few weeks, and he existed on pies and pasties from the village shop. One of the boat owners was looking for someone to keep an eye on his boat while he was away. This was an ideal opportunity for Joe. It was an old wooden lifeboat, which leaked like a sieve, and his main task was to keep the bilge pump running. Even so, oily water frequently swirled over the floorboards.

Joe began to appreciate the regularity and discipline of working in the boatyard, and after a few weeks, he graduated to painting the boats. Far from being monotonous, it was satisfying to complete a job and reflect on achieving the perfect finish, and he enjoyed the banter with the other yard hands despite frequently being the butt of their jokes. Importantly, there was company in the evenings and at weekends when the yard was closed. Many of the larger boats in the muddy creek were houseboats containing a broad mix of residents. Some single men liked to keep to themselves, but mainly they were couples, some with children. They preferred an unconventional lifestyle, and he had a lot in common with them.

One couple befriended him and invited him over for meals. They had two small boys who played on the foreshore and ran free in the woods and fields nearby. Joe longed for sons just like them. If he and Maisie still lived on the barge, this might have happened. Although he hadn't come back to Portsmouth in the hope of seeing Maisie, he often wondered how she was and what she was up to.

The second winter that he lived in the yard was either bitterly cold or pouring with rain. It was miserable on the lifeboat, so Daisy and her husband Russ suggested that Joe move in with them until the weather improved.

'You can sleep in the main saloon,' Daisy told him. 'I'm always in bed by ten, so you won't disturb me, and at least you will be warm and dry.'

This arrangement worked well for a few weeks. Then Joe noticed that Daisy always sat close to him on the sofa and started to stay up after Russ had gone to bed. She flirted with him when they were alone, draping herself suggestively on the sofa while she stroked her body. She was a beautiful woman with lustrous dark hair and sexy eyes, and Joe couldn't help being attracted to her. It was a relief when Daisy took his rejection in good part, and he didn't want any trouble if Russ realised what was happening.

The following day he was laid off by the yard manager, and within weeks he was back to square one. When he reached the park, he remembered the can of Tennants in his coat pocket that he'd bought the previous night. He slumped on the nearest bench and opened the beer to contemplate another interminable day without money or booze.

Once it was daylight, he made his way back to the centre to catch the commuter rush near the station. He found a place to sit outside a department store and began his begging ritual. A steady stream of office and shop workers passed by. Some ignored him and walked as far away from him as they could. Others caught his eye or even smiled and just a few, often the ones who looked as though they could least afford it, would stoop down, and place a few coins on his blanket. Mid-morning, a girl from the supermarket next door, came up to him.

'I thought you might want this.' She held out a plastic-wrapped sandwich.

Joe smiled up at her. 'Thanks, love, have a good day won't you.' It was his stock phrase, but he appreciated the kindness of a stranger.

He packed up when the Guildhall clock chimed ten and counted out just over three pounds. That could be converted into two cans of lager and a bacon sandwich from the café.

266

He made his way back to the park for a sleep. Despite the uncomfortable bench, he fell asleep within minutes and dreamt he was on an ocean liner. When he awoke, it was late afternoon, and it was raining. He scrounged some money from two passing strangers and made his way to the nearest off-licence. When he opened the door, he felt the man's strong hands pushing him out of the door.

'Get out of my shop. I don't want scum like you in here.'

Rain was dripping down his neck as he sat on the steps of a restaurant near the city centre. After a few minutes, the manager appeared.

'Sod off. You can't sit there you're causing an obstruction.'

Joe heard the words scruffy vermin. He didn't blame the guy but didn't have the energy to trade insults. It was best to move on and find a deep shop doorway to shelter from the rain. He was full of gloom about this wretched existence, but happily, rest and relief beckoned in the shape of a shoe shop, and he reached the entrance just before another torrential downpour. He lay on the cold, marble floor near the door and pulled his coat over his head. That was another day taken care of. But he couldn't rely on the begging, and it was getting too cold to sleep on a park bench. He was angry for letting booze get it's hold again. Left to his own devices, he had soon succumbed and was gutted to be so weak.

When morning came, it was bright and sunny. Feeling more positive, he picked up a discarded newspaper from the next bench; it was the twelfth of November, his birthday. He couldn't believe he was twenty-five. He seemed to have been fighting his demons forever, but the last five years had passed in a blur of highs and lows. The other day, he'd seen a woman pushing a toddler in a pram, and she had reminded him so much of Maisie. It made him unbearably sad to think what he'd thrown away. It had been one of the best times in his life on the barge.

It was so typical of him to lose it all. *Why had he done that?* His optimistic streak still kicked in, but as always things tended to fall from his grasp. *Was it down to his own failings or was he just unlucky?* Even the job at the boatyard hadn't lasted. He did a good job on the yachts when he was there, but that old restlessness had kicked in again. Too unreliable, the foreman said. Thus, no job and no money for mooring fees on the old lifeboat.

Over the years he had attempted to sort his life out. He'd tried going back home; he'd stayed with friends and slept on their floors until they grew tired of him and kicked him out. When his head wasn't right, his moods and behaviour frightened people, even Ronnie. At first, the medication had helped to rein in his more disturbing thoughts, but he often forgot to take his pills or simply ran out. In any case, now that he was drinking again, they wouldn't give him lithium. So, it was a catch 22 situation; he could be the zombie on lithium or be plagued by his paranoia.

He made his way to the café and started chatting to a lad at the next table. He was from Manchester he said and was selling the Big Issue. Joe had seen one or two blokes in the city centre selling the paper, but he didn't know much about it.

'How does it work, then?' he asked.

'As from tomorrow I've got a pitch by the fountain. I can keep sixty percent of the money from each paper I sell towards food and stuff plus they help me find somewhere to live. You have to play by their rules, though.'

'How do you mean?'

'Well, for a start, you mustn't beg or harass passers-by, and there's no drinking or swearing allowed. Oh, and you have to declare your earnings to the social. They've got an office on the Kingston Road if you're interested.'

The manager at the Big Issue office asked Joe a lot of questions and showed interest when he told him that he'd done graphic design at college.

'We try to help our vendors to find safe and affordable accommodation, but we also offer training and vocational guidance. We hope to run some creative workshops soon; your skills might come in handy there, Joe.'

'What do I have to do to get started?'

'Well, you must be homeless or what we term vulnerably accommodated.'

Joe smiled. 'Does Victoria Park count?'

'Haven't lost your sense of humour I see. Anyway, if you are accepted, you'll be given a training session, and the pitch system will be explained to you. After that, how well you do is down to you. Stick to the rules, and this could be your chance to get off the streets for good.'

Chapter 37
Maisie
1984

Maisie was in the video shop and there seemed to be a commotion across the road. Peering out of the window she could see flames in the ground floor bay window of a house opposite. The curtains were well alight, and thick smoke poured from the edge of the window frame. She went outside and joined the growing crowd of onlookers. Two young women clung to each other and sobbed on the pavement as more people emerged from the heavy double doors. One man began frantically pressing the doorbells of the flats to alert other tenants in the big Edwardian house.

'Fire; get out, get out' he yelled, the panic and fear evident in his voice.

Maisie frowned and peered into the darkness. A man comforting the two girls looked familiar. She gave a sharp intake of breath and froze, her heart pounding.

'Joe?' The name broke from her lips in an involuntary whisper and echoed in her head. *Joe, oh, dear god. Is it really you after all this time?* She couldn't breathe. *Why was he here, just around the corner from where she lived?* A hundred questions flashed around her brain. Then she lost sight of him in the crowd. People ran around and desperately calling out the names of loved ones. It was a chaotic and frightening scene. *Were people still trapped inside?* Maisie scanned the upstairs windows looking for any sign of life. *Where was the fire brigade?* Staff from the video shop and the Co-op next door handed out bottles of water and put their own warm coats around the shocked tenants. She still couldn't see Joe. Her eyes watered from the acrid smoke. She clamped a hand over her mouth. *Maybe she couldn't see him because he had gone back into the building to make sure no one else was inside?* It was a cold night, and her whole body shook in fear for Joe, for her beloved Joe. She bit hard on her bottom lip. *Where was he?*

After an interminable wait, she heard the insistent blare of sirens as three fire engines arrived. People around her grew noisier as shock turned to morbid excitement. As the firemen jumped from their appliances, the residents of the burning house moved aside, and there was Joe again; there was no doubt in her mind that it was him. He was dressed like some old hippy in loose, striped, trousers and a multi-coloured jacket. The familiar, dark hair was held away from his face in a scruffy ponytail, and deep lines were etched around his mouth, but otherwise, he looked the same lovely, old Joe. Maisie buried her face in her hands and tried to control her breathing as her heart pounded with relief that he was safe. She longed to cross the road to him, but it was an urge that she knew she must resist, and she turned away unseen.

'I saw Joe today.'

Will was at work on the computer. He'd lit a log fire in the large grate in the breakfast room, and Maisie began to relax in its comforting warmth.

'Joe, which Joe?' Will didn't look up.

'Joe Oliver, my Joe.' It was out before she could stop herself. She watched as he slowly turned to face her; she watched him take a deep breath before he spoke.

'And what's he up to? It's a job to imagine him now.'

She struggled to maintain her composure as the long-forbidden image flooded her brain — Joe, with his chocolate-brown eyes and corkscrew curls that flopped around his smiling, tanned face. Joe was always smiling. She knew this wasn't strictly true, but she loved the way his cheeks creased around his mouth. She was shocked at how vivid and raw it still felt, and now there was this new image of the older Joe. She kept her gaze steady to mask the restless excitement that stirred inside her and poured a glass of wine as a distraction from the turmoil in her head.

'I didn't have a chance to speak to him. There was a fire in that big house in Elm Grove, opposite the video shop.

271

He was coming out of there. I don't know if he was visiting or what.'

'And ...' Will leaned towards her. 'Has he changed much after all this time?'

'Not really, he looks much the same.'

Maisie couldn't believe how little he had changed. She had wondered so many times what he might look like now; but that quick snapshot, now such a powerful, such a welcome and delightful image, told her that he was the same Joe. *What was his life like now, three years on?*

She turned back to Will.

'He just looks older, that's all; he's still got a ponytail.'

She gazed out of the window into the darkness as a deep pool of unease

settled over her. Will pushed his fingers through his greying hair and swung his chair around to face Maisie.

'How did it make you feel, seeing Joe again? Think you can cope with the situation now?'

Irritated, Maisie sucked at her bottom lip. *Once a probation officer always a probation officer*, she thought. She nodded, not trusting herself to meet his gaze. Joe was exciting, that was undeniable. He could still affect her, but there was no going back. Even if she could, she didn't want to; she was sure of that. But she owed it to Will to be honest with him.

'I guess so.' She paused, 'No, it was ok, honestly. It was strange seeing him, though. It stirred up a lot of memories. What about you?'

She could see from the look on his face that he was struggling to control his emotions. She ran her hand along his broad, straight back and laid her face against his warm cheek as excitement bubbled inside her. Disgusted with herself, she relished the familiar yearning that she'd kept so firmly clamped over the years as the glimmer of forbidden possibilities made her heart quicken.

For most of the night, she was hot and restless; her emotions heightened in the darkness. It was hard to believe

272

that she had calmly walked away from Joe. Yet she was ashamed of how effortlessly she had allowed her imagination to discard all that she valued with Will. Over the years they had melded as a couple. They laughed at the same jokes; liked the same food and the same people. Will was a determined character. *Had this rounding of the edges been mutual? Or had part of her merely been absorbed?*

And now there was Joe.

Desperate for a distraction she decided this was the time to tell Will about her plans.

'Can we talk?' She smiled at his facial expression. 'Nothing heavy, don't look so concerned. No, it's just that when I had my annual performance review with Shaun, he suggested doing a part-time PhD. It makes sense career-wise, and I need something to get my teeth into. How would you feel about it? I would be pretty tied up weekends etc.'

He pulled her to her feet. 'Come here' he told her. 'I think it's a great idea but just promise you'll save some time for us. What would your research focus on?'

'Well, I've been reading some recent studies on hypnosis research and altered states of consciousness so something along those lines.' She gave Will a quick hug. She'd always known he wouldn't stand in her way that wasn't his style but now she had his blessing she was excited about the whole idea.

It was Saturday, and without warning, Maisie's resolve settled around her like an iron shutter. She had to find Joe. She couldn't bear not to. Long ago, she had acknowledged an unwelcome trait in her character. She possessed a single-mindedness that allowed her to press ahead regardless of who else might be hurt along the way. This was particularly true when men were involved. If she fancied them or imagined herself to be in love with them, that was enough to put aside any remorse. She had slept with Will all that time ago, regardless of her friendship with Fran. She had done the same with Joe despite Chris' warnings about his vulnerability. Her brother had been right about her being a selfish teenager. In many ways, she was a kind and loyal friend and colleague, but she was also capable of using people when it suited her, even Will.

She walked in the direction of the house where the fire had been. It was a dull, depressing day and bitterly cold, but she scarcely noticed in her desire to see Joe. She hugged herself as if trying to keep her heart from leaping out of her chest as she silently repeated, *please let him be there. I so want to see you, Joe; please, please be there.*

The downstairs window of the house was boarded up after the fire. She wasn't sure if the people were still living in the rest of the house. Inevitably, no Joe Oliver was listed on the row of doorbells, but she hoped someone might know him and knocked on the front door. Eventually, an older man appeared with a Jack Russell yapping around his legs.

'No, he doesn't live here; I know who you mean though. He went into the house before the fire brigade arrived to check no one else was inside.'

She smiled at him. 'Thanks for that. You haven't any idea where he went, I suppose?' Her heart was beating faster in anticipation of his reply, and she looked at him encouragingly.

The man nodded across the road. 'He's over there most days if it's not raining, selling that Big Issue paper. You can't miss him. He spreads a dirty great blanket all over the pavement. He's got a nice dog, though. You like him, don't you Perdy.' He stooped to pat the dog's head.

'Oh, that's great.' She struggled to suppress her excitement. 'I'll look out for him. Thanks.'

As she crossed the road, her stomach knotted with a mixture of fear and anticipation. She tried to shut out the clash of opposing thoughts in her head and ignore the small but a persistent inner voice telling her this was a dangerous idea. *But he was here; Joe was here and living so close by.*

Supercharged with impatience, Maisie paced up and down the pavement. *Where was he likely to be?* She walked

briskly to the shopping precinct to check outside
Woolworth's where a girl with several nose rings held up a
copy of the Big Issue. Maisie ignored her. She couldn't bring
herself to ask if she knew Joe. Maisie knew exactly why; it
was that old gnawing jealousy telling her that if the girl did
know him, they might be together. It was inevitable that Joe
would have been with other women since her, and she
couldn't bear the idea.

What's happening to you? she asked herself sternly.
Stop behaving like some lovesick teenager. She was in
danger of being swept up in a dangerous fantasy, and she
needed to stay in control.

Three agonising days later she saw him, just as the old
man had described, sitting on a blanket with his copies of the
Big Issue beside him. A dirty, white terrier rested his head on
Joe's leg. There was no hesitating this time. To his obvious
surprise, Maisie sat down beside him.

'I've been looking for you for days,' she told him.

Joe jumped up. He pulled her to her feet and gathered
her into a big hug.

'Bloody hell, Maisie,' he whispered. The sudden
movement woke the dog who barked loudly. 'Ssh, Murphy;
this is my good friend Maisie.'

She bent to pat the dog. 'He's gorgeous; where did he
come from?'

'I was in a pub one day, and this guy just left him
behind; abandoned you, poor little sod, didn't he? Anyway, I
decided I'd keep him. I was eating a packet of Murphy's
crisps at the time, hence the name.'

She looked up and down the road. 'Got time for a
coffee?' She was amazed at how normal she sounded when
her heart was pounding so much. Joe, despite looking older
and more weather-beaten was as gorgeous as ever.

Over coffee, they chatted about what being a Big Issue
seller involved. He even opened up about his continued
struggles with drink but neither of them mentioned his
mental health issues. Joe seemed to prefer to gloss over that

part of his story and Maisie was still anguished that she'd been such a coward and not visited him in Sturt Priory. She knew she had let him down. She put her hand over his.

'I've thought about you a lot over the years and wondered how you were doing. You are ok; aren't you?'

His face crinkled into a smile. She closed her eyes for a moment and tried to think of Will.

Joe held both of her hands in his. 'I've found a bedsit in one of those big old places in Nightingale Road. Number 34, Flat 7'. Will you come and visit me?'

Maisie lay in bed that night once again unable to sleep; unable to shake the image of his face which flooded her brain in the dark; unable to stop herself silently repeating his name. It was such a bad idea to get involved with Joe again, and she was afraid that it would prove irresistible. That same heart-fluttering excitement when she saw him was still there, and she couldn't bear to lose him all over again.

'How's Will?' Joe asked when they next met up.

'Working too hard. He's the senior probation officer for the area now, and he has to put in such long hours. Still, the money is useful, and we've been able to move to a bigger house. Actually, he's on a course in London this week.' She spoke without thinking.

Joe raised his eyebrows at her. 'Interesting. Is he now?'

A delightfully disturbing image of Joe's tanned and slender body swept over her. Maisie couldn't help but return his smile. She'd forgotten how persuasive he could be, and those beautiful brown eyes bore right to the heart of her.

'I don't think so somehow.' She put a mock frown on her face. *It was best to keep it light and simple.*

'And what about you, Maisie? What have you been up to?

'Nothing exciting. We still go to Pebbles, but it's quiz nights now and very sedate. Do you remember my friend Chris?'

'Yeah, I liked her.'

276

'Well, her husband has been posted back this way, so we see more of each other. We have the odd girly night out when we can manage it, and she often comes to the gym with me in a joint battle of the bulge.'

Joe laughed. 'How's the job? Are you still at the university?'

Maisie nodded. 'I'm doing a part-time PhD now.'

'Impressive.' It was Joe's turn to pull a face. 'What are you researching?'

'Look into my eyes, and I will tell you.' She laughed. 'Stop looking so puzzled. I'm trying to get my head around altered states of consciousness like hypnosis.' Ignoring his bemused expression, she checked her watch. Will would wonder where she had got to. 'Look, I must go now but let's meet up tomorrow. I'll buy you lunch and tell you all about it.'

Lunch was everything she'd hoped. They shared a pizza and Joe stroked her leg underneath the table. He was his old confident self once more and full of ideas. So much so that at times she struggled to keep up with his train of thought.

'I've done some design work,' he told her.

'How come?'

'I've been going to creative workshops run by the Big Issue people, and a couple of times recently I've run the group. I trust you're impressed.'

He lit a second cigarette and launched into an excitable rant about how he'd done some of the artwork for posters. Listening to his expansive plans was exhausting. She ordered another espresso aware she was postponing the time when she had to choose between the sensible course of action and the oh so seductive thought of lying in Joe's arms just one more time. She couldn't cheat on Will and certainly not with Joe. It would destroy him. *But if it were just the once, how would he ever know? It might even bring her closure.* As if picking up on her turmoil, Joe took hold of her hand.

'Come back to the flat with me?' The familiar tilt of the head and the questioning eyes tore at her heart.

'Let's just be together, Maisie, for one last time. We can't just leave things like this and go our separate ways. We need this.'

He was right, and she couldn't help herself.

The house was dark and gloomy and smelled of cabbage. Maisie followed him up the stairs feeling self-conscious and out of place. He chucked his coat on the bed and Murphy looked up expectantly at him.

'I won't be long.' He kissed her on the lips, and she heard him running down the stairs to feed the little dog.

I can't do this; it's all wrong. She grabbed her bag and ran downstairs to explain to Joe. But she hadn't bargained for his crestfallen expression as he pulled her towards him and buried his face in her warm neck.

'Don't go, Maisie.' He put his hands in her hair and held her face close to his as they stood with their bodies pressed hard together. She shut her eyes. This was madness. His body was stronger and more substantial than she remembered. He nibbled her ear as his erection pressed into her thigh. Without warning, she was overcome with shyness. It was a long time since he'd seen her naked. But any doubts quickly vanished as Joe set about seducing her with infectious energy. Locked into the moment and oblivious of anything else, Maisie was absorbed as Joe stroked her body and kissed her thighs and buried his face in her candyfloss hair. Afterwards, they lay in each other's arms, laughing and talking until they fell asleep entwined together.

She woke with a jolt and looked at her watch. It was after eight; Will would wonder where she'd been since lunchtime. There was no choice but to lie to him. In her heart, she had known that sleeping with Joe again could never be a one-off. Throughout the day at work, he was constantly on her mind, and she couldn't wait to see him again.

278

Will was out at a clients' meeting that evening so on her way home, overcome with an urge to cook for Joe again, she stopped off at the supermarket and bought steaks. She knocked at the front door, and an older bloke answered.

'You can try his door, but I don't reckon Joe's in, love.'

She waited in the car. *Perhaps he'd popped out or was still at his pitch.* She waited ten minutes then drove to the city centre, but Joe and Murphy and the dirty blanket were not to be seen. She drove back to his flat, but the whole place was now in darkness. Tears pricked her eyes. *Where was he? This was horrible.*

She drove home feeling disconsolate and headed straight for the bottle of Sancerre she'd been saving for a special occasion. She put the steaks in the fridge; she and Will could have them tomorrow. She was filled with disgust. *God, what am I doing?*

She tried to act normally for Will, but the weekend dragged, and by Sunday night she couldn't bear it any longer. She waited until Will was sound asleep then she grabbed her clothes and dressed in the bathroom. Her heart was in her mouth as she crept down the stairs clutching her shoes. She had no idea what she would say to Will if he discovered she was sneaking out. Softly, she pulled the front door closed and was immediately flooded with a sense of exhilaration. She drove to Joe's bedsit and knocked on the front door. It was two in the morning - *what if she couldn't raise him or he wasn't there or worse that he was with someone else?*

There was a light in one of the upstairs rooms, so she continued to knock until a girl let her in. She didn't make eye contact and grunted at Maisie's flustered explanation. She knocked on Joe's door. There was no response, so she knocked harder and called his name. Eventually, he opened the door, shading his eyes from the bright landing lights. He looked at her with sleepy eyes so full of desire that a shiver ran through her. He pulled her into the room and kissed her fiercely. They half fell onto the bed where they made love with a kind of fierce desperation. Afterwards, they lay curled together. There was no need for words. From time to time, they kissed or stroked each other's hair or face. Neither of them slept.

Soon after five, Maisie slid out of the crumpled bed. It had been a perfect few hours with Joe, but now she was scared that she might not get home before Will woke up. She dressed hurriedly and promising Joe that she would see him soon she ran back to her car. Her heart was thumping as she went back up the stairs at home. It reminded her of sneaking in late when she was a teenager at home, but the consequences of discovery were far greater now.

She stood inside the front door and tried to compose herself.

Before she had an opportunity to see him again, Joe disappeared, leaving Maisie distraught. She was convinced that something must have happened to him and refused to believe that he had gone away without telling her.

Three frantic weeks later, she found him. He had dark circles beneath his eyes, and from the state of his clothes, it was obvious that he was sleeping rough. He was morose, barely looking at her and disinterested in anything she said. Frightened by the swing of his mood, she held him in her arms. She told him over and over how much she loved him, but he was unreachable, and she was powerless to help him.

Chapter 38
Joe

Life for Joe was like wading through treacle. He couldn't focus and felt detached and apathetic. Knowing that he was spiralling into a deep depression, he managed to hitch the twenty miles to Southampton. He rang the bell at Ronnie's flat, but there was no answer, so he tried her friend Sharon on the floor above.

'You're Joe, aren't you? Were you looking for Ronnie?'

Joe nodded. 'Do you know when she'll be back?' He was worried that she might be reluctant to tell him.

'She's moved away, love.'

Crestfallen, he turned to go.

'Not too far, though.' Sharon sounded sympathetic. 'She's got a new bloke, and she and Sam have moved into his place. I've got her address if you like. She lives up by the common now.'

It was dark by the time Joe found the place. His hands shook with anxiety as he rang the bell. It was three years since he'd seen Ronnie. *What would her new bloke think about him turning up?*

When Ronnie opened the door, she greeted him with a quick hug, and he followed her into the cosy lounge where they were in the middle of eating supper. Joe couldn't stop staring at Sam, who sat on the settee in her school uniform. Next to her was a man who Joe presumed was Ronnie's new bloke.

'Phil, this is Joe, an old friend of mine from way back.'

Phil looked amiable enough, and he stood up and shook Joe's hand. 'Alright, mate? Have a seat.'

Joe sat in an armchair while they went back to their supper and continued to watch the television. Feeling disoriented, he couldn't relax and sat in rigid silence. Then Ronnie ushered Sam up to bed, and Phil told them he'd leave them to catch up while he met up with his mates in the pub.

'Are you hungry? Can I fix you something to eat?'

Joe shook his head. He couldn't remember when he had last eaten, but he wasn't hungry. Ignoring him, Ronnie disappeared into the kitchen and came back with a pile of cheese sandwiches and a cup of coffee. Joe dutifully ate them as Ronnie questioned him about what he'd been up to since they last saw each other, and he told her about Marrakech.

'It's an amazing place; you'd love it,' he told her. 'You should try and get there someday.' He didn't elaborate about his experiences with the American religious nutters.

'What about you?' he asked. 'Are you still flogging double glazing?'

'No, but I worked there for five years; then I met Phil and needed a job nearer to this area. I'm working for a marketing firm now. It's my job to book advertising slots on TV.'

'Sounds pretty interesting. Do you like it there?' He was having a normal conversation, but the effort was exhausting.

'I love it. It's like a jigsaw puzzle, booking clients into optimum slots.'

'How do you mean?'

'Well, if there's a link in the programme to the product or the actor used in the ad, I have to make sure I secure the slot. It can be competitive at times, but so far, the bosses are pleased with me. I'm a pushy cow these days.'

He saw her hesitate. 'Is there a but?' he asked.

'Phil and I are having a baby, so I will be taking maternity leave. Things can move on pretty fast in media and advertising, and I'm worried that I won't have a job to go back to.'

'He seems like a good bloke.' Joe said. 'Are you pleased about the baby?'

She nodded. 'Of course, and Sam is so excited. Phil already has two children; he was married for ten years, but he's been divorced for a couple of years. His kids often come and stay at the weekends. It all seems to work well. How about you? Any girls on the scene.'

Joe wanted to tell her he was seeing Maisie again and how screwed up he felt about what they were doing; but for Maisie's sake, he had to keep silent. He wanted to continue their conversation, but he just didn't have the energy. Besides, Ronnie was a stranger now. She couldn't help him any longer and a penetrating gloom settled over him.

It was a freezing January night, but he had no choice but to try and get back to his bedsit where   he had fallen asleep in all his clothes, too apathetic to move. *Whatever that banging was, he was not inclined to get up and find out.* He didn't want to see anyone. He felt nauseous, and his body shook with the cold. He shook his head vigorously, trying to shake away unwelcome thoughts but the notion that he couldn't go on pressed around him. Working slowly with a deliberate determination, he tore strips off the grimy sheets and plaited them to make a rope. The noise was coming from the front door. He heard voices; heard his name as the blood rushed to his head, and he drifted into unconsciousness.

Chapter 39
Maisie

Maisie froze at the terrible sight of Joe hanging from the stairs. Paralysed with shock, she was held in an iron lock, unable to move or scream. As if from some other place, she watched the guy who had let her in swing into action. Unable to support Joe's weight, he undid the noose from the banister, and Joe's body crumpled to the floor. Between them, they put him into the recovery position and Maisie ran to the phone in the hall to call an ambulance. *Was it really her speaking in that calm, measured tone?*

Joe was beginning to come around, so she held his hand and stroked his hair.

'I'm here, Joe. Maisie's here,' she told him. 'It's all ok now, sweetheart.'

She went with him in the ambulance to the A&E department of the local hospital where they checked him over. Apart from some abrasions on his neck and bruising on his lower back, they gave him the all-clear and transferred him back to Sturt Priory. It was gut-wrenching to see him back there, but Maisie knew there was no alternative. First, she rang Lily and Ronnie to let them know then Will who drove straight over to pick her up. When she saw him, her emotions took over, and she clung to him, her breath coming in choking sobs.

When Maisie awoke, she was weeping. Her dream was still vivid. She was floating above Joe's body into the fetid air surrounding him. Possessed with phenomenal strength, her body splits in two. Her arms extend out to one side to a glinting, razor-sharp blade and on the other to dancing, teasing flames. Her face glows with light, and there is a broad smile on her lips. Shocked, she sees that she has no eyes, yet she is looking down on Joe. She throws a rope ladder to him and pleads with him to cling on and climb the ladder to escape from his sordid pit. Joe holds the bottom wooden rung, but the ladder swings precariously and unpredictably. He can't hold on and keeps losing his grip only to fall back again and again on to a maggoty heap of bedding. Joe is calling her as he climbs for one last time. He gathers his strength as the metal slices his palms and the taunting flames prevent him from holding on. His voice grows distant, and with a rush of air, Maisie floats high into the sky and with a long scream of anguish, she drifts away.

'What's up? Why are you crying?' Will cradled her in his strong arms.

'I had such an awful dream about Joe. It was horrible.'

Will made her a cup of tea, but she couldn't shake off the dream nor the feeling of complete exhaustion.

For an entire week, lethargic and queasy, she barely got out of bed. Aside from the trauma of finding Joe, another anxiety was pressing down on her. She was five days late; *she couldn't be pregnant, not now, she couldn't be.*

When she finally emerged from her frozen state, she knew she had to act and do something practical. First, she went to the chemists to buy a pregnancy testing kit which confirmed that she was pregnant. But that was far from the only issue consuming her. She knew she must go and see Joe. When Joe was first sectioned, he had refused to let her see him like that, and to her shame, she had just accepted his decision. She had spoken to him on the ward phone but otherwise, relied on updates from Lily and Ronnie. But she wasn't merely respecting his wishes she knew that she had bottled it and was haunted by the fact that she hadn't been there for him when he needed her most.

Will was away on an overnight course, and Maisie lay awake all night, agonising about letting Joe down. When she was unable to bear it any longer, she got up. The dawn was starting, and on impulse, she drove for two hours until she pulled up at the hospital gate. She was uncertain about what to do next; she couldn't just march in and demand his release.

Just then, a minibus drew up and discharged a group of hospital workers. Maisie made an instant decision and locking her car she merged into the group and entered the foreboding, stone building. She followed the signs to Wessex ward and made her way along brown painted corridors. Like all hospitals, it was overheated and had a sickening stench of diarrhoea mixed with strong disinfectant. Three floors up, she found his ward. There was no sign of any nursing staff, so she scanned the line of beds in search of Joe. She had never been in a psychiatric hospital before and instinctively and filled with shame, turned away from those who squatted on their bed and rocked, and from those who reached out to her with lewd suggestions or gestures. At first, in her panic, she couldn't see Joe. Then, she spotted him; he lay curled on the bed and was covered with a stained, yellowing blanket. She touched him on the shoulder. He didn't move, so she pulled the blanket aside and leaned forward.

'Joe, it's Maisie. Sh! Don't make a sound.'

He turned towards her, but no surprise or alarm registered in his dead eyes. She wasn't even sure that he knew who she was. His lack of response scared her, and she was shocked by his physical appearance. His hair was matted into dull clumps, and his cheeks were pale and hollow. Ignoring the smell, she bent towards him.

'Christ, Joe.' As she held him close, his hunched shoulders relaxed, and he let out a long sigh.

'I've come to take you home, Joe.' She wrapped the filthy blanket around his shoulders. 'Come on; we have to go now.'

She heaved him off the bed. Bewildered, he stared at her, and his legs trembled as if he hadn't used them in a long while. A few inmates, aware enough to be alarmed by a stranger in their midst, began to bang on their beds and cry out. Maisie ignored them and pushed her way through the double doors. Once away from the ward, she could breathe more easily as she half dragged him along the gloomy corridors. A girl was now at the reception desk, but luckily the phone rang at that moment. This distracted the girl long enough to allow them to continue unseen through the main doors. She headed straight to her car; bundled Joe into the passenger seat and drove at speed towards the main road. By now it was raining heavily, and lacking sleep Maisie became mesmerised by each sweep of the wipers. Her heart thumping, she gripped the steering wheel in disbelief as she struggled to concentrate on her driving and push from her mind the enormity of what she'd done.

Joe slept for the entire journey back to Portsmouth. Will was due back from London that evening, and Maisie was apprehensive about his reaction. As she closed the front door, relief flooded through her followed by a wave of acute tiredness. She longed to close her eyes and sleep. Instead, she led Joe upstairs to the bathroom where, without embarrassment, she stripped off the grubby white T-shirt and stained pyjama bottoms he was wearing. She sat him in the bath and let the warm shower water flow over his shivering body. As she washed his hair, she was shocked at how thin he had become. She massaged his scalp with her fingers and, with the help of copious amounts of her best conditioner, she gently untangled the dark curls. Then she washed him all over with a soft, soapy flannel as if he were a young child. When she was satisfied that he was clean, she helped him out of the bath and wrapped him in a soft, warm bath towel. He looked so pathetically grateful that she held his damp body against her. Slowly, his arms curled around her waist, and he laid his head on her shoulder. They stood together, silent, and gently swaying. Then Joe spoke for the first time.

'I couldn't cope with it all. You're the only one who can make it alright, Maisie.'

'I know, sweetheart,' she told him. 'And whatever happens, I'll be there for you, Joe. Always, whenever you need me.'

She sat him on the sofa in front of the television while she made him tea and thick, buttery toast. Then with Joe still wrapped in the towel, they curled together and fell asleep.

Maisie woke to find Will sitting in the armchair opposite staring at them. She put a finger to her lips and gestured towards the kitchen where she told him straightforwardly what she'd done. She watched Will's face carefully. There was no hint of disapproval or annoyance, which she could deservedly have expected, and a huge wave of gratitude flooded through her. He didn't ask, as he might have, what she intended to do next. Instead, he offered practical help.

First, he phoned Sturt Priory, telling the consultant's secretary that Joe was with them and was safe and being well cared for. Maisie heard him ask about Joe's medication. She hadn't even considered that aspect. He was on a high dose of lithium. She covered her mouth with her hand. Christ, she hoped this wouldn't set him back. Will suggested she telephone Lily to let her know what had happened.

She decided to tell Lily the truth. 'I do so hope I haven't done the wrong thing, but I couldn't leave him in that place. To be honest, I acted on impulse and didn't even think about the consequences.' When she'd finished, Maisie went back into the kitchen.

'How did she take it?' Will asked.

'She didn't say a lot, but I don't think she was too happy about it. She's coming down tomorrow if she can get away.'

Next, Will phoned Maisie's doctor friend Tim who explained some of the procedures concerned with sectioning mental health patients. Tim was hopeful that the hospital authorities would allow Joe to stay with them in the short term or at his mother's.

When the phone rang, it was the hospital secretary to inform them that, as it was the weekend, Dr Mooney had agreed that Joe could stay with them. Maisie hugged Will with relief. She'd had terrible visions of men in white coats dragging Joe away in a straitjacket. At least she had the weekend to feed him up and get him as settled as she could. The noise of the phone woke Joe. He wound the towel around his waist and went in search of Maisie. She looked up as he padded into the kitchen. He smiled at her, almost his old grin. Her heart leapt at the sight of him.

'You can stay with us, at least for the weekend', she told him.

'Yes,' he replied with emphasis as if it were what he had expected all along.

'Are you sure it's what you'd like?' She flushed, startled by the sudden renewal of desire.

He smiled and put his hand up to touch her hair. For a moment, he seemed like his old self. He looked rested, and Maisie hadn't heard him pacing around in the night.

Lily arranged to come over on Sunday, so Maisie cooked a roast chicken for lunch. They had agreed over the phone that it would be best if she came on her own. Maisie hadn't seen her since she and Joe split up and she was struck once more by how beautiful she was. True, she was plumper, and her hair was noticeably greyer, but there was warmth in her eyes and a serenity which Maisie envied.

Maisie had been nervous about Lily's visit. *What must it be like for her to have a son in such mental torment?* It would be difficult if her anxiety affected Joe. But she needn't have worried as the meal turned out to be quite a relaxed affair. Lily chatted to Joe, keeping him up to date with news about Jess at university and how Paul had taken up golf. She even managed to raise a smile when she related an amusing anecdote from her class of seven-year-olds. She asked him about his medication and if he was worried about returning to Sturt Priory later that day. She was skilled at recognising when to probe and when to back off, and it was a relief that Joe seemed unperturbed by her questions. He had tucked into the meal with gusto and afterwards spent the afternoon listening to some of Will's records in the lounge. His stillness struck Maisie as eyes closed, he allowed the thumping sound of U2 to wash over him.

Lily helped Maisie with the washing up, which gave them both a chance to air any concerns surrounding Joe.

289

'Are you sure you can cope, Maisie? It's a lot to take on even if it is only at the weekends. Joe seems settled enough at the moment, but you know how changeable he can be'

'All we can do is take it a day at a time,' Maisie told her. 'But I don't want you to think I'm taking over. I couldn't bear to see him in that place and as I told you I acted on impulse.'

'What about Will?' Lily asked. 'It's asking a lot of him as well. Are you sure this is the right thing for any of you, Maisie?'

'Will wants to help Joe as much as I do.' Maisie turned back to the sink to hide her tears. She knew in her heart this was a lie and that Will, lovely unselfish Will was agreeing for her sake. 'I can't turn my back on him, Lily.'

After she had left, Will offered to drive Joe back to the hospital. Maisie held Joe in a long hug when it was time to say goodbye.

'Will is going to fix it so you can come back at the weekends; maybe for longer if they'll agree. Keep strong,' she told him.

He nodded fiercely and followed Will out to the car. A lump came into her throat as she waved them goodbye. Joe was more like a teenager going back to college than a man in his mid-twenties. Time seemed to have stood still for him for the last five years.

For the next few weekends, their lives fell into a pattern. Maisie would collect Joe on Friday evening, and Will made the return trip on the Sunday. In between these visits, Maisie spoke several times on the phone to both Lily and Ronnie. She sensed neither of them approved of the arrangement, but it was Joe who mattered. Yet she was still at a loss to fathom his unpredictable moods. On a Friday he was subdued to the extent that she wondered just how much medication they were giving him at the hospital. She was concerned because he was reluctant leave the house although they both tried without success to persuade him. Maisie had suggested they go to the shopping centre and buy him some new clothes and Will suggested a trip to a wine bar where a band he liked was playing. But Joe was adamant that he was happy as he was. During his talkative interludes, he spoke at length about the staff and fellow patients on his ward. The theme always revolved around some form of conspiracy against him; he couldn't trust anyone as they were all out to get him.

One night in bed, Maisie decided to talk to Will about her concerns. 'Do you think we're doing the right thing for Joe?'

'What's worrying you?' he asked gently.

'I'm not sure this arrangement is helping him. He doesn't seem to be any better, does he? Maybe constantly switching from here to the ward is too unsettling for him.' She sat up in the darkness and hugged her knees. It was a familiar gesture when she was troubled.

'Would it help to discuss it with his doctors? Or maybe Lily could have him some weekends to give us a break.'

Maisie remained silent. Joe was only one of her troubles, but she couldn't confide in Will. At times, with all that had happened with Joe, she had almost forgotten that she was pregnant. Today she was queasy, and anything but calm as the reality of her situation struck her with such force that she shuddered. She closed her eyes and groaned. *What if the baby were Joe's and not Will's? Oh God, it was all such a mess.*

She decided that when Will returned from Sturt Priory, she would tell him about the baby. She knew he would be over the moon. She would never tell him the truth. She risked losing Will altogether if he found out that she had slept with Joe again and she knew that there would never be a happy ever after scenario with Joe playing the doting father. She decided not to confide in anyone, not even Chris. For the first time since she'd met Joe, she was ashamed of her lack of self-control where he was concerned. She reached outstretched fingers into the empty air. 'Joe', she whispered. 'I want my Joe back.'

Maisie was at work on the Wednesday afternoon when she received a call from the hospital.

'This is Doctor Mooney from Sturt Priory Hospital. I wonder has Joe Oliver been in touch with either yourself or Mr Stevens?'

'No. Why? What's happened?'

'I don't want to alarm you unduly', he continued. 'But Mr Oliver has gone missing from the ward. In fact, he's not been seen since Monday, around six in the evening. We've contacted his mother, and his friend, Miss Armstrong, who I believe was still in touch with him, but neither has heard from him.'

'Have you called the police?' Her heart pounded, and her mouth went dry.

'Yes, although he's a voluntary patient, it's our policy to inform the authorities when a patient who is in a vulnerable state has been missing for more than twenty-four hours. I wonder if you would be kind enough to give the hospital a call if you do hear from him.'

'Yes, of course.' Maisie felt numb. *Where was Joe?* The doctor's reference to a vulnerable state implied he might attempt suicide again.

She rang Will straight away and between sobs told him what had happened. They both agreed that all they could do was to wait for news. Without some clue as to his whereabouts, it would be fruitless to try searching for him. As soon as Maisie heard Will's key in the lock, she ran down the corridor. Neither spoke as he held her in his arms. She felt sick and on the verge of tears. She should be looking after herself and eating properly for the baby's sake, but she had no appetite. Unable to sleep for more than an hour at a time, she spent much of her time in bed, sometimes thrashing around in a feverish state or locked rigid with desperation. Her brain went into overdrive imagining the worst. Joe had told her once that if his mental illness returned, his life would become unbearable. A terror gripped her that Joe would give in to his paranoia. She doubted that she could bear it if she were never to see him again. If he were never again to feel the joy of a beautiful sunny day or to feel that physical closeness they had together.

A tortuous few days later, Lily rang to say that Joe had turned up at her house.

'Is he there? Can I speak to him?' Maisie heard the desperation in her voice.

'He's out at an appointment with someone from the housing association; they think there's a good chance that he will be eligible for one of their flats.'

'Why did he take off like that?' Maisie asked. 'Did he say?'

'I think he felt he'd imposed enough on you and Will, especially now you're pregnant.'

'How did you know I was pregnant? Does Joe know?'

'Well, it was actually Joe who told me.'

Maisie listened to the rest of the conversation in a daze. *If Joe knew about the baby, how had it affected him? Had he realised that there was a chance that he could be the father?* She was puzzled about how he had found out. They hadn't told anyone else. She went cold; if Joe knew then Will must have told him. It couldn't be anyone else.

As soon as he came home from work, she confronted him. 'You told Joe that I was pregnant; didn't you? What were you thinking?' She clenched her teeth and pulled away as he tried to stroke her hair.

'I was worried about you. You were having a hard time and seemed so anxious I just wanted to make it easier for you.'

'Easier for you; you mean. What did you say to Joe?' She made no attempt to keep the sarcasm from her tone.

'Don't be like that. You know how thrilled I was that you were pregnant, and I rang Joe and suggested a break from the weekend visits until you were over the morning sickness.'

She rounded angrily on him. 'When? When did you ring Joe?'

293

'It was on Monday. Why? What difference does it make?'

'You stupid bastard. Don't you see your little bit of news may well have triggered his disappearance? You know that; don't you?' She spat the words out angrily.

Will looked devastated. She hadn't meant to sound so harsh and could tell by the look on his face that he was aware of the possible consequences.

'I'll never forgive you if anything happens to Joe because of this.'

She couldn't stay in the house with such turmoil inside her head, so she grabbed her coat and set off towards the seafront. She walked slowly and deliberately making a conscious effort to be aware of her surroundings in the hope that it would calm her mind. She inspected the menu at Truffles, which was one of their favourite restaurants. Then she walked across the common. Here, the light was more intense than in the gloomy February streets of the crowded city and her spirits lifted.

She padded across the soggy grass, avoiding a sparse array of yellow crocuses. Pulling her scarf tighter around her neck, she sat on a bench on the seafront and watched the grey waters of the Solent. The Isle of Wight looked distant today, not like that sunny holiday she'd had with Joe in the beach house at Bembridge. Her life had changed so much since then. She had grown used to her comfortable life with Will. It would never have the same excitement as being with Joe, but she had come to appreciate being in a loving relationship. Now, the uncertainty of her pregnancy had changed all that. Apart from morning sickness, she was lethargic and preferred her own company. Will had tried to cheer her up, suggesting a visit to the cinema or having friends over for dinner but Maisie always found an excuse.

Since Will's promotion, he had to work until late most evenings. This arrangement suited Maisie who slumped in front of the television. While Will was out, she took the opportunity to speak to Joe on the phone. He had been in his bedsit in Bath for six months now and was coping well.

'Yeah,' he told her one evening. 'Having mum close by helps. She's finally got the message that I don't want her to interfere in my life, and she knows when to back off.'

'How are you getting on with Paul?' Maisie asked.

'He a good bloke and he makes mum happy. He's driven us over to see Jess in Cardiff a few times. I can't believe that she's married. Did I tell you Paul's fixed up some work for me with a friend of his who runs a sports clothing business? I help out a couple of days a week. It might be more if they get a big order.'

'What sort of work?'

'Mostly designing logos on tracksuits and so on; I quite like it.'

She was pleased that he was doing something creative. *But I miss him, I miss him so much.* Lily had told her the consultant had finally sorted out his medication and that he was less prone to mood swings. Phone calls were better than nothing, but Maisie was tormented by the lack of physical contact with Joe and was glad that she was still working. At least it provided a distraction. Once the morning sickness had stopped, she felt well physically. She wanted to share in some of Will's excitement about the baby, but she just couldn't and tried to explain her snappiness and lack of emotion on hormones.

Maisie eventually saw Joe at Lily and Paul's wedding. She was eight months pregnant and exhausted from a lack of sleep. Scenarios continued to play themselves out in her head. *What if Joe had guessed the baby might be his? What if Will ever found out?* It was so wrong to keep silent, but she didn't know what else to do.

The reception was in an upstairs room of a pub by the river in Bath. She saw Joe standing by the window. She longed to talk to him on his own but never got the chance and the whole day proved an almost unbearable strain.

Bent double with pain, Maisie struggled to the loo for the third time that night.

'Will, wake up.' Maisie prodded him with some urgency. 'I think I've started; my waters have broken, and the pain is worse.' With that, she doubled up in agony and collapsed on to the bed.

Will slung a dressing gown around her shoulders and led her downstairs and helped her into the car. He decided it was quicker to drive than to wait for an ambulance. Maisie gulped at the gas and air and tried to focus on something other than the pain. They decided not to tell either set of parents that she was in labour until they were sure that the baby was alright. She was grateful for Will's calm reassurance as he stroked her hair and encouraged her with her breathing until, after an agonising ten hours, Maisie gave birth to a daughter.

'Yes, nearly four weeks early', Will was on the phone to her mother. 'But Maisie's fine, and the baby's fine. 5lbs 1oz which is a good weight for a premature baby. She's beautiful; tiny but beautiful, as you might expect.'

He was grinning hugely. 'Isabelle Maria.' Maisie heard his voice choke with emotion.

'Make sure you phone Lily as well, won't you,' Maisie told him.

Maisie had to stay in hospital for five days. She was glad that her mother was coming to help out for a week as this meant that Will could go back to work. She knew how excited he was to have his little family back home. He had told her enough times. She tried to match his enthusiasm, but she felt distant from him; from anyone except her baby, her Izzy.

'Please let me help more, Maisie. You can't do it all, and it makes me feel so useless.'

Maisie knew he felt excluded, but she couldn't help herself. Shaun's wife had suffered from post-natal depression after their second child was born, and she suspected that Will was worried about it happening to her. She spent most of her time, when Izzy was awake, just looking at her. She inspected every crease and dimple trying to decide if she resembled Joe. But the baby had wispy light brown hair and blue eyes, which were bright and clear, like Maisie's own. There were no physical clues; if the baby were Will's that would be wonderful and what they'd always wanted. But in her heart that she was desperate for this baby to be Joe's, a part of him that she could keep close forever. She knew her love for Joe was unhealthy and obsessive, but as with any obsession, it was often overwhelming and all-consuming.

She lay on the bed as Izzy slept in her carrycot alongside. Her behaviour towards Will shocked her but she would never regret her affair with Joe and refused to feel guilty. If only she'd been brave enough to give up her job and go travelling with Joe when she'd had the chance none of this might have happened. *How could she have been stupid enough to let the difference in their ages and her pathetic need for stability to influence her?* Tears ran down her hot cheeks. She would never love Will in that way, yet he was kind and thoughtful, and she knew how much he loved her. He would do anything for her, and she suspected that he would even be prepared to let her go back to Joe if it were what she truly wanted. But that had been before Izzy was born. She sighed deeply; this tangled web was all her own making.

Izzy stirred in her cot. Maisie picked her up; she cradled her against her chest and breathed in the warm milky smell. For days now, a dangerous idea had been forming – she wanted Joe to meet Izzy. *How Joe would love his beautiful daughter.* Several times she had picked up the phone to dial the number *but what would she say?* Dangerously, the idea grew and took hold of her to the extent that she could barely function. Will had been working late at the office most evenings and when he was home was distant. All my life I have done this, she thought – pushed away the people that love me the most.

297

After agonies of indecision, she gave in and rang Lily, who was understandably protective of her vulnerable son.

'I'm so sorry, Maisie. I appreciate how much you've done for Joe but seeing you is not what he needs right now. He's settled at his flat, and he's coping. You know what he's like, that constant craving for company but for the first time he seems to be ok about being on his own.'

Maisie fought the urge to tell her that Izzy was Joe's child. *Was she strong enough to keep that secret locked away, or did Joe have the right to know that he was a father?* She bit her lip to hold back the tears. Part of her rationalised that it could be just what he needed to help him sort his life out. But the uncertainty surrounding his mental illness lurked persistently.

After the phone call, Maisie sat motionless for a long time. Emotionally she kept coming back to her need for Joe. Gradually the pieces came together, and with a heavy heart, she accepted that Lily was right. She was not what Joe needed, and for his sake and the sake of her marriage, she had to learn to deal with her obsession. It was dangerous for all of them.

She rang Chris, who was the one person who knew that Izzy might not be Will's child. They spoke for a long time.

'I know you are struggling and vulnerable right now, but the Maisie I know is strong and decisive. You can do this, Maisie; you've got to let Joe go once and for all.' Chris told her.

'I've tried, Chris. But I just can't do it.'

'You have to. It would destroy Will if he ever found out. You can't do that to him, Maisie. You need to let Joe find himself and find the strength to cope with his demons. You can't do it for him.'

'I know you're right, Chris.' Her voice betrayed the deep emotions flooding through her. 'But it's more than I can cope with. I can't stop thinking about him; he's everywhere.'

298

'Look, why don't you and Will take Izzy and have a holiday somewhere? You need something to distract you, and I think you both need to put some fun back into your lives.' Chris suggested.

Maisie was exhausted, and the phone call hadn't helped. On one level she agreed with Chris, but it wasn't what she wanted to hear. When she suggested the idea of a holiday to Will, he had been curt with her, claiming he was far too busy at work. She didn't have the energy or the inclination to cajole him and soon after she had heard the front door bang and his car start. No goodbye kiss then, not even one of his warm smiles.

At nine that evening the phone rang.

'I won't be in for supper as you've probably gathered, and I think I'll stay at Shaun's tonight as I've got an early start tomorrow.' Will informed her.

Maisie tossed in bed. A few times she fell asleep only to wake with a start drenched in sweat. She couldn't remember the last time that she had slept alone and her mind rampaged. Recently, Will had often stayed late at the office but staying away all night was new. A persistent voice niggled. *Was he telling her the truth about staying at Shaun's? Surely, he hadn't fallen for somehow else. Not Will, not her Will;* it was an uncomfortable realisation. She had treated him badly all the years she'd known him. She had ridden roughshod over his emotions, kept hidden her innermost feelings and worst of all, she had lied to him about Izzy. She reached her hand across the emptiness beside her. Tears welled up in her eyes and the horribly familiar lump in her throat, which to her surprise was for Will, for her lovely handsome husband – not for Joe. For the first time, not for Joe. She would always love Joe, and she would be there for him if that were what he needed, but she belonged with Will. They needed each other; they had a life together, a future. She sat up and hugged her knees. 'Please let me feel like this in the morning,' she whispered.

Printed in Great Britain
by Amazon

24616181R00169